Other People's Heroes

Revised and Expanded Second Edition
With Bonus Content

Blake M. Petit

DEDICATION

For Erin
Who reminds me how to fly

CONTENTS

AUTHOR'S NOTE

A true and sincere thank you to everybody who has purchased this eBook. *Other People's Heroes* is near and dear to my heart – it's the first major work I ever completed, and it was a long fight to get the rights to it back. In the years since it first saw print a lot of things have changed, both personally for me and in the world of publishing in general, but one thing that has never changed is my love for the superhero genre and my enthusiasm for everything the medium could potentially be.

If this is your first time meeting the heroes of Siegel City, welcome! I hope you enjoy what you're about to read. If you read this book in its original form, welcome back. Most everything is where you left it, although you may notice we've tidied up a bit and added a few new rooms in the back. If you listened to this book in its podcast form, you'll still have a chance at a little new content, as I've included two additional short stories to this edition, the Christmas-themed tale "Lonely Miracle" and the prequel short story "Inciting Incident." If you've already read both of those stories in their previous eBook editions (in my own *A Long November and Other Tales of Christmas* and the first edition of Flying Island Press's *Flagship* anthology, respectively)... well, then this author's note is the only new content for you. But thanks anyway for your purchase, I could use the cash.

Special thanks to Jacob Bascle for providing the cover to this edition of the book, my uncle Wallace Faucheux for providing the original cover (I really loved it, but I wanted to differentiate this edition from the first one), my sister Heather Keller for the logo for the *Evercast* podcast, my brother Jeff Hendricks for the *Evercast* theme music and for unending faith and support, to Eric Barrett for being the last line of defense between me and the world of typos, and to my Erin, for poking and prodding me until this story was finally available to everybody again.

This book is not the end for my stories, or even for the tales of Siegel City. You'll be able to keep track what I'm doing at my website, www.EvertimeRealms.com, for as long as I can keep updating it.

Okay, enough of this. Let's get to what you came here for. Close your eyes, take a deep breath, and enter a world of heroes... and those who just wish they were.

FIRST ISSUE

RESCUE

Sometimes I still look at the sky and remember what it was like from the ground. I remember what it was like to stand on solid Earth and gaze at bodies in flight, not knowing what it was like to be a part of them. Sometimes I am lost in amazement at what I have become.

And sometimes I just tell myself I think way the hell too much about all this.

When I got out of high school, I wanted nothing more than to get a journalism scholarship to an Ivy League university. When I got out of college, I wanted to write for a major news magazine. When I got my job at *Powerlines,* my wish was to win a Pulitzer Prize and have hundreds of scholarly-minded women hurl themselves at my feet.

While that last one never happened, the rest did. Back when I worked for my college newspaper (I usually covered student government meetings and other riveting events, like watching administrative paint peel), I came to the conclusion that most of my colleagues who wrote about sports were aspiring athletes who lacked either the skills or the talent to be pros themselves. Unable to compete with people who had real ability in their chosen field, they decided to content themselves with turning out cliché-ridden yarns of missed goals and big games that were lost at the last second.

I can't particularly blame them. I did the same thing. Except that my obsession wasn't with Michael Jordan or Mark McGuire. My idols were the types that strapped on capes and tights, rushing out -- I always thought -- in a valiant battle against the forces of evil.

I wrote about superheroes.

We've all got our favorites... the Defender or Alien Angel... Even lame ones like Superconductor have their fans -- usually the ones they sweep in and save from the clutches of Herr Nemesis or Agent Orange or the Aryan Ape.

And I know it's gone out of style, but my favorite was Lionheart.

When I was ten years old, I was saved from a burning building by the man who used that name. He'd been active for fifteen years by that time and this was a few years before he was the victim of what would become the most talked about Hero Vanishing in history. I still remember how that rescue felt -- I was holed up in the bathroom of the tiny apartment I shared with my parents and I filled the tub with water, hoping it would keep the flames back. It was an old claw-foot tub, though, and the flames were licking at the porcelain like a pot on the stove. I don't know if the water actually approached boiling, but it was a lot hotter than I was comfortable with. I tried splashing some out onto the fire, but it didn't make a difference and before I knew what was happening there was a veil of smoke and orange hell between me and the door.

Then I felt a rush. The water, which by now was beginning to bubble, wasn't burning me anymore, and my muscles were filled with an energy, a *strength* I'd never felt. That's when the smoke parted and Lionheart appeared. He was tall and strong, with his red, military-cut coat tucked into his black slacks. His blue cape and mask were buttoned securely to the tunic, and the proud yellow lion's head he wore on his chest seemed to be looking straight at me as he approached.

"Are you all right, little guy?" he asked as he lifted me out of the tub. I was surprised -- he had a British accent. I would have expected a full-out, All-American Hero. Not that it bothered me. He was *there*.

"We're getting you out of here, okay?"

I nodded. He dipped his cape in the water and wrapped it around me, made sure that I had no exposed skin and flew me out of the burning building into the chilled night air. When I dared to brush the cape from my eyes and look, I saw we were dropping down to the paramedics below -- but medical attention was the last thing I needed. I had never felt so good in my life.

"Cool-*ness*," I whispered while in the air. There was sort of a tingle and my rescuer smiled down at me.

"Got the heart of a lion yourself, don't you?"

When he handed me over to the paramedics, I didn't want to go. "Don't worry, little guy," he said. "You'll be okay now." Then he gave me a wry grin and a quick, dry salute, put his drenched cape back on, and flew back into the inferno. As soon as he was gone, the energy rush I felt subsided and I collapsed into the medic's arms. I suffered some smoke inhalation, they later told me, but there was no permanent damage. I would be fine.

Except that once you've been saved by a Cape, you're never quite the same again. Once you've flown with a man like Lionheart, you can't be satisfied back on the ground.

APPOINTMENT

When I was born, my mother called me Joshua Corwood. My *father* called me a slew of other names, the kindest of which was "Little Bugger." But then, the man was fairly unpleasant to begin with and, soon after he fell asleep with a cigarette in his hand and burnt down our entire apartment complex, Mom divorced him. We considered ourselves better off for it.

I was given my second name by a man named Morris Abadie. The first time I spoke to him I was 23 years old, still a reporter for a superhero-focused newsmagazine called *Powerlines*. I'd been there for nearly a year and I was still stuck on feature articles and follow-ups. Nothing that could gain me much attention, nothing that would get me out in the field, with my heroes.

I was plodding around in my cubicle (which at least was against an outside wall and offered me a window), polishing up my retrospective piece on the LightCorps when Morrie called me. His calm, sensitive demeanor was a comfort right from the start.

"You Cordwood?" he asked.

"*Cor*wood," I said. "Yes it is. What can I do for you?"

"I hear you're looking to do a story on Doctor Noble," he said. "I'm his publicist."

"His publicist? Since when does a guy like Doctor Noble need a publicist?"

"You're new, aren't you, kid?" Morrie grumbled. "Look, there are only two ways to get a hold of any of the major Capes in this town. You either gotta catch 'em while they're putting a Mask in the slam or you go through guys like me."

"Okay," I said. "I'd be happy to go through you, Mister Abadie." I'd been working on the Dr. Noble profile piece for weeks, but without an interview with the man himself it would never make it beyond a sidebar on page 64, only to be read by guys on the can too preoccupied to turn the page.

"Here's the deal, then. I can give you fifteen minutes at a time and place of my choosing. *We* supply *you* with the photographs -- Doc doesn't trust your camera guys -- and we get approval before you turn the story into your editor. Oh, and no questions about the incident with Photon Man, the Doc doesn't like to talk about that."

Photon Man was one of dozens of energy-based Masks who operated in Siegel City, and all I really knew about him is that he had not been seen since his last public battle with Dr. Noble, a few weeks ago. I wasn't thinking about that, though, I was just thinking about how slick Morrie was. "You *aren't* new at this, are you?"

"Look, you want the interview or not?"

"Yes!" I interjected. "Of course. Sure, you get approval and no questions about Photon Man. I can do that."

"And *no photographers!*"

"Right, of course. I wouldn't dream of bringing a photographer."

"All right, then. Roof of Simon Tower, 1 p.m."

"Thank you, sir, of course sir." I hung up the phone and took a glance at my watch. It was already 12:50 and Simon Tower was about fifteen minutes away. Fortunately, cab drivers in Siegel City are notorious for driving at three times the posted speed limit, so after bolting out of the office and nearly dying in the attempt to get one, I made it to Simon Tower just in time.

INTERVIEW

I hadn't even made it to the glass doors that looked out from the lobby when I heard a whistling sound. I looked up, hoping to see Dr. Noble. The more I looked at the humanoid shape, though, the less he looked like he was flying and the more it looked like falling. Then I started to wonder where Dr. Noble's cape had gone. And when he'd grown four extra arms. And why there were two of him.

I ran from Simon Tower just as a pair of orange, gelatinous creatures splattered into the pavement. Their viscous flesh coated the sidewalk, the building, the cars parked in front and about half a dozen people like they'd been dipped in orange wax. It also managed to splatter directly in my face like a pie in an old Three

Stooges routine. All around, innocent bystanders began flinging goo from their faces and limbs.

"Ah geez..."

"Look at this *mess*."

"Guy's a menace I tell you..."

I had written about these two before -- the Gunk and his companion, the Goop, were basically a pair of skeletons covered in thick, orange slime rather than flesh. The slime, however, was now covering the sidewalk, the building and the spectators. Gunk's appreciative public stood around much the way I did, trying to clean themselves off. I wiped away the orange ooze from my eyes and shook my limbs, spraying the goo everywhere.

Looking towards the point of impact, I thought for a moment that Gunk had landed on some people. As the figures in the epicenter of the slime reached up with three bony arms, though, I realized I was looking at Gunk and Goop's skeletons -- the only solid part of them. As they stood up, the orange slime began to pull away from the bystanders and surroundings, reassembling on the form of its respective owner.

As the slime pulled off me I felt a little weak in the knees, odd considering the incredible adrenaline rush I had. As energized as I was, I couldn't seem to make any of my muscles obey me, and I fell over. A six-armed shadow looked down over me.

"Gunk... hurt... man?"

The monster's vocabulary wasn't the particularly good, nor had it been since the experiment that turned him into an arachnid slime creature. His brain, it seemed, was the first thing to "gunkify." Still, for all the mayhem he'd caused, there were those of us who believed he was more like a confused child than a malevolent beast, and the look of concern in his eyes would seem to bear that out.

"Is he okay, Gunk? Huh? Is he?" Goop, Gunk's mysterious buddy, had appeared some years after Gunk first burst onto the scene. No one had ever been able to figure out who he really was or where he came from. His story was a total mystery, but not one most folks worried about, since the smaller slime man -- despite having a slightly higher vocabulary than his boss -- showed all the intelligence and loyalty of a good dog.

"Heeeeeeey..." Goop said, strolling up to me. "You're a little guy. Who're ya? Y'okay? Y'weren't *hurt*, wereya?"

"I'm... okay," I said, forcing myself up on one elbow. For some reason, that arm felt incredibly wet. I wanted to chuckle at Goop calling me "little guy" -- I was 250 pounds easy and stood at six-one when I hadn't been knocked to the ground by a couple of slime-monsters.

"Okay," the Gunk moaned. It was painful just to *listen* to his slow, tortured speech.

"Yeah. It's okay, Gunk," Goop said, bounding around. "It ain't our fault, it ain't, you see that." He glared at me a bit. "I think I know ya from somewhere."

"That's... nice," I said.

"Gunk... go... now." The quasi-monster looked around at the blazing eyes of the public, crouched, and with a mighty leap returned to the air, Goop in tow.

Once they were gone, my muscles seemed to solidify and I sat up on the pavement.

"You okay, mister?" asked another of the now-clean bystanders who'd just been bathed in Gunk's body. "You want me to call an ambulance?"

"I'll be fine," I said. And I was. I felt perfect again already. "Besides, I've got to get upstairs." Scrambling to my feet, I rushed into Simon Tower.

When I stepped out of the elevator onto the observation deck I was greeted by a man in a pit-stained white shirt and suspenders. His tie was crooked and his scalp was flaking out a few clumps at a time onto his snow-covered shoulders. I maneuvered myself upwind of him so as not to inhale the smoke drifting from his cheap cigar. As a publicist, the guy was awe-inspiring.

"You Cordwood?"

"*Cor*wood," I sighed. "Mr. Abadie?"

"Yeah, that's me. The Doc will be here in a minute. Here's yer press packet." He handed me a red, white and blue folder with Dr. Noble's insignia on the cover. Inside was a press release, a profile and about half a dozen staff photos, mostly headshots. There was only one full-body shot, and it wasn't even a photograph -- it looked like Abadie had hired a comic book artist to draw it.

"Where *is* Doctor Noble?"

"Gettin' a cat out of a tree," he said, flicking ash from his cigar over the railing. "Keep yer pants on, kid."

"Is it okay if I record the interview?"

"Audio or video?"

17

"Audio," I said, taking out my hand-held recorder.

"Yeah, that's okay."

It was actually more like ten minutes before the Doctor showed up. After a few aborted attempts at conversation with the great publicist, I used the time to review the press packet. I'd read the information a thousand times, but I went over his again. Dr. Noble had been an ordinary MD before his alien abduction some years back. He managed to feign unconsciousness as he was taken into some spacecraft, and watched as the visitors began their experiments. Somehow (the press packet was vague on this point) he managed to escape the aliens' clutches, free his fellow captives and pilot the spacecraft back to Earth. He was the only human left on the ship when he set the engine to self-destruct. Instead of killing him in a dazzling display of self-sacrifice, though, the alien energies gave him superpowers, including flight, telekinesis and limited electromagnetic manipulation. Endowed with these abilities, he embarked on a neverending battle for truth, justice and all the rest of it.

The next release in the packet was concerned more with his accomplishments since donning his tights for the first time: kidnapping victims saved, one-man rescue operations in the wake of natural disasters, terrorist attacks averted and a nearly endless list of Masks he had brought to justice. Photon Man, I noticed, was conspicuously absent from the list.

"Standard stuff," I said out loud.

"It is in *my* life, son," said a commanding voice. I turned my attention away from the packet and looked up to see the man who had just landed on the roof. He was broad-shouldered and the red and white cape he wore draped down from his mask. Wrapped in the colors of the flag, he stood erect, his jaw tilted upwards, with a smile that indicated he knew some great secret, some mystery of the universe that had never occurred to anyone else. I looked at Abadie and, in two words managed to convey the awesome respect and grandeur I felt at that moment.

"He's *fat*," I whispered.

"Hey, neither of us is gonna get a call from the Mister Universe competition either, pal. Just ask him your questions."

Okay, I was a 44-inch waist and in no danger of going down. But at least I was *proportionate*. The weight was fairly evenly distributed, so I just looked like a typical, jolly fat guy. I'd even played Santa Claus a few times. Noble, on the other hand, had a slim, svelte frame with a distended belly that seemed to indicate when he wasn't putting the bad guys behind bars he was throwing back a few brewskis with the Arrow Ace and Silverfish.

This was the first time I'd made contact with one of our superhuman protectors since Lionheart rescued me thirteen years before, so I was going to take advantage of it. I extended my hand and he took it in a firm grip. When we shook, I felt that rush again, that excitement, that burst of energy I'd gotten during my rescue.

"Wow," I said.

Noble grinned and an errant ray of sunlight sparkled off his teeth. "I get that a lot," he said.

POWER

About five minutes after I got back to the office there was a tap at the entrance to my cubicle. A head poked around the corner with a warm, welcome smile. "Hey," she said, "How did the interview go?"

Sheila Reynolds, my copy editor at *Powerlines*, was a cute brunette with deep brown eyes. I'd considered asking her out when I was new at the magazine, but she seemed to be perpetually torn between our star reporter, Scott Elliott, and the solar-powered hero, Spectrum. In fact, she often suspected Elliott and Spectrum and being one and the same, until someone pointed out to her that Elliott had a beard and Spectrum didn't. She finally gave up on it.

"It was... interesting," I said.

"You don't sound too enthused. What happened? I thought Doctor Noble was always one of your favorites."

"Well... you know how I've always been really into the big, tough, beyond reproach heroes?"

"Like Lionheart and the United Statesmen?"

"Right. I admire guys who do the right thing just *because* it's the right thing. No thought of reward, no ulterior motive... that's my kind of hero."

"And Noble?"

I flicked my computer on. "He's the most pompous ass I've ever met."

"That bad?"

I took my tape recorder out and hit the "play" button. Noble's tinny voice filtered out.

"...shortly after I single-handedly put away the Bloodsucker Gang I returned to the homeworld of the aliens that originally gave me my powers and liberated their slave class from the aristocratic *bourgeois* elite which I learned has been manipulating governments on Earth for some time now. I drove them all away by turning the Washington Monument into a giant negatively-charged magnet but this suddenly left Earth without some vital energy programs, so I rounded up all the villains I could find with electrical powers and used them to power the entire town of Luling, Texas for six months. Well naturally they gave me the key to the city which I later used as bait in the ingenious trap I set for Colonel Coldsnap and his Refrigerator Rangers--"

I shut the recorder off. "The entire fifteen minutes was like that," I said. "One long, rambling run-on ego-stroking session. I have *no* idea where to insert the punctuation marks in his quotes."

"Geez," Sheila said. "How many questions did you get to ask?"

"Just one."

"What was it?"

"'How are you?'"

She grimaced. "Ow. I'd better let you work, then -- you've got it cut out for you."

"Thanks. Hey, are we still catching a movie tomorrow?"

"You bet."

Sheila left and I turned my attention back to the interview. I was contemplating turning the story into an attack piece, but that wasn't really my style. Besides, I'd promised Abadie approval. While I sat there trying to figure out how to make him look like less of a self-absorbed cretin, I felt that same rush *(could it be adrenalin?)* I'd gotten when I met the caped bozo on the roof. Even before I turned my head to see him hovering there, I knew I would find Dr. Noble outside my window.

I raised the glass. "Can I help you?" I asked.

"Morrie forgot to give you this. It's my favorite." He reached out and handed me an 8 by 10 glossy of himself, a full body shot. He was lean in this photo -- you could count his abs if you wanted to, and my immediate reaction was to assume it had been retouched. Then I saw a billboard in the background featuring a cigarette mascot that had been retired six years ago and I suppressed a chuckle. The guy was using outdated publicity shots because he couldn't keep himself in shape.

"Thanks," I said. "I'll--"

"Where's Elliott?"

There was a sound like a wall being ripped apart and the partitions that made up my cubicle began to tremble. I tried not to worry -- when I got the job I was warned that irate super-villains had a tendency to show up at the office hunting reporters who made them look bad, although this was the first time since I'd been there that one of them was tearing up *my* floor.

Before I even left my chair, Noble blasted in through the window and flew into the hall. I followed just in time to see him catch a rather satisfying blow to the jaw, sending him tumbling.

"Where's that slimeball Elliott?" shouted his attacker. A shock of blonde hair fell across her eyes and she brushed it back with one blue glove, finally allowing me a good look at her masked face. It was Miss Sinistah, late of the Malevolence Mob. My mental reporter's file clicked to her entry -- she'd been part of an illegal program to genetically enhance athletes, but it was only a partial success. She had highly increased strength, endurance and durability, but the more the used her powers the weaker she got and had to resort to periods of almost no physical activity to recharge. Still, when fully energized she was invulnerable, super strong... and *shorter* than I'd imagined.

"*You!*" She grabbed me by the front of the shirt and lifted me into the air. "All right, big boy, where is he?"

"Who--"

"Elliott! Scott Elliott!"

"He's not here--"

"Stop trying to cover. He's hiding, right? He *knew* I'd be coming after him for that piece he wrote about the Mob. We were *never* brought in by that milksop Lionheart! I never even *met* him! I'll rip his *arms* off when I--"

She was only halfway through the rant when the sudden burst of energy broke us apart. I fell safely to the floor and she went crashing into a cubicle wall, making it collapse on Danny Cardigan from the graphic design department.

"What was *that*?" she spat out as she scrambled to her feet.

"It looked like Noble used his telekinesis to break them apart!" Sheila shouted.

Sinistah grumbled. "How is it somebody *always* has the time for expository dialogue during these fights?"

Her next announcement was cut short when Noble slammed into her. I pulled myself to my feet and half-walked, half-stumbled to the stairwell. I wasn't concerned about the fight, Noble would catch her. Those guys *always* did. All I wanted was for the rush to fade, which it did as I put some distance between myself and the superhumans.

It was logical to accept Sheila's explanation, just as it was typical of a winning fella like Noble to take credit. But she was wrong, I knew it. The whole time Noble had been there, I'd felt the rush. When Sinistah showed up, it lanced upwards on me, and I felt stronger than ever before.

Then, when she insulted Lionheart -- a genuinely *good* hero -- I'd felt a veil of anger like I'd never experienced. And when that happened, something inside me exploded.

The teke-burst that bowled over Miss Sinistah didn't come from Dr. Noble. It came from *me.*

ISSUE TWO

ACCIDENTS HAPPEN

How many people ever stare at a quarter? I mean really *stare* at it? Do they wonder why Washington is facing the left instead of the right? Why it looks like he's not wearing anything but that stupid bow in his hair? I didn't think about any of those things either, until I spent the better part of an hour staring at a twenty-five cent piece that night, trying to make it move with my mind.

"It's just sitting there," Sheila observed.

"I *know* it's just sitting there," I hissed. "Maybe it's a magic quarter or something."

"Yeah, there are lots of those in circulation."

"Hey, we've seen stranger things. In this office. Today. Sheila, I *know* I fired off that telekinetic burst this afternoon."

"Doctor Noble did that."

"That overstuffed moron couldn't hit anything that didn't come from a keg. *Move*, dammit!"

"Maybe you should try being polite to it."

"Oh be quiet." I slapped the quarter away and it rolled under the desk. "Maybe it needs to be sparked by anger or something."

"You're not mad *enough* at it?"

"*You're* getting on my nerves right now. How do you feel about being a guinea pig?"

Sheila sighed and planted a light, sisterly kiss on my forehead. "Aw, Josh, sweetie, we all know how bad you want to get into the game. Heck, that's why most of us came to work here in the first place. But sooner or later, you're just going to have to accept that it's not going to happen, okay?"

"Hey, Sheila," Danny said, poking his head into my cubicle. "We've got a rumble in the streets between Deep Six and Flambeaux. You might want to pull out those files to prep the story."

"Okay, Dan. Where's the rumble, anyway?"

"Right outside. I think Flambeaux read Scott's last column."

"I *tell* him to think before he writes that sort of thing. Later, Joshie-bear." Sheila patted my hand and left me alone.

"Darn quarter," I mumbled, fishing in my pocket for another one. I cleared everything else off my desk, sweeping it into my already-cluttered top drawer, and placed the quarter dead center. As I concentrated on it, I heard a whistling sound outside -- Flambeaux used his fire powers to make himself lighter than air. The result was, he could fly, and apparently he was doing so right outside the building. I didn't catch this yet. I was staring at the damned quarter.

I didn't notice it at first, but as the whistling sound rose and fell, I started to feel minor peaks in energy -- like the rush was starting to creep up on me. With each minor scale in the energy I redoubled my concentration. Finally my eyes were beginning to hurt and I was ready to *throw* the blasted thing just to get it to move. I didn't listen to the whistling outside, paid no attention to the crescendo of a human body hurtling through the air at supersonic speeds. I paid no heed at all to the fact that it was getting louder and louder and I was feeling stronger and stronger.

Two things then happened at once. The first is that the whistling got so loud, so intense that Flambeaux *must* have flown directly past my window. I could hear this, even though I was paying no attention to it.

The second thing that happened was, as the whistle reached its loudest point, a massive burst of flame erupted from my eyes and charred off the top of my desk. My concentration broke immediately -- in part because the flames were threatening to burn my face off -- and I fell back in my chair.

The fire alarm went off just as I flopped out of my cubicle shouting incoherent syllables with the intent of alerting people to the situation. "Fire! Gha! Cubie! Fire!" were my exact words. Fortunately, between this and the four-foot wall of flames that was roaring behind me, Sheila was able to translate the message.

She grabbed the fire extinguisher and rushed into my cubicle. There was a spitting sound and the light was replaced by smoke. Sheila came back out and shoved the extinguisher in my hands.

"Some hero," she chuckled. Crisis averted, the rest of the staff was returning to work. This sort of thing happened *far* too often around here.

"How did Flambeaux blast you like that? The window is still closed," Sheila said.

I dropped my voice and leaned into her. "It wasn't Flambeaux. Sheila, it was me."

"Josh..."

"No, come on, I *swear*. I was trying to move that damn quarter again and... the quarter!" I grabbed her by the arm and dragged her into my slightly-used work area. The top of my desk was black and burnt, except in the center. There, puddled on the desk, were the molten remains of twenty-five American cents.

"You see *that*?"

"Okay, Josh, this is going too far. Maybe you should see the company counselor--"

"Dammit!" I grabbed her by the arm again and tugged her into the stairwell, hitting the steps and going straight for the roof.

"Josh, what are you doing? Let go!"

"I'm proving my point! I *know* I've got something going on!"

When we made it to the roof we could see Flambeaux smoldering at the top of Barks Plaza across the street. Deep Six's partners in the Spectacle Six had arrived, and he was getting a lift from the robot called V3OL.

"Look! I'll bet I can send up a flare." I thrust my hand towards the air and started thinking *hot, heat, fire, flame*... even *mad* and *angry* when nothing else worked.

"Josh, you look like an idiot."

"Did Edison look like an idiot when he invented the light bulb? The Wright Brothers? Eins*teeeeaaaaaiiiigh!*"

The scream wasn't of pain, but of shock -- my hand was rocketing away into the air. I didn't go *with* it, mind you, I stayed right there on the roof. Nor did the hand separate itself from my body. Instead, my arm stretched out to a length of at least twenty feet. The flesh hung in the gap like overstretched taffy.

When I realized what was happening, I shouted even louder, falling back into Sheila's arms. She didn't catch me, though. Instead I puddled through her fingers into a gooey mess on the roof.

"Josh! Josh, what's going on? *JOSH!*"

Taking a deep breath (and feeling my lungs inflate like balloons) I tried to imagine myself whole again, 44-inch waist and all. I thought of myself as *solid* as *human* as *complete*.

And when I managed to stop panicking, I felt my body pull itself back together, and I was *me* again.

"Oh God, Josh, what the hell *was* that?"

"I don't know what's going on, Sheila. I don't. I--"

As I rambled, a purple-gloved hand stretched up onto the roof, pulling behind it an overly-long individual, wadding all over the place like mint and purple Silly Putty. As he stretched up onto the roof and solidified, we managed to place him as another of the Spectacle Six, DoubleGum Man.

"You people shouldn't be up here," he said. "It's not safe. Get back inside the building and let us handle it."

"Right," I gasped, feeling that same old rush and, at the same time, feeling my knees turn to jelly -- literally. "We'll... we'll get downstairs." I grabbed Sheila and headed for the door, just as DoubleGum bounced away towards the rumble. Once we were back inside, the door slammed behind us. I dared to test my limbs, flexing all my muscles and waving my arms around. They were solid. I was normal.

"Josh, what's going on?"

"That's what I've been trying to tell you!" I shouted. "Sheila... it's *happening.* I've got *super powers.*"

"But so *many*? Teke-bursts and fire and stretching and... Josh *nobody* has powers that diverse, they say it's *impossible.*"

"That's not it, Sheila, don't you see? I don't have *any* of those powers."

"I just *saw* you stretch."

"But I can't do it *now.* And I could only do the teke-burst while Dr. Numbskull was in the room, and that fire thing only worked while Flambeaux was *right outside the window.* Don't you *get* it?"

"Get *what?*"

"*That's* my power. I can duplicate *other people's* powers, so long as they're nearby. It's like I'm... I don't know, picking up on ambient energy or something. Man... if I could get around a big, mess of heroes at once I'll bet I could do *anything.*"

"Well... what *are* you going to do?"

I felt another rush this time... not the one that meant I had powers welling up on me... one of pure adrenalin. And I gave her a smile to indicate I knew *exactly* what I was going to do.

"You're going to get yourself killed," she said.

CALLING HOME

I spent the rest of the day shopping, getting materials together for my uniform and facing more than a little ridicule from Sheila in the process. I was ready to put the whole thing together, but there were a few things I was more than a little curious about -- and for all my reporting skills there was always one method of information gathering I turned to when all else failed.

"Hey, Mom, it's me," I said when she finally picked up her phone.

"Joshie! How are you, sweetheart?" she asked.

"Not bad--"

"If you're calling to remind me of your birthday next month, I'll have you know I already got your present, so you can just stop hinting around, mister. And no, it's not as good as the Defender footie pajamas you got when you were seven, so you'll just have to lump it."

"Nothing like that, Mom." I had her on speaker phone so I could work with the laces and accessories I'd bought while I talked. "I was just sort of wondering about... things."

"What sort of things, honey?"

"Well... I had a normal childhood, didn't I?"

"Let's see, your father was creep, you nearly died in a fire, you were saved by a Cape... I guess you'd call it normal in a 'Daytime Talk Show' sort of way."

"No, I mean... did anything really *bizarre* ever happen to me? Or did I ever *do* anything really bizarre?"

"You used to pour 7-Up in your chicken soup before you ate it. Does that count?"

My cat, a plump tabby, tried to hop up into my lap as I spread out my tunic. He looked up at me with big, wondering eyes (wondering, no doubt, if what I was working on was food and, if so, how was he going to get some). I called the cat Achilles. To this day I don't know what he called himself, but he certainly never responded to his given name.

"Down boy," I said.

"What?"

"Not you, mom. I can't really say that's what I'm looking for. I never... I dunno, started to float around the room or got bathed in some kind of highly-experimental radioactive fluid, did I?"

"Josh--"

"Mom, I'll cut to the chase, am I the product of a top-secret government conspiracy?"

She gave me the sigh that let me know I had gone too far. "Josh, I *know* you've always wanted to be a superhero. I blame your father."

"Dad never said anything to me about superheroes."

"Your dad never said much of *anything* to you, that's why you adopted guys like Lionheart as surrogates. I promise you, Josh, you have led a perfectly normal life, utterly devoid of radiation baths, magic spells and alien abductions. I'm sorry to disappoint you."

"Meow," said Achilles. He still wasn't convinced my latest project wasn't edible.

"That's okay, Mom."

"Why are you bringing all this up now? Did something happen at work?"

"Yeah. I was writing a story about Capes whose powers didn't manifest until late in life and I was just thinking..."

"Maybe you could *be* one, right?"

I held out the tunic I'd just finished stitching my superhero emblem. "Yeah. That's it exactly."

"All I can say, son, is that if you start emitting radiation, it's not my fault."

"Okay. I guess I should go; I've got work to do. Oh, and I'm sorry if I wasted your time."

"Any time, Josh. Oh, and son?"

"Yes?"

"If this is the last time I hear from you before your birthday, you don't *get* a present."

"It's a deal, Mom."

After the line was disconnected, I wiggled into the half-finished uniform I'd been stitching. It was exactly as I'd envisioned it. "Well, Achilles?" I asked. "What's the verdict?"

"Meow," he observed.

"My thoughts exactly."

PATROL

You write about superheroes long enough and you learn that the first thing, the most *important* thing any new hero needs is a good costume. Something proud and strong. Something that makes a bold statement. Something that strikes fear in the hearts of evildoers and inspires awe and respect amongst the peace-loving general populace.

"You look like a dork," Sheila said.

"Is it the trenchcoat? Is it too much?"

"Oh, I think you crossed the 'too much' line when you decided to go with the gold trim," she said.

I turned back to the full-length mirror Sheila had in her apartment and ran my eyes along the improvised get-up. Wisely choosing to eschew the tights, I'd elected for black trousers and boots and a pair of black leather gloves. My domino mask was the same royal blue as my tunic and a line of gold trim formed the initials "GP" on my chest. I'd topped off the whole ensemble with a black trenchcoat -- partially to give myself a more imposing look and partially in the hopes that any evildoers I ran across would find it distracting enough not to notice they were being jumped by a 250-pound reporter.

"I think it looks pretty good," I said.

"You look like a dork," she reiterated.

"You know, my mother always says that clothes do *not* make the man."

"Your mother is far more forgiving than our editor will be if you turn in a story about some geek in a trenchcoat with gold laces."

"I'm not going to *write* about this! A reporter who's really a superhero and turns in stories about *himself*? How unethical would *that* be?"

To be perfectly honest, I kind of *felt* like a dork, too, but there was no way I'd admit that to Sheila. Instead I just flexed my leather-clad fists and said, "Open the window."

"The *window*? For *what*?"

"So I can go on my first patrol."

"Josh, you've read way too many comic books. What happens if you come across a mugger? Or a bank robber? Someone with no powers for you to duplicate? You could get killed."

"So I only go after Masks. No non-powered opponents."

"Oh, *that*'s better. Now it's between you -- a novice with *no* clue as to what he's doing -- and people who have dealt with these abilities every day of their lives."

"Come on, Sheila. It'll be a massacre."

"That's exactly what I'm afraid of."

Frowning at her skepticism, I went and opened the window myself. I had already scrambled halfway out onto the fire escape when I felt her warm hand wrap around my arm.

"Josh, just... be careful." She placed a chaste kiss on my cheek and gave my arm a squeeze. I smiled back at her.

"I'll be fine," I promised.

To my chagrin, I soon found that "fine" was a relative term. Usually the urban superheroes without some method of flight or propulsion carried cables and grappling hooks that allowed rapid transportation from rooftop to rooftop. In *my* case, what you had was a fat guy scrabbling up and down fire escapes with a pair of binoculars banging against his chest. I wasn't going to be instilling fear in any crooks anytime soon, but I was hoping I'd at least have them paralyzed with laughter long enough to leap down and take them out with their own powers.

Remembering what Sheila said about a bank robber, I decided the primary place to survey on my patrol would be the First National Bank. Two fire escapes and a pulled shoulder muscle later, I decided that was way the hell too far away and I'd go to the Fourth National Bank instead. After nearly slipping on a ladder and falling to a grisly death, I cut my losses and held patrol over a nearby ATM.

I sat on the fire escape glaring at that ATM for about three hours -- most of which I spent trying to concoct a story to feed to Sheila to avoid ridicule: "Well there I was, surrounded by Herr Nemesis and the Tantric Trio, when I remembered Aura's weakness to magnifying glasses..."

It was about two a.m. at this point and the worst crime I'd seen thus far was a stray dog peeing on a fire hydrant. I was ready to pack it in and go home when God smiled on me and the woman in the brown coat showed up. She had short-cropped blonde hair that fell into her face every so often, and she'd brush it aside with her blue-gloved hand. Her mask was familiar, but it wasn't quite clicking where I'd seen this tiny woman before.

Standing on tiptoes, she glared into the two-way mirror that masked the ATM's security camera, as if she was making sure it saw her. Then she tossed her coat aside and I realized where I'd encountered her before. It was that afternoon in the *Powerlines* office.

"Miss Sinistah," I hissed.

The villainess craned her arm back and shattered the face of the ATM with a superhuman punch. Cash was flying everywhere. I didn't know how she'd escaped Dr. Noble, nor did I care. It was going to feel *great* to bring in a Mask that had evaded our Beloved Champion.

As I scrambled down the fire escape, I began to feel the now-familiar Rush (it was important enough, I'd decided, to capitalize) come over me. My muscles toughened and the exhaustion drained from my limbs. I was ready to take her down.

Apparently, though, one of Miss Sinistah's powers was *not* super-coordination, because my attempt to leap from the fire escape and land in a dramatic pose wound up with me dangling from the ladder by one foot and my head rattling around inside a garbage can.

My head clunked against the metal and I grunted, more from habit than from any actual pain. I hung there, banging my head against aluminum and smelling what must have been a mix of orange peels, coffee grounds and certain feminine hygiene products, and the only thing I could think of before a hand wrapped around my ankle and lifted me out was, "Well *this* is stupid."

I stared at a pair of red boots and wondered why on Earth anyone would choose stiletto heels for combat. Despite the blood rushing to my head, I managed to bend my neck until I was looking at her knees. Then the blue trunks that only *just* covered her thighs. Then her bare midriff. And then slightly higher I saw...

"I'm up *here,* lunkhead," she said.

With Herculean effort I bent my neck a bit farther so I could look into a pair of the iciest blue eyes I'd ever seen.

"And who are *you* supposed to be? I wasn't told there were any new guys on this assignment."

I twisted my leg, breaking free of her grip, and somehow rolled myself into a standing position. "I'm one of the *good* guys." I grabbed the lid off a trash can and, using Sinistah's own super-strength, drove my fist clean through it. This, along with my brilliant dialogue, was intended to be impressive. Instead, as Sheila doubtlessly would have informed me, I looked like a dork with my fist in a garbage can lid.

"One of the *good* guys? Please." There was a new Rush and a shape descended from the sky. He took a spot next to Sinistah, folded his arms and frowned.

"Doctor Noble!" I suddenly felt lightheaded, trying to imagine myself slugging it out with Siegel City's Sweetheart. "I knew you were a jackass," I said, "but I didn't think you'd be in league with the Malevolence Mob!"

"Don't tell me..." he mumbled.

"I think so," she said, frowning. "What's your name, honey?"

I steeled myself and spat out the introductory line I'd rehearsed in Sheila's apartment.

"You can call me," pause for dramatic effect, "the *Great Pretender*!" I pointed a thumb at the insignia on my chest. "And I'm going to use your own powers to put you both out of commission!"

There was a long, hideous silence.

And then Noble started to laugh. Not quite as loudly as Sheila had.

Sinistah slapped him on the arm. "Now cut that out," she said. "He doesn't know."

"Know *what*?" I shouted. "Look, I don't *need* to know any more than I already do. People deserve to know that their 'hero' is corrupt. You're *not* walking away from here."

I launched my fist at Noble's jaw, but it stopped in midair some inches from his face. That's when I knew guys with telekinetic powers really honked me off.

"Amateur," he said in the tone of voice you use to describe intestinal discomfort. He squinted and I felt a pinching inside my neck. The world swam around me, dissolved into a haze, and I collapsed.

"What did you *do*, Todd?" I heard Sinistah ask.

"Don't get 'em in a bunch," Noble growled. "I just cut off the blood to his brain to knock him out. He'll be fine."

"Should we take him to Morrie?"

"Standard protocol," he said. "Hey... his eyes just moved. I guess I didn't whammy him good enough."

The pinching resumed, and the last thing I wondered before I blacked out was where I'd heard the name "Morrie" before that day.

ISSUE THREE

OFFICE PARTY

I awoke to the gentlest brushes on my cheek and a sweet voice saying, "Preten -- um -- honey? Whatever your name is, come on, wake up. It'll be okay, I promise."

The voice alone was enough of an incentive for me to pry my eyes open. As the universe returned to me I saw an incredible woman wearing Miss Sinistah's costume. She looked warm, tender -- it was like having my own personal angel to welcome me back to consciousness. As my head began to clear I realized it *was* Miss Sinistah. Somehow I hadn't recognized her without her mask.

Dear God, she was beautiful.

"Are you all right?"

"Oh, sure," I said, hoping I sounded more sophisticated than I felt. "That's the last time that train will try to hit *me*."

"I'm sorry about To -- Doctor Noble. He's not aware of this new technique we have called 'talking to people'."

"Oh, like *he* would have listened," Noble grumbled, alerting me to the fact that Sinistah and I were not alone. I blinked a few more times, extinguishing the sleep in my eyes, and I was in an office, lying back in a swiveling chair in front of a desk. I was turned to the side so I could see the door to my right and the desk to my left. Noble was sitting on a couch next to the door, mask down, moping. With his mask off I saw that he had, in addition to his nasty attitude and ugly, stupid eyes, one massive eyebrow marching across his forehead. Actually, that's not doing it justice -- it looked like his lauded aliens had grafted a mutant caterpillar to his face while they were busy giving him his powers. It felt slightly gratifying.

I could still feel the Rush coming from Noble and Sinistah (actually, I felt considerably more than just the Rush from Sinistah), but I was also feeling more power hitting me from the left. Standing next to a desk was a woman in magenta robes with a blood-red medallion around her neck. Her skin was a lighter shade than her clothing but still quite a satisfactory purple and her eyes were white and pupil-less -- she looked like some bizarre mutation of Little Orphan Annie. Her pointed ears probably could have been covered by her hair if not for the fact that she was completely bald. A guy who didn't work for a superhero news rag probably would have found her familiar but be unable to place a finger on her identity. One of the first things you go through when you get a job at *Powerlines,* though, is an intense rundown of all known Capes and Masks in the city -- this girl in particular, because people had an interesting tendency to "forget" her. She was the mysterious heroine known as Mental Maid.

And, of course, sitting behind the desk, gnawing on an imported *la repulsiva* cigar, was my old pal Morrie Abadie.

"Mister Cordwood," he said, "a pleasure to speak to you again."

"For the last time, it's *Cor*wood, not -- hey! How did you --" My hand went up to my face and traced the outline of my domino mask, still firmly set.

"You don't *really* think that's much of a disguise, do you?" he chuckled. "I can still see your eyes, nose, cheekbones -- every distinguishing feature. That kind of mask gives you about as much anonymity as a pair of glasses."

"Yeah? What about guys like Hotshot? Jackal? The Marauder? It's good enough for *them*."

"*They* have a gal like Mental Maid to make sure nobody pays too much attention. You don't got that yet, kid. Even half-masks wouldn't protect you for long without her doin' her thing." He expelled a gray-blue ring of smoke into the air from between his fleshy lips. "So, 'Pretender,' what do you do, anyway?"

My intended response was to invite him to perform a certain anatomical impossibility, but instead I found myself answering, "I can duplicate other people's powers if I'm in close range."

Morrie's eyes lit up and, for the first time, I detected a hint of cunning behind them to match his greed and lack of scruples. "*Really*?" he said. "And can you do *anybody's* powers?"

"Everyone I've tried so far."

"Yeah? Gimme a list."

"Miss Sinistah. Flambeaux. DoubleGum Man. The Gunk, now that I think about it. Doctor Dunderhead here." Noble blanched at that, but I saw a sly grin trace its way across Sinistah's face.

"And I'm not sure how they work," I finished, "but I can *feel* Mental Maid's powers running through me right now." A light went off. *"That's* how you're doing this, aren't you? *She's* forcing me to answer your questions."

"Better than any truth serum," Morrie said. "So how long have you been aping powers off my boys?"

"I only realized I *could* do it today," I said. "But I think I did it once when I was a kid. When Lionheart saved me from a fire."

"Oooh, Lionheart. 'Course, you're still practically a kid now, musta been just before he took a powder."

"Bite me." I'm still not sure if Mental Maid's truth powers made me say that or not. I rather hope not.

"Don't get cocky, kid, I haven't made up my mind about you yet."

"What are you babbling about? Look, I don't know how you warped these heroes into your schemes, but if you're going to kill me just go ahead and do it or I'll --"

Morrie and Noble exploded into laughter. Sinistah shot them both a dirty look.

"What? What did I say?"

"I'm sorry," Sinistah said. "They *never* act civil to people from the outside."

"What the hell is going *on*?" I shouted.

"Morrie?" There was a knock at the door and a man in red, black and gold poked his head in. Even if it weren't for the sunburst emblem on his belt buckle and the freshly-ridiculed half-mask, I would have recognized this guy. He was Hotshot, the last active

43

member of the now-defunct LightCorps, the team Lionheart had founded.

And in his hands was what appeared to be a script.

"Hey, Minister Malice and I had some questions about Tuesday's rumble. Have you got a minute?"

"Not now, 'Shot," Morrie said. "We're having a discussion with our friend Mister Corwood. We'll go over it later."

"Okay, Morrie." He grinned straight at me on his way out. "Good luck, kid," he said.

"What..." I said.

"The *hell*..." I continued.

"Was *that?*" I added for clarity.

"That was Hotshot goin' over his next fight with Minister Malice. And it's a damn good thing, too. Usually it's like pulling teeth to get any decent rehearsal time outta Mister 'I Was In the Original LightCorps...'"

"No," I said. "I mean... what the *hell* was *that?*"

"It's like having a parrot isn't it?" Noble smirked.

"He's a *hero!*" I shouted. "He's not supposed to be in cahoots with people like Minister Malice or... or *you*."

Morrie sighed. "You still don't get it, do you kid?"

"What is there to *get?*"

"It's all a fake. A fraud. The battles are staged. The villains are actors. The stuff you've spent your life following and reporting on has all the legitimacy of a pro wrestling match."

"*Liar!*"

"Afraid not. There hasn't been a real superhero battle in Siegel City for nearly ten years."

LUNCH BREAK

Morrie's office, as it turned out, was part of a much larger underground complex that housed dorms, studios, laboratories, various workout, training and rehearsal areas and, apparently, a first-rate cafeteria, all buried in the superstructure of Simon Tower. Miss Sinistah took me for some food to ponder the offer Morrie had laid on the table.

"I just don't know about this," I said. "It seems so... dishonest."

"We're just actors, Josh," she said. "It's like being on a movie or on a soap opera."

"Except that the audience knows a soap opera is fake. Superhero rumbles don't get interrupted by Proctor & Gamble ads."

We were in the food line with about a dozen other Capes and Masks getting their late-night lunches. Many more were already seated and eating. This was a nocturnal crowd, I realized. I recognized the Squid and DeVinity right away, and Merlin Junior was sitting with his legs crossed, hovering along and picking up food as he went.

Swordplay and Whipstar, supposedly mortal enemies, were in line ahead of us, laughing and clapping each other on the back like they were kids in summer camp, and the Justice Giant had his massive arms wrapped around the death-masked Solemna, a villain I *knew* had tried to kill him at least seven times in the past week. I'd even managed to get a telephone quote from the guy: "When I get my hands on that horror movie reject, I'm going to send her back to whatever unmarked grave she crawled out of."

He was saying considerably different things to her in the cafeteria line. "More pudding, sweets?" for instance, and, "Of course I don't mind if your mother comes for a visit." I kept expecting Rod Serling to make an appearance.

Aside from the sudden surprises I'd gotten just from a *visual* standpoint, I was feeling a stronger influx of power than I'd ever known before. Each time one of these guys walked past me I felt a new Rush, a new power, that faded as they moved away. Now I could walk through walls. Now I could disintegrate them. Now I could speak any language ever written. Now I could dance the Alligator faster than anybody in the world.

"The Alligator?" I muttered to myself as that particular ability faded.

"Hey," grumbled a frosty voice behind me, "you wanna keep the line going, pal?"

I looked back to stare straight into the arctic-blue eyes of Icebergg, one of the city's more notorious villains.

"Um, moving, sir."

Turning my attention at last to the food, I found a few more items of interest. While the cafeteria featured all the normal foods you would expect -- sandwiches, chicken, salads and the like -- there was an equally plentiful assortment of foods I'd never seen. Glowing fruits and crystalline lumps. Bubbling metallic soups and milkshakes of no color found in nature.

Merlin Junior levitated a plate of sky-blue mush onto his tray, and further down the line I saw Fourtifier munching on what looked like a broken shard of stained glass. Icebergg, at least, had *human* foods, but what an assortment: hot peppers and pizza with the cheese still bubbling, a sizzling enchilada and a café latté that was more steam then coffee.

"What are you looking at, new meat?" he asked in an arctic tone.

"I was just... admiring your dinner," I said.

"You wasting time with punks like *this* on top of your other nasty habits now, Sinistah?"

"Oh, chill out, Simon."

"Bad joke. Awful joke."

"You know you love me," she giggled.

"Yeah... whatever. Just keep your new pet away from me, okay?" He picked up his tray and ambled off.

"Nice guy," I commented.

"He's really a sweetheart once you get to know him."

I nodded, but I was getting the feel Sinistah had that impression of just about everybody. "So why does he eat like that, anyway?"

"Keeps him from freezing up," Sinistah said as she placed a tuna melt on her plate. "Although frankly, I think it's psychosomatic." Come on."

She led me to a table near the middle of the cafeteria and we sat down. From every direction I could feel rising and falling energy levels. On any other day I'd be falling all over myself trying to see how many powers I could duplicate, but sitting that close to her...

well... the powers just didn't seem that important anymore.

"Miss -- I'm sorry, I feel ridiculous calling you 'Miss Sinistah.' Can I ask your name?"

"No real names with rookies," she said. "Sorry."

I adopted a hurt puppy dog look and she rolled her eyes. "No fair, I'm a sucker for that sort of thing."

"I got that vibe."

"Tell you what, why don't you just call me 'Sindy'? With an 'S'."

"Sindy with an S? Is that your name?"

"Nope. But it's the best you're gonna get for now." She said it in sort of a teasing, singsong voice that seemed to imply I'd have a shot at her real name later. She smiled and I once again began feeling an entirely different sort of Rush from her.

Damn. Those *eyes*.

"Okay, Sindy then. All ethics of misleading the public aside, what if somebody gets hurt during one of your *faux* rumbles? This isn't the safest job in the world."

"Oh we train. And we rehearse. A *lot*. Morrie's tough on Hotshot but he really does take it seriously. The chances of one of us getting legitimately injured are pretty slim and, on those rare occasions it *does* happen... well, he knew the risks."

"What about innocent bystanders?"

She almost laughed at that. "Josh, you're a reporter, right? When's the last time you heard about an innocent bystander getting hurt during a rumble?"

"Well yeah, it's rare, but it *does* happen. About once or twice a year we get a report--"

"Plants," she said. "Every so often we slip one of our own into the crowd to fake an injury or a death. It keeps up the necessary drama and maintains the public distrust of super-villains.

"And what's more, at every scheduled rumble we have a few speedsters or fliers or tekes hanging out incognito, just in case there's an accident. You know, the type that could jump in and lend a hand but still have a fairly small chance of being noticed."

"And if they *are* noticed?"

She grinned. "Haven't you ever wondered why there are so many superhero team-ups?"

"Well what about property damage? You guys are *always* wrecking things."

"We've got under-the-table deals with every insurance company in Siegel City. Anyone whose property we wreck is covered, whether they know it or not."

I let out a sigh and sank my teeth into the corned beef sandwich I'd gotten (which, I had to admit, was pretty good. I wondered if there was a Cape in the back with food preparation powers.)

"It just... it seems so *wrong.*"

"A lot of people feel that way at first, but eventually they realize it's just a form of entertainment, not that different from pro sports or kid's cartoons. Plus, we all get some pretty nice residuals when our likenesses are licensed for toys and books and the like. That's also how Morrie bankrolls this entire operation, by the way

-- the merchandising. You'd be surprised what people are willing to pay for a Miss Sinistah Action Ace figure."

No I wouldn't. I had one on my nightstand. Paid $16.95 for it at a comic book store. "And nobody *ever* figures you out?" I asked, rapidly changing the subject.

"Mental Maid's powers are strong enough to cast a field of susceptibility over the entire city."

"A *what*?"

"A susceptibility field. It makes the general populace a bit more susceptible to suggestion."

"They'll swallow any line Morrie feeds them, in other words."

"If you want to be blunt about it. And should anyone find out find out the truth, Mental Maid can blank that part of their memory."

"You mean... like *I* just found out?"

For the first time, her lovely smile left her face, replaced with a look of concern. "I *really* hope you take the job," she said. "I'd hate to see you... damaged."

"Damaged?"

"Mental Maid's the best, but even *she* goofs up sometimes."

I felt an audible gulp arise in my throat.

"Come on, Josh. It's not so bad, really."

There was a squelching pat on my back and I nearly jumped out of my skin. There were too many Masks around for me to be really comfortable yet and the rapidly rising and descending Rushes had me confused -- I was still waiting for Dynaman to show up and blow me to smithereens or something.

"Sorry about that, chap. I just wanted to apologize for nearly bowling you over this afternoon."

I looked back at the man attached to the arm on my shoulder. And the three other arms it was attached to.

"Gunk?"

"Everybody *always* reacts like that," the Gunk said. "Really, my boy, you've already learned we just play parts. We're *actors.* You didn't *really* think I was that monosyllabic brute that bounds around the city, did you? By the way, you may want to think about your costume, that's not much of a mask you know."

He smiled, patted me again and walked off with a tray of what looked like oatmeal, except it was green and something was moving in it. I turned back to Sindy.

"The Gunk..."

"Is a Rhodes scholar. He *was* a scientist before the accident that gave him his powers, you know."

"Then why such a... drastic act?"

"Morrie says that people *expect* a monster to sound stupid."

"That's awful."

"Not really. Gunk actually enjoys playing the part. He says it challenges his thespian skills."

"And Goop?"

She swallowed. "You know, even *we* don't know just where Goop came from. The older guys tell me he just started hanging around the Gunk one day."

"No, I mean... is he playing a part or is he really... the way he is?"

"Hey! It's *you* again!"

The smaller, slimy Goop squished into my lap and threw an arm around his neck. "Hey, there, little guy. Good to see you again. I *never* forget a face, did you know that? You might wanna change the mask though. I can see right through that. Gunk! Wait for me!"

He mussed my hair with one gooey hand and bounded off to the table where the Gunk was already eating with Nightshadow.

"Goop is pretty much himself," Sindy said.

"This is a lot to take in. I just... I wanted to *help* people, you know?"

"You don't think we help people? We usually provide *much* better role models than, say, NFL pros. And Morrie lets us do a little freelancing on the side -- anyone in Cape can stop a legitimate crime or help put out a fire -- anything they want, so long as it's not out of character."

"And the Masks?"

"They can help as long as they can do it without being noticed. And under *no* circumstances can they commit unsanctioned crimes."

"Sanctioned crimes, *uns*anctioned crimes," I muttered. "Do you realize how this all sounds?"

"Of course."

"Some role models we are. I always wanted to be one of the good guys -- Lionheart, the LightCorps... and now to learn all of this--"

"Well *they* were legitimate."

"What about Hotshot? *He's* part of your little menagerie."

"He wasn't always a... well... one of us. None of the original LightCorps members were. Not Tin Man, not Oriole, not the Defender. When Lionheart vanished, the rest of them lost their spirit and, one at a time, decided to retire. Finally, only Hotshot was left. That's when Morrie came to him with his original proposal. Once the deal was made, most of the remaining heroes in the city signed up."

"And those that didn't?" I asked.

"Mental Maid wiped their memories and planted the urge to leave Siegel City for good."

"So not every city on Earth is stuck with fake superheroes?"

"Most of the major ones are scripted now... New York, Washington D.C., Boston... oh, and Los Angeles, naturally. We mine a lot of our writers from Hollywood."

"That explains why most of the fights seem exactly the same."

"Every so often we even do a trade with another city. V3OL, the robot, came from Detroit, for instance. We traded for the Cluemeister and a sidekick to be named later."

"What about the villains? How did you get *them* to sign up and play nice?"

"Well it's not like it was me *personally,* Josh, I've only been here for a few years. I'm only 22 myself."

"Okay, not you, I'm sorry. How did it happen?"

"Well, from what I learned, Hotshot and the heroes rounded up most of the really hardcore villains -- the sadistic, violent ones and the world-conquerors -- and put them away. Security was beefed up and, although one of them may still escape from time to time, when that happens he's got Morrie's whole force after him. Escapees never last long."

"And the non-world-conquerors?"

"The rest of them -- bank robbers and publicity-seekers, mostly, were offered the same deal as the heroes."

"Sign up or get the hell out of Dodge?"

"Most of them signed up. A guaranteed paycheck and no jail time? How could they refuse?"

"No jail time? Don't tell me you've got the cops in on this, too."

"Not most of them. But we do have... friends... in every precinct."

I must have been wearing the hurt puppy dog face again, because she placed her hand on my arm and for what may have been the dozenth time said, "It's really not that bad." At least, that's what I *think* she said. The moment she made contact with my arm an electric jolt raced through my entire body and every sensory device I was equipped with was suddenly focusing on the fact that a beautiful woman was voluntarily touching me.

When my head finally began to clear I gave her a weak smile. "I feel sort of silly now, I guess. I thought..." my voice trailed off as I tried to figure out how to express what I thought without looking like even more of a dork than my costume would seem to convey. She rescued me.

"You thought you'd be able to help people. There's nothing wrong with that."

It was then that I realized she was leaning remarkably close to me.

"You know, that is a *great* trait for a guy to have."

"It... it *is*?" I felt the sweat beginning to pool in my hands.

"Yeah. Concern for other people is *very* desirable."

I steeled myself like a man staring down the barrel of a gun and gave her the suavest, most sophisticated line of my life: "Abbabbabbabbabbabbabba..."

"Seriously, sometimes I think my boyfriend wouldn't show concern if his own mother got body-slammed by the Gunk."

Have you ever actually *felt* your tongue swell to the size of a sea lion? It's really a rather interesting sensation.

As she turned her attention back to her tuna melt, my rapidly-disintegrating brain tried to process what she'd just said. This was horrible. This was terrible. This was the worst thing that could possibly happen. The only way this could be any worse was if--

"You done with this loser yet, babe?" said Dr. Noble, approaching the table. He spun the chair next to Sindy backwards, plopped down and threw an arm around her shoulders like a caveman protecting his territory. I'd always believed God had a sense of humor. Now I had evidence.

THE CONDUCTOR

If Sindy's presence had me drunk, that of her boyfriend was the world's best hangover cure. I couldn't get another bite of my sandwich down -- part of me wanted to rip open my esophagus to escape the lump that suddenly appeared there. "Listen," I said, "is there a 'Little Cape's Room' around here?"

Noble stuck his thumb towards a pair of doors in the far corner of the cafeteria and I quickly picked myself up, wanting nothing more than to get away as soon as possible.

The doors to the bathroom were revoltingly inappropriate -- one had a picture of an overly-muscled cartoon hero bursting out of his tights, the other featured a generously-endowed heroine whose halter top was in serious danger of being torn apart by the "forces of evil," if you get my drift. I ducked into the men's room, washed my face a dozen times and proceeded to stare into the mirror as though that would change me into an entirely different individual.

"What does she *see* in that asshole?" I finally asked the man in the mirror. He didn't know, either.

As I stepped out of the bathroom I caught another Rush and a wave of empathic powers. Somebody nearby was feeling genuinely sorry for somebody else. And there was music playing... it sounded like a trombone disturbed by a cup mute -- a sort of *"wha-wha-wha-whaaaaa..."* such as you'd hear right after the coyote fell off the cliff trying to catch the roadrunner.

"Tough break, man," said a Cape in what looked like a modified drum major's uniform. He had his blue bucket hat tucked beneath his white-clad arm, and a blue cape dangled behind him. His pants and boots were black, and the whole, military-cut ensemble had blue and gold trim that didn't look nearly as ridiculous on him as it did on me.

"For what it's worth," he said, "you're not the first guy around here to notice that Miss Sinistah is settling for a guy that the term 'weasel excrement' would flatter." He stuck out his hand. "Men call me the Conductor. Women never call me. I blame my mother. And you?"

"The Great -- Josh."

"The Great Josh? Got kind of a high opinion of yourself, huh?"

"Josh. Just Josh. I had a code-name, but I'm rethinking it now." I accepted his hand and we shook. "I don't think I've ever heard of the Conductor. What do you do?"

He frowned. "Oh, like a hero named 'Josh' is all the rage?"

"Um... I'm sorry, I--"

A smile broke his face. "Relax, rookie." He let out a good-natured laugh and I realized I liked this guy already.

"I've got the strangest form of telepathy on Earth," he said. "I sense people's emotions empathically."

"That's not that strange. I mean... comparatively."

"Yeah, but then I translate the emotions into music and mentally broadcast it to everybody nearby."

"You mean like the '*wha-wha-wha-whaaaaa*' a minute ago?"

"You felt like you fell off a cliff. I wouldn't need powers to tell that."

"So what you're telling me, essentially, is that you do superhero theme music?"

"Now you know why I'm not famous," he said. "What's more, since my music is telepathic, it can't be recorded. The only way it can be reproduced is if someone remembers it, picks up an instrument and plays it himself."

"Bummer."

"Yeah. I don't really have many chances for the spotlight." He sighed and his shoulders slumped. "I shouldn't complain, though. Morrie sends me out to all the really epic battles so I can broadcast to the crowd. Says I add the 'necessary ambiance.' So, you're the guy who can copy other people's powers, huh?"

"Word travels fast."

"So are you going to sign up or what?"

I cast my glance back to where Sindy was sitting, alone again. "I'm thinking about it."

"So I see."

As the Conductor's gaze followed mine, I caught another emotion from him, using his own powers. It was fondness, laced with the slightest thread of regret, and I realized he was right, I *wasn't* the first guy to want to give Sindy what she deserved instead of what she was stuck with. A strain of music swelled. It sounded vaguely like rock and roll, but it was slow and nostalgic -- the kind of song the radio stations play to death every time high school graduation season rolls around.

The Conductor was taken aback for a moment, realizing the music wasn't coming from him, then he looked back and chuckled.

"Damn," he said. "You're good."

Blake M. Petit

ISSUE FOUR

JOSH'S CHOICE

Five hours and about five minutes of sleep later, I was behind a fresh desk (when Masks routinely break into your offices, maintenance keeps a supply of extra desks handy) at *Powerlines*, staring at my computer, wondering why I should even bother with my assignments. The LightCorps retrospective was one thing, *they* were legitimate, but the rest of it...

A "Secret Origins" piece on Nightshadow, the dark avenger with the tendency to leave criminals dangling upside-down from 20 story buildings. And, according to the Conductor, a Donna Summer fan in his spare time.

A follow-up on the arrest of the Buzzard -- who I now knew retired from active criminal behavior to join Morrie's writing staff.

Profiles on the entire Spectacle Six: First Light, DoubleGum Man, V3OL, Fourtifier, Five-Share and Deep Six. The Great Superhero family of Siegel City. Not a one of them had even *met* before two years ago, when Morrie slapped them together and the public relations staff made them out to be an unbreakable band of brothers, sisters and friends.

A "Whatever Happened To?" piece on Swoosh, formerly Siegel City's preeminent super-speedster. "Whatever happened" to him, as it turned out, was that Nike sued him for trademark infringement and rather than take it to court Morrie made him change his identity to LifeSpeed.

All of it was meaningless.

"Come on, Josh, perk up." Sheila's head rounded the corner into my cubicle and she shot me her best, "You okay, sweetie?" look. "You look like the Gunk ate your Lionheart Underoos."

"Nah, he only eats Omega Oatmeal," I mumbled.

"What was that?"

"Nothing." I buried my head on the desk, pretending to pay attention to some paperwork.

She glanced around, looking for people in the adjoining cubicles, then stepped into mine and lowered her voice. "Josh, what happened to you last night? I was worried sick."

"Nothing happened."

"Mmm-mmm. I've *seen* the kind of depressed you get when nothing happened. When *nothing* happened you get all pouty and obstinate as if the universe *owed* you a little adventure. Right now you're being all quiet and brooding. That means *something* happened and you're waiting for someone to ask what it was so you can pretend you don't want to talk about it."

"What, were you bitten by a radioactive Sigmund Freud?"

"What happened?"

"I don't want to talk about it."

She stuck out her bottom lip and plopped herself at the edge of my desk. "Come on... you *know* you want to."

"I *don't* want to."

"Did you let some crook get away? Get caught in some over-complicated deathtrap and needed

Nightshadow to save you? Doctor Noble call you an amateur? Ooh, I know, you asked Miss Sinistah to the movies and she shot you down."

"Hey!" I banged my fist on the paperwork I'd been attempting to do. Sheila looked a bit taken aback by my sudden defensiveness. To be honest, so was I.

"Whoa, hit a nerve there, huh?"

"Just don't make fun of Miss Sinistah, okay?"

"We *always* make fun of Miss Sinistah. Remember? How she's such an airhead that even Llamaman caught her once? How her costume perpetuates every negative female stereotype? And that *stupid* origin -- I mean, channeling the sprits of Lizzie Borden, Typhoid Mary and Delilah? What kind of--"

"Cut it out!" I was more adamant this time, and I think Sheila was starting to realize this was more than your typical down-in-the-dumps.

"Josh, what's come over you?"

"She's not like that, okay?"

Her jaw dropped. "You really *did* meet Miss Sinistah last night."

"I met a *lot* of people last night," I hissed.

"Oh my God, Josh, you're *serious*. What happened? How did you... *who* did you..."

"Sheila, *relax*. Man, it happened to *me* and even *I'm* not that jumpy about it."

"But... Miss Sinistah? Did you catch her? Are they reforming the Malevolence Mob?"

"Can't you drop *anything?*"

"I work for a newsmagazine, I'm naturally curious."

Other People's Heroes

"You're a *copy editor*, Sheila. Your job is to stop us from printing stupid things like 'Bismarck is the capitol of North Dakota'."

"Bismarck *is* the capitol of North Dakota."

"Don't change the subject."

"Look, Josh, we both know what's going to happen here. You're going to be stubborn, but I'm going to beg, plead, persuade, needle, cajole and, if necessary, tickle you until you finally break down and tell me what happened last night. So why don't we just take all that as a given and skip to the part where you're a big weenie and spill your guts?"

"*This* is how you persuade?"

"Next I start in with the 'Yo Momma' jokes."

I slumped down at my desk and let out a deep, full-body sigh. "If I tell you just the tiniest bit of what went on last night, can you promise to keep it to yourself?"

"Promise."

"You *swear*?"

"I swear."

"This isn't like the time you promised not to tell that Justine in payroll was pregnant and we wound up getting photocopied invitations to a baby shower in our in-boxes, right? You're *really* going to keep it to yourself?"

"I *promise*, now *tell me!*"

"Sit down."

"I *am* sitting down."

"In a *chair.*"

63

She slid off my desk and landed in the tiny chair on the other side. I felt like I had a kid in my cubicle waiting for me to give her Santa Claus' phone number.

"Yeah, I ran into some Masks last night," I said. "They took me... back to their hideout."

"And you fought them?"

"No. You see, they thought I was *one* of them, and they offered me... a position in their organization."

"And you turned them down flat and blew up the compound!"

"No! They're already a *very powerful* group. They've got their hands in a *lot* of things."

"Oooh, graft! This just keeps getting better and better. Do they know where Lionheart is buried?"

I shot her a look she correctly assumed was an invitation to shut up, and she did.

"They aren't *all* bad people. Some of them are just in over their heads." I thought of the Conductor, with his friendly, quirky grin and his calm, understanding demeanor. I thought of Hotshot, once one of my idols and now part of this terrible, deceitful machine. I thought of Sindy, and her wonderful, *wonderful* smile.

And then I thought of Dr. Noble, and how that smile was wiped off her face every time he walked into the room.

"Some of them, though, are monsters," I said.

"So what are you doing?"

"I'm going back tonight. And I'm going to join up with them."

"*What?* Josh are--"

"Relax. I'm not *really* joining up."

"You're not?"

"Uh-uh. I'm just going information-gathering. Then, once I've got what I need, I'm bringing down the biggest con game this city has ever seen."

INDUCTION

I walked into Simon Tower that night and entered the elevator, trying to remember the sequence of buttons Sindy told me to hit to activate the secret entrance to Morrie's complex. At first I wondered how they avoided sewer workers and other underground folks, then I remembered Mental Maid's contribution and put that particular concern out of my mind.

I know what most people would think in this situation. I was going undercover to blow the lid off a Rembrandt of a con artist who happened to have a pet telepath. What's more, Sindy told me Mental Maid was perhaps the strongest telepath ever to walk the Earth.

The thing is, all that stuff they say on TV and in movies about telepaths having to hold back and undergo years of Zen training to keep from overloading on other people's brains? That's crap. Telepathy -- at least in Mental Maid's case -- didn't work that way. She had to make a conscious effort to link her mind with someone else's. I figured as long as I didn't give her reason to get suspicious and scan me, I would be fine.

I got to Morrie's office. "I'm in," I said.

"Great!" he said. "Mental Maid, scan 'im."

"What?"

"Nothin' personal, kid. We scan all the new recruits."

"But--"

"Especially with you bein' a reporter and all. We gotta make sure you ain't plannin' on blowing the whistle on us or somethin'. You don't have a problem with being scanned, do you?"

"Who, *me*?" I asked.

"Of *course* not!" I lied.

"What reason could I *possibly* have for not wanting to be scanned?" I warbled, wishing for divine intervention to answer precisely that question for me.

"Good. Just sit down and relax. I promise, you won't feel a thing." He looked over at Mental Maid, still in her prescribed spot next to the desk, and nodded towards me.

As she stepped forward I saw her eyes begin to dance with a purple glow. My fingers dug into the arms of the cheap vinyl chair and a thousand scenarios raced through my mind at once, most of them culminating with me as a vegetable, dribbling my lips and playing patty-cake with the Goop.

I tried to force good thoughts into my head, hoping I could veil my intentions with images of strength and nobility. I thought of Lionheart, proud and strong, the pinnacle of what a superhero should be. And I thought of these people... of what they were doing to his legacy... of the lunch boxes and coloring books and all the junk they hawked with superhero pictures on them, and it made me sick and it made me just wanna--

Stop it. That wasn't going to work.

So I decided to think of Sindy. Sweet, beautiful Sindy. So gentle, so warm, so special... and then I thought of her idiot boyfriend and how he disgusted me and how this whole endeavor would be worth it if only I could find a way to get him *away* from her and--

Not helping.

I thought of my mother. How can anything bad happen to a boy who's thinking of his mother? My wonderful, loving mother, who always looked out for me, always protected me, always *told* me that my nosy streak would get me into trouble someday, and here I was about to get my brain fried by the most powerful telepath on--

The light in Mental Maid's eyes faded and she stepped back, nodding. That was it. That was the signal that I was a spy a fraud, an infiltrator--

"Took ya long enough," Morrie said. "Double-Em gives ya a clean bill. Welcome aboard, kid."

I managed to squeeze out a "Thanks," but I never took my eyes off Mental Maid. Had she *really* sensed *nothing?* It seemed impossible, the way my thoughts kept drifting back to my stupid plan. And there was no way to read her face, she continued wearing that cold, impartial glare she always had, as if nothing and no one in the world mattered to her one way or the other.

"Okay, kid," Morrie said, "the first thing we gotta talk about is your name."

"What's wrong with my name?"

"It sucks. I mean... 'Great Pretender'? Ugh. First rule of Cape names: if you get it from a song title, it sucks."

"It's a good thing I rejected 'Judy's Turn to Cry,' then."

Morrie bristled. "We don't really need to worry about that now. You'll be using stock names for a while yet."

"What do you mean?"

"Well we can't very well make ya a superstar right out of the box, can we? Listen, every so often a Mask can get away. It adds to the drama, right? But more often than not, if they don't get caught, people start to lose faith in the Capes. We got two options here. We can employ three times as many Masks as are actually available and only work 'em a third of the time, or we hire people to be Masks whose powers are diverse enough to do multiple characters without drawing suspicion."

"You gotta be kidding me."

"You think so? You know the Jackal?"

A furry little Mask with claws and a lousy disposition. "Yeah, I know him."

"What about Headgame?" A non-powered Mask who left jokes as clues to his crimes. I nodded.

"And the Rapier?" Three Musketeers wanna-be. I confirmed.

"All the same guy," he said.

"That's impossible."

"Haven't you ever noticed that there are some Masks that never operate at the same time as certain other ones?" I nodded assent, even though I never had.

"Now there are *some* Masks big enough to operate full-time as one character. Saint Sinister, fer instance. But he wasn't always *just* Saint Sinister. For a while there, he was the original Herr Nemesis."

"What about the guy who's Herr Nemesis now?"

"Does double-duty as the Shell. Now you... *you*, my little friend, are a *goldmine.* With *you* all I gotta do is have the right people nearby and I can give you any combination of powers I *want*! Think of it! I get Deep Six and Flambeaux in the crowd and you got fire an' water powers at the same time!"

"Won't it be difficult to get those two to work together? They're usually at each other's throats."

Morrie laughed. "Look, kid, I know you're new and all, but you got to stop thinkin' like that. I know you never seen Deep Six without his helmet, but him an' Flambeaux are *brothers. Twins*, even."

"*Twins*? But... don't tell me, the Element Clan, right?"

"The same." The Element Clan was a villain family that had vanished about two years ago, before Deep Six showed up. There were four members: the matriarch Earth, her daughter Air and the brothers, Fire and Water. They hadn't been seen in a long time.

"When the clan broke up, Fire became Flambeaux and Water became Deep Six," I said.

"Yeah. The brothers got their powers from... I dunno, space rays or somethin'. I got writers who keep track of that for me." Morrie took a long drag off his cigar. "Hey, that reminds me, what's *your* story? How'd you get juiced up?"

"Actually, I don't know. I just started feeling them one day. I guess I was born with my powers."

Morrie coughed so hard at this I thought he was going to spit a lung into my lap. *"Born* with 'em?

Nobody'll buy a crap-ass origin like *that*! That's the sort of thing a lazy writer comes up with because he can't be bothered to cook up an original origin story. I'll talk to the guys. If and when you get your own character, they'll have a decent origin cooked up for you."

"That's generous of you, Morrie, really," I said.

"Anyway, now that you're in, Mental Maid is going to include you in her susceptibility field. That means no one who don't already suspect somethin' about you is likely to make any connections between you and any Cape or Mask in the city. Not unless you give 'em *reason* to, that is. That's why nobody's ever figured out that Spectrum is really your buddy Elliott, even though his only disguise is that nappy beard."

I sputtered. "*Scott* Elliott? After all these years... Sheila was *right?*"

Morrie had a good belly-laugh at that one. "All this time an' it *still* cracks me up. Think about it, kid. Spectrum has *hologram powers*. He just whips up a fake beard to turn into Elliott. His secret identity could be a friggin' *armadillo* if that's what he wanted. Sheesh."

"You paint quite a picture."

"I'm gonna get your paperwork together, kid -- contracts, insurance forms, I'm sure you know the drill. You go take a load off in the lounge."

I managed to suppress a chuckle at the thought of an organization like this requiring paperwork. "Sure thing, Morrie," was all I said.

And as I left the office, I felt Mental Maid's cold eyes following me.

WHERE THEY LET THEIR CAPES DOWN

At first I'd expected "Lounge" to be a euphemism, thinking I'd find some reinforced rumble area, or maybe a seedy bar. Nope. The Lounge had couches, snack tables, vending machines, video games, pool and ping-pong tables and a television area where several Capes and Masks were deeply engrossed in a repeat of some basketball game on late-night ESPN. Flux, apparently a big Georgetown fan, was using his gravity power to squeeze the Marauder against the ceiling.

"Say it..." Flux hissed.

"No!"

"Say it was a foul!"

"Never!"

If nothing else could have convinced me that gaining super-powers didn't change a person's fundamental guyness, this did the trick.

"Hey, 'Pretender'! Over here!"

I glanced in the direction of the voice to see the Conductor waving me over with a pool cue. Sindy was there too, along with the ugly growth she called a boyfriend.

"So did you do it, man? You in?"

"Yeah, bro. I'm in."

"Whooptie-freakin'-doo," Noble said, chalking up a pool cue. "Break out the goats."

"C'mon," the Conductor said. "You know we don't use goats until after his first rumble." He took another cue from a rack on the wall and held it out to me. "You play?"

"A little."

"You any good?"

"Nope."

"Good, I suck too. You can be on my team."

Noble got to break. As he hunched over, cape woefully inadequate at disguising his beer belly, he piped up with, "So what pissant Mask ID is Morrie giving you for the big debut?" I could almost *see* the venom dripping from his voice.

"I haven't been assigned yet," I said.

"Small wonder, with such a wealth of powers to choose from." The cue ball rocketed forward and broke up the cluster, sending two solids straight into the pockets.

"Nice break," I said.

"I know."

"Why are you so congenial, anyway?"

Sindy frowned. "He's like this to anyone who doesn't have a solo character." She turned to Noble. "Not *everybody* gets one right off the bat, you know."

"I'm still surprised *you* did," he snapped.

She sort of buried her face and half-whispered, "so am I."

I found myself first glaring at him, then smiling at her. I grasped her shoulder in a friendly gesture and said, "Well, *I'm* not."

"What?" she said. At the table, Noble finally missed and the Conductor stepped up to take his turn.

"I'm not at all surprised you're not mucking around in a bunch of different costumes. You're powerful, beautiful, talented..."

"Talent? What talent do *I* have?" She began chalking her cue as the Conductor missed.

"Well, you're obviously quite an actress. Hey, you had *me* believing you were a cast-iron bitch." She smiled and took her cue to the table.

"That's not acting," Noble grumbled. I ignored him.

"I don't remember the last time I met someone so genuine," I offered. It was my shot now, her boyfriend's supportive words had caused her to miss. "If someone like you can convince *anyone* to dislike you, *that's* talent. Um... green stripey ball in that pocket over there." I promptly scratched.

"You are *so sweet,*" she said in a voice that indicated surprise more than anything else.

"Just relentlessly honest," I said.

"Relentlessly cornball, maybe." Noble stepped back to the table and ran it, sinking each solid in turn. Finishing with the 8-ball, he knocked the chalk from his hands and stuck his cue in my face.

"How's *that,* loser?"

"It's just a game, man."

There was a wheezing noise as a voice called out Noble's name and told him to cool it. Morrie was walking across the lounge with a manila envelope in his hand. Next to him, as always, was Mental Maid, looking straight ahead, not registering anything. "Your next assignment, Doc. Practice is tomorrow at four p.m. Don't be late this time. How about you, kid?" he said, clapping me on the shoulder. "Makin' friends?"

"Yeah, it's great, Morrie."

"Good, good. Come on, Em-Em." He filtered away, leaving Noble standing there, holding the envelope, staring through me like I'd just run over his puppy with a steamroller and invited him to the barbecue.

"Come on, girlie, I don't like the company around here." He grabbed Sindy by the hand and dragged her away. On the way out, Sindy looked back at me with a glance that said, "Sorry, what can I do?" Then she waved, and then she was gone.

I turned back to the Conductor. "Have I mentioned lately how much I hate that guy?"

"That was the greatest thing I've ever seen!"

"Are you kidding? He *had* to have been using his telekinesis on those balls..."

"Not *that*. You actually stood there and complimented her in *front* of him. *No one* does that."

"How could anyone *not* compliment her?"

"Because they're all afraid of *him*."

"What, are they afraid he'll crush them with his enormous ego?"

"Hey, Noble may be scum, but he's also probably the most powerful guy in Siegel City since Lionheart vanished. Physically, anyway."

"So what? There's bound to be enough guys around here to take him *together,* right?"

"Maybe, but after what happened to Photon Man..." As soon as the words were out of his mouth, the Conductor clapped his hand over it. "Forget I said that."

"No, wait a minute, what's the big secret about Photon Man?"

"Let it go."

"Uh-uh. You can't give me pizza and then say no pepperoni, bunky. Cough it up."

The Conductor sighed and put his cue down. "Every so often somebody... does something bad. I mean, a serious crime, something against one of our own. A while back, someone discovered that Photon Man was skimming money from his heists. Normally the cash our Masks steal is subtly returned to its owner, who then 'forgets' the whole thing. When wrongdoing is discovered, the suspect is taken before a review board."

"Review board?"

"Okay, Mental Maid. The *concept* is the same. You get up, you state your case, someone is appointed prosecutor, and Mental Maid passes judgment. But sometimes... and this is what Photon did, sometimes they rabbit."

"Run away."

"You're quick on the euphemisms, for a reporter. When someone runs instead of facing the review, we go after him and bring him in."

"I'm guessing that's not quite what happened in this case."

"Noble was the one that finally caught up with Photon Man. Unfortunately, no one figured on what Noble's electromagnetic powers, at full force, would *do* to a guy who was essentially made of energy particles."

"*Made* of energy particles?" I said.

"The things you learn on this side, eh?" He chalked up his cue a little more, trying to find the proper words. "Noble caught him, and... Photon Man *exploded.*"

"Oh. Um. Ew."

"Right. Anyway, Noble got cleared of any wrongdoing, but he's still... there are some of us who think it may not have exactly been an accident."

"Wouldn't Mental Maid have caught wind if he did it on purpose?" I asked, remembering the way she'd waved me through my scan.

"Have you *looked* at her, Josh? Those eyes, that skin... hell, just those freaky powers. There are some of us who think *she's* got an agenda of her own, too."

"Oh."

"Since then, Noble's been even less popular around here than he was before. And folks are even *more* frightened of him." He shook his head clear. "Another game?"

"Yeah, I guess. I guess I find it hard to be scared of someone so... so..."

"So *Deliverance*?"

"Bingo. It gets me sick, the way he talks about her." I didn't think I needed to specify who "her" was. "What's worse, he's been brow-beating her for so long she's started to *believe* his crap."

"Well, if it makes you feel any better, he doesn't like *you* very much either."

"I get the impression he doesn't like *anyone*."

"Yeah but *dude*, the minute Noble saw *you* just now his emotions went all nasty and sour. It was like listening to emo rock in my head." He started arranging balls on the table. "He's scared of you, man."

"Scared? Of *what*?"

"My guess? That she's gonna open her eyes and realize she can do better than *him*."

"And how does *she* feel about all this?"

"Confused. She thinks you're a real sweet guy -- and you *are,* Joshie, you *really* are," he quipped, "but she's also been convinced for months now that she *deserves* that SOB."

"So what do *I* do?"

"Hell if I know. But if you figure *that* out I'll personally sponsor you for 'Smartest Man on Earth'."

I laughed at that, but my reporter's instincts welled just then, squeezing out the one question I really wanted the answer to at that second.

"Hey, Conductor... when Noble killed -- I mean -- when Photon Man *died*... was there anyone else there? Any witnesses?"

The Conductor shook his head. "Nope." he tossed me the cue ball. "You break."

GUIDED TOUR

"Come on in, kid," Morrie said a few days later, waving me into his office. I was there to begin my official training, but Morrie asked me to show up an hour before my session. In fact, I came in even earlier to hang around the lounge and take in everything I could -- it's amazing what you can learn just sitting on a couch and listening.

I also encountered the Gunk again. He sat down and tried to hold a conversation with me concerning an article I'd written about the United Statesmen, but as he buddied up to me his powers turned my limbs to goo and I found it hard to concentrate. I managed to maneuver my way out of the conversation when it was time to meet Morrie.

Morrie was at his desk, cigar smoke filtering through his nostrils and curling past his eyes. Mental Maid was by his desk as usual, still staring at me. I caught a nice chill off that. "Gettin' yourself situated?" he asked.

"I'm doing all right," I said.

"Meetin' people? Learnin' your way around?"

"More of the first."

"Well, I'm gonna help you with the second. Hotshot's waitin' for you in the lounge. Guy volunteered to take you around the joint. The grand tour, as it were."

"Sounds good, Morrie." I left the office, still feeling Mental Maid's eyes boring into the back of my head.

Hotshot had a big smile on his face when I met him in the lounge. "Hey, new guy! Nice to meet you -- officially, I mean. I'm Hotshot."

"Yeah, I said, I know. Member of the original LightCorps. You knew Lionheart, didn't you?"

"Everybody always asks that."

"I'm Josh Corwood."

"I know. The kid who duplicates other people's powers. You're either going to make a lot of friends that way or tick a lot of people off."

"Don't worry, I seem to be well on my way to both. So why did you volunteer to take me around?"

"I don't know. Just caught a friendly vibe from you, I guess. Come on, let's get a move on."

It started out amicably enough. We started at Morrie's office and began to make our way through the bowels of the complex. The first thing I asked him was about Lionheart -- what *really* happened to him.

"Let's not talk about that," Hotshot said. "Sore subject."

"But you knew him, right? You were his friend."

"We were pretty close."

"Was he as... as great a presence as he seemed?"

"Greater. There's not a decent person on Earth who could have met Lionheart and not be willing to put himself on the line for the guy. He was the sort of person you would do anything to follow -- the sort that inspires courage and confidence just by walking into the room.

"One time the Sinister Squadron had deactivated the Tin Man's armor and trapped him in it, disarmed the Defender, caught Condor and Oriole in cages and put Lightning in this null-time sphere so she couldn't use her speed powers. They had me trapped in a gravity bubble, too, so I couldn't reach anything to charge up. Nobody had a plan, nobody had an idea. We were all doomed.

"Then, bam! Lionheart shows up. He doesn't lift a finger to save us because he knows he doesn't *have* to. He charges after the Squadron and in about ten seconds, Tin Man has escaped from his dead armor and deactivated the traps Lightning and I were in. We freed the rest of the guys and wiped up the Squadron just in time to stop them from launching the Omega Device."

"The Omega Device?" I asked.

"One of those contraptions old Masks used to use to try and conquer the world. I think this one would devolve the entire eastern seaboard into plankton or something, they sort of blend together after a while."

"But that doesn't sound like Lionheart actually *did* anything," I said. "He *had* to have done *something*."

"Why?"

"Because... because he was *Lionheart*." It was the simplest thing in the world to me, why couldn't his old teammate see it?

"You're not getting the point, Josh," he said. "There were plenty of times when Lionheart saved this planet by himself and saved *our* lives in particular. In this particular instance, though, he didn't have to. Not directly, anyway. When we saw him, it jazzed us up again, enough for the Tin Man to break out and free us. From there, victory was a foregone conclusion." He let out something of a sigh. "I miss that -- the excitement of a real rumble, not knowing the outcome beforehand. That was a *real* thrill, buddy."

"Why did it stop?"

"Long story. After Lionheart was gone, Morrie tracked me down and said, 'Hey, kid, I got me an' idea,' and we started to build this little organization. It just sort of snowballed from there."

I didn't like the direction this conversation was taking. Hotshot, Lionheart's own teammate, was one of the guys who *started* this mess?

"What would Lionheart say about all this?" I asked.

"Lionheart? He wouldn't have liked it at all. The guy didn't have a deceptive bone in his body. The closest thing I ever heard him say to a lie was one Christmas when he tried to convince Lightning he liked this *incredibly* ugly sweater she gave him. You could still see the truth in his eyes, though. Those always gave him away. He was good at a lot of things, but the worst liar I've ever met."

"He was a good guy, then?"

"The best. You didn't just follow him, you didn't just respect him... you would do anything, *anything* not to let him down." He sighed. "Y'know, there's a reason you don't see his picture stuck on t-shirts or cereal boxes like the rest of us. Morrie wanted to use him – begged me to, actually. It'd be like having an Elvis shirt or something. But I won't let him. That was my one condition for going along with this – no Lionheart merchandise."

By now I was furious. This guy was Lionheart's *friend*, his *teammate* for God's sake, and he'd betrayed him by constructing this organization, *knowing* Lionheart wouldn't have approved. The rage I felt was nearly blinding. How could he? *How could he?*

"But hey," he said, "we're supposed to be on a tour of the complex, not the cobwebs of my screwed-up head." We'd ridden an elevator to the second level in the complex. As big as it was, the top level of the underground system only consisted of Morrie's office and a few storage rooms and bathrooms. That was because everything on the second level extended up to just beneath the surface.

Right off from the elevator, and right beneath the lobby of Simon Tower proper, was an auditorium with lush wood paneling, flags of the United States and Siegel City flanking the podium, and tables set up for when used for arbitration.

"Whenever somebody here breaks the rules, commits a 'crime against a Cape', Morrie calls it, we take him here for his hearing. There are enough seats in here for every Cape and Mask in the city."

"I hope you don't get to use it much."

"Only once in the last three years," he said. "At least, only once for that purpose. We also have meetings here, general assemblies, that sort of thing."

"Exciting?"

"You can't imagine. Let's keep going."

Next down the hallway was a steel door with a keypad to open it. "The Arena," Hotshot said. "It's where we practice our rumbles."

"Don't I get to see it?" I asked.

"Particle runs the practice sessions. He likes to show rookies the Arena for the first time. Next door is the gym -- we have plenty of ordinary workout machines -- treadmills, bikes, a pool, weights, and we've also got specialized stuff for folks with unique talents. Morrie will probably have you practice using other people's powers in there before he actually sends you into the Arena."

"Thoughtful of him." I was aware that my responses to his tour were becoming rather cold. I didn't care.

"One last stop on this level," he said. "Our arboretum."

He took me into a large, greenhouse-like area full of lush vines, bushes and trees, some like nothing I'd ever seen. There were plants with orange leaves and striped petals -- big, dripping white fruits and beautiful flowers. It was like standing in God's flower garden.

The ceiling, like in the auditorium and the gym, extended past the top level where Morrie's office was and all the way to the surface. Here, though, the ceiling was glass, allowing sunlight to filter in from the sky above. We must have been standing beneath the courtyard behind Simon Tower.

"The glass is polarized," Hotshot said, answering my unspoken question. "It lets all the light in, but nobody can look through the glass and see us down here. It's safe."

"What's this place for?" I asked.

"We've got some people here with unusual dietary needs," Hotshot said. "Aliens, mystical creatures, that sort of thing. When Morrie built this place, he wanted to include a greenhouse so we could grow the foods they needed. As time went by, though, the whole thing got bigger and bigger until... well, until we got what you see here."

I was standing underneath a tree that almost looked like a willow, but had strange, puffy flowers budding all over it. The buds resembled chrysanthemums, but the petals were in concentric rings of red, black and gold. There also a blue cactus in here, I noticed. And a crystal palm. And over there...

"Wow."

The centerpiece of the arboretum was a beautiful topiary garden, full of careful, hand-crafted sculptures made from cut leaves. Some were animals, but others were carefully-detailed recreations of Capes and Masks. There was a nice sculpture of Lionheart.

"Who does all this?"

"We've got a couple of guys who dabble in topiary sculpture," Hotshot said. "Morrie likes everybody in his employ to be happy."

"What a prince, that Morrie."

I was already accustomed to the third level. It was the living area, where the lounge and cafeteria were located. We breezed through there and I saw Miss Sinistah, who gave me a smile and a wink before Dr. Noble showed up with a scowl and a snarl, dragging her away.

"Level four," Hotshot said as we stepped off the elevator, "the dormitory."

He led me down to an unoccupied apartment -- it consisted of a living room/kitchenette combo, a bathroom, and two single bedrooms. The furniture was plain and the decor Spartan.

"Morrie lets you decorate as you please," he said. "Everybody is entitled to quarters, but some people prefer to live outside of the tower."

"I've got my own apartment," I said. "I think I'll stay there for a while. Besides, my cat hates to move."

The bottom floor was pretty frigid. "What's down here?" I asked.

"Storage," Hotshot said. "Of all kinds."

"What does that mean?"

"This is where we keep all of our supplies and merchandise. Y'know, the stuff we haven't gotten out to the stores yet. You should see how packed it gets in October, just before the Christmas rush. This is also where we keep prisoners waiting for arbitration upstairs. And, when the situation demands it, the morgue is right down the hall."

"I don't suppose you mean 'morgue' in any sort of newspaper sense, do you?"

"The most writing you'll find in there are on tags."

"Beautiful. I *really* hope you don't have to use *that* often."

"It's been years."

"Good to know."

"And that's pretty much it," Hotshot said. "Any questions?"

Yeah. How long did you wait after Lionheart was dead before you drove the knife in his back?

"No, I think I got everything."

"Great." We wandered back to the lounge area and he clapped me on the back. "It was nice getting to know you, Josh."

"Mmm-hmm."

"If you need anything else, let me know."

He was friendly, courteous and a real nice guy to be around. But one little thing overshadowed everything else. As he left, my eyes followed. If anybody nearby had heat vision, I would have wound up frying the guy.

It was the kind of stupid, irrational anger that has no explanation and, once it has passed, you simply cannot understand. But while you feel it, none of that matters.

For what he'd done to Lionheart's legacy, I *hated* Hotshot. I couldn't help it. Although, to my credit, I *was* sorry for it later.

THE ARENA

Part of me, the stupid part, wanted to be matched against Hotshot for my first professional rumble. I *really* wanted to hand him his head. Then I thought for a while about Hotshot's main power -- the ability to take any solid object and break down the atomic bonds within, turning it into a particle stream whose strength was proportionate to the mass of the original object. In short, he could turn *any*thing into a zap-ray. So a much larger portion of me was relieved to draw a match against half of the Spectacle Six. First Light, Fourtifier and Five-Share were supposed to meet me outside the room called The Arena.

I spent a week practicing the powers I would use in that first rumble. I copied both Flux's gravity powers and the inertia-controlling abilities of LifeSpeed. Between the two I could pretty much contradict everything Isaac Newton ever said. Fortunately, rather than dressing me up like a giant apple or something, Morrie gave me the semi-respectable stock name "Shift."

First Light, a thin, albino woman in gossamer robes, was the first to meet me outside the training room. She was practically glowing, and there was a Tolkienesque look about her somehow, with her pointed ears, high nose and narrow eyes. "You, then, are the new Shift?"

she said in a high, hollow voice that made me think of elves.

"For the moment, anyway," I said. "Josh Corwood, nice to meet you." I stuck out my hand to shake, but she blanched away, eyes bulging in terror.

"No! I must not sully myself with human contact. It would shatter the purity of the Light."

I dropped my hand, bashful. "Sorry. I guess that makes swing dancing difficult, right?" She raised an eyebrow in confusion and I surrendered the lame jokes.

There was an intense grinding noise sidling up to us and a gruff voice said, "*I'm* the dancer on this team, boyo." The rock-creature called Fourtifier smiled a dusty grin at us, sounding all the time like someone dragging a chunk of granite across a cement patio. I couldn't help thinking any attempt this guy made to move faster than a 12-year-old boy at a junior high dance would drown out any music.

"Aren't we one short?" I asked. "Or rather, five short?"

Just then, though, turning the corner down the hall was Five-Share. He was a skilled martial arts master with the ability to divide into five independent bodies at a time. I was surprised to see him approach me as a mob -- I would have thought he'd have stayed consolidated until he entered a combat situation. Instead it was like watching a group of kids on their way to a stickball game.

"Josh Corwood," I said to all of Five-Share. "Nice to meet you."

They answered as a mob, talking over each other, making it almost impossible to tell who was saying what. "Hi.--Hiya.--Yo.--Wassup?--How's it going?--Hey man."

I froze.

"*You're* Five-Share?"

"Yep.--Uh-huh.--You betcha.--Bingo.--Heard *that*.--Bright, ain't he?"

Something was still bothering me. I turned it over in my head half a dozen times before I realized what it was.

"There are *six* of you," I said.

"Smart guy.--Swift...--Quick study--"

"Now *cut that out!*" I bellowed. "What's the deal here?"

The one in front reached up and pulled off his full, blue and red face mask, revealing an athletic-looking man with brown hair and eyes and a nicely-cleft chin. "I don't know what you're talking about."

"Why can somebody called *Five*-Share split into *six* people?" I asked

"Actually," said the next one over, pulling off his mask, "we *are* six people." His face was the same as the other, at first, until I realized his chin was full. A definite resemblance, but *not* the same guy.

"The amazing Cochinsky Brothers," said the third, pulling off his mask to reveal a blonde.

"Our *real* power is to teleport," said Four, whose hair was black. "The problem is, we can only teleport to a location where one of us already *is*."

"If we do it right, it looks like we're one guy with multiple bodies," Five said. He had the pocked remains of an old scar on his cheek.

"One of us sits out each fight here at Simon so the others can teleport home in an emergency," said the last one. "It was Morrie's idea."

Six sported the same brown hair and eyes as One, Two and Five, but I couldn't help noticing a fundamental difference.

"You're a *girl!*"

"Boy, nothing gets past you," she said. "It's a padded suit, genius."

"Man, this place is just one fake after another, isn't it?"

"Ah, what *is* 'real'?" asked Three.

"Just a state of mind," Four said.

Two piped up. "Sophocles said--"

"Do you guys *always* talk like this?" I moaned.

"Yeah.--I suppose.--Pretty much.--It's a gift.--It would seem.--You got it."

It was beyond a blessing, a few seconds later, when Flux and LifeSpeed finally arrived. With them was another Cape, one I hadn't been told to expect -- the veteran called Particle. He'd been on the front lines as long as anybody -- even as long as the LightCorps, and although he'd never officially joined any teams he was well-known and respected in the Cape community as a technological and biochemical genius. Particle had the ability to shrink himself down to near subatomic levels. At least, that's what I'd always been *told* his power was

-- the way *my* day was going I was probably going to learn that he just made everything else *big*.

"Nice to meet you Josh," he said. "Or do you prefer 'Shift'?"

"Well, since we don't know how long 'Shift' will last, let's stick to 'Josh' for now, okay?"

"Good deal. Did Morrie explain to you how this was going to work?"

"He said we'd rehearse the combat in a replica of Siegel City, and that the two guys I'm drawing power from would wait it out on the side. What I don't get is where this replica comes from... do we have a hologram room or virtual reality setup or something?"

"What is this, a Keanu Reeves movie?" Flux said. Particle let out an amused chuckle.

"Nothing quite so elaborate, son," Particle said. "Here, it's best to show you."

Next to the door was a computer keypad, into which Particle fed a series of numbers. Then he was given a palmprint, retina scan and voice analyses. "Only Particle can access the rehearsal area," LifeSpeed said to me as we waited. "He runs all the training sessions, so Morrie's got the whole system keyed into him. Only two or three people can get in."

"Is he afraid of someone stealing all the high-powered equipment or something?"

"Nah, he's just such a tightass he's afraid we'll break the thing if we go in without a chaperone."

Finally, Particle was finished with the ridiculously over-elaborate entry sequence and the steel doors glided open along their tracks revealing an empty doorframe and a tunnel. We headed down a hall and Particle waved Flux, LifeSpeed and one of Five-Share (they'd put their masks back on, I couldn't tell which) into an observation area off to the side. Finally, Particle led us to another steel door.

"Your first day in the Arena, Josh," Particle said. "Hope you like it."

He slid the portal open and I saw it for the first time -- Siegel City. A perfect duplication. Oh, it was empty of people and movement and, well... life, really. But there were cars and street signs and billboards just like the real Siegel. The gleaming presence of Simon Tower, the subtle elegance of Barks Plaza, the peaceful centerpiece of Lee Park. It was incredible.

"It's two feet tall," I said.

"How else do you think we could duplicate an entire city in this complex?" Particle said.

"How do we rehearse without pulling a Godzilla all over Kirby Square?"

"You forget who you're talking to, Josh. I'm Particle. I've been doing this for *years*."

He wasn't even scolding me, not really, but for some reason being spoken to in that tone by him made me feel small. Very small.

"You're shrinking me, aren't you?" I said.

I was looking, at eye-level, directly at Particle's belt buckle. Then his knees. Then his boots. Behind me I could hear a similarly shrinking Five-Share chuckling at me.

"You didn't think I could only shrink *myself*, did you?" Particle said, his voice booming. He wasn't coming down on me, he just enjoyed his job and didn't mind having a little fun with the new guy. It sort of made me more comfortable to know that not everybody I encountered would be a Dr. Noble. "How do you feel, Josh?"

"Like G.I. Joe," I shouted.

Particle sat down at a control panel at the edge of the mock city. He hit a couple of buttons and a small, open-topped transport with long rows of cushioned seats along the sides rolled up beside us. It may have been a foot long. To our perceptions, it was like a bus.

"Hop in," Particle said. "The transport will take you to the rumble site."

TRAINING EXERCISE

My first rumble was scheduled for the tall, glass-and-steel structure of the First National Bank -- the same one I decided not to stake out that first night when I'd met Sindy. The plan was for me to go in, steal some quick cash, allow an unsuspecting teller to trip the alarm and rush outside just in time to meet my opponents from the Spectacle Six, who would subsequently "capture" me.

I was worried, at first, about doing this dry run with no actual civilians involved -- "How can I prepare for the bystanders?" I'd asked Morrie.

The manager simply blew a smoke-ring and scowled. "No point in worrin' about our audience, kiddo. There are only two things civilians *ever* do during a rumble. *Nothing,* or something so ridiculously unexpected that there's no way to prepare for it. Either way, you're gonna just have to play it by ear."

I smiled and nodded, trying to remember his precise phraseology so I could write it down later. I had a notebook of all the illicit activities I'd run across in the week since I'd been there. I didn't have a plan or any idea how long I'd be there. Until I got everything I could use, I supposed.

Or until Mental Maid decided to point the finger at me.

"Nervous, kid?" asked Fourtifier in his rock tumbler voice.

"A little," I said. "Be kind of stupid *not* to be, don't you think?"

"At first, maybe," he said. "But you get used to it."

"Goody."

The transport dropped me off outside the miniature replica of First National and pulled away, taking my "opponents" to their own starting location.

"How are you over there?" asked Particle. I was hearing his voice, now, through a micro radio woven into my mask. With more experienced, more reliable Capes, full scripts were sometimes written, because guys like Hotshot could be counted on to stick to them. I was the rookie, though. In order for the battle to be both spontaneous *and* realistic, we were going to improvise large chunks of it, with Particle giving us commands at various points that would take us to the preordained conclusion -- my defeat.

"I'm doing fine," I said. On the horizon I could see what looked like a mile-high wall of glass, through which was the observation area. LifeSpeed and Flux were flanking the last member of Five-Share. Apparently my diminutive size had no effect on my powers -- even though those guys seemed miles away I could still feel the Rush they provided as if I were standing at their gargantuan feet.

"Okay," Particle finally said. "They're in position. Go ahead and rob the bank."

"Do you know how bizarre it is to hear you say that?"

He laughed. "You're on, kiddo."

It was a typical robbery, worthy of any poorly-scripted movie. I was supposed to barge in, scream out some supposedly intimidating phrase and begin juggling around security guards to prove my point. To be perfectly honest, I wasn't sure what my point *was*, but I was going to prove it regardless.

I kicked the miniature door open and shouted, "Everybody on the floor, this is a stick-up!" The scene was not exactly what I was expected. The scene was, in fact, a shoebox-sized room full of paper dolls. Some with smiley faces. There was laughter outside and I wondered if this was part of some hazing ritual or something.

"Oh, *veeeeeery* droll," I said. Still, sticking with the plan, I used Flux's gravity power to hurl one security guard doll against the ceiling and simultaneously used LifeSpeed's inertia powers to slam the other into a wall more than hard enough to incapacitate even a non-cardboard opponent.

Behind the counter one of the teller-dolls was already holding out a tiny bag with the words "This is money" written on it.

"Uh-oh," Particle said in my ear. "Some well-meaning teller has just triggered the silent alarm. What are you going to do about it?"

I played along, pretending to roll my options over in my head. "Well... let's see... Herr Nemesis would probably blast her head off and call her an 'insolent dog'... the Squid would trip over his own tentacles in the escape attempt... but something tells me *Shift* would simply... *take the money and run!*"

I think I did a pretty good job, too. I grabbed the cash (that doll didn't even put up a fight), clocked the guards together and got the hell out of there. I still think it was *totally* uncalled for when a Five-Share clotheslined me on my way out the door.

"Clumsy, pal. You've got to watch that."

"Yeah. Same to you." In an eyeblink I hit him with the gravity and inertia powers. During my training with those particular skills I'd developed just enough control to spin his arm through the air, causing him to punch himself in the face. As soon as he was down, I found myself hoping it wasn't the girl. For some reason, I felt like Lionheart wouldn't approve at all.

There was only the one Five-Share there -- the others were waiting nearby to teleport in and give the illusion of bifurcation. I turned around to bolt and wound up facing the observation room, way on the horizon. I saw we had a few more spectators now. Sindy and the Conductor were there, applauding me, and the Goop was bouncing around the room with a big doofy grin on his fluid mug.

Off to the side was Mental Maid, her eyes glowing, glaring at me.

Seeing her froze me in place. I couldn't even move, and the ground began to quake beneath me. It wasn't just *her* making me stiff -- I just hadn't noticed that one of the other Rushes I was feeling was now coming from beneath.

"Not so fast," a flinty voice growled. A shield of solid rock grew up around my feet and I realized I'd been *standing* on Fourtifier's spread-out silicon form. My body was beginning to copy his rock-powers, and my joints began to growl when I moved. "Ain't so easy to get away, is it?" his voice rumbled.

"I don't know," I said, trying to shake Mental Maid. "Let's see."

One thing that always bugged me about certain Capes or Masks was the limited ways in which they used their powers. I mean... here we had LifeSpeed, a guy who could control something as fundamental as inertia itself, and he almost always used it for something as petty as simply running fast. When Fourtifier's rock-form crackled up around me, I poured the inertia *down*, into his very molecules.

A quick mental review of 10th-grade science reminded me that solid objects are only those forms where the molecules are moving too slowly to pass through them. You speed up the molecules of a solid, it becomes a liquid. Speed them up even more, you've got a gas. So when I poured inertia into Fourtifier...

"Hey! I'm *melting*!"

"Quick study," I said.

I hopped out of the puddle that Fourtifier was quickly becoming, only to slam face-first into Five-Share.

"You get one freebie, Shift," he said. With a pop of his fingers, I was surrounded by the entire quintet. I was impressed -- if I didn't know better I would have sworn he *did* split apart. My eyes began darting around for an out.

"Time to make your escape attempt," Particle said. "Your route is straight up."

I looked up the side of the bank building, totally clear, and smiled at a couple of the Five-Shares. "Catch you later," I said as I cut off gravity's effect on me. I pushed off the ground and rocketed up, up and away.

I glided along the side of the silicon and steel construct (more likely plexiglass and aluminum in this miniature form), viewing myself in the window as I went. At about the fourth floor I caught a glint of light. Two floors higher and I saw First Light arching down towards me, robes swirling around her. In the eighth floor window I saw her hand explode in a veil of light and, by the time I reached the roof of the bank complex, she had completely blanked out my vision.

I was racing upwards, flying blind. I couldn't turn my gravity back on because, without seeing my way down, I'd most likely splatter along the side of the bank -- and that was assuming I didn't get impaled on its spire.

I caught a breeze on my back. First Light was rushing past me in the air. I reached out instinctively and grabbed her robe.

"No!" I heard Particle shout in my ear.

"No!" First Light screamed.

"Yaaagh!" I howled as she flipped me through the air. I don't know if it was because I was blind and new at this or if she was just a lot tougher than she looked, but somehow, with no leverage whatsoever, she made me lose my orientation. I had no idea what direction I was drifting in, but I knew I was moving fast.

"Shift! Josh, dammit, *look out!*"

My eyes picked that moment to begin to clear. I saw several humanoid shapes in front of me and thought, for a second, that Particle had sent a squadron of fliers to pull me down. When I saw the way the shapes -- Five-Shares, I now realized -- were thoughtfully scrambling out of my way, I decided it was far more likely that I was about to crack my skull open against the ground.

"Crap! Crap! Crap! Crap!"

I reached out at a lamppost, hoping to regain my control, but it slipped right away from my hands.

"Crapcrapcrapcrap..."

I was ten feet from the ground now. Eight. Five.

Then, out of sheer terror, I reached out with Five-Share's powers and teleported.

My stomach turned inside-out and the entire world fell apart and reassembled itself around me. Suddenly I was upright, on the ground and standing next to a Five-Share.

And then I was rocketing straight up again because teleporting failed to do two rather important things: cancel my inertia, or restore my gravity.

"CRAPCRAPCRAPCRAP..."

"Josh!" Particle was shouting. "Josh, calm down!"

I had trained for days to gain control over gravity and inertia, and I wasn't that bad if I do say so myself. If I had paused long enough to think about it, righting myself would probably be child's play. Unfortunately, by this point I'd already taken the perfectly rational precaution of panicking like a teen slasher movie actor with a pimple.

"MOOOOOOMMMMYYYYYYYY!"

"Retrieve him, Aquila," Particle said.

Even before I could react (suspected reaction: "*Crap! Mommy!*") there was a twirling in the air around me and a pair of clawed hands clasped my arms. The skin on the hands was rough, like the feet of a chicken, and the sudden burst of speed cleared my head. I saw the ground rising back up to me -- I was being guided.

"Wha--"

"Calm yourself, my friend." My rescuer was a tall, powerful figure clad all in white and brown feathers. Around his neck dangled a tiny wooden bird, carefully hand-carved and painted. His eyes were blue and wise, the wings on his back full and lush, his beak and talons sharp and vicious. I recognized him immediately as one of my old favorites. He was among the proudest, noblest of Siegel City's protectors. He was Aquila, the Spirit of the Eagle.

"Geez," I said.

"What is it?"

"I-- nothing." I couldn't bring myself to say, "I can't believe someone like *you* got caught up in this mess, too."

Aquila placed me on the ground. "Thanks for the save," I said. He nodded and his cheek muscles pulled back into what may have been a smile -- it was too hard to tell through the beak.

"Particle often keeps me on call when training newcomers."

"*God*, I feel stupid."

"Don't," said the gravel voice. Fourtifier ground up to me and clapped a dusty hand on my back. I felt my limbs begin to stiffen again. "It happens during a first rumble sometimes."

"And I'm *really* sorry, First Light," I called up to the floating Cape. She was shivering in the air.

"Perhaps... I overreacted. You merely grasped my robe. I remain clean." I noticed she kept her distance, though.

"Hey, you did fine, kid," a Five-Share offered.

"Yeah." Fourtifier shuddered a little. "That melting thing was inspired."

"It's not a big deal," Particle said, "but you certainly have room for improvement. Let's

reset everything and try it again."

ISSUE FIVE

ANIMAN

After three run-throughs I satisfied both Particle and myself that I wouldn't go flying off the handle (so to speak) for the actual rumble, and he was ready to call it a day. He enlarged the Six-ers and me, then Aquila, who waited nearby just in case. Normal-sized, we joined the others in the observation room. Mental Maid, I was relieved to see, had gone, but the rest of our audience remained -- most of them being abnormally sympathetic.

"Hey, it's okay..."

"Happens to everyone..."

"First time out..."

"Geez, it's like talking to Five-Share," I muttered. I felt like an Olympic gymnast being comforted by his team after smashing his personal region into the pummel horse.

"Okay, that's enough," Particle said. "We're not looking at this as anything more than one bad run-through and three good ones. And for a first-timer, that's a pretty good ratio, as any of you can attest."

"Yeah!" Goop barked, slinging one dripping orange arm over my shoulder. "Leave the little guy alone."

"Initial snafu aside," the Conductor said, "it w*as* pretty good, Josh."

"I was so *proud* of you," Sindy said. I could feel the glow well up around my ears. It rapidly diminished when the cell phone on her belt buzzed.

FLO

"It's Todd," she said, turning on the phone and completely oblivious that she was using Noble's real name in front of a "rookie."

"Why's he texting you?"

"He just wants to know where I am."

I had to fight back a snarl. "What, he doesn't trust you to be by yourself?"

"He's just concerned," she said, letting out a depressing, full-body sigh. "I'd better see what he needs. I'll catch up with you later. Nice run-through, Josh."

She walked away, steel door to the Arena gliding shut behind her. There was a beat and then myself, the Conductor and no less than three of Five-Share mumbled the word "Jackass" simultaneously.

"Good run, Josh. Now go rest up. You'll be doing the real thing in a few days." Particle gave me a firm, reassuring handshake and walked out, Flux and LifeSpeed close behind. I gave congratulatory handshakes to the Six-ers, all but First Light, and they left too.

"You're gonna be *good*, little guy," Goop said. "*Goodgoodgoodgoodgood*!" He complimented me with a squishy hug, interjected "See ya 'round," and happily bounded away.

Aquila, the Conductor and I walked out into the hall, me shaking off a little Goop residue. "Want to head to our room and clean yourself up?"

"Yeah, I'd appreciate that. Wait a minute, 'our' room?"

"Yeah. Animan here is my roommate."

"Who?"

Aquila smiled as much as he could with a beak and wrapped a hand around the little wooden eagle-totem around his neck. He closed his birdlike eyes and bore down. There was a twinkling of light and the towering figure next to me began to convulse. The long, proud wings folded in upon themselves and his beak and talons lost their points, shrank and eventually morphed into an ordinary face and hands.

Once the transformation was done, the brilliant figure of Aquila was gone, replaced by a short, happy-looking man with mocha-colored skin surrounding his jet hair and eyes. He wore a simple green shirt and blue jeans with white Keds and, except for the eagle dangling from his neck, there was nothing out of the ordinary about him at all.

"Ah," he said, stretching his muscles. "The real me. This is a much better fit, right, bud?"

"Yeah," I said. "Much. Geez, with the wings and beak and all, it never even occurred to me that Aquila *could* have a secret identity."

The newcomer cast a wry glance at the Conductor. "He don't know me very well, *do* he?"

"Native American eagle totems *and* Bugs Bunny imitations," I said. "The culture in this room is astounding."

"Come on, Josh," the Conductor said. "Have we got something to show *you.*"

As we turned the corner into the dorms, Hotshot rounded the corner. Just as fast as I felt the Rush from him I also felt a well of disdain. The Conductor must have felt my emotion, because he raised an eyebrow and glanced at me.

"Hey guys," Hotshot said. "How'd the rehearsal go, rookie?"

"I survived," I said in the coldest voice I could muster, and I sped up, tromping down the hall.

Animan waited for him to leave hearing range. "What was *that* about?"

"Let's just get to your place. I need to get cleaned."

I saw the quarters on Hotshot's tour, but I hadn't seen one decorated yet. Straight through the front door was a living area, complete with a kitchenette, TV area and couch that more than likely had been discovered on the side of the road. In short, it looked like any of a dozen post-college apartments I'd seen.

"What am I here to see?" I asked.

"This way." Animan led me to an abbreviated hallway in the back, which featured a bathroom in the middle, flanked on either side by a sleeping area. I caught a glimpse of what I figured was the Conductor's room. The stacks of *Classical Thunder* CDs and the Phantom Regiment Marching Corps banner were the giveaways.

The other bedroom, Animan's, was like stepping into the Discovery Channel. The walls were covered with ornithological and ichthyological charts, the bed was barely visible beneath the zoology textbooks and the shelves were lined with cutaway models of birds, whales and mountain cats. The only spot that didn't belong in a college zoology class was the full-length mirror hanging from the back of the door.

A work-desk ran along one side of the room and nearly the entire wall behind it was covered with pegs. Small wooden totems dangled from many of them, each about two inches long, carefully crafted and hand-painted. Many more pegs stood empty, as though they were waiting for a totem to occupy them. As I examined the rows of creatures -- a falcon, a puma, a dolphin, a starfish -- Animan removed the eagle-totem from around his neck and hung it from one of the empty pegs.

The totems were some of the most beautiful carvings I'd ever seen. I couldn't even imagine the precision of the blade used or how fine a paintbrush was needed to create those lines. "This is incredible stuff, man."

"Thanks," Animan said. "I carve and paint it all myself, once I finish researching an animal."

"Animan's an expert on every animal he crafts," the Conductor said. "By now he's got enough rattling around that otherwise-empty head to rack up half a dozen PhDs."

Animan nodded. "Check out my new one -- it's on the desk."

I looked down and saw a half-whittled shape that I could tell, even in this preliminary stage, was going to be an antelope. It was crude and had no details yet, but it was already a remarkable piece of work.

"You do all this yourself?" I said, turning to face Animan. "You've got some serious talents, ma--"

I shouted out an unintentional expletive as I turned to see Animan gone, replaced by a snarling, snaggletoothed beast with flashing eyes and gaping, salivating jaws. I fell backwards into a bookshelf and a frog model slipped from its peg, bonking me on the head.

In the doorway, the Conductor was laughing so hard I thought his band uniform would pop open. He wheezed and held onto the doorframe for support. In front of me the carnivorous visage that sent me crashing backwards calmed itself into a smile and began to utter a low, guttural canine chuckle.

"I *am* sorry, Josh," the Conductor said, gasping for breath. "Oh, geez, but if you had seen your *face*..."

As calm returned to my limbs I examined the hairy, fanged creature in front of me with his tattered, brown shreds of clothing and short snout sniffing at the air. For the first time, I noticed the animal totem about his neck -- it was a dog, I thought. No, a...

"You're *Wolph*," I said. Wolph was a Cape in the same vein as the Gunk -- widely considered monster by the general public, but who, more often than not, wound up helping the very people who despised and feared him.

"I apologize for frightening you, friend Joshua," he said in a sudden British accent. (A werewolf with a British accent. I felt like I was in a movie.) "Sometimes my passion for the dramatic overwhelms me."

"You're *Wolph*," I added for clarification. By now they were probably wondering if I was sitting on a parrot totem. "And you're also *Animan*," I pointed out, just to break the monotony.

"And Aquila," said Wolph. "And many, many others. Each totem you see here represents another champion." He grasped the wolf-totem at his neck and concentrated. The fur went back beneath the surface of his skin, his teeth dulled and he was once again the good-natured guy I'd met a few minutes ago.

He handed me the wolf-totem. "Fact is," he said, "I'm pretty much any animal-based Cape you can think of. Llamaman, K-9 Kop, Moray..."

"And that's why they call you Animan?"

"Yeah. 'Manimal' was taken."

I examined the wolf-totem closer. "Hey, you know, the first few times I was around Capes who couldn't turn off their powers, you know, like the Gunk or DoubleGum Man, I automatically shifted to whatever form *they* were in. That didn't happen just now."

"Didn't happen when Goop was around either," the Conductor said.

"Maybe I'm getting better control over my powers. I *do* feel a Rush from you, though."

"Maybe it's that the forms I take aren't really *powers*," Animan said. "The forms are what happen when I *use* my powers. My only *inherent* talent is to absorb the characteristics of my magic totems."

"They're magic?"

"Yeah, it was some Indian Shamen or Mayan priest or something, I forget what Morrie's guys suggested. Truth is I just research the animal, make a carving and I use it to bring out their phenotypes on my own body. I'm not quite sure *how* I do it, but I do it."

"Can anyone else use them?"

"Nope. They're attuned to me. I make 'em, I study 'em, only *I* can use 'em."

"Really?" I said. I raised the Wolf-totem to eyes and imagined myself... *hairier.*

Suddenly my skin began to itch and my teeth pricked my lips. I was consumed with smells and sounds I never even conceived before -- Conductor and Animan each had distinctive heartbeats and scents -- Animan smelled of wood-chips and paint, the Conductor like slide grease and brass. I felt the need to hunt, to prowl... I lost my ability to speak in contractions and my thoughts suddenly had a European tinge to them. I w*as* Wolph.

"Sheee-oot," Animan said. "*Nobody's* supposed to be able to do that."

"And it is probably for the best that they cannot," I said. "It *is* rather... seductive." I touched the totem again and deactivated my... *Wolph's* powers.

"How can you *do* that?" Animan said.

"That's *my* power," I said. "If *you* can do it, *I* can do it."

"Oh," Animan said, smiling. "You know, I like you man."

"Well thanks, I--"

He took the wolf-totem and put it back on its peg. "I just wanted to let you know that before I tell you to never do that again."

SHEILA OBSERVES

A few days later, on the day of my first rumble, Sheila wandered into my cubicle again. I was going over an archive piece on Nancy Drake, the reclusive romance novelist who had a weird talent for writing stories involving Capes. It wasn't exactly my kind of article, but you took the assignments you got. Sheila poked her head into my work area and opened up with the sort of warm, sisterly concern I had grown to expect from her.

"What the *hell* are you doing?"

"Nothing. Just having a cup of coffee," I said, drinking straight from the pot I'd stolen -- along with several packets of sweetener and cream -- from the office snack area as soon as I got to work.

"Where were you last night? We were supposed to go to the coffee shop together and make fun of the other people who didn't have dates."

"I was... at work."

"You know, your *mother* called me last night. I have no idea how she got my number."

"Mom's resourceful."

"But she hasn't heard from you in a week and she's getting worried."

"Moms *always* worry."

"Well I'm worried too."

"You'll make a good mom someday."

"These nocturnal activities of yours are starting to wear you down, Josh. Maybe you should back off."

"Are you *kidding*? I'm getting absolutely *golden* material here. We're talking guaranteed Pulitzer, Sheila."

"But it's *dangerous*, and you're not in any shape to really watch yourself. Plus you're exhausted."

"Well sure, now, but -- You know, it's funny, but I'm *never* this wiped when I'm actually *there*. It's like that constant influx of powers I feel prevents me from getting tired."

"Until you come down off your high. Then you can barely lift a finger to write with."

"Come on, Sheila, you make it sound like I'm an addict." I chugged more coffee.

"Your caffeine fix notwithstanding, what if you wind up getting hurt, Josh? Or worse? You know, the average 'permanent retirement' age for your new profession is pretty low."

"Yeah, but Heaven's retention rate for us *sucks*." In fact, I had discovered, about ninety percent of the superheroes and villains who "came back from the dead" were retirees who thought they could live the high life with the money they had stowed away, then squandered it all on magic beans or the like, so they had to come back. It was only about ten percent that *actually* returned from the grave.

Sheila gave me a look I interpreted as "You *male*," and stomped off. As usual, after one of these conversations, I was left both smiling and thinking. Sure, it was worth it to irritate her on occasion, but she *did* have a point. I was dead on my feet and I had been for nearly a week now. Maybe after my rumble with the Spectacle Six I'd keep away from Simon Tower for a while -- just enough to get my energy back. Then I'd be able to dive straight back in.

The rumble. *Crap.* What time was it?

I looked down at my watch, but the face and hands had totally vanished. Upon closer, examination, and drawing upon detective skills that would have made

Nightshadow proud, I determined this was, in fact, because I was wearing my cat's flea collar on my wrist. Achilles was no doubt scratching up a storm back home. I was more tired than I thought.

"Danny!"

Dan Cardigan was walking past my cubicle at that moment and my eyes were firmly fixated on his wrist. "Dan, I left my watch at home, what time is it?"

"What's that on your arm?"

"Don't ask stupid questions! Just tell me what time it is!"

"Josh, relax. Geez. I've got... eleven-forty-five."

Of *course* it was eleven-forty-five. Because I was due to rob a bank at high noon (Morrie thought it would add a "classic" flair) and I had to get way the hell across town.

I snapped my briefcase shut and scrambled for the hall. "Thanks, Dan, I'll see you later."

"Josh! Where are you going?"

"Um... I got a tip on a... bank robbery?" Crap. Probably shouldn't have said that. "I'm going to check it out."

"Well check your in-box first, I think you've got an assignment in there."

I cursed the editor under my breath and grabbed a couple of paper-clipped sheets from my inter-office mailbox on the way out. I got in the elevator -- alone -- and hit the lobby button.

As the doors to the elevator glided shut, I looked down at the papers in my hand. It was another profile piece, like the Doctor Noble mess I suppose had started this whole thing... but the *subject.*

"Well what do you know?" I mumbled.

That's how I went to my first rumble -- not concerned with my choreography, not hoping I'd be able to put on a good show. Instead, I was wondering how in the hell I was going to write a profile piece on the Goop.

JOSH'S FIRST CRIME

I changed into the Shift costume in an alley on the way to the bank, proving again the glamour of the business. To cover it up the rest of the way Morrie gave me the two least conspicuous articles of clothing ever designed: a trench coat and a fedora to pull down over my face. Practically everyone I passed on the street pointed or glared or simply tried to avoid my gaze, while a couple of kids actually pulled out decks for a *Capes and Masks* trading card game and tried to see if they could find a Shift card as their mother hurried them away from me. The kid's face and shock of blonde hair looked kind of familiar to me, but I didn't have time to try to place it.

I was still a block away from the bank when I could feel the Rush starting to come over me from Flux and LifeSpeed, who were supposed to be nearby. I switched on my mask-radio. "This is Shift, do you read?"

"I read you, Josh," Particle said. He was back at Simon Tower with microphones connecting him to all the "combatants," as well as a readout of the bank's security system so he would know when the alarm was tripped. That would be the clue for the Spectacle Six to come crashing in and capture me. "Are you in position?"

"Almost. What about the Six?"

"They're just waiting for the alarm. It's all on you."

"Okay. Tell Fourtifier to slip on his dancing shoes. I'm going in."

I stood outside the tall, glass doors of the Siegel City First National Bank. I took several deep breaths. And then, in one smooth, practiced motion, I burst through the door, tossed the hat from my head, threw off the coat, got my arms tangled in the sleeves, thrust it aside in frustration, hit a small child in a stroller, sheepishly apologized to a furious mother and finally managed to shout, "Everybody freeze! This is a stick-up!"

There were only three or four customers and three tellers there, all of which hit the ground as soon as my trench coat was clear. They got bored waiting for me to get it off, though, and most were now sitting cross-legged, patiently waiting for me to begin the robbery. Meanwhile the two guards bolted straight for me as they reached for their firearms.

I yanked my left arm up, hand cupped, and cut off the gravity to the first guard, sending him to the ceiling. With my right arm I punched straight out at the other guard, charging him with backwards momentum and plastering him to the wall. Neither of these hand motions were particularly necessary, mind you, but they added to the dramatic effect and I rather liked the way they looked.

As I approached the teller on the end I saw two guys on the floor near a credit card display grinning like maniacs and giving me a thumbs-up. Flux and LifeSpeed. Real subtle. I pulled a canvas sack from my coat and thrust it at the first teller in the line. "Fill 'er up, sweetheart," I said, "and *no funny business.*"

As corny as the dialogue was, saying it *did* give me something of an adrenal jolt. I was beginning to understand what actors mean when they say it's more fun to play the bad guy. As long as it's fake, as long as no one gets hurt... God help me, I *enjoyed* it.

The panicked teller handed the bag back to me, filled with cash. I grinned and cocked my head back. "Well," I said, "ta-ta for--"

"Shift," Particle's voice echoed in my head, "we've got a problem. Nobody tripped the alarm yet. The Six can't go in."

"What?" I shouted.

"I didn't say anything!" the teller squeaked.

"Stall!" Particle shouted.

"Um... okay, you! Next in line! Gimme whatever *you've* got."

I shoved the bag at the next teller over and snarled. This one had a little more fire in her than the first one, though. "If you think I'm going to cooperate with the likes of *you*--" she began. I sent out another stream of inertia, this one in pulses and directed at the guard plastered to the ceiling. As a result, his head began bobbing up and down, banging against the ceiling like a metronome.

"All right, all right!" The teller began feeding money into the bag and I lowered the poor guard to the ground, hoping I hadn't actually hurt him -- I calibrated the pulses so they shouldn't be more than an annoyance.

"How're we doing?" I asked.

"Fine, fine," said the teller, thinking I meant her.

"We still haven't got an alarm!" Particle said.

"What is this, your first day?" I shouted to the tellers. "Okay, keep it going. Um... change, too. You got any of those quarters with states on them? Gimme a few. I'm still missing Vermont."

"Nothing!" Particle shouted.

"This is the *worst bank ever!*" I howled to the staff and patrons.

"Well do *something!*" Particle said.

The bag was almost overflowing now, there was no way the next teller could fit any more cash in it. She was a cute blonde, though, and kind of reminded me of Sindy. There was only one delaying tactic left that I could imagine. "Hey baby," I said, doing my best Doc Noble imitation, "what're *you* doing after the robbery?"

She smiled and giggled and shuffled her foot. I heard a click.

"That did it Josh!" Particle said. "She just stepped on the alarm switch!"

I frowned, picked up the money sack and slung it over my shoulder. "Your gender is all alike," I hissed on the way out.

After three run-throughs at the arena we'd settled on a routine that *didn't* include me getting cold-cocked by Five-Share on my way out of the bank. Instead, as I stepped onto the sidewalk outside I made sure to create at least three feet of clearance. There was a clattering of heels and I spun around just in time to get punched in the jaw.

I rolled with the punch, hitting the ground at just the right speed and angle that it didn't hurt, but I pretended to be dazed as Five-Share -- all five of him -- hovered over me in a circle.

"Didn't you learn your lesson *last* time, Shift?--Dope.--Dork.--*Please* pick the hard way.--Some guys never learn."

I rolled to my feet. "Sorry to disappoint, you walking barbershop quintet." I jutted both arms from my sides, sending a ring of inertia out, knocking all of the Five-Shares away.

"It's time for the Shift school of combat," I said as practiced. "Lesson one, don't make yourselves such an obvious target."

"Lesson two," rumbled Fourtifier's voice. "*Always* keep your guard up when you're line dancing with the Spectacle Six!" A pair of rock arms wrapped around me and fused together, binding my arms to my side, in theory to keep me from using the inertia powers. Fourtifier may have *admired* my melting technique, but as we soon discovered, he didn't particularly *like* it. Of course, I didn't *need* to use my arms, but it made for a better show.

"Wow!" shouted one of the boys I'd seen swapping cards earlier. "The Spectacle Six!"

"Check your deck, Tom!" the other one shouted. "Maybe we can get their autographs."

"Lesson three," I said to Fourtifier, trying not to laugh at the kids, "binding a man's *arms* is pointless when he can always escape *up*!"

I cut my own gravity -- the only part of this entire routine I was still a little nervous about -- and gave myself a burst of upwards thrust, squirting out of Fourtifier's grip like a greased banana.

As I rose I dared a glimpse upwards, only to find myself zipping straight towards a field of low-flying meteors. "Sweet crap!" I shouted, more for effect than anything else. After all, I knew what was going on. I twisted through the air, applying momentum as needed, and tried to navigate my way through the meteor field. I did okay for a while, too, dodging the three or four biggest chunks before flying headfirst into one...

Which I naturally passed straight through without harm. The entire field blinked out of existence as "Shift" realized the whole thing was an illusion conjured by First Light.

The albino Cape swept down at me. "This is a pointless exercise, Shift," she said. "You cannot escape us. You never have before."

"First time for everything," I said. Then, with a gulp, I restored my gravity and dropped towards the ground. Between careful bursts of inertia and lowering my gravity I managed to make a perfect landing on the sidewalk, quite a distance from Five-Share and the slow-moving Fourtifier. The kids, I noticed, had followed me rather well.

"You're doing good," Particle said. "Don't do *too* good, though. You're supposed to get *caught,* remember?"

"Right." I turned and bolted through the crowd, where I was scheduled to run into Five-Share, only it *wasn't* going to be Five-Share, it was going to be a hologram created by First Light, who was at that very moment landing behind me, ready to create it.

"Hey, Miss First Light!"

I spun around at the child's voice, and thank God I did, because otherwise I would have kept right on running through all of what happened next. I would not have seen as one of the kids -- the one whose blonde hair and face looked familiar to me earlier -- charged up to the Six-er, begging for her to autograph his trading card. I would not have seen him reach up to get her attention, firmly wrapping his hand around her bare wrist. I wouldn't have seen the flesh-to-flesh contact cause her to recoil and instinctively lash out with a burst of concentrated light in the child's face and I wouldn't have watched the kid, blind and shrieking, stagger into the street. Although to be perfectly fair, my attention probably would have been drawn a second later as the kid's mother began to scream like a falling missile and as the driver of the big rig that was roaring down the road began blaring his horn at the poor boy as if it were at all possible for him to get out of the way in time.

ISSUE SIX

WIRING

I've always believed that a lot of the way people behave is instinctual, especially in split-second cases. Some people are simply programmed to react a certain way in a given situation, no matter what they would normally do if they had time to think about it. Some people are constructed to flee from danger, some leap in face-first. Some will risk their lives without thinking and others just freeze to the spot.

This doesn't make them good or bad people, you understand, any more than the quality of a car's wiring makes the rest of it any more or less functional.

I've got a point to this. It wasn't *me* that saved that kid's life. It was my wiring.

The truck was inches from his face, zooming in my direction, and he was too terrified to move -- not that it would have mattered, human beings aren't built to move as fast as he would have needed to get out of the way.

Without taking an instant to think it over, I charged the kid with momentum -- but not to the right or the left. Even using LifeSpeed's powers I couldn't possibly have moved him fast enough to even clear the truck's massive grill that way, it was just too close. Cutting the gravity and hurling him up wouldn't have done any good, either, that would have only resulted in the paramedics scraping him off the windshield instead of the grill. The momentum I threw into that terrified boy with the familiar face was going in the *same direction as the truck.*

The kid jolted off his feet and hurled through the air, keeping pace with the truck well. I gave him bit more momentum, increasing the gap between him and the cab to a few feet rather than a few inches. Whenever I saw an opportunity to hurl him away I'd need to have the clearance at the ready. In the meantime, I rocketed myself down the street, next to the truck, and managed to match the kid's position and speed. To my perceptions, it looked like he was simply hovering in front of a still cab as the world zipped past us.

"Don't worry!" I shouted to the screaming boy. "You're gonna be fine!" I looked up into the cab, boring my gaze into the driver. "Stop the truck!" I shouted. "Stop the damned truck! *Stop!*"

The driver stared at me with a confused look. He couldn't see the kid from his angle and had apparently decided the absence of a "thud" meant I'd pulled the boy free somehow. Over the wind and the groaning engine, he couldn't hear a word I was saying. I began hurriedly looking for any potential landing spot for the kid, there would be no time to do this delicately.

Across the street we were coming up to a vegetable market. If I could send the kid into the lettuce bin or something it might just cushion the impact. The avocados and apples scared the hell out of me, though. Now if only I could only find a break in the traffic...

As the kid and I lined up with the lettuce bin a green Subaru in the other lane cleared it. There was about four empty feet of space before the next car, a red Jeep whose driver was looking somewhat perturbed.

Four feet at about forty-five miles per hour. It would have to be enough.

I cut off all forward momentum for both the kid and myself, simultaneously shoving him across the street as hard and as fast as I could. My vision was cut off as the truck that should have pulverized him raced past. There was a screeching sound and the cars in the other lane roared to a stop in a domino effect, with more than one fender-bender down the line.

The truck cleared my vision just in time to see the lettuce bin across the street collapsing in on itself, leaves being sprayed into the air, The tomatoes and cabbage on either side tumbled down on the boy and for a quick, horrible second I imagined the headlines: "SHIFT A MURDERER, BOY TOSSED INTO SALAD."

And then he sat up. He was scratched and scraped. He was probably bruised a little from the impact. But he was in *one piece.*

As soon as I knew he wasn't dead I felt a twang deep in my core. I'd actually done some honest-to-God superhero stuff. Now *there* was a Rush I hadn't prepared for.

It wasn't until I knew the kid was safe that I realized two things. First of all, Particle had been shouting at me through my earpiece during the entire ordeal. Whatever he'd been shouting before, though, had been replaced by shouts of "Woo-hoo!" and "That was *spectacular!*"

The second thing I noticed was that I was too far from the bank to feel Rushes from either Flux or any of the Six-ers, but I was still using LifeSpeed's powers, which meant he had to be nearby, following. As it turned out, he was directly behind me, apparently having changed into his costume, with the kid's horrified mother and brother in tow. All three were wearing looks of total amazement on their faces.

"I surrender?" I offered.

"You... I was..." LifeSpeed was babbling. As he struggled to figure out how to delicately arrest a man who had just pulled a ten-year-old back from Street Pizza Heaven, in full view of a city's worth of witnesses no less, a crowd began to form. He finally managed to compose himself. "I happened to be in the area and... and... what the hell did you *do*?"

"I think he saved my son's life," the mother said, understandably stunned. After all, I *was* the guy she'd just watch rob a bank (and I suddenly hoped that one of the Spectacle Six had retrieved the money bag I'd dropped rather than some upwardly-mobile passerby). But I had just rescued her son, who wouldn't have even been *in* danger if not for the direct actions of one of our *protectors*.

With traffic ground to a halt the four of us -- LifeSpeed, Mom and bro and myself -- made our way across to the stunned kid with no problem.

A couple of the rubberneckers seemed put off by my presence. "Keep him away from the kid!" someone shouted.

"Hey, cut him some slack!"

"He saved that kid's life!"

"Kid wouldn't have been in danger if it weren't for *him*!"

"It wasn't his fault!"

As we approached the child, one of the more vigorous critics of my performance started to find small objects he didn't require. A soda bottle glanced off my back, and when I looked up again I saw a rock zooming for me. His aim was off, though, and it angled in towards the mother. She didn't see it coming. I could have just cut its inertia, but I was getting pissed. Remembering my trick with Fourtifier, I sent it back at the thrower, sped up the molecules and allowed the rock to fall, puddling on the ground, splattering onto a couple of people who ventured too close.

"That's enough!" LifeSpeed shouted. "The situation is under control!" He got us to the boy's side, ignoring the bizarre mixture of rants and accolades. Mom, of course, got there first. "Tom? Tommy, are you all right?" She pulled him from the rubble, brushed a lettuce leaf from his hair and clutched him to her chest like a helium balloon trying to escape. The fear in her voice was slowly being replaced by relief.

"I'm okay," Tom said, still a little unsure of what happened. "I can't see very well, though."

"Your eyes will clear up," I said. "I've been zapped by First Light before."

"Is that *Shift*?" Tom asked, squinting at me. "Did *he* save me?"

"Yes," his mom said, "he did." Then she looked up at me, still unsure how to take all of this. He looked a bit

Blake M. Petit

like his mother, I realized, and she looked even more familiar than *he* did. *"Why?"* she asked.

My mind scrambled for a moment, finally settling on something I vaguely remembered hearing in a movie once. "Hey, lady," I said. "I'm just a crook. I'm no killer."

"Come on, Shift," LifeSpeed said. "You're going in. Maybe I can get you some leniency... um... you know, considering."

"Yeah. Thanks." I held out my hands and prepared to be led away.

"Mr. Shift?" It was Tom. "Wait a second, please, sir." He pulled his trading cards from his pocket and started to shuffle through them. "Darn it," he said, squinting, "I can't--"

"Wait, let me, squirt," his brother said. He looked through Tom's cards, finally pulling one out and holding it up to me. "I think he wants you to sign it for him."

The three of us tall enough to ride a roller coaster were momentarily stunned. After a few seconds, though, Mom regained her senses. She dug into her purse and produced a pen.

I glanced at LifeSpeed, who raised his eyebrows in a "hell if *I* know" expression. Still feeling a little strange about it, I took the card and pen, scribbled the word "Shift" on it, and gave them back.

"Thanks, mister," Tom said.

"Uh... yeah, Tom. Anytime."

We started to push our way through the developing crowd, me playing the part of LifeSpeed's prisoner.

"Clear the way!" LifeSpeed shouted. "This guy's got a one-way ticket to jail! Clear out!"

The sight of me being led by a Cape seemed to galvanize the audience against me. "Yeah! Get him out of here!"

"Damned menace..."

"Better off with 'em *all* in jail."

But I still noticed, for every three or four adversaries I had in the crowd, there was at least one person who didn't seem quite convinced that LifeSpeed was leading away the right combatant.

As we moved along and the people began to keep their distance, LifeSpeed leaned forward and whispered, "The others have calmed First Light down and returned her to the tower. The money is already back in the bank."

"Good," I whispered back. It was like he'd read my mind.

"That was some stunt, rookie," LifeSpeed said. "Morrie isn't going to like it at *all*."

"Morrie isn't the one who would've had to live with a child's death on his conscience when he could have done something to save him."

"Whoa, relax! I didn't say I *agreed* with him. You did *great* out there today."

"Oh. Well... thanks."

"So... how does it feel?"

I thought about it for a moment before coming to a conclusion. "Strange," I said. "But pretty good."

"Yeah," LifeSpeed said. "That's how it *should* feel."

We walked in silence for a few more moments.

"Do you think you could teach me that melting trick sometime?" he asked.

REPRIMAND

I don't know exactly what I expected when LifeSpeed returned me to Simon Tower, but it certainly wasn't the reception I got. We walked into the lounge amidst a barrage of applause, cheers and catcalls. It was like I'd just won the Miss America pageant, while in actuality I felt like I'd bombed out in the swimsuit competition.

Particle was the first to actually approach me. "Well done, Josh. *Well* done! Any veteran here couldn't have done any better."

"Are you kidding? That kid could have been killed."

"But he *wasn't*," Hotshot said. "Not only did you save the kid, but you gave Siegel City a show it's not going to forget anytime soon. That's how the game is played, pal."

"Yeah," I grumbled. "Where's First Light? Is she okay?"

"In her quarters getting 'purified'," Flux said. "Morrie's already talked to her."

"And he's going to want to talk to *you*," LifeSpeed said. "Relax here for a while, I'll try to gauge his mood for you."

LifeSpeed left and the mob of Capes and Masks dissipated amongst a flurry of pats on the back and trumpeting praise. Bit by bit, people returned to what they were doing before my celebrated entrance, but they were still coming up to me one-on-one, some of them with a simple "Good job," some whispering how they'd always wanted to do that sort of thing but Morrie wouldn't have liked it. Even the ever-cheerful Icebergg grumbled out, "I guess ya did okay." Then my muscles began to water on me and I felt my flesh sag. Even my head hurt a little, like someone had shoved a bag of water up there. I knew who it was.

"Hey Gunk," I said.

"Hello, my boy."

"You... you heard about my little... adventure?" Maybe it was because I felt my body turning to mush, but I was started to get some major heebie-jeebies every time I encountered the Gunk.

"Quite the attention-grabber, laddie-buck. I knew you'd be one to look out for, I have an instinct about these things. I *knew* you would be one of those rare supra-normals that electrifies the mundane populace from the moment of your debut." He laughed. "Why, I wouldn't be surprised in the slightest if a series of Shift action figures were rushed into production post haste."

"Yeah... thanks." It was like holding a conversation with a thesaurus, armed with a copy of *See Spot Run*. I needed out of this situation. "Um... Gunk?"

"Yes, son?"

"Would you mind... going somewhere else? I get... I mean... no offense, but... I get kind of... *slimy* when you're... you're around."

"Oh! My deepest apologizes, lad." He gave my disintegrating shoulder a fraternal squeeze and a mushy pat. "I should have realized the detrimental effect my particular energy-signature would have upon you. I'll leave you alone. Again, well done, Joshua."

As my body returned to its previous semi-solid state, I tried to force a little clarity back into my skull "God, I *hate* when he does that." I grabbed my own shoulders and squeezed them a couple of times, just to reassure myself that they were again as firm as they'd ever been.

Flambeaux and Deep Six were next. With his flame turned off, Flambeaux was a very pleasant-seeming fellow with a wide grin and a shock of white hair. Deep Six was still in his costume -- a diving suit complete with a bronze dome helmet that covered his entire face, but I assumed the twin brothers would be identical.

"Pretty good, fella," Flambeaux said.

"Yeah, that was sweet." Deep Six's voice was hollow and resonant in the helmet. "I'd never have tried anything like that myself."

"Well," said Flambeaux, "not unless you count that time Miss Sinistah--"

"Oh, shut up."

"Thanks guys," I said. "Your support is appreciated. Weird, but appreciated."

As they wandered off, the next member of the sudden Pro-Shift Society came up to me. "Hey there, Goop," I said. As I'd noticed back at the Arena, he wasn't affecting me. As soon as his boss was around I took on the consistency of runny Jell-O, but I wasn't getting an erg of power from the second-string Gunk.

"Um..." I said. As unnerving as the effects of the Gunk's powers were on me, the Goop's *lack* of energy was starting to make me even *more* ill at ease. I tried to sound pleasant. "So... you heard about the kid, huh?"

Goop approached me, his body squishing around, making a sound like a water balloon. He walked up until he was staring me in the eye. Then he raised both arms and, with a squish, dropped a hand on each of my shoulders.

"I'm proud of you, little guy," he said. Then he jerked his neck a little, blinked and added, "Proudproud*proud*!" He pulled me into a decidedly unsolid hug. Then he gave me a sloppy kiss on the cheek and walked away.

I've got to profile that*?* I thought.

"Dude!"

I didn't even have time to turn around before I was practically concussed by Animan and the Conductor, both beaming like they'd just seen their little brother hit his first home run.

"Spectacular!"

"Rock!"

"Five-star performance, man!" Animan pulled me into a friendly headlock while the Conductor drummed "Charge" on my temples.

"Thanks, guys," I said, breaking free. "Hey, Conductor--"

"Ted," he said.

"What?"

"My name. It's Ted Ossian. If anybody calls you a rookie after *that* stunt I'll *personally* hand 'em their ass."

"No you won't," Animan said.

"Yeah, I won't," Ted grumbled. "But they'd *deserve* it."

"You *rule*, brother," Animan said. "I'd give you my name, but nobody uses it anymore. I'm just Animan."

"Animan it is, then," I said. Unable to contain my smile, I shook their hands and embraced them as though we were meeting for the first time.

"Yo, Shift!"

I turned and saw LifeSpeed coming up behind me, his mask pulled off his face and his lips tightened in a grimace.

"Morrie wants to talk to you now, Josh."

"Hey, don't take any crap from him, man," Animan said.

"Yeah. You did the only thing you could," Ted chimed in.

LifeSpeed managed a grin. "And you pulled off a hell of a show in the process. Let's go, buddy."

Much as I'd enjoyed my prior visits to the office of Morris Abadie, I could positively *feel* the outpouring of love when I walked in that afternoon, what with the blackened gaze boring straight into my soul. Actually, what I felt was the Rush from Mental Maid's powers, stronger than I'd ever felt it before. Was she angry? Pleased? Was I disrupting whatever scheme she had or playing right into her hands?

The power was so intense that even the source I was drawing it from was feeling more diffused, as if Mental Maid's powers were not confined to her body. It was almost as though they were bleeding into Morrie. I tried, just for a second, to reach out and try to feel my way through her powers, to *understand* them, the way I had with some of the others, but it didn't do any good.

Didn't matter much anyway. I didn't have another chance to try. The look I was getting from Morrie cut me off from any bold moves I had left in me.

"What," he said.

"The *hell*," he continued.

"Was *that?*" he finished, giving me a sensation of *deja vu*. As he fumed, Mental Maid glared.

"I saved that kid," I said. "I'm not making any apologizes for that."

"Somebody *else* could have saved the kid."

"Nobody else was in position."

"That wasn't your call! Do you know how long Flux and LifeSpeed have been doing this sort of thing?"

"Yeah? Are they coordinated enough to use their powers like they've got one brain? And what were you thinking, sending someone as unstable as First Light into a *combat* situation?"

"If that kid hadn't touched her, she would have been *fine*."

"Well I guess if you don't bother to *plan...*"

There was a crackle and I dropped into the chair across from Morrie. My limbs froze into place on the arms and my jaw snapped shut. I was still able to look from side to side, though, and I saw Mental Maid's eyes shining that damnable purple glow.

"*I* am going to talk," Morrie said. "*You* are going to listen." He was leaning over his desk now, his cigar resting between his index and middle fingers sending tendrils of smoke up to circle his head like a halo. His eyes flashed and he over-enunciated each word like a pissed-off father who has tried every other method to the point of exhaustion in his quest to drill a point into his son's thick head.

"It was not your call to make," Morrie growled. "When you are in Mask you do not -- repeat -- do *not* do anything even *remotely* heroic. You will trust that, should the need arise, someone wearing the *proper damned uniform* will handle the situation. Bank robbers do *not* save kids from who are about to get run over by an eighteen-wheeler. *Capice*?"

I felt the mental control freezing my mouth in place relax. This, apparently, was my cue to agree with Morrie, call him a god and so forth.

Instead I squeezed out the words, "Why not?"

Morrie was momentarily stunned that I didn't just crumble. "*What?*" he said.

"Why *wouldn't* a crook save a kid? If he could?"

"Cause -- because he's the *bad* guy. Because -- dammit, *do you get me?*"

"Yeah," I spat out. "I get you."

"Good." His eyes dimmed and he inhaled through four inches of Cuban tobacco. "That said," he hissed, "I gotta admit, that was some kinda showmanship out there."

"Huh?"

"You gave those rubes a spectacle they ain't gonna forget for a *long* time. You got a knack for that, kid. And *remember* that, it's the *only* thing keepin' me from making Mental Maid wipe yer brain and throw your candy-ass out of town. I haven't seen a job fouled up like this since the Photon Man fiasco."

My limbs were reawakening and I found myself finally able to move again. "I'm *real* sorry to have let you down, Morrie, you just don't know."

"Yeah, right. Okay, get out of here, kid. Yer welcome to hang around the complex whenever you want, but I ain't gonna need you again until Tuesday. That's when you start training for your next show."

"Shift again?"

"I don't think so. Time you tried on a different Mask."

"Got you." I stood up and turned towards the door, but that Rush... that feeling I was still getting from Mental Maid... it was just too intoxicating not to try.

Not really understanding how the power worked, I thrust out at Morrie and I *felt*. I felt the truth. Morrie was mad at me, to be certain... but I'd also impressed the hell out of him. I was still uneasy as I left the office, but carrying that knowledge made me walk just a little taller.

REWARD

Hotshot was waiting in the hall when I came out. "How was the riot act?" he asked.

"Nothing I can't handle," I said, exactly as snappish as I'd intended. I headed towards the lounge, but Hotshot cut me off -- he pulled a plastic shaft from a pouch on his belt and used his power on it. Since the shaft had a focal point, he was able to fire an ion stream into the air, blocking my way. If it had been an object with no point, such as a ball or a particularly regular stone, it would have continued to break down until it finally exploded, like a grenade.

At any rate, the result was an ear-splitting energy beam lancing in front of me as I reached for the door, only millimeters from branding a streak across my chest. It was enough to get my attention.

"What did I ever do to you, Josh?" he said. "I've tried to be a pal to you from the minute you walked into this complex, I even took you around like I'd known you all my life, but you treat me like something you'd pick out of Doctor Noble's ingrown toenail. *Why*?"

I gave him a stare colder than anything even Mental Maid could conjure up. "Lionheart isn't around," I said. "*Somebody's* got to be disgusted at what you've done to his city."

Before he could babble out another word, I shoved past him and into the lounge. It was mostly deserted now, but Animan and the Conductor -- *Ted,* I had to remind myself -- were waiting for me.

"You still got your brain?" Ted asked.

"As much as ever," I said.

"Good."

"So... Have you seen Miss Sinistah here?"

"Wondering if she'd heard about your impromptu heroics, huh?"

"Aw, *no*," Animan said. "Don't tell me we got *another* one with a crush on Miss 'I'm-Slow-Dancing-With-the-Scum-of-the-Earth-and-I-Deserve-It'."

"You've seen it before?" I asked.

He pointed a thumb at Ted. "Hey I *lived* through it with *this* one."

"She's not here," Ted said. "She left a few minutes ago to make a phone call."

"Not Doctor Nimrod again--"

"Family emergency this time. I tell you, bro, *this* should blow her mind."

"Actually," Animan said, "I think she's back already. Feast your eyes, man."

He pointed over to the television area, but Miss Sinistah was already racing towards me. I didn't even get to blurt out a "hello" before she hit me with a flying hug at breakneck speed. If not for the stamina I got from her powers, she probably would have knocked me down. Her arms wrapped around me and hugged me tighter than I'd ever been held in my life. I decided that if there was a Heaven, I didn't want to go if those arms weren't waiting there.

"You..." she said, her voice cracking. "You are so... *incredible*. Do you know that?"

"Lil' old me? What did I do?"

She pulled her head up and kissed me firmly on the cheek. When I finally saw her eyes, they were red and puffy. "Hey... hey, have you been *crying*?" I wiped a tear from her face (Lord, how could invulnerable skin feel so soft?) and pulled her in for an even tighter hug. "What is it? What's wrong?"

"I'm just... I'm so *proud* of you."

"Thanks, Sindy."

She squeezed harder. "It's Annie," she said. "My name is Annie."

Geez, even her *name* was cute.

"Okay, then," I said. "Annie."

"I can't stay," she said. "I have a family crisis to get back to. But... when I heard what you did for that little boy..." her eyes welled up again and a fat tear rolled down her cheek. "I must be a mess."

"I think you're beautiful."

"I know you do." She kissed me again and finally took her arms away. I never wanted anything as badly as I wanted them back around me.

"Thank you," she said, and she was gone.

"What was *that* about?" I asked Ted.

"I don't know, man, but if you don't *use* this..."

"Are you sure there's something to use?"

"God, even *I'm* not *that* stupid." He wrinkled his brow. "You want to hear the music she was giving off?"

I didn't even answer, the tune simply welled up within me. It was a soft piano riff, quiet, gentle and majestic. The kind of music you only hear in movies. The kind of music you fall in love to. Ted smiled.

"Nice, isn't it?"

"Beyond nice. But *why?*"

"Hey, rookie!" Nightshadow waved at me from a computer terminal across the lounge -- there was an entire bank of them we could use to access the Internet or the Simon Tower media archives.

"No rookie over here!" Ted shouted back. "We got a grizzled veteran, I'll have you know!"

"*Josh*, then," Nightshadow said. "The first newsfeed from your little tango just showed up on the web. Come take a look."

Ted placed a hand on my shoulder and led me over to the computer, where he started reading over Nightshadow's shoulder. Ted read highlights from the report out loud. "Notorious thief Shift... Spectacle Six... saved the life of ten-year-old--" He audibly gasped. I thought people only did that in comic books. "Josh... the kid you saved is named *Tom Harmon*?"

"Yeah. What, does that mean more to you than to me?"

"Did Sinistah tell you her real name?"

"Yeah, it's Annie. Why?"

"Annie *Harmon*," Ted said. "No wonder she's falling for you, man. As of this afternoon, she owes you a brother."

DOWNTIME

It was about 7 p.m. when I finally made it back to the *Powerlines* office. Nearly every evening edition newspaper in Siegel City led with the story of the hardened criminal who saved the little boy's life: "SHIFTING GEARS?" asked the *Star*. The *Ledger* proclaimed "SHIFT'S SAVING GRACE." The *Post* even worked in a tossed salad joke. The only paper I could find with any negative coverage was the *Trumpet*, which practically crucified poor First Light for putting Tom Harmon in danger to begin with. It was a bit unfair, but not really unexpected, given the publisher's well-known bias against Capes. Of course he usually reserved his ire for guys like Nightshadow and the Arachnid, rather than the high-profile, much-beloved Spectacle Six.

Sheila came by as I was clipping the article out of the *Ledger*. As soon as she saw me, she raised an eyebrow. *"You're* in a surprisingly good mood."

"What makes you say that?"

"Well, for one thing there are no circles under your eyes and you're not drinking the annual caffeine intake of Juan Valdez in one sitting."

"I had a good night's sleep," I returned.

"Since this morning?"

"Time warp."

"You're also smiling like a jackal on nitrous oxide."

"It's a wonderful, sunny day."

"You're humming."

"I've got a song in my heart."

"You're humming songs from *Disney* movies."

"I've got a *sappy* song in my heart."

She finally broke. "Spill, Josh. What happened this afternoon? And why are you clipping all those stories about Shift? Were you there when he saved that kid? Did you have anything to do with it?"

"Four questions in one paragraph. You'll be a reporter someday yet."

"You're stalling."

I was, really. Sheila was the closest friend I had, without a doubt, but somehow I just couldn't see my way clear to filling her in on my misadventures. A big part of me was regretting even telling her I had powers in the first place.

"I was the one who tipped off the Spectacle Six," I said. "Anonymously, of course. I knew Shift was going to try pulling a job and I knew somebody had to stop him. And the Spectacle Six aren't listed in the phone book."

"Well... you *do* look better than you did before."

I stood up and gave Sheila a hug. "I'm telling you, I'm *fine.* I'm starting to learn how this whole thing works. Once I've got that, I can put a stop to it."

"So why can't you *tell* me any of it?"

"Because it would be dangerous for you to know too much. Look, I'm keeping a notebook of every activity that goes on there. As soon as I've got enough info, I'll show it all to you and we'll put this story together as a team. Deal?"

"All right." She smiled and we hugged again. As we stood there, our arms around each other, she pulled her head back with a surprised look on her face. "Josh, are you losing weight?"

"What makes you say that?"

"Well, your pants just fell down around your ankles, for one thing."

That explained the sudden draft I caught. I yanked my trousers up and cinched my belt. The worn notch, the one I usually used, was several inches from the one I'd unconsciously buckled that afternoon when I changed out of my Shift costume. Even the last notch on the belt was a tad loose.

"I guess it's all the exercise I've been getting," I said.

"Exercise?" she said. "What exercise?"

"Well, my trai-- um... my... um..."

"Your *training*? Training for *what*?"

"Training for... the... Olympics?"

"Josh..."

"I'm sorry, Sheila, I really am, but I can't say too much."

"This silent game of yours is starting to bother me, Josh."

I patted her on the shoulder. "I don't like it much either, but..."

She sat down and began wringing her hands in a worried, grinding motion. "You know, we *never* hang out anymore. We never *do* anything, we never see each other outside of work. Now you're not even telling me what you're doing all the time. You're my *best friend*, but it feels like you're cutting me out of your life."

"Sheila..."

"I don't want to lose you. I don't want you to become... I don't know... one of 'them'."

I frowned. "One of who?"

"You know, one of those people that works all the time and has no life and never makes time for his friends."

"Oh. *Them*." I sat back down. "You can't really accuse me of having no life, Sheila. I've been keeping myself plenty busy. But I *do* miss you. It's the masochist in me. Tell you what, I don't have to do anything tonight. It's Friday and I know you don't have a date with Scott or Spectrum or anyone else because if you did you'd have walked in here waving a banner."

"You see why I love you? You know me so well."

I smiled. "So tonight, it's gonna be *us*. You and me, two best buddies out for a night on the town. What do you say?"

"Sounds great."

"I'm glad you think so. Because you're not getting out of it. We start as soon as we get off work."

"Okay," she said. "And the *first* thing we're doing is taking you shopping for some new pants."

And we did. I bought three pairs that evening, a size smaller than what I'd been wearing. We caught a terrible movie and made fun of pretty much everyone associated with it, up to and including the producer's dog. We split a greasy pizza and then we leaned back and listened to our arteries clog. It was a great time.

But as much fun as I had with Sheila, Annie was in the back of my mind all night long.

ISSUE SEVEN

VISITING HOURS

The next time I saw Annie, she composed herself enough to inform me the kid I saved was her brother. (I didn't let her know I'd already heard.) I smiled and asked, "Why didn't you just tell me the other day?"

She smiled back, that tiny smile she had. "I'm not sure," she said. For some reason, this made me feel incredibly hopeful -- almost as hopeful as a few seconds later, when she asked me to go home with her and meet Tom and her family as myself.

"You saved his life," she said. "I think it's only right that he see your real face. Even if we *can't* tell him it was you." It took me about half an eyeblink to agree to go with her.

"The funny thing is," she said as we walked through Siegel to her parent's apartment, "Tom is convinced I'm a *Cape*. He thinks I put on a black wig and a mask and go around as Glamour Girl. It's never even occurred to him that his sister could be the big, bad Miss Sinistah."

"Well can you blame him? I mean... if I didn't know better I would *never* place you in the same category as Sinistah."

"No?"

"Uh-uh."

"What *would* you imagine me to be?"

I stopped on the sidewalk and looked her up and down. She was wearing khakis that day, and a cargo vest over a green top. On her feet were a well-worn pair of gray sneakers with a yellow trim. Her blonde hair was pulled back by an orange band, away from her face, and her eyes reflected the sun like marbles. She looked silly and innocent and beautiful, and somehow the first two contributed even more to the third.

"Elementary school librarian," I said.

"*What?*" she smacked me with her purse and we kept on, together, walking along a concrete ribbon glittering in the sun, only occasionally broken apart into the detritus of some rumble or another.

As it turned out, Tom had long suspected his sister's involvement in the world of superhumans. He had caught her, on occasion, using her strength to lift up her car a bit when she couldn't find a jack, pick up a sofa with one hand so she could vacuum underneath and, on multiple occasions, utterly failing to be cut by knives and razors. Sindy -- *Annie*, I had to remind myself -- repeatedly denied any sort of connection to the Capes, but Tom was too sharp a kid to be dissuaded.

Like everyone else he was under the influence of Mental Maid's citywide susceptibility field, but since he'd seen evidence of his sister's powers with his own eyes its hold wasn't as strong. Most people trapped in the field could no longer even *fathom* putting two and two together when it came to us. In Tom's case, he knew two and two were *supposed* to go together, but he didn't quite know what the result should be.

"It actually makes things a bit easier to understand," I said, "him being your brother. I was wondering how a 10-year-old could be reckless enough to interfere with a rumble like that."

"I suppose Tom figured, if I was part of the whole Cape and Mask crowd, it couldn't be something that would hurt him," she assented.

"The kid loves you, huh?"

"You'd think an 11-year age difference would cause a pretty big gulf between us, but Tom and I have always been close. He's my little buddy. He even tries to protect me all the time."

"Protect you? How?"

Annie bit her lip and nibbled, like she was trying not to say something. When she *did* break her silence, it was to indicate a three-story brownstone walk-up, with the perky announcement, "we're here."

The Harmon family lived on the second story of the walk-up. It was a fairly small place, with a kitchen/living room combination and a hallway that I assumed led to an assortment of bedrooms and probably just one bath.

"I could afford a better place for the whole family," Annie whispered, "but not without letting them know what I really do for a living."

"What *do* you tell them you do?"

Her lips curled into a playful smile. "They think I'm a receptionist at *Powerlines.*"

I stifled a laugh. "You're *kidding.*"

"I figured if I ever slipped up and let out too much information I could tell them it was something I heard at the office."

"I wish you *did* work there. It would make my job a lot--"

I stopped talking when Tom's mother came in from the hall. I hadn't bothered to examine her during the previous day's chaos, but now that I took the time to check, she really looked a *lot* like her daughter. She was a small, blonde woman with only a hint of white in her hair, and she carried herself with an air of dignity. She was fairly young -- I'd guess mid-forties -- and her face was as yet unmarked by major wrinkles, the light not yet gone from her eye.

"Well, what have we here?" she asked.

"This is my friend Josh, Mom," she said. "From work."

"Ooooh, *Josh*," she said in an "I-know-something-you-don't-know" voice. She held out her hand and gave mine a firm shake. "I've heard a lot about you, Josh. It's nice to finally meet you."

"Likewise, Mrs. Harmon."

"Oh please, it's *Cynthia*. But never 'Cindy.' I *hate* 'Cindy'." I once again found myself suppressing the urge to chuckle. As I glanced over at Annie, she was doing the same.

"Is Tom around, Mom?" she asked.

"At the park with Quentin. They should be back soon. Make yourself at home, Josh. Would you like some lemonade? I just made a pitcher."

"That would be wonderful." Annie and I situated ourselves on the sofa as Cynthia went to the kitchen.

"Who's Quentin?" I whispered.

"My other brother."

"Oh," I said. "Autograph Boy. Does he suspect..."

"Quentin? No, I don't think so. He's 13, he spends a lot more time on basketball and girls than Capes and Masks."

"Girls? Poor kid doesn't know what he's getting into." This prompted another laugh and a dirty look from Annie that probably would have led to an incredibly sarcastic (and therefore adorable) remark on her part, but at that moment Cynthia called her from the kitchen to ask for help. Their backs were turned to me and, with their similar voices, I had trouble picking out who was saying exactly what. I did get a *few* snippets of conversation, though.

"Seems very nice..."

"...handsome thing, isn't..."

"...reminds me of Tom..."

"...oh cut that out..."

"...very sweet..."

"...*stop* it!"

They turned around, Cynthia holding a tray with three glasses of lemonade, Annie holding a half-full pitcher and wearing a look that anyone who has ever known a girl between the ages of 14 and 23 could translate into "if you embarrass me I'll kill you in your sleep."

Cynthia handed me the lemonade with a wide, warm smile. "So Josh, Annie tells me you're a reporter at the magazine, right?"

"That's right."

"That's such a good job," she said. "It must be exciting."

"Well, it's not like I'm out there covering wars or anything, but it pays the bills."

"Pays *well*, does it?" The Look returned to Annie's face and her eyebrows arched up. She was probably getting furious with her mother, but I was starting to enjoy the hell out of this conversation.

"Hey mom!" There was a slamming door and the two boys came running in tossing a basketball back and forth. "Hey, Annie!"

"How's your game, squirt?" she asked.

"Hah! Quent's got *nothing*. I took him in three sets." He tossed the ball to Annie, who deftly began twirling it on her finger.

"Impressive," I said.

"This is my friend Josh, guys. He works at *Powerlines*. Josh, this is Tom and Quentin."

"Hey," Quentin mumbled. "Mom, did Heather call?"

"Thrice." She handed Quent a handwritten message from her pocket. He gave the rapid-fire "Howyadoingnicetameetcha" of a teenage boy with a teenage girl's phone number and vanished.

"What do you do at the magazine?" Tom asked.

"I'm a reporter."

"Cool. Does that mean you get to meet a lot of Capes?"

"Well... well yeah, recently I have."

"Did you ever meet LifeSpeed? He was there yesterday when Shift saved me."

"Yeah, I *have* met LifeSpeed. Nice guy, that one."

"Will you be staying for dinner, Josh?" Cynthia asked.

"Um... I don't know, am I?"

Annie nodded. "I think we can pencil you in."

"Then we need to start cooking, Annie. Tom, can you keep Josh entertained?"

"Sure," he said.

"You don't mind, do you Josh?" Annie asked.

"Not at all. I think Tom and I will get along great."

The Harmon ladies left Tom and me alone as they began rifling through cabinets and refrigerator drawers.

"Have you ever seen a rumble?" Tom asked.

"A couple. Once I got *real* close. You really like these Capes, don't you?"

"They're great! I wish I could do what they do."

"Disrupt traffic and cause wanton property damage?"

"No! They stop Masks and they save people and... look what Shift did yesterday. Did Annie tell you about that?"

"Yeah. I heard."

"I think, maybe, he should be a Cape instead of a Mask. If he was all bad, he wouldn't have saved me, would he?"

"I don't know, Tom. Just because someone's a crook, does that mean he'd let an innocent person die?"

"Maybe not, but... I don't know, the way Shift acted -- he seemed concerned, you know? Like he actually cared what happened to me."

"You know what?"I said. "I think maybe he did."

Tom grinned at me. "Want to see something?

"Sure."

He took me down the hall to a bedroom that obviously belonged to a couple of boys whose ages were just creeping into the double digits. There were a couple of beds with blue sheets and a floor littered with sports equipment, comic books, and tons of toys, clothes and school supplies littered with the images of various Capes and Masks. Morrie probably made enough money for a new car just on this room alone. On the wall were posters of the Spectacle Six and Spectrum and a somewhat provocative shot of Glamour Girl near Quentin's bed. I knew it was his because that's the bed he was lying on, chattering away on a cordless phone, when we walked in. He gave us a glare as to indicate that we had interrupted an incredibly meaningful conversation about who was dating who since third period and he quickly left the premises.

Tom must have noticed me looking at the Glamour Girl poster because he wrinkled his nose and said, "I don't like that one."

"Why not?"

"I... I just don't." It hit me as he went to his desk -- he honestly believed that was a poster of his sister on the wall.

On his desk was a binder full of plastic sheets. In each sheet, arranged in a clear little envelopes, were nine "Capes and Masks" game trading cards. Spectrum. Flambeaux. The Shell. Swoosh -- an old card, before he changed his name to LifeSpeed. At least four cards of Animan in various guises.

Tom flipped through until he got to the last page. "Hey," I said, "is that the card Shift signed for you yesterday?"

"How'd you know about that?"

"Your sister told me. Cool card, man."

"Did you ever get an autograph from one of them?"

"Nah, it's not really considered proper etiquette to ask for signatures when you're interviewing somebody." I flipped through the pages a bit -- DeVinity, Goop, Deep Six, Colonel Coldsnap... knowing the truth about the people on those cards gave the game a whole new dimension. "So which one's your favorite?"

Tom took the binder and flipped to the first card on the first page. The card was printed to look old and yellowed, with fake frays on the edges. Across the bottom was a silver banner that read "Vintage Series."

"I had to swap my brother for a First Light, a Justice Giant and a Doctor Noble for him," Tom said. "I still miss Justice Giant."

It was Lionheart, one of the few items ever allowed with his picture.

"Are you okay?"

I nodded. "Yeah, I'm... how do you even know about Lionheart, Tom? You must have been a baby when he disappeared."

"I read a lot," Tom said. "Old magazines, books, comics... he was the best of them, you know. The best of them all." He took the card out and looked it over. As he admired the hero for what must have been the thousandth time, I felt a rise from him. There was a swell of energy and a Rush.

He handed me the card to look at, and I took it, shaking. Tom had powers. They were raw, undeveloped... no way to even tell what they *were* yet. But they were there. It made sense, I suppose -- if his sister had powers, why *not* Tom? I'd have to remember to ask Annie if Quentin had ever displayed unusual talents.

My hand quivered a bit and I dropped the Lionheart card on top of a picture of the Goop with a big, dopey grin on his face. Tom slid Lionheart back into the plastic and closed the binder. "Can I ask you something?" he asked.

"Sure, buddy."

He slid the binder back on its shelf. "Are you dating my sister?"

I regret not having brought my glass of lemonade with me, because I've never had such a wonderful opportunity to perform a spit take. "No," I finally said, more than a little wistfully. "No, I'm not."

"Oh," he said. He sounded disappointed.

"Why? Did she... um... did she say something to you?"

"Not really. But she talks about you a lot, and I thought... once I heard her tell Mom she wishes Todd -- that's her *boy*-friend -- saying she wishes Todd were more like you." He said the word "boyfriend" the way most people would say "dung beetle."

My head simply nodded. My heart, on the other hand, was resisting the urge to physically leap from my chest and perform the "Red and Black" number from *Les Miserables.* "Oh," I said. "I see."

"It's a shame," he said. "I like you a lot better than that Todd guy."

"You're a wise, wise young man, Tom," I said.

RESEARCH

Foosball, it seems, is one of the most intense, strategic sports ever devised by the human mind. At least, that's what you'd think if you saw the way Ted was cleaning my clock at it the next day at the lounge. Not that it was entirely a fair game, mind you. He kept distracting me by talking about Miss Sinistah.

"It sounds to me like you've got the brother *and* the mother on your side," he said, scoring his fifth consecutive goal without me even getting my little twirly guys near the ball. "Dude, you're in good shape."

"Brother... mother... Ted, I could have the Pope getting a piggyback ride from Lionheart dragging a 'Josh loves you' banner behind them through the air. As long as she's with Doc Noble, there's nothing I can do."

"Why *not*?"

"Because I don't do that sort of thing. If I was the 'reason' they broke up, if I got her *that* way, I'd feel so damn *guilty* about it that I'd never be happy."

"That is an *incredibly* warped perception."

"Oh, like I don't *know* that."

Ted stopped moving, stood straight up and glared at me with a "you moron" look on his face.

"What?"

"I'm just thinking that maybe we've got the wrong guy in the Doctor Noble suit." Without bending down or even looking he twirled a row of foosball players and scored another goal.

"Are you sure you're not telekinetic?" I asked. "Why are you so stunned, anyway? You think I'm not telling the truth."

"Empath, remember? I *know* you're telling the truth. That's what bothers me. That and the fact that you're scared of something and you don't want anyone to find out about it." He shot another goal.

"If you must know," I said, "I got a *Powerlines* assignment to profile the Goop and I didn't know quite how to go about it. Do they have air hockey here? I'm *good* at air hockey..."

"Is that all?" Ted gave me a look that indicated he didn't for an instant believe that *was* all, but he respected me enough not to pry if I didn't want him to.

What he was really sensing, I suppose, was my growing apprehension about my notebook. I'd filled it with more than enough info to expose Morrie's little charade once and for all, but I just couldn't bring myself to start on the exposé. I told myself I needed more info. I told myself I could make it better. I told myself there was a deeper story here.

Truth was, there were only two reasons I hadn't gone ahead with the story. First, I was afraid if I blew the whistle, I'd never see Annie again.

Second...

Second...

Dammit.

Second, I was just having too much fun.

"If that's all you're worried about," Ted said, "why don't you look in the archive?" He scored again.

"Archive?"

"Yeah. The computer system here can tell you everything there is to know about every Cape and Mask since Morrie took over -- both the legitimate stories *and* the 'official' spin jobs we release to the public." He pointed me toward the row of computers Nightshadow had read my news article from a few days earlier and scored another goal. "Check it out. This game is getting too easy anyway."

I migrated over to the computer and clicked on the "archive" icon (which, I was irritated to see, was Hotshot's emblem.) Once in the program, the computer asked me for the name of the Cape or Mask I wished to study. The program was rather bland, without the sort of flashy graphics and colors and animated features you get accustomed to with a computer.

"It's a beta version," Ted said. "Morrie just wants to make sure he can get all of the info in and the mechanics working properly. When he releases the full version to the mass market on CD-ROM, it'll blow your eyes out. Of course, it'll be *sans* the non-official files."

I typed in "Goop" and hit the send button. The computer hummed and whirred for a minute, then asked me "official or unofficial version?" With Ted standing right there, I decided it would be more prudent to simply look at what I'd need for the story. I clicked on "official."

The computer sang to itself for a few more seconds before a somewhat lengthy document appeared on the screen. I glared up at Ted, who shrugged. "That's what you asked for," he said. "Hey, Animan! Feel like getting your butt kicked?"

I turned back to the screen and began reading the ludicrous story of the Goop, according to Morrie's spin writers. This is it, in a nutshell:

During one of the brief periods the Gunk regained the intellect of Dr. Richard Newell, his original identity, he abducted a brilliant young biochemist by the name of Edward Plante. Gunk forced Plante to try to help him find a cure for his condition. The two slaved away for weeks, analyzing samples of Gunk's body and trying to figure out a treatment that would restore his DNA to a human state.

Plante finally developed a serum he believed could revert Newell back to human form. Unfortunately, by that point, Newell's mind was again retreating into the personality of the Gunk. The slime-beast raged when Plante tried to present him with the treatment, destroying the laboratory and bathing Plante in the serum. The doomed researcher managed to escape the lab, only to be struck by lightning.

The next morning the Gunk, now with Newell's identity completely submerged, found Plante lying unconscious outside the complex. The serum, combined with the lightning, had transformed him into another slime-creature like the Gunk.

Gunk felt a kinship to this new, familiar creature and took it under his gooey, dripping wing. The childlike Goop had no recollection of his former life, and was probably better off not knowing what he'd lost.

I turned away from the screen and looked at Ted. "This is total crap," I said.

"Most of the 'official' stories are. Score!" As he shot Animan cursed and pounded the table.

"It doesn't even make sense. If Goop doesn't remember his old life and Gunk doesn't 'officially' have the brains God gave sea algae, how did this story get out at all?"

"That's probably one of the reasons the official story never became that popular," Ted said.

The rest of the document was just a rundown of all the known activity Goop and Gunk had taken part in since his debut. I gave it only a cursory glance before scrolling all the way to the bottom of the document, where there was a link. "Unofficial history," it read. I clicked on it, read every word in the new document and looked over at Ted, who was pissing off Animan at the foosball table.

"Hey, Ted... 'unofficial' histories *are* the real ones, right? I mean, the stuff that actually gave people their powers?"

"Yeah, why?"

"Have you ever read Goop's?"

"No. Why, what does it say?"

I turned back to the screen to make sure I got the wording right.

"He followed the Gunk home one day," I read.

"And then?"

"No 'and then'," I said. "That's all it says."

"Hey, little guy." I jumped nearly a foot into the air when I heard Goop's fluid voice behind me. When I turned to face him, he had his typical, friendly grin plastered across his face.

"Oh. Hey, Goop."

"Good story, huh?" he said. "I like the part where I get hit by lightning. And Morrie says it really happened, too."

I shuddered. For the first time, I started to get the feeling Goop was feeding me a line, whether he intended to or not. "Yeah... I'll bet he does. Goop, does the name 'Edward Plante' mean anything to you?"

He reached up in a motion to scratch his head that resulted in his bony fingers digging into his flesh and scraping his skull. "It sounds right, but... it's like there's something..."

"Wrong?" I offered.

"Missing."

The lights fell suddenly and turned blue and there was an alarm. It fired off three high-pitched, staccato beeps in rapid succession, then repeated. Everyone else in the lounge jumped up, some looking angry, but most dismayed.

"What?" I said. "What's going on? Is it a fire?"

"I wish," Animan said.

Ted kicked the table. "It *can't* be. Not so soon after Photon Man, who'd be that stupid?"

"Ted, what the hell is going on?"

Ted picked up his helmet. "We've got a rabbit, Josh."

"A *what?*"

"Remember what I told you happened to Photon Man? Somebody did... *something*. A crime against a Cape, that's what Morrie calls it."

"So you sound an alarm?"

"No. The alarm means the guilty party, whoever the hell it is, is rabbiting... running away. And that means *we've* got to catch him."

HE'S A COLD-HEARTED SNAKE

As we rushed down the halls to the main auditorium, I kept trying to hustle information out of Ted and Animan. "What do you mean *we've* got to catch him?"

"If one of us goes bad, Josh, who else can take him down? A cop? No, when we have a rabbit, we send out the big guns."

"Isn't this a bit of an overreaction, though? The guy hasn't even been proven guilty yet."

"Think about it, buddy," Animan said. "We have a telepathic arbiter that can clear any innocent man."

We headed into the auditorium and took our seats. Ted fumbled nervously with his helmet. "We still have a hearing and all, you know, after the rabbit is caught--"

"*Usually*," Animan broke in.

"--but anyone who bolts... it's as bad as confessing on tape, Josh. He might as well hang a 'Guilty' sign around his neck and have a seat next to O.J. Simpson."

As the last stragglers filtered in, Morrie took the podium. As usual, Mental Maid flanked him to the left. On the other side, First Light took a place. She had a green band wrapped around her wrist where Tom had grabbed her. Some part of the 'purification' process, I supposed. As everyone yammered, waiting for Morrie to start, I noticed the conversation dominated by a variety of questions that asked the same thing.

"Who is it?"

The room was finally ground to silence when Flambeaux, sitting in the front row, jumped and shouted, "Dammit, Morrie, we're wasting time! He could be *anywhere* by now!"

"Relax, Ben. You know perfectly well he can't leave the city."

"Why can't he leave the city?" I whispered.

"Mental Maid," Ted hissed back. "As soon as the alarm goes off she sends out a subconscious command that keeps us all within the city limits. None of us could leave now if we wanted to."

"Why doesn't she just do that to the guilty party? In fact, why doesn't she just make *him* come to us? Why do we have to scour the city at all?"

"Morrie says her powers aren't that precise. Not from long range."

I frowned and settled back in my chair. At this point I had decided that the preface "Morrie says" could very easily be translated into "This is utter B.S."

Morrie looked out over the crowd and inhaled sharply. "Icebergg is on the lam," he said. There were the requisite gasps of shock and someone even managed an overly-dramatic "It can't be!" I simply sat with my arms folded and scowled.

"Apparently there was some sort of disagreement--"

"It was a *fight*!" Flambeaux spat.

"An *altercation*," Morrie stressed. "Flambeaux was the witness. Um... First Light, if you will?"

First Light raised her unbandaged arm and a hologram of Deep Six and Icebergg appeared in the air. "Mental Maid takes the image from Flambeaux's mind and gives it to First Light," Ted whispered. "We're seeing the whole scene through his eyes."

The hologram shimmered in place and we watched Icebergg and Deep Six, still in full gear, standing in the dorm-level hall and flailing their arms at each other. There was no sound, but it was the sort of encounter even a deaf man couldn't mistake for a friendly exchange. In fact, I couldn't recall Icebergg ever moving so fluidly before.

Deep Six opened his hands and fired a cannon of water at Icebergg, but the frozen Mask trapped the water in midair, turning it into a column of ice. The stream of water continued to freeze, the iced-over portion flowing backwards until it finally captured Deep Six's hands. The ice block then began to grow, spreading across his chest and down his torso.

"Why the hell isn't Flambeaux doing something?" I asked. "Isn't Deep Six his *brother*?"

As if in answer, a burst of flame erupted from the bottom of the hologram -- the "camera," as it were -- and lurched in at Icebergg. The flame met with a wall of ice and its creator pointed his cold, blue finger to meet the fire's point of origin. A block of ice leapt from his hand and the hologram went momentarily black.

"He knocked Flambeaux out?" Animan whispered.

The images flickered back in a few seconds, although to be fair there was no way to tell how long the time-lapse really was. When we could see the combatants again, Icebergg was standing by a Deep Six completely encased in ice, except for his diving-helmeted head. He grinned a blood-chilling smile and the ice closed in around the helmet.

"He's got air in there, right?" I asked, getting worried despite myself. "He can still breathe in that helmet?"

As it turns out, it didn't matter.

We watched as the ice began to contract around the helmet. Even *I* was feeling sick at this point. The helmet, inside the ice, began to shrink, and then dent, and then crack.

Then there was a red stain against the ice and the hologram ended.

"He rabbitted," Morrie said. "He was last seen heading towards the vicinity of Lee Park. I want everyone in a Cape after him. Animan, Hotshot, Corwood, don't go anywhere yet. Everyone else, do what you gotta do."

I glanced over at Animan while the rest of the Capes and Masks began filtering out of the auditorium, most visibly distressed. "What do you think he wants?" I asked.

"Me, he probably wants to tell which identity to use. You? Hell if I know."

As the two of us and Hotshot approached our boss I noticed that First Light wasn't going out either. The rest of the Six -- DoubleGum Man, Fourtifier, Five-

Share... even the robotic V3OL -- were all fuming, enraged and ready to grind Icebergg into a daiquiri. First Light headed off quietly in the direction of the dorms.

"Animan, you're gonna be using that polar bear totem of yours today," Morrie said.

Animan grumbled. "Man, I *hate* Great White..."

"Corwood, you're gonna tag along with Hotshot."

"But--"

"Shut up. Head to the locker room, we're gonna suit you up as Stinger -- Animan's wasp-character. You're gonna partner with Hotshot and use his flight and ion-blasts to simulate Stinger's powers."

"How about I just use the wasp-totem and hang around with Animan?"

"Hey brother, just because you *can* don't mean you *do*," Animan said. "Those totems are my babies, I don't want 'em getting all scuffed up."

"Go," Morrie said. *"Chase."*

"I'll wait for you here," Hotshot said.

I didn't try to disguise the dirty looks on my face after I stormed away to the locker room.

Once there, I found the Stinger costume waiting for me in the empty room. It consisted of a gray bodysuit (which I was finding myself less and less embarrassed to get into as my weight continued to fall) and several pieces of red armor -- boots, a codpiece, a chestplate with slits down the back, gauntlets and a helmet I *knew* was going to be hot as hell. Rather than metal, though, the armor was made of hard, lightweight plastic and the bodysuit was a flexible ceramic mesh. The gauntlets extended into points -- "stingers," I suppose -- with ports for the bioelectric sting he fired. I, on the other hand, would have to fudge the points of origin for my blasts.

As I snapped the chestpiece into place I realized that, even though it was a trifle loose on me, it was still obviously not intended for Animan, who now that I thought about it wouldn't have needed the armor anyway, his totem would create it. That meant that Morrie had the armor made already, intending this little Hotshot expedition to be my next fight all along. Jackass.

Well... at least I was a Cape this time.

I was dressed, tucking the helmet under my arm, when I turned to leave --

And damn near ran smack-dab into Mental Maid, just standing there, eyes dim and expressionless.

"Christ! You scared the crap out of me."

And she just stood there...

"What do you want, anyway?"

... cold, unemotional...

"Why do you keep *staring* at me? What do you know?"

... completely without a soul...

"Dammit! Will you for *once* in your life *say* something?"

... until she opened her mouth.

"Watch," she hissed. "Learn. Help."

I was too surprised to do anything but stare as she closed her mouth again, gathered her robes and left. I popped the helmet on and followed.

ISSUE EIGHT

WHAT HAPPENED TO LIONHEART?

I met Hotshot and we took the express elevator to the roof of Simon Tower. It was dusk and the sky stretched out in front of us, a field of orange and pink and red that was slowly receding into purple.

"Okay," said Hotshot, "if we were a six-foot tall ice sculpture, where would we hide?"

"Wedding receptions."

"Oh, before I forget..." he tossed me a utility belt identical to his own; red with black pouches.

"What's this for?"

"Your 'stings.' There's stuff in those pouches you can convert to blasts-- plastic shafts, mostly. Golf balls, too, but you should probably steer clear of those. The energy grenades don't quite mesh with Stinger's powers."

"Lovely." I clipped the belt on. "All right, Hotshot, I guess you're the boss here. Where are we going?"

"Let's start at the park."

I flicked a switch on my chestplate and a pair of fake wings snapped out of the slits in the back of the red plastic. They swiveled into place and began humming. "*These* things are supposed to pass for flight powers?" I asked.

"They work for the *real* Stinger," Hotshot said. "Come on."

I wasn't exactly pleased to be with Hotshot but I had to admit, flying was an experience well worth the poor company. I'd done a little of it in the gym, working with various powers, but *nothing* compared to hitting the skies over Siegel City, the buildings stretched out below me, the sky stretched out above. From this vantage point I could see a lot of the other Capes scouring the city. LifeSpeed was racing around in concentric circles, trying to smoke Icebergg out. The Gunk and Goop were bounding around as usual and, in stark silhouette against the falling sun, I saw the Spectacle Sled bearing its four passengers. (Most of Five-Share, obviously, had stayed behind and would teleport in if the situation demanded it.)

"Hey, I said, "Is it just me or is Doctor Noble conspicuously absent from this little fox hunt?"

"You don't care for Noble much, do you?"

"Nope," I said, "but I don't think I'm exactly in the minority there."

Hotshot actually chuckled. "No, I suppose not."

"Of course, *he's* just a jackass. He, at least, didn't betray everything he should have held sacred."

We flew silent for a moment.

"Land," Hotshot said.

"What?"

"Land. *Now,* Junior, or I take off and you can try to ape powers off a nearby pigeon."

I reluctantly swept down to the empty roof of Barks Plaza, Hotshot right behind me. He yanked his mask off and growled, "The helmet."

"What?"

"You say that a lot, kid. The helmet, take it off. We're gonna do this face-to-face."

165

I popped the helmet off and dropped it to the ground. "Go ahead," I said.

"No, *you* go ahead."

"Wh--"

"I swear to *God,* if you say 'what' one more time I'm gonna feed you to the Gunk. This is your chance. Whatever it is that's eating you, whatever it is you have against me, you get it off your chest *right now.*"

I was momentarily stunned. Momentarily. "You want to know what my problem with you is?"

"I'd *love* to."

"You were *there!*" I shouted. "You were *one* of the LightCorps. You *knew* Lionheart, you fought with him, and now... now..."

"What, you're *jealous,* is that it? That I stuck it out with him and you never had the chance?"

"No. I'm not jealous. I'm *mad!* How *could* you? After *knowing* him, *fighting* with him, *learning* from him, how could you buy into Morrie's scam? How could you disgrace his memory like that? No, this is beyond disgrace, this... this is *blasphemy.*"

His eyes grew wide and his jaw fell. "Oh my God," he said. "Of course. You're one of the children, aren't you?"

"One of who?"

"Lionheart saved you once, didn't he?"

"How did you know that?"

"It was the nature of his powers, Josh. Lionheart never forgot *anyone* he rescued, but every so often he'd come across someone special, someone... like him. Do you know where he got his powers?"

"No."

"He was chosen. By who, I don't know, he never really elaborated, but once in a generation, a champion is chosen, someone who possessed what he called, 'The Heart of the Lion.' Someone brave, and honest, and incapable of a malevolent action."

"Yeah, well... that *sounds* like Lionheart, at least."

"Along with his position came his power and he became a protector. That was a different procedure -- powers don't *always* accompany the Heart of the Lion, but it doesn't hurt."

"You *are* aware of how ridiculous this sounds, aren't you?" I asked.

"No more ridiculous, I think, than a man who copies someone else's power by walking in the room.

"I stand chastised. Go ahead."

"Every so often, while Lionheart was out stopping cosmic menaces or getting cats out of trees or whatever, he'd encounter someone else who could just as easily have been chosen, someone else with the Heart of the Lion. And what's more, when one Child of the Lion saves the life of another, they become bonded somehow -- blindly loyal and faithful and willing to do *anything* to protect each other. Or their legacies. God, Josh, *that's* why you hated me so much? You thought I was disgracing what Lionheart built?"

I felt myself choke. "Well... well *aren't* you?"

He sat down, back to the railing along the roof, and buried his face in his hands. "You can't know what it was like out there, when we lost him."

"Then *make* me understand. What happened? *What happened to Lionheart?*"

"The same thing that happens to every *real* hero, sooner or later," Hotshot said. "He died.

"We were fighting a Mask who called himself Carnival -- some heavily-armored lunatic we'd never seen before and haven't seen since. The entire LightCorps was there -- Lionheart, Lightning, Tin Man, the Defender, Condor and Oriole... and me. I was still the rookie then; I'd only been a Cape for maybe a year and I guess I didn't really believe anything could hurt one of us.

"I still don't know how it happened, but Carnival took over our minds... made us do things... the Defender, the kindest man I ever met, nearly beat a *child* to death. Tin Man blew up factories and army bases. Condor nearly murdered Oriole, his own *wife*. And I..."

Hotshot began to stammer and tremble. I choked as the memory of his own actions welled up inside of him.

"Lionheart was the one who broke Carnival's grip. He had to fight his way through the rest of us, but he finally took on that psychopath. There was this incredible burst -- people all over the city were blinded for days. Once it cleared, Carnival was gone. All we found of Lionheart was... was his..." He bit down on his lip so hard he nearly drew blood and pressed a tight fist to his forehead.

"You don't have to--" I tried to say.

"His *skeleton*," he hissed out. His wet cheeks were very red now, and his voice escaped only in brief intervals.

"We didn't want to tell people he was gone. Every crook and scumbag we'd ever put away would have come crawling out of the woodwork. The crime wave that would have resulted -- we didn't even want to *think* about it. But soon enough people realized he was missing. I even tried wearing the suit a few times to throw people off, but I was no good at the charade. Heh... ironic, huh?"

"No. Not really."

"The rest of the team... they decided they couldn't do it anymore. They went into retirement and I was all alone. And then..."

"And then Morrie came to you."

"Yeah. I didn't like his plan, I didn't want to go along with it, but the city was falling apart. Violent crime was the highest in the country. Burglaries were peaking... people were starting to get scared to go outside in the *day*time."

"So how did turning all the Capes into pro wrestlers *fix* things?"

"You're looking at it from the wrong end, Josh. We didn't do this because of the *Capes*. At least, *I* didn't. I did it for the Masks. We put all of the real threats behind bars for *good*. As for the minor crooks, the ones that were only in it for a quick buck... well, they got what they wanted. Good money, relatively *honest* money, and nobody had to go to jail. Even those who just wanted the rush of adventure got a fix out of

Morrie's plan. And you know what? Most of them aren't half-bad guys when you get to know them. When you're not trying to kill each other. Sure, they aren't all rushing out to pull kids from burning buildings or anything, but neither are the *Capes* -- except for the pure, tried-and-trues that would have gone that route anyway. Folks like you."

I felt my legs give way beneath me and I slid to the roof, sitting next to him. "I never realized--"

"How could you? But *think*, Josh. This city is no paradise, but it's not bad, either. Almost zero *real* crime. A ready brigade of heroes to fight off any *natural* disaster or calamity that should hit. And if the price for that is that we've got to put on a show for the sake of Joe and Jane Average? That's not such a bad trade-off."

There was a cry and a streak of light blue in the now-darkened sky. We looked up to see what, at a glance, was an azure comet. But in the head...

"Noble," muttered Hotshot. "Come on. After what happened with Photon Man I'll be damned if I let *him* get to Icebergg first." He pulled his mask back into place and scrambled to his feet.

As I stood, brushing the dust from my helmet, I asked, "Hotshot... did Lionheart ever save... besides me, I mean... did he save any other Capes with this Heart of the Lion?"

"Only one that I know of," he said.

"Who?"

"Me."

We escalated into the night to resume the search. One man had died today. One was enough.

CONFLAGRATION

By now the red-purple sky had given way to darkness and stars were beginning to glitter. The efforts of various environmentally-conscious Capes over the years had eliminated much of Siegel City's pollution concerns, and once you got above the city lights you could see practically to the ends of the universe.

We weren't using our eyes to look up at the stars, however. Instead our gaze danced the streets looking for a sign -- a lump of ice, a frost-covered streetlight -- *anything* that would indicate Icebergg's passing. But flying was still totally new to me, so I think I can be forgiven if my stare occasionally craned up to the sky.

We flew, buzzing the towers and swooping into the alleys, almost totally silent, for about a half an hour until one of those moments when I ogled the sky and I saw a patch of orange on the horizon, eradicating the stars above and illuminating the ground more than any electric light could. "Hotshot," I said, "is that what I think it is?"

He followed my gaze to the point in the distance where orange light touched the sky. "Dammit," he said in the affirmative.

"What do we do?"

"See if there's anything we *can* do. Hope they don't need us. Then, most likely, we help anyway. Welcome to the Cape-club, pal."

We turned in the direction of the lights and poured on the speed. In a few seconds we'd covered several blocks worth of sky, crested the buildings and saw tongues of flame trying to lick the stars. The burning structure was an apartment complex, a three-story walk-up, and for the briefest of instants I had a vision of Tom, clothes aflame, hurling himself off the balcony and screaming like the Goop during Final Jeopardy. I had to clear my head. We were nowhere near Annie's house. Tom was safe. But there were almost certainly others in that building that *weren't*.

Hotshot and I landed by the fire chief, a mahogany-skinned man of about my mother's age, whose look of relief was almost immediate. "Thank God," he said. "We were getting worried for a minute, Hotshot."

"Can your men handle this?"

"My men are the best, but I always breathe a little easier when there's a couple of you guys on the job. Who's your partner?"

"Stinger," I said, extending my hand. He took it.

"Oh yeah, the wasp-guy. Hey, you're experienced with this sort of thing too, aren't you? A buddy of mine uptown tells me you pitched in at that warehouse fire a couple of months ago."

"Um..." I said. "Yes. That was a hot one."

"What's the problem?" Hotshot asked.

"Oh, you know how these stupid buildings are put together. No windows in the back rooms, and of *course* that's where the children sleep. I've got my boys trying to make sure there's no one left in there, but--"

"It'll go faster with the two of *us*, right?" Hotshot frowned, but nodded. "Let's go, Stinger."

As we rose into the air, he asked me, "Do you know how far you can be from me and keep the powers?"

"I've been working on controlling my range. I should be cool as long as you don't leave the block."

There was a nasty backdraft and a ball of flame erupted from one of the apartments.

"Cool, of course, is a relative term..."

Some kids probably would have had a lifelong fear of fire instilled in them if they'd gone through what I had. I guess Lionheart's timely appearance had saved me from that phobia, because I dove straight into the conflagration without so much as the bat of an eye. The first two units I searched were empty. In the third I came across two howling yorkies that got fur twisted in my gauntlets as I flew them to safety. As I launched back into the building to check room number four, I caught Hotshot's eye. The veteran Cape was carrying a basket full of kittens and sneezing uncontrollably.

"Don't these people take their pets *with* them when their houses catch on fire, dammit?" I shouted. Under any other circumstances I would have been ecstatic to be involved in a real, honest-to-God rescue. As things stood, though, I just wanted to get this over with so we could get back to looking for Icebergg.

Apartments four and five were clean, too. When I kicked my way into six, though, I could hear shrieking coming from -- of course -- the back.

My "wings" turned out to be good for something after all. They beat away the smoke and cleared my vision enough to follow the sound of a voice shouting, "It's okay, Joanie! We're gonna be okay!"

The voices were coming from the other side of a door with a towel stuffed under the crack. My gloves were insulated, so I didn't feel the heat as much, but the doorknob must have been red-hot. I yanked the door open and crashed in to find a small bathroom, water all over the floor. There were two girls in the tub, clad in soaked pajamas that clung to their bodies as they flailed about. The older one was trying to calm the younger down and they were splashing everywhere.

"*Deja-freakin'-vu*," I said.

The smaller girl screamed as soon as my wings shoved away enough smoke for her to see my wasp-armor. I hadn't considered what a frightening visage I'd be to small children. The older one, God bless her, was keeping her head about her much better.

"No, Joanie! I saw him on the news! He's a friend!"

"That's right, I'm a friend, Joanie." The girl kept screaming, though. I took a quick glance down the hall to make sure no one was looking, then I fell to one knee by the tub.

"It's my face, isn't it?" I said. "Sweetie, I know it's scary, but *look*." I popped the helmet off and set it down. "It's not real, see? It's just a mask. Like for Halloween."

"See, Joanie? He's not a monster."

Joanie's howls regressed when she saw my bare face. She couldn't have been older than three years old, her sister no more than eight. Why the hell were they *alone?*

"What's your name, sweetie?" I asked the older girl.

"Katie."

"Katie, where's your mom?"

"She went to see Miss Elsie -- she lives downstairs -- and she said she was only gonna be gone a minute, but then there was all this smoke, and--"

"I know, I know. You did the right thing, honey. But don't worry, I'm going to--"

There was a scream of bending metal and the howl of burning wood falling collapsing on itself. I looked back at a blocked hall and said a word that consisted of precisely four letters.

"Mommy doesn't like that word," Katie said.

"Sorry, your mom's right. Come on." I lifted the girls out of the tub, closed the door to the blazing hallway and put them behind me. "Hold tight."

I pulled a handful of plastic shafts from my utility belt, tucked them into my gauntlets and charged them up. An ion stream erupted from my hands and I blasted the wall behind the bathtub. The wall was scorched and a small indentation appeared, but nothing more.

I brushed the dust that remained from the plastic off my gloves and managed to refrain from swearing again. Those things were meant to be stunners, they just didn't have enough mass to do any serious damage. I could probably charge up the whole wall, but the explosion would kill me *and* the girls. I patted myself down, looking for something, and felt a bulge in one of my belt-pouches.

"Girls," I said, "you promise not to tell anyone what I'm about to do?"

Katie nodded, but Joanie just quivered. I took that as a "yes" and pulled one of the golf balls from my belt. I charged it up, tucked it into the hole I'd created and put my own body between it and the girls.

"Keep your faces covered!" I shouted just before the golf ball exploded. My back was showered with dust and small chunks of debris. When I turned around, though, there was a small hole, not nearly big enough for even Joanie to wiggle through.

I sputtered out two false starts before my diction settled on "Crap! I need something bigger."

My eyes danced around the room, looking for something I could jam into the wall that was big enough to blow us free. No hair dryer, no curling iron -- this was a kid's bathroom. I could only find one thing with real mass.

"Ah, geez, Morrie's gonna *kill* me." I snatched my helmet up, charged it, and jammed an antenna into the hole. I spun around and blocked the girls just before it exploded.

The side of the tub was blown off and water rushed out, hitting my feet in tiny waves. Chunks of plaster fell into the puddles and wiring sparkled, then died. Through a hole quite large enough for the three of us I saw the bathroom of another apartment -- one that wasn't quite an inferno yet.

I snatched a blue gel beauty mask from the sink in the next room and slid it over my face. "Katie, sweetheart, can you get on my back?"

"You've got *wings*!"

"Aw...." my brain searched for a non-swearing swear word, finally settling on "*pumpernickel*!" I reached back and snapped the wings off, tossing them aside. "Climb on."

With Katie on my back, Joanie in my arms and their neighbor's beauty mask on my face, I darted through the apartment and kicked the door open, getting a quick running start before I flew away from the building. A few seconds later I handed them off to their hysterical mother, who looked like she had been crying for years and didn't stop when her girls fell into their arms.

"We're okay, Mommy," Katie said. "The wasp-man saved us."

A few seconds after *that,* Hotshot landed next to me. After a long moment of trying not to laugh at me, he sputtered out, "That's a good look for you."

"Oh shut up. Is the building clear?"

"Yeah, it's clear. Come on, lets--"

"Hotshot! Stinger!"

We looked to the air and saw Spectrum flying overhead. He pointed hard in the direction of Kirby Square and made a desperate "N"-shape with a thumb and two index fingers. Seeing this, Hotshot said a word which, while not as severe as the one I'd said, Katie's mom would almost certainly have disapproved of.

"What's wrong?" I asked.

"They found him" Hotshot said. "And Noble got there first."

THE BATTLE OF KIRBY SQUARE

Kirby Square, along with the observation deck at the top of Simon Tower, was one of the major tourist attractions in Siegel City. Lined on all four sides by what the brochures called "quaint shops and outdoor cafés," the Square itself was about an acre and a half of open spaces frequented by street performers, vendors, young lovers on romantic moonlight walks and anybody looking for an open bar.

In short, it was the most dangerous place in the city to hold a superhero rumble.

The fight had already begun when Hotshot and I arrived. One of us -- probably me -- groaned an "Oh *crap*" when we swept down into the Square to see Icebergg standing atop a three-story mound of snow and frost. He was dueling Spectrum, but the Gunk and Goop were also there, trying to scale the mound and sliding down off the ice. The Conductor must have been nearby too, because as I approached I heard the low rumble of kettledrums and a French horn fanfare that reached a miniature climax each time one of the combatants fired at each other. Spectrum's lasers were evaporating chunks of the mound, but Icebergg's frozen darts were merely passing through Spectrum's light-form and shattering to the street below.

As I got in range I began to feel rushes from each of the fighters, particularly the Gunk. My limbs turned to mush and I felt my body begin to seep through the ceramic mesh of the Stinger armor. The stupid elastic on the beauty mask I was wearing contracted violently and the gel-pack was sucked into my slimy head, tight against my skull.

Cursing, I landed on the roof of a flower shop as Hotshot jumped into the battle. This was getting ridiculous -- I'd always felt Gunk's powers, from the first time I'd met him outside of Simon Tower, but every time they washed over me they got a little harder to assimilate and I began to feel my mind slipping away. Even with the greater degree of control I was getting over my own powers, with my brain scrambled I couldn't seem to get away.

I drove my gooey fist into my own head, wrapped my fingers around the mask and pulled it out. I managed to extract my own body mass from the thing and tossed it aside. Then, drawing on one of the other Rushes I was getting -- Icebergg's, to be specific -- I shoved most of the heat-energy out of my body. I wasn't thinking straight, all I knew was that I wanted to be *solid* again.

Somehow, it worked. With the heat expelled I not only felt my flesh crystallize, but my head started to clear again. I removed one of the gauntlets to look at my own, frozen hands. The orange slime-flesh froze a deep red, almost matching my armor. Losing the helmet wasn't such a big deal after all -- my face probably looked monstrous enough by now. The cold, crystalline sensation I felt was unusual, to be certain, but it was a hell of a lot better than being made of slime.

My perceptions back together, I turned my attention to the battle. Hotshot and Spectrum were using their powers in concert to try and melt a trap into Icebergg's mound (Spectrum with a steady laser-burst, Hotshot having to constantly refill his blasts and mostly laying down cover fire.)

179

I leapt from the roof, my joints cracking with each motion, and flew at the mound, pulling shafts from my utility belt as I went. "Can you guys use a hand?" I asked. At least, that's what I *tried* to ask. My frozen vocal cords didn't exactly vibrate, though, they just kind of chattered together and the resulting sound came across like a Zamboni attempting to belch in coherent sentences.

"What?" Hotshot shouted. Then, seeing the plastic in my hands, nodded. "Oh. Yeah."

As I charged up the shafts and fired I realized I was having the same disadvantage with the mound of ice as I did with the burning building -- these shafts simply didn't have enough mass to do much damage. All Hotshot and I were really doing was herding Icebergg towards Spectrum's trap, and I wondered offhandedly how Hotshot used these things in combat. Then I figured it probably didn't matter how strong the blasts were, his opponents could doubtlessly fake a much stronger result.

The Gunk, meanwhile, was still slipping and sliding up and down the mound. Goop, on the other hand, was making some headway towards the battle.

As Icebergg fell backwards into Spectrum's pool, I found myself counting the combatants. Gunk, Goop, Spectrum, Hotshot, the Conductor... who was I missing?

"Spectrum!" I shouted, but it came out, "Shhhrreeecccctttttrruuuuuukk!"

"What is it, Stinger?"

"Whhhheeerrreee'ssshhhhNnnruuubbbulllh?"

"What?"

"Drrrraaaaakkkttttrrrrr Nnnruuubbulllh!"

"I can't understand you!"

"NNNRUUUBBULLLH!"

"Hey," Hotshot yelled, "where's Doctor Noble?"

And, according to the rules of dramatic effect, that is the precise moment the ice mound began to crack.

"Stinger!" Hotshot shouted, "the civilians--"

"Aaaahnneeett!" I growled. *On it!* The two of us pulled away from the man-made glacier and began snatching bystanders from the Square, getting them to shelter. I grabbed a couple walking from the cathedral, a pretzel vendor, a caricature artist -- I didn't even regret saving the mime before the mound exploded like a hail-bomb. The ominous violin music in my head stopped when the Conductor got nailed by a chunk of ice the size of a baseball. Doctor Noble, at the epicenter of the blast, brushed some ice chips from his hair and grumbled, "At least that stupid music stopped."

"Dillweed," Icebergg muttered.

"I'll kill you, you overgrown Popsicle!" Noble snarled. "I'll grind you into a snowcone!" He was oblivious to everything but Icebergg now -- I wasn't really to his left, the Goop wasn't almost directly behind him, Spectrum and Hotshot weren't really in the night sky.

The lamp posts in the Square -- those that hadn't broken when the ice mound detonated -- each cracked and popped and electricity arched in towards Noble. He thrust his hands out and shoved at Icebergg with a teke-blast that hit the Mask in the gut. There was a terrible cracking sound and, for the first time, I saw there was actual, pale flesh beneath his sheathe of ice.

"You know what, Noble?" he said, spitting out a couple of ice cubes. "I always *did* hate you."

He fired off a blue bolt of energy at Noble that I knew would freeze whatever it hit. Noble probably knew it too, as he telekinetically lifted himself into the air, leaving a new target in his wake.

Goop, get down! I tried to shout, but the clattering, grinding syllables sounded like I'd just dumped an ice sculpture down the garbage disposal. I lunged at the addle-brained sidekick, hoping to get him down before the bolt struck, but when I slammed into his cold, hardened body, I knew I was too late.

"Whhhaaattt'ssshhaappinnneeeenngg?" Goop's body twisted and crackled like red ice in stop-motion animation. He reached a creaking arm in my direction. "Iiiisssthaaaatttchhooooleettoolllghhiii?"

"Shhpeeehktrruuummm!" I yelled. Somehow the message got across. As Noble and Hotshot engaged Icebergg, Spectrum turned towards us, cutting off his laser and instead firing high-intensity sunlight. The beam melted our bodies back into slime.

"Hey, not *me*--" I started to protest, but as my muscles thawed out and returned to their normal temperature, I realized I had become flesh again. The Gunk was gone.

"Hey, where's your boss?" I asked Goop. Instead of answering, though, he clasped me in a mushy hug.

"Thanks for trying to help me, little guy," he said. "I heard ya try to warn me!" I nodded and slid from his far-too-receptive grasp.

Hotshot, meanwhile, had managed to get Icebergg into a full nelson. "Calm down, Frosty," he was saying, "or I'll charge up that charming little snowcap you wear on your face."

"You idiot," Icebergg growled, "do you really think you can *bluff* me? You were one of Lionheart's original peons. You won't kill me."

I was about to rail against him in defense of Lionheart, but Noble broke in, growling, "Nah, but *I* might." He grasped Icebergg's head between two powerful hands and started to compress them. The ice cracked rather quickly.

"Noble, let him go!" I shouted.

"Buzz off, wasp-boy," he said.

"Noble!" Hotshot released Icebergg and grabbed Noble's hands, prying them off. Icebergg dropped to the ground between them and rolled away.

"Crazy son of a bitch," he hissed.

Noble pulled out of his tangle with Hotshot and dove at Icebergg, who responded by blasting at Noble with razor-sharp spike.

Noble threw up a rampart of telekinetic force and the spike bounced away, flying through the air and going straight for Hotshot's face.

"Hotshot! Look out!" I bellowed.

It's amazing how natural this stuff was coming to me at this point. I reached out with Noble's own teke field and caught the spike inches from Hotshot's eyeball. I let it hang there for a second, then looked a Noble with a glare of pure fire. With a twist of my arm, I used the teke field to grind the spike into slush and then let it fall to the ground.

"Nice save," Hotshot gasped.

"Thanks," I said, failing to add, "and I'd do it again." I never apologized to him for being such an ass earlier, either. I never *needed* to after that. He knew I was sorry, and I knew he forgave me.

He was right. When one person with the Heart of a Lion saves another, the two become bonded. Loyal and devoted to one another. For life.

"You want to finish this?" I asked him.

"Let's shall," he said. We both pivoted at the same time, pulling darts from our utility belts and charging them up. The ion streams surged forward, striking Icebergg in the face and melting holes in his frost helmet. He slumped to his knees and then rolled over, unconscious. He was stunned, but not seriously hurt. We'd focused our blasts just right.

There was a trumpet fanfare and a still woozy Conductor approached us, clapping. "Heil the conquering heroes!" he called.

"Heil my ass," Noble said.

"Not even if you got a crucifix tattooed on it," I returned.

"You *maggot.* Never, *never* copy my powers again, do you understand?"

"If you knew how to use your powers properly in the first place, there wouldn't have been a *need* to copy them you pompous--"

"Gentlemen!" Spectrum said, stepping between us. "Perhaps we can settle this later? The rubberneckers are gonna be back any minute now."

"Yeah," Noble spat, slinging Icebergg over his shoulder. "We'll finish this later. We are *so* gonna finish this later." He took off, the others close behind, but Hotshot clapped my shoulder before I could take to the air.

"Jason," he said.

"What?"

"My name. It's Jason Lear. My friends call me Jay."

I smiled, but I don't think I've ever called him that except if we were in civilian gear in public. He's always been Hotshot, where I was concerned.

ISSUE NINE

THE SOUL RAY

Unlike many residents of Simon Tower, Morrie Abadie's skin tone was perfectly normal. Not green, not orange, not blue, but a simple, healthy fleshtone. So I was fairly impressed at the way he turned six shades of purple when I told him what happened during the hunt for Icebergg.

"You used Noble's powers?" he shrieked.

"Hotshot could have *died*!"

"When are you gonna get it through your skull? These guys are *pros*. Somebody else woulda stopped that ice. Noble *hisself* might have done it."

Not damn likely, I thought, but I managed to hold my tongue. As Morrie sat down behind his desk, his cheeks returned to a more healthy tone. Mental Maid, on the other hand, just stood there looking as alien as ever.

"This is even worse than *last* time. At least *then* you were using the right powers. Are you *trying* to blow the lid off this whole operation or something?"

I just gulped at that and dared a glance over at Mental Maid, who was still displaying all the emotional range of a mannequin on Ritalin.

"And you *lost your helmet*!" Morrie continued, still sputtering. "Do you know how many people may have seen your face, kid?"

"Oh come on, how many of them going to recognize dumpy old Josh Corwood?"

"All it takes is *one*," he said. "Or even worse, what if one of those rubes had a *camera*? Or a camera phone? People get their picture taken pickin' their nose at every stoplight these days! Did you ever think of *that*?"

I hadn't. In this confrontation with Morrie I was feeling less like James Dean and more like Wally and the Beav getting chewed out by Ward.

"I still think I did the best thing I *could*," I grumbled, looking at my feet.

"You're thinking *too much*, kid," Morrie said. "That's yer problem." He sighed and rubbed his eyes. "All right, get outta here. We got Icebergg's hearing to deal with now, I'll decide what to do about you after that."

"What, right *now*?" I said. "We only brought him in a half hour ago."

"Whaddaya think this is, the Federal Court system? Nah, when we got a crime against a Cape we hold the hearing immediately, none of that screwin' around."

When I left Morrie's office I found the Conductor and Miss Sinistah waiting for me, both with sullen looks on their faces.

"How'd it go?" Ted asked.

"Could have been worse. He could have had Mental Maid wipe my brain right there."

"You don't think he'd really kick you out?" Annie said.

"That's got to be at *least* three strikes at this point," I said. I told them what Morrie had said about "deciding what to do with me." Ted's face lit up at this.

"You see? He didn't say he was kicking you out!"

"He may as well have."

"You've got to be more positive, Josh," Annie said, taking my arm (which did far more for my demeanor than Ted's pep-talk could.) "A lot of people have messed up a lot worse than *you* have and Morrie's kept them around. Just look at the Photon Man fiasco."

"Annie!"

Our heads all spun around at once. "Oh great," Ted moaned, "the moron patrol is here."

Dr. Noble came up to us and thrust his own face in Ted's. "What did you say, Ossian?"

"I said, 'Look, here comes Todd," Ted replied, his voice somewhere between angry and quivering.

"You better. And *you*," he said to Annie, his blazing voice resonating through a barrel-chest, "I don't want to see you hanging around with these two wanna-be Capes anymore. I'm sick of 'em shoving ideas into your head."

"Oh yeah," I hissed, "God forbid she have any ideas *you* didn't put there, right?"

"Back off, little man."

"The hell I will! Annie, are you actually gonna let this stupid prick tell you who your *friends* can be?"

"You think *you* can take me, worm?"

"You're forgetting," I said, "you aren't dealing with an inferior here. You're not dealing with a normal human and you're not dealing with someone who's scared of you. For *once* you're dealing with someone who can give you *exactly* as good as he can get."

We stared at each other down for a long moment and I briefly worried he would take me up on my challenge, but he finally turned on his heel and stormed away. "Come on, Annie!" he shouted over his shoulder.

"I'm sorry, guys, I'll talk to him," she said. "He's really not that bad."

"Not that bad?" I asked once they were gone. "What is she waiting for, some accident to scar his face so he can wear sinister-looking armor? Or maybe it'll just make his hair fall out and he'll declare himself my arch-enemy. Christ, he's as bad as they come!"

"You have got *serious* gonads, my friend," Ted said. "I thought you two were going to throw down right here in the hall."

"Yeah, well, you know how it is. My mother always said a bully will stand down if you face them on *your* terms. Thanks for backing me up, by the way."

"Heh. Sorry about that," Ted said. "Come on, the hearing must be half-over by now."

"So fast?" He nodded.

We made our way to the auditorium, where Icebergg was being held by a pair of what looked like handcuffs from the starship *Enterprise*. "Power dampeners," Ted explained as we grabbed a couple of seats in the back. Icebergg was clothed in a robe now, his ice-sheathe having melted away. His skin was very pale and there was no visible hair on his body, not even eyebrows or lashes. His only distinguishing features were his eyes, blue and freezing.

They had already replayed First Light's holographic recreation of Deep Six's... termination. No one was saying a word, but the looks on people's faces spoke volumes. This was a crowd that wanted blood.

Flambeaux got up and testified in a voice cold enough to re-freeze Icebergg, and Doc Noble and Hotshot each made statements about the rumble in Kirby Square. Once everybody who had something to say had done so, Morrie took the podium. "Well, Icebergg? Anything to say in your defense?"

Icebergg grinned. "Yeah. I got something."

"Well? This is your only chance. Spill it."

The grin just got bigger. "You make me wanna vomit."

"Fine. Mental Maid?"

She stepped up to the podium, robes swirling around her, and turned to stare Icebergg straight in the eyes.

"What happens now?" I whispered to Ted.

"Mental Maid holds judgement. If she finds him innocent, he's let free and life goes back to normal. If he's guilty... punishment."

"Has anyone... any *rabbit* ever been found innocent?"

Ted covered his face. "No. I don't want to see this."

"See *what*? Ted, what's the punishment?"

"The Soul Ray."

The Soul Ray, I later learned after already having seen it in action, was Mental Maid's strongest power. The Ray totally obliterated a person's physical form, vaporizing their body and reducing the matter that comprised it to dust.

It then took their emotional essence, what a person really *was* in the bottom of their soul, and gave *that* physicality. Someone who is inherently good will become strong and handsome and a wonder to behold. Someone with an evil heart will become a monster. Once someone hit by a Soul Ray morphed into a giant insect. Another literally became a snake. If the Soul Ray hit you, you became what you always really *were*, effectively making it perfectly safe to judge a book by its cover.

That's what I found out *later.*

What I *saw* was *this*:

Icebergg was taken before Mental Maid. Both stood there without a trace of human feeling.

A beam of the purest white light I'd ever seen poured from Mental Maid's hand, bathing Icebergg.

The light stopped.

Where Icebergg had been was a screaming, agonized, humanoid mass of fire.

"Makes sense," Ted said, finding the nerve to uncover his eyes. "Icebergg was always one of the angriest people I knew."

"What did they *do* to him?" I gulped.

"Reduced him to who he was."

"What happens now?"

"He gets exiled. We've got an arrangement with this space federation, they'll take him to an intergalactic penal colony."

I raised an eyebrow. "Does anyone around here ever listen to himself talk?"

Judgement passed, Particle and Justice Giant escorted the smoldering mess that was once Icebergg from the chamber. The assembly broke apart and went about their business, no doubt trying to forget the whole damned affair had ever happened.

Not that *everyone* could forget... Flambeaux and the Spectacle Six -- or Five, I supposed -- each walked around with looks on their faces that betrayed the deep wound each carried that otherwise would not show.

I took a deep, strengthening breath. "Well, I guess it's time to face the music."

"What do you mean?"

"I've got to see Morrie, Ted."

The Conductor recoiled and I heard a bugle dirge stir within me. "Taps," to be specific.

"Your vote of confidence is staggering," I said.

"That's how *you* feel, buddy."

I moved up through the dispersing throng until I got to the big boss. "Hey, Morrie."

"Oh yeah. Corwood."

"Not to sound pushy or anything, but... have *I* got a verdict yet?"

"Yeah," he said. "Yeah, I suppose I do. Yer trouble, kid. You've only been on two ops and you've given me more headaches than some of these guys have in ten years."

I gulped and nodded, unable to meet his gaze. Behind him, though, I could see Mental Maid's eyes glowing and I began thinking, *This is it, this is when she blows the whistle. It's the Soul Ray and the penal colony for me.*

"But yer also good," Morrie said. "Damn good. And Morrie Abadie ain't the type to cut off his nose to spite his face. Thing is, I can't have an ulcer worryin' about which powers yer gonna use every time you leave the Tower!"

"What are you getting at?"

"Come back Tuesday, like you were gonna do anyway. We'll fit you for a new costume then."

I let out the breath I hadn't realized I'd been holding. "What character this time?"

"I dunno yet. I'll have the boys work something up this weekend."

My eyes lit and my heart jumped into my throat. "You mean--"

"Yeah, yeah. I'm givin' you yer own character. But don't go gettin' a big head about it. Yer still gonna be a Mask -- I don't know if you got the stage presence to be a Cape yet. But I'll see to it you got a character that can ape anybody else's powers. If for no other reason than to cut down my expenses on antacid. Now go. Have a good weekend. And don't let me have to see yer mug again before Tuesday or I might just change my mind."

I left. *Fast.*

INTRUDER

I practically tap-danced all the way home that night -- anybody watching would have presumed Gene Kelly was a Cape and I had found a way to duplicate his powers. *My own character*, I kept thinking, over and over. *Me*. It was like getting three BARs on a slot machine: Jackpot! I was still concerned about Annie -- the way the good Doctor browbeat her bordered on the criminal -- but I also knew that with my own character as an excuse to hang around Simon Tower I'd have

193

plenty of opportunities to talk to her, hang around and, hopefully, break her away from that smarmy piece of filth.

It was a little after eleven o'clock when I got home. As I turned the key I felt the lock click shut. My first thought was, *Darn it, forgot to lock the door again.*

My second thought was, *I* never *forget to lock the door.*

I quickly opened it into an already-lit apartment. In the front room, which consisted of a kitchenette and a living area, I saw David Letterman chattering away on my television and a plate with crumbs and a puddle of ketchup sitting on the counter. I knew I hadn't done it. For one thing, I'd washed all the dishes before I left and, for another thing, I watched Conan.

"Make yourself at home, why don't you?" I asked my unseen visitor. I headed down the short hall to the back. The door to my bedroom was closed, but the bathroom was open and I heard the telltale hiss of a toilet running. I ducked in and jiggled the handle and the gasping noise stopped.

"Damned inconsiderate intruders," I muttered, heading for the bedroom door. In retrospect it was probably a stupid move, barging in like that. A typical burglar wouldn't have had any powers for me to duplicate and he more than likely would have had a gun. I didn't have any special training, I wasn't Nightshadow. I could have been killed. All things considered, I should have been *relieved* when I opened that door without meeting up with some crook. Instead,

I was furious to find Sheila Reynolds, sitting on my bed, flipping through my notebook.

"What the hell is *this*?" she asked, fanning the pages.

"*That*? What the hell is *this*?"

"Is what you've written here true?"

"You broke into my apartment!"

"And why did you draw little curlicues around the name 'Sindy' every time?"

"What the hell are you *doing* here?"

"And why are you misspelling 'Cindy' all of a sudden?"

"Have you *no* regard for anyone else's privacy?"

We both stood there in infuriated silence for a long moment.

"I think you owe me an explanation!" we shouted in concert.

"It's *my* apartment!" I said. "You first!"

She dropped the notebook on the bed. "I came because I've been *worried* about you, Josh. Something just hasn't been right with you lately. Now I think I know what. Is the stuff you wrote in there true? Is the whole Cape scene in this entire city a *front?*"

"Of course not!" I sputtered. "I mean... I've been writing that stuff because I thought it would be *funny*... maybe for an April Fool's edition. I mean, heh, Nightshadow as a disco freak? A female Five-Share? And who's gonna believe Doctor Noble is a jackass?"

"When you interviewed him last month the first thing you told me is that he *was* a jackass."

"I was delusional. I'd been hit by the Gunk."

"You mean the guy who makes Mensa members look like Sesame Street rejects?"

"Now you're making things up."

She picked up the notebook and flipped it open. "'And the Gunk, previously believed to be a practically mindless beast, is actually a scholar who makes Mensa members look like Sesame Street rejects'," she recited.

"I'm awful with a metaphor, you know that."

"Why are you sitting on this, Josh? This could be the biggest story since Watergate! Why haven't you blown the whistle? Unless..."

"Unless? Unless *what*?"

"Unless you've started to buy into the whole thing. That's it, isn't it? You *enjoy* playing dress-up and running around with these headcases."

"It's not like that--"

"And this Sindy chick -- you've got it for her, don't you?"

"She's not at *all* like Miss Sinistah, Sheila, that's just a character."

She gasped and I slapped my own face, realizing I'd said too much. "Sindy is *Miss Sinistah*? You're in love with *MISS SINISTAH*?" She let her slick, curious look slip and replaced it with a wry grin. "Okay, Josh, confess, is *everything* about her super-strong?"

"Now cut that out!" I snatched the notebook from her hand. "Sheila, you can't tell *anyone* about this!"

"And why not?"

"Because it's not what you think. It's not what *I* thought it was, it's... it's something more."

"*Now* who sounds like the after-school special?" She jammed her finger at the notebook. "And what about all the stuff about using the merchandizing to payroll this? How do you think people will feel when they figure out how they've been footing the bill for all this?"

"It's not that big a deal."

"Your notebook has *a picture of Spectrum on the cover*!" She turned and tried to dart around me, towards the door, but I pivoted and kicked the knob with my foot, slamming it shut. I think we were both surprised that I managed to do it.

"You're not leaving until I have your word that you won't spread this around."

"Why should I?"

"Because if you don't I'm gonna... oh God."

"What?"

I felt the blood draining from my head as my anger subsided. I had come dangerously close to pulling a Doctor Noble.

"Please, Sheila," I said. "Sit down. Let me talk to you. Let me explain to you why this has to stay a secret."

She stared at me for a while, without saying anything. "All right," she said, finally. "But *only* because it's *you*, Josh."

"I know, I know, and thank you," I said. So we sat down and we talked for a very long time. I told her everything. I told her about that first night and how I met Sindy. I told her about the Arena and my first adventure as Shift. I told her about Tom and Icebergg and the Soul Ray. And I told her what happened to Lionheart.

But I didn't tell her about the Heart of the Lion. I didn't know why.

When we finally finished talking, it was nearly one o'clock in the morning. My head hurt and I'd run out of coffee, but except for the odd question and her one outburst about me trying to fool the great telepath Mental Maid, Sheila remained annoyingly silent.

"I don't know," she finally said.

"Oh come on, Sheila! That *had* to be enough to convince you!"

"I'm sorry, Josh. I can't make you any promises. I need to think about this." She stood up to leave, but when her hand touched the doorknob, instead of turning it, she looked back at me.

"Josh?"

"Yes?" I said, anxious to say anything that might make a difference.

"You *were* going to use all that, weren't you? I mean... you wouldn't have written it all down otherwise."

"Yeah," I said. "I *was* going to use it. So?"

"When did you decide not to?"

I couldn't help but smile. "Hell I don't know. Part of me decided a long time ago, I think. Another part decided when Hotshot told me what happened to Lionheart. But I didn't *realize* until I came in and saw you holding that damn notebook."

She nodded, tight-lipped, and left. I sat up the rest of the night, eyes fluttering, unable to sleep.

A WALK IN THE PARK

I was still awake the next morning when the telephone rang. I picked up the receiver with a groggy, "Sheila?"

"Who's Sheila?" asked Annie's voice on the other end.

"She's nobody!" I shouted, the exhaustion draining from my head. "I mean... just this woman I work with. I was expecting to hear from her."

"Really?" Annie asked. "Young, voluptuous type?"

"Hairy old bat with a wart on her nose," I lied. "What's up?"

"Well I was wondering, if you're not too busy waiting for a call from *Sheila*--"

"She knows how voice mail works."

"What would you say to a picnic in Lee Park? You know, to celebrate your impending promotion?"

"I would say, 'Hello, picnic in Lee Park. It appears God has finally relented and is allowing me a modicum of happiness'."

She giggled. "That's an awful lot to say to a *picnic*."

"It's a very *literate* picnic. What time?"

"Eleven-thirty, bring some sodas."

"Deal." I then did the following things in the following order: I hung up the phone, choreographed and performed a little happy dance all by myself, showered (while still dancing), shaved (I stopped dancing for that), got dressed, realized my *new* pants were now entirely too big for me, bought newer pants and a six-pack of sodas and finally got to the park.

"Josh!" I turned in the direction of the voice to see Annie, picnic basket and a blanket tucked under her arm, in a pair of cut-off blue jean shorts and a white top that had a very similar effect upon me as copying the Gunk's powers.

My limbs rapidly solidified, however, when I saw the *other* little package she'd brought with her. It was a surprise, to be sure, but at least it was a welcome one.

"Hey, Tom!" I said.

"Josh!" He rushed me from Annie's side, red backpack banging against his side, and darted in for a high-five.

"I couldn't keep him from coming," Annie said, laughing. "He's always asking about you these days -- you and Shift are all he talks about."

"How are you, buddy?" I asked. "Discovered any latent superpowers lately?"

"Not yet," he said, "but I'm working on it." He pulled out a brown portfolio he had in his backpack. "Hey, I brought something to show you."

"Did you know Tom was an artist?" Annie asked. "He's going to be the next George Perrin when he grows up."

"That's *Perez*," Tom said in that tone of voice that 10-year-olds use to indicate that everybody in the world except the person they just corrected already knew that. As Annie unrolled the blanket she brought, Tom opened up his portfolio and started pointing out some of his favorite sketches. He was pretty good, too -- a lot better than *I'd* ever be. There were drawings of the skyline and of Simon Tower. Some sketches of birds and a particularly impressive drawing of a lion he'd done at the zoo.

"I always bring my sketchbook when I'm going outside for a while," he said. "You never know what you're going to see."

"I'll bet."

Then, of course, came the super-heroes. Lots of them. Drawings of Hotshot and the Spectacle Six and an airborne Aquila, backlit by the sun. I smiled at a drawing of Justice Giant capturing Solemna, and I felt a knot at a sketch of Lionheart fighting back-to-back with the Gunk.

The most recent sketch ground me to a halt. It was Shift, in midair, racing alongside a speeding truck with a small boy in front of it.

"You like that one?" Tom asked. "I wish I knew how to get in touch with Shift, I'd like him to sign *this,* too."

"What are you looking at there, boys?" Annie asked. I looked up from the sketchbook and, despite the size of the lump in my throat, managed to explain to her the concept of "Ghangaghangahgangahgang."

"What?" said Tom.

"Nothing. It's just... it's really good, man."

I never learned who wore the Shift costume before me, but I can promise no one ever drew a picture of *him* like this. Tom's rendition of Shift was strong, proud and majestic and, even though the costume still had the menacing presence it intended to convey, someone who didn't know better would have sworn it was a picture of a Cape rather than a Mask.

"Wow... Tom, that's great," Annie said.

"Thanks. So what do we have to eat?"

Annie broke out the basket of cold chicken, potato salad and cole slaw, and Tom had triple helpings of everything before spying a bluebird in a tree and darting off to sketch it. Annie and I stayed back, finally able to talk. Tom was a great kid, don't get me wrong, but he had a tendency to stifle the conversation.

"Did you *see* that drawing of Shift?" I asked her, still flabbergasted.

"He's a really good artist, isn't he?"

"Well yeah, but... I mean the *way* he drew it. It was like... Whoa, here comes Shift, saving the day!" I thrust my arms in front of me like I was flying and "banked" in the "air" a few times. Annie practically doubled over with her wonderful laughter. Within a few seconds I had joined her and it was a good, long while before either of us was able to catch our breath.

"So..." I finally asked, "How does Todd feel about you having a picnic with this 'lowly maggot'?"

"I don't know," she said. "I didn't tell him. Frankly, I don't care."

"Woo-hoo! Two points for Annie!" She laughed a little at that, but then her face fell. Slowly, and probably with more fear than anything I'd done in my entire life, I placed my hand over hers.

She let out an agonized breath. "It's not like it's *all* bad."

"It's not? Come on then. Give me one reason you stay with him and I'll drop the whole subject."

"Because--"

"And any reason that includes the phrase 'he used to' doesn't count."

She was quiet for an eternity. Finally she said, "I can't. I should be able to, but I can't."

"Can I ask you something?"

"I suppose."

"Why *him*? I mean... what did you see in that guy in the first place?"

"Oh come on, Josh, think about it. I've just been drafted into this world of super-heroes and tights and fame and -- all of a sudden *the* hero, the one everybody in the world looks up to... all of a sudden he's paying attention to *me*."

"Couldn't you tell what kind of guy he was?"

"He wasn't like this then. He didn't start... acting the way he does--"

"Like a jackass, you mean."

"-- until... well... until..."

"Until he knew he had you," I finished. She nodded.

"You're better than him, Annie," I said. "You *deserve* better. I..."

"You what?"

I looked her straight in the eye and felt my voice break. "I..."

"Josh! Annie!" Tom broke in, waving his sketch in the air. "What do you think?"

"It's great, buddy," I said, barely looking at it.

"I saw a turtle by the fountain! I'm going to go draw it."

"Okay, squirt," Annie called back as he jogged away. She smiled at me. "What were you saying?"

"Just that... you amaze me," I finally wheezed out.

"Aw Josh... Thank you." She threw her arms around my neck and gave me a solid kiss on the cheek, and that was the best I'd felt since I saw Sheila sitting on my bed reading my notebook.

When I got home that afternoon I locked the book in a big trunk at the foot of my bed. Although it *was* taken out once more, I never wrote in it again. I spent that night, as the night before, wondering. This time I was wondering what would have happened if I *had* managed to say "I'm falling in love with you" to Annie. I was outraged at Tom for interrupting, and at the same time I was wholly and incredibly relieved that he *did*, because if she'd heard that statement and didn't agree with me, I don't think I would have been able to take it.

ISSUE TEN

COPYCAT

Cats with a mouse being dangled before them. Kids on Christmas morning, waiting for their parents to wake up. Me waiting for my costume. The three most anxious creatures I can imagine. When I made it to Morrie's office that Tuesday, he greeted me with a smokey expression that was half frustration and half amusement. There was a white plastic garment bag hanging from the coat rack with a picture of a black domino mask printed on it. My eyes landed on that bag like it was Annie in a bikini.

"Hey there, Morrie," I said as though I just happened to be passing through his office directly in front of his desk. ""How's it going there, man? Heh?"

"Yer terrible at playin' things aloof, Corwood, you know that?"

"My mother says it's my best quality."

"Must be a killer with the ladies. Come on in. Lemme show ya what we've got."

I closed the door and sat, completely oblivious to Mental Maid for once, and waited as Morrie got the bag and laid it on his desk.

"Yer name," he said, "is Copycat."

"Copycat, sounds great, I love it."

"You're what our boys down in the writer's shop call a revenant."

"A what?"

"A revenant. A ghost that rose from the grave to exact revenge."

"Oooh, spooky. I like it so far."

"Ten years ago, during Lionheart's last battle--"

"Whoa! I'm tied in to *Lionheart*?"

"You want this suit or not?"

"I want! I want!" I raised my arms in surrender. "Go ahead."

"Lionheart's last fight happened in January. In the middle of it, you got thrown through the ice on the pond in Lee Park. You were countin' on Lionheart to save ya, but he never got around to doin' it, what with him vanishin' and all. So ya died."

"Sounds like fun."

"But ya couldn't rest, see, because that Carnival guy, the last one anyone saw Lionheart fightin'? *He's* the one that killed ya, the way *you* figger, y'know, with him knocking ya through the ice and all. So you were brought back from the dead to hunt him down an' kill him, and you don't care who you gotta get past or what you gotta destroy to find that guy. Understood?"

"Yeah, I got it, Morrie, great origin. But why 'Copycat'? And how does the revenant thing explain my duplicating other people's powers?"

"When you was alive, you didn't *have* no powers. Now that yer a ghost, all you can do is *copy* other people's shtick. That's the 'copy' half of yer name. Oh, except that you can turn into smoke."

"Smoke?"

"Yer a ghost, accept it."

"Farfetched," I said, "but I've heard worse."

"As fer the 'cat' half... heh... I think you'll understand when you see yer costume. It's lined with kevlar, standard precaution for folks that aren't invulnerable, and there are compartments in the belt for yer smoke bombs. Go ahead. Try it on. "

I snatched the garment bag from him and raced to the locker rooms fast enough to justify anyone asking me if I was copying LifeSpeed's powers again. When I got there I unzipped the bag and pulled out a mass of black and gray fabric with a pair of black boots at the bottom. I knew immediately where he got the 'cat' from, and I was simultaneously honored and saddened.

It was Lionheart's costume.

Not an exact duplication, of course, the colors were all off. The pants and boots were the same jet black as his, but the brilliant red tunic he always wore, with its crisp, military cut, was the same black as the pants. His sky-blue cape, which buttoned to the tunic with gold buttons and connected to the brilliant Lion's Head emblem on the chest -- was thundercloud grey. The Lion's Head itself, a wonderful yellow on Lionheart's costume, was a deep, blood-red on mine.

I almost couldn't put it on.

But I did.

"Ya look sharp, kid," Morrie said when I returned to his office in full regalia.

"I'm kind of uncomfortable dressing like this," I said.

"What, are you worried about disrespectin' Lionheart? Don't be. Y'see, yer one of those Masks who's got a sense of honor. Oh, you'll steamroller anyone who gets in yer way, but you don't wanna see nobody *else* get hurt if you can help it." He laughed and expelled a cloud of cigar smoke. "I told 'em to add that part. This way if you do somethin' stupid like save a life or somethin', nobody'll think there's anything strange about that."

"Beautiful."

"You go in the Arena tomorrow. Hotshot is gonna be the one to take you in. We figgered it would add.... what did they call it? Pathos! That's it. Y'know, since he knew Lionheart an' all."

I stepped into the lounge and was greeted by a round of applause, led by Hotshot. It was the first time I'd ever noticed how much *his* costume resembled Lionheart's (and, by extension, mine). It was almost a reverse, with red pants. His cape was connected to the front of his black tunic by a patch of color (yellow instead of blue) and the masks were identical -- they covered most of the head, but opened for the eyes, nose and mouth. The tops were open, too, letting the hair breathe free.

"Looking sharp, junior," he said.

"Not so bad yourself, old-timer." We shook hands and clapped each other on the back, then I wandered over to a stunned-looking Animan, Conductor and Miss Sinistah.

"Since when are you and Hotshot so buddy-buddy?" Ted asked. I opened my mouth to answer, but something stopped me. I knew somehow that possessing the Heart of the Lion was the sort of information you kept to yourself, something you only discussed with those who were a part of it. I never talked about it with anyone, and I know that Hotshot never did, either.

"Things change, Ted," I said, simply enough. "People grow up."

The Goop sidled up to me, still completely failing to give me a Rush. Instead of bounding all over me for once, though, he just looked me up and down and gave me a sloppy grin. "Nice threads, little guy," he said, before sliming away. I just shrugged and turned to my friends.

"So how do I look?"

"Sharp," Animan said.

"*I* wouldn't mess with you," Ted added.

"Like a big ol' scary ghost."

"*With* a cape."

They broke into chuckles and Annie scowled at them. "Well, *I* think you're *very* handsome."

"Yeah? Not too much of a bulge around the middle?"

"*Bulge*? Josh, when's the last time you looked at yourself in the mirror?"

"When I put this costume on, why?"

"Okay, when's the last time you really paid *attention* to yourself? Come here."

She pulled me over to the juice bar, which had full-length mirrors along the wall behind it. "*Look* at yourself, Josh. You may not be skinny, but you're certainly not *fat.* Not by any means."

She was right. My sagging gut was gone, my jowls were lean -- even my lovehandles were a thing of a past. When I checked the label in the pants later, I realized they were only a 34-inch waist.

"What the *hell* is this?"

"Metabolism," said Animan, slurping a kiwi juice.

"What?" I said.

"A lot of the folks in here have superefficient metabolisms as part of their powers. I figure God didn't want 'em looking too silly in Spandex. You copy other people's powers. Hanging around here is slimmin' you down, boy!" He patted my no-longer-protruding stomach.

"Of course, not *everyone* has a super-metabolism," said Ted, jamming this thumb towards the door. There was Doctor Noble, pot-belly and all.

"Sinistah!" he shrieked in a voice so high that it bordered on the effeminate. "What the hell do you think you're doing?"

She looked over at me with a frightened glare in her eyes, but I just opened mine wider. *Tell him* exactly *what you're doing.* I thought.

"I'm congratulating my friend," she said.

"I thought I told you not to hang around this twerp anymore."

Don't let him tell you what to do, I pleaded silently.

"You can *not* tell me who my friends are!" she shouted. It was probably the first time in memory that anyone had yelled at Doctor Noble like that -- particularly not in front of everybody in the lounge. We were beginning to draw a crowd.

"Do you know what you're saying, little girl?"

Her eyes blazed. "I know *exactly* what I'm doing." She placed a single index finger on his chest and shoved him out the door. Ted, Animan and I began hurriedly looking at each other, unsure of what to do next.

"She's breaking up with him, dude!" Animan half-whispered.

"Come on, you don't know that."

"What *else* could she be doing out there?" Ted asked.

"*Tons* of things. Apologizing... wimping out..."

"Uh-uh. No. She's finally had it with that walking mound of cow vomit. The three of us are gonna wait right here until she comes back."

So we did. We waited three hours. Ted and Animan repeatedly trounced me at foosball, ping-pong and multiple video games. I could feel the bile in my stomach scouting out a location for the ulcer like prospective homeowners counting the bathrooms. Finally, sullen and red-eyed, she returned.

"Did you?" Ted asked.

"Did you?" Animan asked.

"Daaaaah?" I asked.

"I did," she said. "If you don't mind, guys, I'd really like to be alone right now."

"Oh yeah," Animan said.

"We understand," Ted said.

"Abbahahah," I added.

"Thanks." She turned and walked out. Then Ted and Animan, moving with the kind of precision and single-mindedness that the United States Congress can only *dream* of, turned to me and shouted, "Go after her!"

"What? She just *said* she wants to be alone."

"Don't listen to what she *said*," Animan explained. "Listen to what she *didn't* say."

"What she... *didn't* say?"

"Yeah," Ted said. "She *said* she wants to be alone..."

"What she *didn't* say is, 'I need a shoulder to cry on'."

"*You* have shoulders!"

"You could *be* that shoulder!"

At that point they began babbling incoherently about my upper anatomy and backing me towards the door. I got shoved out into the hall, where I was alone, except for Annie, leaning against the wall, arms wrapped around herself, crying.

I stepped up and hugged her, and she did, indeed begin crying on my shoulder, as though she'd been waiting for me after all. "You're better off without him, you know," I said.

"I know."

"You're going to be fine. I swear."

She sniffled and wiped her eyes. "Oh, Josh, you're so good to me. I'm so lucky to have a friend like you."

I held her as she said that, even though it felt like a knife between my ribs, through my stomach and arching straight up towards my heart.

"And I know I'm going to be fine," she continued. "It's just going to take some time."

"I know. I know."

I held her until she didn't need me anymore, and then she left to return to her quarters. I went back to the lounge, a large wet patch on my shoulder making the dark gray even darker. Ted grinned like a maniac.

"So?" he said. "How would you like to thank us?"

"I know *precisely* how to thank you," I said, smacking him on the back of his head.

EMBERS

My relationship with Dr. Noble didn't particularly improve after that. He went from being merely surly and rude to downright belligerent. When I passed him in the hall he'd glare at me, when he walked in the lounge and found me there he'd stare until I acknowledged him and then walk away gritting his teeth.

Annie didn't stay depressed for very long, but neither did she open up to me anymore. I knew Noble was still harassing her, trying to reconcile with her, but she assured me she was handling the situation. I didn't believe that for an instant, but at the same time I knew it wasn't my place to interfere until she wanted it. She was hurt and angry and it was all totally justified.

The only thing she *wasn't* was... *ready.*

Now that I think about it, everything got kind of tense those next few weeks. Copycat made a spectacular debut, battling Hotshot in full view of all the major networks and talking in a creepy, Bela Lugosi type of voice. I "escaped" that first night to continue my quest to find the murderous Carnival. ("Pathos!" Morrie insisted. "This has got pathos out the yin-yang!")

Back at *Powerlines* I finally relented and turned in a story about Hotshot's epic struggle against Copycat. It ran in full color and earned me a dirty look from Sheila, who had agreed not to blab the secrets but didn't quite seem up to looking me in the eye anymore.

Copycat made a few more appearances in the following weeks, including battles against Justice Giant and Particle, LifeSpeed and a debut match-up against Animan's new deer totem, Stag. Every time I turned in a Copycat story, Sheila got a little more distant, and I decided it was, indeed, a good thing that I hadn't jotted down Spectrum's double identity in that blasted notebook -- she would have never spoken to Scott Elliott again.

Ted was cool with me and Animan was friendlier than ever, but Mental Maid still stared me down every time I saw her and, frankly, she was continuing to give me the flaming heebie-jeebies.

Everybody's mood seemed to change after the Icebergg incident. The Spectacle Six was only venturing out on solo missions or in pairs -- never more than two at a time -- until Morrie could find a replacement for Deep Six. First Light finally completed her "purification" and was participating in rumbles again, but she made a concerted effort to stay in the air whenever possible, avoiding the civilians.

Flambeaux was the worst. He seemed to retreat from human contact entirely. It was bad enough that he couldn't stop his brother's murder, but he didn't even get to be in on the capture of the killer. He showed up for practices and had a perfectly adequate, if bland and spiritless, rumble against the Arachnid. He didn't speak to anyone unless absolutely necessary and he never put in an appearance unless officially mandated by the boss. It was like having an extra ghost around Simon Tower.

The afternoon of my "climactic final battle" with Hotshot ("Pathos!"), I was walking past the arboretum, the glass doors wide open. There were flashes coming from inside and I heard a steady hiss of breath accompanied by low grumbles.

I stepped into the large, open area. I had more than once walked through the fronds and foliage, admiring the quality of the topiary beasts and figures, including the particularly impressive hedge-sculpture of Lionheart, but I'd never known who created them.

The flashes I had seen were brief bursts of flame spitting from Flambeaux's fingertips, cutting into an unformed bush. He got it into a humanoid shape in the same rough, arms akimbo as the Lionheart topiary, but he hadn't added any details yet and it looked less like an actual person than a formless body.

Flambeaux was wide-eyed and stuttering to himself as he worked. "Icebergg," he kept saying over and over. There were other syllables in between, but I couldn't make out what they were.

"Flambeaux? You need something, man?"

"N'Icebergg. S'not. Find 'im... Icebergg..."

"We *did* find Icebergg, Flambeaux. He's gone."

"No!" he shrieked, sending out a burst of flame that wilted the head of his topiary. "*No.* Find *him.* Stop *him!*"

"Stop *who*? What are you talking about?"

"Find *him.*" He pointed at his topiary. "Stop *him,*" he kicked at the burnt leaves at his feet. "Icebergg..."

"We *did* find Icebergg."

"I DON' MEAN ICEBERGG!" he shouted. "He... he *wan's* me to mean Icebergg." He pulled me very close. His eyes were glowing orange like a Jack-o-Lantern and his breath smelled of burnt meat and roasted marshmallows.

"You... you're dressed like him... *another* him... *He* would have stopped *him* if *he* wasn't... weren't..."

"If Lionheart wasn't dead he could have saved your brother?" I asked.

"No!" he shouted again, shoving me aside. "I's not... I's not *about* Lance... Six... Icebergg..."

"If this isn't about Icebergg, why do you keep *saying* Icebergg?"

"He *wants* Icebergg... in my head..." he gasped. "But *here* -- my plants -- in the topiary I can *concentrate*. I can *think,* for a li'l while. While I work... while I work... I can *focus*."

"Focus on what?"

"Get *him*. Stop *him*. Save *him*." For the first time I realized he was talking about "multiple" hims, but I could tell neither how many nor who they were.

"Flambeaux, what--"

"Hey, Junior!" It was Hotshot, coming into the arboretum. "Ready for the big grudge match?"

"No!" Flambeaux shouted. "No more!" He burst into flame and blasted towards the ceiling, leaving a circle of fire on the grass. I was bathed in fire and I heard Hotshot shout.

"Josh! Are you all right?"

"Yeah, he's immune to his own powers. Go stop him, I'll put this out."

As it turned out, neither of us had to do very much. I started absorbing the flames to kill them while Hotshot flew after Flambeaux, but the arboretum sprinklers suddenly kicked in. The flow from those really shouldn't have been enough to douse Flambeaux, but it was like the falling water drowned what little spirit he had left. He cut his flames off and allowed himself to fall. Hotshot caught him before he could hit the ground, but when he brought him to me (and later, to the infirmary), he was catatonic. He just laid there, mouth open, eyes blank, still orange, but the fire behind them was gone.

"What's going on, 'Shot?" I asked. "What the hell is happening?"

"I don't know," he said, "but we don't have time to worry about it now. We've got a rumble to stage."

He took Flambeaux away for treatment and I was left alone with the ruined topiary, the one I still couldn't quite place. It was funny, though -- between the wilting and the water from the sprinklers weighing down the leaves I could almost make out some of the details I hadn't seen before. It wasn't really a shapeless mass, Flambeaux had been sculpting someone in particular, and for a second I knew who it was. And then I dismissed that thought entirely because it didn't make any sense at all.

"I WILL NOT BE DENIED!"

My rumble with Hotshot was planned for the Siegel City Cape and Mask Museum. Allegedly, Copycat was going there in the hopes of finding a clue that would lead him to the infamous Carnival. Truth be told, Morrie just wanted to ensure there would be plenty of security cameras around. (I was good television, it seemed. That very morning Morrie had shown me the prototype of a Copycat action figure. I wondered if Tom would ever ask me to autograph one of *those*.)

The only "inherent" power Copycat had was the ability to materialize out of smoke, a power I faked with smoke bombs tucked into pouches along my belt. When I got to the museum I snuck in through a hole Morrie had created in the security system, cutting through the air ducts and diving into the Lionheart wing in a veil of smoke.

There were two guards when I arrived, both -- I would guess -- real cops trying to pull in some extra cash. When they saw me they both went for their nightsticks, no firearms for these boys.

"Where is Carnival?" I moaned in my creepy horror-movie voice.

"It's that ghost guy!" one of them shouted.

"Aw *crap*."

"Where is Carnival?" I reiterated. I felt kind of lousy about dropping a couple of smoke bombs and taking them out while they couldn't see, but I'd been taught by Nightshadow exactly how to strike to render them unconscious without doing any real damage.

"*Where is Carnival?*" I asked for clarification. I proceeded to the monument of Lionheart's last battle, which was a wax sculpture of him fighting the crimson-armored Carnival and a glass display in which Carnival's helmet -- all they'd retrieved of him, it seemed -- was interred.

"Wheeereee iiiiiis Caaaaarr-niiiii-vaaaaaaal?" I backhanded the sculpture of Lionheart's killer, sending the wax head rolling away. It was rather cathartic. Keeping with the plan, I moved over to the glass case with the actual helmet and raised my fist.

"WHERE... IS... CARNIVAL?" I bellowed.

"Why don't you try asking someone who was *there?*"

Hotshot had charged in from the front entrance (the way legitimate patrons would, I thought). He landed only a few yards from me, planted his arms firmly on his hips and scowled. "Welcome back, Copycat."

"Hotshot!" I shouted in the required overly-dramatic fashion. I turned away from the case. "You and your ilk have delayed my quest for far too long." I threw a punch, which he easily countered, and he returned. I caught his fist in midair and we twisted, launching into sort of an acrobatic wrestling match that didn't pay much heed to the laws of gravity.

"My 'ilk'?" he whispered.

"I'm playing it up for the cameras, deal with it."

He doubled over on himself and threw me, judo-style, into the case with Carnival's helmet. Glass shattered, scattering in every direction. A blaring alarm klaxon went off and I felt a sharpness in my back. For a second I was worried I'd been stabbed by one of the

219

shards, but as I felt around I could tell I was just feeling the extreme coldness of a sharp, flat-edged piece. I wasn't being punctured, I was being refrigerated.

I started grabbing shards, charging them up and firing them at Hotshot. He dodged them with little problem, but took cover behind a bronze memorial to Lionheart as my blasts got closer.

I'd fired off maybe a half a dozen of these chilled glass plates when I picked up one that was particularly heavy and thick. A quick glance revealed it wasn't a piece of glass at all, but rather a shard of Carnival's helmet that somehow broke off in the crash. It wasn't metal, like I'd thought, but some sort of super-dense crystal. I tucked the shard into an empty smoke-bomb compartment and returned to firing glass at Hotshot.

A particularly large shard broke in my hand before I got a chance to charge it up. Hotshot was finally returning fire.

"I will not be denied!" I roared. Then, after a quick glance to make sure I was in view of the cameras, I lunged forward, kicking in the flight powers, zipping in under the fire and delivering a body-slam to the gut.

"Go crawling back underground smokey!" he shouted, kicking me in the jaw and sending me flying.

"Smokey?" I whispered again.

"Just *take the cue*," he hissed back. He was right, this battle had gone on long enough.

I reached into my pouches and discreetly pulled out a few more smoke bombs, smashing them to the ground. Fingers of mist swirled up to grasp me and I started to emit a corny, B-movie style moan. "Ooooooooooooh..."

"Gotcha," Hotshot said. He whipped out a gray canister about the size of a aerosol can. "Little care package I borrowed from the Spectacle Six," he said. "Pleasant dreams."

He hit a red switch on the canister and a vacuum kicked in, sucking up the smoke. "No!" I screamed, trying to sound as horrified as possible. *"I WILL NOT BE DENIED! I WILL EXACT MY REVENGE!"*

The crappy dialogue taken care of, I dove directly into the stream of smoke. I concentrated all my mass inwards and began to shrink down. Hiding in the smoke, I'd made it down to about an inch of height before I flew into a hidden chamber in the canister. At the bottom were a couple of seats with tiny safety harnesses. I sat down in one and strapped myself in. In the other, Particle was waiting with a grin.

"Nice finale," he said.

"Why thankee, kind sir."

We waited in the canister as Hotshot dealt with the cops, repeatedly assuring them that he would be taking "that dangerous revenant Copycat" to a spectral containment facility maintained by V3OL, resident genius of the Spectacle Six. Finally, all the explanation taken care of, they left the police to clean up and took to the air.

"Hey, can I come out now?" I asked.

"Of course not!" Hotshot called. "How's it going to look if people see you flying around Siegel City with me after I've caught you?"

I looked over at Particle, who just nodded. We sat there a few more minutes, experiencing a turbulent flight, before we finally felt a harsh thud.

"Are we on the roof?" I called. "Can we come out yet?"

"Not yet!"

I looked at Particle again. "That felt like a landing to me."

He shook his head. "Just some nasty turbulence."

"And what was that sound?"

"What sound?"

"That dinging sound."

"The one that sounded like an elevator door?"

"Yeah, that one."

"Didn't hear it."

I listened a little more. "Now it sounds like he's walking."

"Just your imagination, son."

There was another thud and the canister stopped moving entirely. "Okay!" Hotshot called, "come on out!"

"About time," I said, unstraping my harness and scrambling out the exit. I leapt into the air and I grew back to full-size, executing a perfect 10-point landing in a kung-fu stance intended to display for Hotshot how incredibly intimidating I could be despite the fact that I looked like a total dork in that pose.

I did all this.

In the middle of the lounge.

Surrounded by Capes and Masks with big smiles on their faces.

And a cake.

And a big banner that said, "Congratulations, Copycat!"

Oh yeah. And they were all yelling, "Surprise!"

"What the hell is *this*?" I shouted.

"Tradition," Particle said.

Hotshot grinned. "Whenever someone gets their own character we always have a little celebration at the end of their first campaign."

"It was *my* idea to surprise you," Annie said, stepping forward and kissing my cheek. "Congratulations, Josh."

"Aw... I don't know what to say."

"Try 'Thank-you'," Ted said, giving me a hug (with the requirement of pounding me fraternally on the back -- the only way that males are allowed to hug one another unless at least one of them has a fatal disease). I made the rounds, accepting congratulations from Particle, DoubleGum Man, Five-Share, Animan, V3OL, Five-Share, Spectrum, the Arachnid, Fire-Share, Nightshadow, Five-Share, the Justice Giant and Solemna, the Goop, Five-Share, Fourtifier, LifeSpeed, Flux, and Five-Share. There was cake and snacks and Miss Sinistah kissed me on the cheek at least twice more, the second one turning me to jelly and making me wonder where the Gunk was once my head cleared. Not that I was complaining -- the last thing I needed was him pulping my brain.

Finally I managed to get Annie by herself. "This is so sweet," I said. "Thank you."

"Hey, for the sweetest guy I know."

"Cut it out, you're gonna make me blush."

"Yeah?" she said in that teasing voice she used sometimes (particularly, I suspected, when she knew it would drive me the craziest). "Maybe that's what I'm going for."

I couldn't believe my ears -- nor could I keep the smile from spreading across my face. "Now why would you want to do something like that?"

"Oh, I don't know," she said. "Maybe I'm just starting to see things a little clearer."

"Maybe," I said, suddenly aware of how close our faces were. And that she was slowly closing the gap.

"Stay *away* from her, puke!"

We broke apart and looked towards the door -- along with literally everybody else in the lounge. I chided myself for my foolishness. How could I possibly have only noticed the *Gunk's* absence from the party?

But the crowd was complete now. Dr. Noble was there.

BIG MISTAKE

"Well hi there, Todd," I said. "Somehow it just didn't seem like a party without you."

"Todd, nobody asked you to come here," Annie said. The wonderful, magical smile she'd worn only seconds ago was gone, and I was seeing red.

"I'll go anywhere I damn well please," he snarled. "Stay away from her, Corwood."

"What makes you think you can barge in here and start ordering her around like that?" I asked.

"Please, Josh, I can handle this," she insisted.

"Are you *sure*?" I asked, pleading with my eyes for her to let me flatten this slug.

"I'm sure," she said. "Please, he's *my* problem. Let me deal with him."

I stared at her for a moment, not wanting to leave her alone with the beast. But she *needed* to do it. *That* I understood.

I looked at Noble. "Hurt her," I said. "Give me an excuse."

Then they stepped out of the lounge. They must have been right outside the door, because I could still hear them talking. I turned and walked away.

"You're a strong man, Josh," Ted said. "I think almost anyone else would have thrown a punch there. You're calm, you're reserved--"

I grabbed the nearest pool cue out of Nightshadow's hand and broke it over my leg.

"You're venting," Ted continued.

Nightshadow was about to say something, but after glancing at my face he turned away, grabbed another cue and began chalking it up at a considerable distance from me. In fact, except for Ted and Animan, everyone was pretty much keeping their distance. I think they understood.

"You know, that lounge equipment didn't do anything to you," Animan said as I put my fist through a steel garbage can. I didn't know whose strength I was using, and I didn't care. I'd never felt such an urge to commit a violent act in my life.

"I need to break *something* worthless!" I shouted, "and Noble's in the hall!" I picked up a beer bottle and ground it to powder in my hand. Alcohol was running down my sleeve. I didn't care.

"How dare he... how *dare* he take away her smile?" I raised my fist, poised to bring it down on the pool table, when a black-gloved hand wrapped around my wrist.

"Watch it, pal," Hotshot said. "I'm kind of partial to this table."

"Did you *see?*" I hissed at him. "Did you *see* what he does to her? How he makes her feel?"

"I know, buddy," Hotshot said. "We all feel the same way about Doc Noble."

"The *scale* of those feelings may vary," Animan said, twirling the broken pool cue.

"You have to calm down," Hotshot said. "In a place like this, with power like yours, anger is more than just self-destructive, it could be *catastrophic.*"

"*I DON'T CARE!*" I shouted. "Why do I have to play the nice guy here? Why *can't* I get mad for *once?* Don't you think he *deserves* it?"

"He *deserves* to have a volcano dropped on him," Ted said, "but that doesn't mean you can *do* it."

"*Somebody* has to. Before he hurts her again. Before--"

"It's just words, Josh," Hotshot said. "That's all he has in him, that's all he has going for him. But as long as it's just words, there's *nothing you can do.* If she's going to listen to him, you have to *let* her."

"I *KNOW* THAT! Why do you think I'm so upset?" I charged the door, pointing towards it and hissing under my breath. "And don't pretend words don't hurt, Hotshot. Don't you even *try.* But I swear to you, if he does anything else, if he so much as lays a *finger* on her--"

"Did you hear that?" Ted asked.

"WHAT?"

We fell silent and I was close enough to the door to hear them talking again. And what I heard was Annie's voice. And what she said was this:

"Todd, let go. Todd -- Todd, that *hurts*. Todd--"

LifeSpeed himself couldn't have stopped me in time.

I ripped the door from its hinges on my way through. They had progressed maybe five feet down the hall. Noble had one beefy paw clamped around her arm, the other with a single finger extended in her face. He turned and looked at me and probably would have said something of great import and intelligence if my fist hadn't chosen that precise moment to impact his face. I felt his nose crunch and blood flowed onto my glove. I don't think I've ever felt anything so satisfying.

"You libble PUNG!" he hissed through a stream of red. He rocketed his fist at my head but I easily caught the blow, flipping him not just over my back but straight through the wall and into the lounge.

I jumped through the hole he made, amidst a hail of plaster and dust, and looked around to see where he'd landed. He actually hit the pool table Hotshot had saved a few minutes ago, splitting it in two.

By now the others were trying to hold me back, although whether it was for Noble's good or my own I wasn't sure. Nightshadow was the first to reach me, but I hurled him into the wall using the very techniques he had taught me. I swatted the Arachnid aside and rolled past Flux before Fourtifier, Justice Giant, DoubleGum Man, Merlin Junior and at least half of Five-Share managed to pile onto me, dragging me to a halt. I was still struggling against them. If I had been thinking clearly, I probably could have figured out a way to slip away with some combination of powers or another. That's an enormous "if."

"Josh, *calm down!*" Hotshot shouted. "Todd, what just happened?"

"The libble sigo jus' unloabed on me!" he said, wiping his nose. "He oughtta be pud away!"

"You piece of filth!" I shouted. "He was hurting her, I *saw*--"

"He's nuds! I woulden' lay a figger on her!"

"No?" Annie stepped through the hole in the wall and held out her arm. "What do you call *these*, Todd?"

Around her upper arm were a series of deep, finger-shaped red marks. One of them was already beginning to purple. And considering her invulnerability -- how tough she was -- to think of how much pressure he must have applied... I again tried to break free, but the others held me in place. I don't exactly think all of them *wanted* to, though.

"*How?*" I asked, my voice quivering. "How can someone claim to care about her and then do *that*? ANSWER ME, NOBLE!"

"Why do you eben *care*?" he blurbled.

"BECAUSE I'M IN LOVE WITH HER, YOU STUPID SON OF A BITCH!"

Nobody moved.

Nobody breathed.

Nobody spoke.

A tumbleweed rolled by.

"Get out of here, Todd," Hotshot finally said. "Get out and go away for a while. I'll handle this."

"Yeah, I'm goin', I'm --" he was headed for the door when Hotshot caught him on the shoulder and pulled him in very close.

"Oh, and Todd?" he said sweetly. "Next time, we don't stop him."

Noble ripped his shoulder from Hotshot's grasp and left, though the door. Before he was gone, though, he made it a point to shoot me an enraged, murderous gaze, which I gladly returned.

With him gone my blind fury subsided. "You can let me go, I'm all right now," I gasped. Arms of rock and taffy and flesh relaxed and I was free to move again. Everyone was staring at me -- some in horror, some in admiration, most in simple amazement.

In Annie's face, I saw all three.

"I have to go," I said to her, and I ran out of the lounge. I ran down the hall and stumbled into the arboretum, the only place I could think of to do what I was about to do without interruption.

I ran past the alien plants and past the gardens and past Flambeaux's ruined topiary, which still looked a bit like someone I knew. I ran until I was as close to the center of the arboretum as I could estimate.

Then I fell to my knees.

And then I screamed.

I screamed for a very long time.

CONFESSIONAL

By the time I finished screaming I was ready to collapse. My energy was gone, my spirit was empty and every iota of strength I'd had seemed to void itself from my body. I didn't think I would ever be able to move again. My cheeks were tear-stained and my neck hurt. The worst thing that could possibly have happened was if someone had shown up just then.

Which is why I was not at all surprised, as I slumped against a tree and buried my face in my lap, to hear footsteps and feel a Rush approaching me.

"Go away, Ted," I moaned.

"It's not Ted," Annie said, "it's me."

"I know it's you. I'm talking to Ted. He's hiding in those azalea bushes."

The bush in question cursed, rustled and moved away.

"I figure I at *least* owe you a conversation," I said to Annie.

"Yeah, you do," she said, unable to disguise the quiet, hurt rage in her voice. "Did you *mean* that?"

"When somebody is about to assault the city's best-loved Cape in a maniacal rage you can probably take anything he happens to blurt out as gospel."

"Why didn't you ever tell me?"

"Oh come on, like you didn't know. The way I look at you? The way I hang on your every word in the desperate hope that you'll say *anything* to make me believe you're in the same place I am? You haven't noticed *any* of this?"

"Even if I *did,* Josh, why didn't you ever say anything? And *don't* say you never had the chance, you had a *thousand* chances these last few months."

"I had the *chance,*" I said, "I didn't have the *right.*"

"What does *that m*ean?"

"You were with Noble. Maybe it *was* a stupid, destructive relationship, but I *couldn't* be the one to point that out because I didn't know if I'd be doing it because it was the best for you or because I wanted you for myself. Besides, I realize this places me in the minority these days, but I was raised with a certain set of values that includes 'don't steal someone else's girl.' Not even a jackass."

She came to my tree and knelt next to me. "So you just kept it to yourself, then. How long were you going to leave things bottled up like that, Josh?"

"As long as it took! What, do you think I *liked* that? Do you think I liked watching you with him? The way he treated you... the way he made you feel whenever he walked into the room... it's a *sin,* Annie." I rolled to my knees so I could stare directly into her eyes.

"Get out of here, Ted!"

"Geez, all right," said a topiary giraffe with a band director's hat, which bobbed away.

"Josh," she wept. "You don't even know me, you're in love with the mask."

"Don't *know* you? I don't give a damn about the mask. You've never been so beautiful as you were that day in the park. And as for who you are, your name is Annie Harmon. Your mother's name is Cynthia. You've got a brother named Quentin who's only interested in girls and a brother named Tom who's only interested in Capes. You've got a scar on your knee from a bike accident before your powers kicked in. You always wanted to be a dancer but you didn't think you had the legs for it. You think the Smurfs get too preachy sometimes. Tell me some more of what I don't know."

She covered her face and bent over, weeping.

"How long were you with Todd, Annie?"

"About... eleven months."

"Eleven *months*? It didn't take me eleven *minutes* with you to tell how sweet and amazing and incredible you are. He had eleven *months* and he *still* treated you like that? The man's a bigger idiot than I thought."

She stood up, wiping her face. I followed suit. "Stop saying that, Josh, you don't know what he was like then--"

"Are you *still* defending him? What is it going to take, Annie, is he going to have to *kill* somebody? *He doesn't deserve you*. You're too good for him. And I'm not saying I *do* deserve you -- God knows I haven't earned any miracles lately, but let me tell you what I *do* know. If I had the chance, if you *gave* me the chance, I would never, *never* stop trying to make you happy. You're wonderful, you're beautiful, you're funny -- and stop trying to argue that point with me, you *are*. And you're everything, *everything* I could ever want. I'd lose the powers, I'd burn the costume, I'd leave the whole damn city behind if you wanted me to. If it was for you."

I don't know which of us was more stunned that I'd said it, me or her.

"But I guess that's not enough, is it?" I asked.

"I don't know, Josh. I don't know what's enough or what's too much or -- God, I'm so confused."

"When I met you, Annie, when I first began to learn who you are underneath that mask, I was thanking God for finally bringing someone that wonderful into my life. And then I found out about you and Todd, and I've spent every day since then raging against Him for placing you out of my reach."

She began to tremble, still crying. I placed my hands on her shoulders and turned her to face me. At first, she tried to look away, but when I started talking, her eyes met mine.

"I love you, Annie. I'm sorry it came out this way, but I'm not sorry it came out. I love you. I need you. I'd do *anything* to make you smile or to hear you laugh. When you're not around, I wish I was with you, when I *am* with you I never want it to end. I love you. And I'll *never* regret saying that."

She smiled, just for a second, then began to cry again. "You don't know. You've got me on a pedestal--"

"No! That is *NOT* it. I know your faults. Some of them -- such as your incessant tendency to put yourself down -- *really* upset me. But dear *God,* I wouldn't care if you had no powers, waitressing in the filthiest greasy spoon in Siegel City and always had a *hairnet* on, as long as it was *you.*"

"I don't know... I don't know *what* to think. I don't know what I want. I need to sort all this out."

"Then go ahead. It's okay. I'm not afraid of waiting, I'll wait as long as you need."

She put her head on my shoulder then and we both squeezed out the last of our tears. As I felt her, the nearness of her, I never wanted to let go, because I was scared I wouldn't get her back.

This must be love, I thought, *I can hear violins playing.* And then I noticed the fir tree with the white-clad arm giving me a thumbs-up. I opened my mouth, but Annie beat me to punch.

"Go away, Ted."

"Darn it," said the tree. Once he was gone, we just stood there for a while longer.

We just stood there.

ISSUE ELEVEN

THE CALM

It's amazing, how sometimes the simplest things can be the hardest to do. For instance, ringing Sheila's doorbell the next day. I thought it would take my arm off. It was almost as hard as standing there, on the steps of her apartment building, waiting for her to click the damn intercom button and acknowledge my existence.

Finally there was an electric hiss and Sheila's scratchy voice crackled, "Who is it?"

"Sheila, it's me. It's Josh. Come on, I need to talk to you."

There were several more moments of quiet static before she replied. "I'm sorry, the sneaky bitch you have requested is no longer in service."

"Oh come on, Sheila! I never called you a sneaky bitch."

"You were thinking it."

"Sheila, please, this is important! I need your help."

"Why, all of a sudden, do you need *my* help? I wasn't good enough to trust with your little secret about the Magical World of Morrie Abadie."

"Look, I'm sorry about that, okay? I should have trusted you and I'll never make that mistake again, I *promise.* But Sheila, listen, I've gotten myself into a real mess here. Noble wants my blood, Annie's as stable as a nuclear power plant with Homer Simpson on staff, I've got to buy a new pool table if you can believe that and any minute now a swarm of pissed-off troll dolls with

235

neon blue hair from the center of the Earth are going to attack the city, so I don't have a lot of time!"

No response.

"Okay, I'm making up the part about the troll dolls, but the rest of it is all true. I *need* you, Sheila. I need your help. I can't talk to anyone who can be *objective* about this whole, stupid mess! Please, just hit the buzzer and let me come up there."

No response.

"You want me to beg? Is that what you want? I'll do it! I'll make a fool out of myself in front of the entire street! Sheila, I was wrong and I'm sorry. I'm a blithering idiot. I'll do whatever it takes to make it up to you. I'll cook! I'll clean! I'll bear your children! I'd be down on my knees if I could reach the intercom button from there! I'll erect a shrine to the wonderfulness that is Sheila Reynolds, if you'll just let me *talk* to you!"

I was in the middle of composing a ballad entitled, "Why I Think Sheila is Really Keen-a" when the door opened and Sheila stepped out. "Hey."

"How long have you been away from the intercom?"

"I started down the stairs as soon as you said you were sorry."

"So I've been begging the *door* for your forgiveness?"

"I suppose. Why, what did you say?"

"Nothing. Why didn't you just buzz me up?"

"Because we're not doing this here. We're going for some frozen yogurt. You have until we get back here to convince me you're really sorry."

"Okay. But it's on me."

"You're damn right it is. That's not quite going to be enough, though."

"Didn't think it would."

It didn't even take me until we got to the yogurt place to finagle forgiveness out of her -- Sheila's always kind of had a sisterly soft spot where I'm concerned. I bought her a cup of strawberry cheesecake. It wasn't enough to rebuild the bridge entirely, but it sure as hell laid the foundation.

While she satisfied her sweet tooth I told her what happened with Annie -- the blowup with Todd, the tearfest in the arboretum, all of it. She listened with attention so rapt I thought she'd burst. Finally, she put down her cup and spoon.

"It's obvious, isn't it?" she said. "All you *can* do is give her time."

"Time is going to *kill* me one of these days, you know that?"

"Time kills all of us. You've just got to live with it."

"Time or Doctor Noble."

"Don't let that guy bug you. Sounds to me like he's all bark and no bite, Josh. If he was really going to go after you, he'd have done it by now."

"Tell that to Photon Man."

"Do you *know* what really happened to Photon Man?"

"Well... not exactly, no. I know he did... *something* bad, I can't really get people to talk about it. They chased him down and Noble found him, *alone.* He 'accidentally' hyper-intensified Photon Man's powers and made him blow up."

"Ew."

"You're telling me. That's why Hotshot was so adamant about trying to find Icebergg before Noble got to him last month."

"Is *that* what happened to Icebergg?" she said. "I'd noticed he'd gone missing."

"You've really been paying attention, haven't you?"

"Well... once I learned it was all fake it's sort of like watching a soap opera."

"You *hate* soap operas."

"That's because Eric Braden doesn't wear tights. So, what *did* Icebergg do?"

"I don't know if I should be telling you this, Sheila," I said, but she shot me a look that seemed to indicate she knew precisely where she could hide the bodies, so I relented.

"Okay, okay. But you don't report--"

"I don't report any of this, I know. Go on."

I launched into another storytelling session, this time beginning with First Light's holo-reproduction of Deep Six's murder and concluding with Flambeaux's incoherent babbling in the arboretum.

"That is *so* weird," she said. "Did you ever figure out what he was trying to say?"

"You know, right after that was Copycat's 'capture,' and right after *that* I threw Doctor Noble through a wall and confessed to Miss Sinistah that I was in love with her. I didn't even *think* about Flambeaux again until just now."

"Josh, how could you *not*? It sounds like something *huge* is going to happen, you can't keep this to yourself!"

"Sheila, I *have* to keep this to myself. No reporting, remember?"

"Oh, yeah. But still, how can you just *sit* on a mystery like this? I'm *already* climbing up the walls."

"I'm no detective, Sheila, I wouldn't know how to *begin* digging this up."

"There's only one way *to* do it. You've got to go to Flambeaux and pick his brain."

"He's catatonic!"

"Ah, how long can *that* possibly last?"

I laughed. "Sheila, as grateful as I am that you haven't told anyone – Anderson Cooper, for instance -- about Morrie's little playhouse, I've got to ask something here. How can someone as inquisitive as *you* be sitting on a story this big and *not* go insane?"

"I thought about that," she said. "I guess the truth is I'm content to keep the secret as long as *I* know it. Solving the puzzle is more important than showing it off."

"*Really?*" I said with a ridiculous level of skepticism.

"Well... also, I guess I'd rather have my best friend than a Pulitzer."

I blushed. "Aaaw... Sheila. I don't know what to say."

"Just accept the compliment. Jackass."

"Whore."

"Creep."

"Skank."

She hugged me and we both fell into outrageous fits of laughter which, now that I look back on it, may have saved my life. Or at least my sanity. I was happy there. It was quite some time before I was happy again.

BEFORE THE STORM

"What *I* don't get," Ted said to me the next day, "is why you're going to visit the catatonic pyro instead of trying to talk to Annie."

"We've talked, man. *Believe* me, we've talked. Fact is, we both need some time to decide what else there is to say."

"Pessimistic way to look at it."

"Realistic, I'd say."

We were back in the lounge and, although I had no more rumbles on my docket for a while, I was in costume, like most of the others. While I was in Simon Tower it made more sense to be Copycat than Josh Corwood.

The broken pool table had been replaced and the only sign that there had been a scuffle at all was a white patch on the wall that hadn't been painted yet. Morrie's repair crews were even faster than *Powerlines'*. Still, staring at the new pool table, I found myself desperately praying the Copycat action figure would be a top seller -- there was going to be a big hole in my royalty checks until that thing was paid for.

"Still, why talk to Flambeaux? The guy's practically a vegetable."

"He was trying to tell me something back there, Ted, before he blanked out on me. Maybe if I can snap him out of his... trance, whatever it is, he can finish."

"I still don't know what you hope to find out. Icebergg is gone, Deep Six is still in a block of ice in the morgue -- case closed. Come on, stick around here and help me break in the new table."

"Very funny."

"Josh, think about this. Morrie's got the best doctors and psychiatrists in Siegel City on his payroll. What makes you think you can snap him out of it where they all failed?"

"I'm going to try something I'll bet they never even considered."

"What's that?"

"I'm going to bring him flowers."

I went down to the infirmary with my recent purchase resting comfortably in my hands. It was a bonsai tree -- one of those little things people could trim and shape. I remembered how Flambeaux said working on the topiary garden somehow helped him to concentrate -- clear his head. Since I couldn't bring him to the garden, I figured this would be the next best thing.

The on-call nurse simply waved me through to Flambeaux's room. "Who knows?" she said. "Maybe you can get a rise out of him. It certainly can't hurt."

I sat next to Flambeaux's bed and placed the bonsai on his nightstand. Except for some beard stubble, he looked very much like he had when Hotshot brought him in -- cold, empty and not really there. His eyes were still orange, but even moreso now, as though it were fluid gushing around inside the vitreous humor and not just an energy build-up.

"Hey man," I said. I glanced down at his chart to remind myself of his real name -- Benjamin Costanza. And his brother, Deep Six, was Lance. I wondered if they had any family besides each other. I wondered if the rest of the family knew.

"Hey, Ben. I brought you something." I slid the bonsai closer to him, hoping at least *some* part of his vacant brain could see it. "I realize it's no giant topiary giraffe, but when I tried bringing *that* bad boy in, the nurse gave me such a dirty look... I tell you, it'd chill your blood to *ice,* man."

I found this joke considerably funnier than Flambeaux did.

"Look, I know you're probably busy and all, but I was wondering if maybe you could shed a little light on the whole 'find him' thing we were talking about the other day. Ring any bells? Wanna share anything else? Come on, Benny, who is *'he'*? Who do I find? Who do I *stop*? Who do I *save*?"

Flambeaux just lay there, beeping periodically through a monitor. It was like watching the world's most boring pinball machine. In exhaustion, I buried my face in my hands and groaned. "I give up. I could have a more meaningful conversation with the Goop."

"Josh?"

The voice was slow and soft, like someone learning to speak the language, but it was *there*. My ears pricked and my head shot up. Flambeaux had turned his head and was staring at the bonsai tree. His eyes *looked* the same, like an orange hurricane was playing itself out in there, but all the same there was a presence, a *consciousness*, that wasn't there before.

"It's nice." He raised an arm in a slow, tortured movement. It was in the air just long enough for him to brush a leaf with a fingertip before he had to drop his arm to the bed again.

"Thank you."

"Hey, any time, man. Just glad I could help. So come on, can you talk? How do you feel?"

"Scared," he said. I hadn't heard him sound so totally *sane* since before his brother died. "Is *he* still out there?"

"I don't know, Ben. I don't know who he *is*. You've got to tell me."

His eyes fluttered and his face contracted in on itself, down his neck, as though he were trying to cough up something. "Gha," he said. "Glarg." His face relaxed and he exhaled with a long, low moan. "Can't tell you. He won't let me."

"Then how can I possibly find him?"

His head rolled to the side again. "Tree?"

"Huh?" I looked at the small plant, wondering how there could be a clue *there*, but when he whispered "Tree?" again, I realized he was *asking* for it. I took it from its spot on the nightstand and placed it on his bed, near his hand. With Herculean effort, he lifted his hand and began to burn off a leaf here, a branch there, giving the tree its shape.

"See... my brother," he said clearly.

"Your brother? Ben, your brother is--"

"*See him.* And *not* the costume. See *him.* See th' *truth.*"

I shuddered as I realized what he was asking. He wanted me to go examine a corpsesicle.

"Ben, are you sure? Isn't there some other way?"

"*No* way! Can't *say* it, even now, even with a clear head. You'll see. You'll *know.*"

The look in his eyes had changed dramatically. It had gone not only from vacant to occupied, but now conveyed a wealth of emotions ranging from terror to grief to desperation.

"Okay, Ben," I said. "I'll go to your brother."

His eyes shifted to relief in the split-second before they closed and he slumped back against the bed, exhausted. He waved at the bonsai tree with a finger, asking me to take it away, and I returned it to the nightstand.

"Thanks, Benny," I said. "I hope I can find whatever it is you want me to."

"Wait--"

"What? Is there something else?"

"He's *here*," he whispered. "Part of him. With *you*?"

"What?"

"*Look*," he said. Then his eyes rolled back in his head and the expression of sanity was gone. Flambeaux was empty again.

"Get some rest, man. You've done your part."

Three hours later I was sneaking into the Simon Tower morgue.

THE FIRST BAR

An interesting thing about Morrie Abadie was that as much as he liked to splurge on certain amenities like the lounge or the gym, there were other things he didn't spend a nickel more than he had to on. At 9 p.m. not only was there nobody at the morgue, but there wasn't even a fancy security system in place, just a deadbolt.

Even the few lessons I'd gotten in subterfuge from Nightshadow were enough to get me into the morgue and to find the drawer Deep Six was in. I steeled myself as I gripped the handle, took a deep breath and slid it open.

He was literally still a corpsesicle -- they hadn't even bothered to thaw him out before the put him in the drawer. They just chipped away enough of the ice to fit the poor guy in there. "I'm gonna regret this," I mumbled to myself. I dug around until I found a screwdriver to use as an icepick and a paper towel to wipe off the ice chips that would undoubtedly spatter my face.

The body was closest to the surface of the ice around the head and, even with the helmet cracked, it would still keep me from accidentally jabbing into... well... anything *soft*. There was a scarlet cloud in the ice surrounding Lance Costanza's head, where his blood had leaked out of the broken helmet and frozen. Of course, it was right where I would be chipping.

I raised the screwdriver into the air and jabbed it into the ice. Shards flew everywhere and I wiped the water from my face. The towel was still white then.

I kept chipping, kept wiping. The towel was getting wet but it wasn't changing color. Once I started chipping into the crimson, I stopped looking at the towel.

Finally I heard a clang as the screwdriver impacted the helmet. It didn't really take as long as I'd thought it would. I used that point of contact and chipped outwards, finally exposing the crack in the armor. I wondered how so much blood could flow through such a small crack.

I'd decided to just pry open the crack and hope I could see, through that mess, whatever it was Flambeaux had sent me after. The screwdriver fit into the split easily and prying it open it was not difficult, but when I looked in all I could see was a mass of red with vaguely skull-like shadows at the core.

In frustration I grabbed the towel and wiped at my face again, trying to ignore the bloody orange stains and --

Orange?

Why were Deep Six's blood-stains *orange?*

I chipped out a hunk of red from the ice and cupped it in my hands. The red ice was melting, not into blood, but into a gooey orange slime. The orange looked *exactly* like the bodies of a certain pair of monsters. While frozen it *did* look like it could be blood, but it also looked like the same color *my* flesh had been when I froze myself during the battle with Icebergg. The same color as--

People usually compare solving a mystery to putting together a puzzle -- finding all the pieces and teaching yourself how they go together. I suppose some mysteries are solved that way, but for me this was more like hitting the jackpot on the slot machine -- first one BAR slides into place, then the second. Then, as the last roller spins, the wait is intolerably long -- until finally it hits and everything becomes clear.

The first BAR came when I reached into my belt-pouch there in the morgue. I'd had my costume cleaned but I hadn't bothered to replenish my supply of smoke-bombs. I remembered how cold the glass case was during my rumble with Hotshot and how I pocketed a shard of Carnival's blood-red armor and forgot about it.

I slid my fingers into that canister, hoping I'd wrap them around a hunk of red crystal, but instead I dipped them into a puddle of orange goo at the bottom of the compartment.

The glass case had been refrigerated. Carnival's armor had been made of frozen Gunk-flesh.

"I thought I saw you slip down here."

I jumped straight up when I heard the voice, half-expecting the Gunk to be waiting to decapitate me, but it was only Nightshadow. I should have known -- not only did he have the stealth skills to get in unnoticed, but only someone with no powers could have snuck up on me without my feeling it.

"Thank God you're here," I said. "You've got to see this."

"What the hell have you *done*?"

"It's not what it looks like--"

"First that stupid, pointless, destructive fight with Dr. Noble and now *this*? You're *insane,* Josh."

"No! It's not like that!" I rushed past the frozen body and grabbed Nightshadow by the cape. "You're not leaving until you hear me out!" I shouted, getting a sensation of *deja vu.*

"Get off me, you psycho!" He spun and kicked me in the side, but somehow it didn't hurt. In fact, his foot kind of collapsed that side of my body, like he was hitting a water balloon. My flesh was melting and turning orange and my brains began to scramble.

I think Nightshadow tried to say something, tried to get away, but at this point my head was so messed up I wouldn't have recognized Annie kissing me full on the mushy lips. I just wanted to be *me* again, *solid* again.

I grabbed Nightshadow around the ankle and moaned, writhing in confusion. He cursed and tried to kick me off, but I held on. Then I tried, again, to do what I'd done while we fought Icebergg -- I pushed *out,* trying to become solid.

My limbs hardened and my torso filled out my costume again. My face stopped dripping through the mask. I was *me.*

I wish I could have said the same for Nightshadow.

He was standing there, trying to hold himself together, gushing through his costume as an orange fluid. He finally collapsed in an orange puddle, nothing more than a skeleton in a costume. He never even had time to scream.

That's when I heard the clapping.

I looked up at the doorway to the morgue to see the Gunk standing there, applauding with all three sets of limbs.

"Very nicely done, my boy. Do you have *any* idea how interesting your powers are?"

"What's going on here, Gunk? What *is* this?"

"It's quite simple -- my powers build up on me. Every so often they build up so much I need to dispel some of the energy by transforming some lout into an orange behemoth who -- once he manages to pull himself together -- will obey any command I give him."

I was dumbstruck. Whatever was going on (and I was starting to believe I *knew* what) was *not* an unusual practice for him.

"What really *astounds* me is the fact that you were able to transfer my excess energy *for* me. It had been quite some time since I'd duped poor Deep Six over there, and I was starting to get a bit addlepated. Thank you."

"Then... the Goop?"

"Oh, the good Dr. Plante? Once I transformed him I thought it would be useful to keep a 'sidekick' around. The ruse was pleasant for a while, but it's grown tiresome. Time for a new ruse, I think."

"How could you *do* this?"

"It's quite easy, actually, especially when you consider that I don't need to wait for an energy buildup to capture someone's *mind.* I have several drones out there that will obey my commands -- although I *will* have to punish Flambeaux for alerting you to me."

"Who else have you... *taken*?"

"Oh, the odd Cape and Mask. Icebergg, obviously. And Flambeaux and Deep Six. Mental Maid has been particularly difficult to keep a hold of -- it must be the nature of her powers. Her brother, though, *he's* so simple that he doesn't even realize he's been enthralled.

"Her *brother*? Who's her *brother*?"

Gunk knelt down by Nightshadow's still form. There was a strange cracking, gushing sound and his four extra arms fell off. He placed the bones next to Nightshadow, then turned his remaining hands into shears and began cutting Nightshadow's costume off the skeleton. "Oh, didn't you know?" he said sweetly. "Mary Abadie, and her amazing brother Morris. They used to be quite well-known as 'mentalists,' had a stage show together." He absorbed Nightshadow's costume into his body. "On to the next game, eh?"

"And what's *that*?"

"Oh, please, Joshua. I've seen far too many spy movies to give away my master plan at the bottom of act two. Suffice it to say, it won't matter to *you*. You'll be on a prison planet in a few days, serving hard time for the murder of the Gunk."

It was a good ruse. Lying there in a pool of slime, a skeleton with four extra arms, Nightshadow didn't even enter my mind.

"I'll tell them the truth," I said. "I'll stop you."

He laughed the kind of nasty, evil laugh I thought you only heard in Vincent Price movies. Then he began to flex his sloppy muscles. His flesh began to solidify. His torso turned red and his legs black. A shock of raven hair erupted from his skull and a blue cape flowed down his back. Perfectly human, a brilliant yellow emblem appeared on his chest.

"Really, my dear boy. Who do you think they're going to believe? *You?* Or *LIONHEART?*"

ISSUE TWELVE

IS THAT YOU?

There was a moment of blind panic when it seemed like the entire universe was going to collapse in on us with the Simon Tower morgue as the focal point. He *couldn't* be Lionheart, I told myself, he just *couldn't.*

Then I realized I was right, he *really* couldn't, and for two reasons. First, someone who possesses the Heart of the Lion was incapable of committing a malevolent act. (It never even occurred to me to doubt this, I accepted it as a simple scientific fact, like the world is round and that God created women for the express purpose of giving me an ulcer before I turned 30.)

Second, Lionheart had saved my life, and I had been loyal to him ever since. Far from being loyal to this abomination, I wanted to rip him into so many pieces it would take all of Five-Share and half of the United States Marine Corps a week to find them all. Once this realization sunk in, my panic was replaced by pure rage, and I wasted no time informing him that I did not believe his parents were married.

"Tut-tut," the Gunk-as-Lionheart chuckled. "Such *language.*"

"How can you *do* this?"

"Oh, my boy, it's easy, I'm a shapeshifter. One that, thanks to you, now has enough dominion over his own body to again to control the shifts. I'm *very* grateful, by the way."

"Nobody will believe you're Lionheart. They all know he's dead."

"*Missing*," he reiterated. "The only person who was present for that battle is Hotshot, and he's never told anyone that he *watched* Lionheart die."

"He told *me*."

"Well aren't *you* special? As for my credibility... Morris and Mary are *mine*, remember? And so is the susceptibility field. In terms of legitimacy, child, *I* am Walter Cronkite. *You* are Jerry Springer."

"Yeah," I said. "But I've also got *your* powers." I bore down and concentrated, shifting the colors on my costume, slimming myself a bit more and broadening my shoulders. My hair darkened from its natural brown to Lionheart's jet black. I gave him a smile that Lionheart once gave me, drifting away from a burning building.

"*Now* who are they going to believe?" I asked.

We both lashed out at the same time, deflecting each other's blows. He swept at my legs with a low kick but I leapt over him, coming down and landing my elbow on his neck. The first strike was mine.

Second, third and fourth were all his, as he snapped a fist up into my face, down into my gut and hurled me into the wall. As I felt my bones jar against steel, I realized that, while the blows *hurt,* they didn't seem to be doing any actual *damage*. The malleable shapeshifter body we both had was acting as a cushion -- only my skeleton was solid now.

He charged me, but I countered by rolling onto my back, catching him in the gut with my feet and flipping him. He crashed into the bank of steel drawers and crunched his jaw down on the ice-block that contained poor Deep Six.

I followed his head down, smashing it with both fists. "Still think you got what it takes to be Lionheart, you son of a bitch?"

"More than *you,* boy." He launched an elbow into my crotch and I winced. I was immensely relieved, a second later, when I realized that the blow didn't hurt any more than the others. Even my sensitive areas were nice, spongy shapeshifter-flesh for now.

I grabbed him by the scruff of the neck and hurled him over Nightshadow's skeleton and into the door, which smashed open under his weight. I leapt out after him and followed into the hall, where he tangled his legs with mine and pulled me to the ground.

"Give it up, boy! You haven't got a prayer!"

"Would Lionheart give up, greaseball?" I brought my elbow down hard on his knees and I heard a pleasant crunch. The Gunk rolled over and howled in pain. I scrambled to my feet and delivered a solid kick to his face, which briefly showed signs of flowing back into its natural, orange state, but he managed to keep his wits about him enough to resolidify.

"Josh? Is that you?"

A voice echoed down the corridors from around the corner -- Ted. He must have decided to come looking for me.

"I'm getting some strange music from you, man, is everything all right?"

The music in question began to well up inside of me -- it was a fast-paced low brass rhythm, pounding out staccato riffs over and over again -- the kind of music you hear during heated battle scene in a movie.

"Ted, get the hell out of here!"

"Why? What's--"

"No, Ted!" the Gunk shouted in the same voice I'd used. "Get in here, quick!"

"Will you make up your--" he turned the corner and the music exploded into one loud, high-pitched blatt as though everybody in the orchestra had screamed into their instruments at the same time.

"Sweet Jesus," he whispered.

The Gunk and I simultaneously pointed at each other and shouted, "Stop him! He's an imposter!"

"Ah... ah... ah--" Ted turned on his heel and bolted down the hall.

The *faux* Lionheart and I glared at each other, then down the hall where Ted had charged. At the same time, we began to run.

I don't know how he did it -- between a bum leg and the fact that I started standing up, but somehow the Gunk got ahead of me as we raced. Before long we were in the more populated areas of the complex, charging past a series of perplexed Capes and Masks and one *thoroughly* confused-looking Goop. Even Dr. Noble wasn't wearing a smirk as we charged past him and LifeSpeed into the lounge.

Where Annie was watching a movie on late-night cable.

The Gunk made a beeline for her.

"Oh, the *hell* you are!" I screamed, hurling myself at him and "borrowing" a burst of inertia from LifeSpeed. I hit him at the waist and he crumbled like a lousy quarterback. I began to pound him with both fists as hard as I could, insane with rage, shouting, "Take it *off*, you monster! Take off his face! *TAKE OFF LIONHEART'S FACE!*"

I felt hands surrounding me and pulling me away -- it was like fighting Dr. Noble all over again. Once I was back on my feet Gunk/Lionheart pulled himself up and just stood there. He didn't need anyone to hold *him* back.

"All right, all right, I'm coming!" Morrie shouted, pushing his way through the crowd. "Will somebody please tell me what the -- oh my God."

He had as much amazement on his face as anyone else and I remembered what the Gunk had told me, he was so "simple" that he didn't even know he was being manipulated.

"That's Copycat!" the Gunk shouted, "and he murdered the Gunk!"

"That's the Gunk!" I returned, "and *he* murdered *Lionheart!*" As soon as it was out of my mouth I realized how unlikely it sounded. Not that *his* story had much credibility, but... what had I told Sheila once? "Heaven's retention rate for us *sucks.*" And the Gunk was counting on that well-earned stereotype to carry his line of crap through.

Heads began to turn in my direction, most of them with scowls, rage or simple disbelief in their eyes. Only Ted, Annie, Animan and Hotshot looked like they were struggling with the Gunk's story -- and Hotshot looked like he was going to have an aneurism.

"No way I'm going to convince you guys, huh?" I asked. I switched the shapeshifter powers back on and made my body incredibly slick, gliding away from my detainers. Before they could make another motion to grab me I jumped forward and attacked.

"Change *back*," I shouted, driving a roundhouse punch to the Gunk's jaw before bolting out of the lounge with a burst of LifeSpeed.

I darted into the express elevator and thumbed the button for the roof. As the door began to close I saw an entire mob rushing towards it. I thought I would make it, too, but in the second before it closed a humanoid mass blasted through the crack. I had company.

The pneumatic lifters the elevator used fired and we began our rapid ascent to the roof. The mass next to me began to regain its shape -- stolen, of course, from Lionheart.

"You see, boy?" the Gunk hissed. "They all *love* me. By the time I'm done with *you*, the only one on your side will be your mother."

"*Your* mother!" Even in the confines of the elevator I somehow found the maneuvering room to deliver a blow to his gut and a few more to the head before the elevator doors opened and we spilled out onto the roof.

We danced out onto the gravel, trading punch for punch, kick for kick, until we made it to the edge. I fell back against the railing, nearly destroyed by exhaustion.

"Give up, Joshua. I'm going down in the history books, while you won't even merit a footnote."

"You're going down in history, all right," I spat. "Attila the Hun, Adolph Hitler, the Gunk."

"King Arthur, Robin Hood, Richard the *Lionhearted...*"

I bristled at the names – according to legend, they were three of the heroes whose spirits gave power to the real Lionheart. Whether it was true or not, I didn't even care at this point. This guy comparing himself to a Plantagenet would have been bad enough. Comparing him to Siegel's last real hero made me snap, and I launched at him. He backhanded me and I caught a glimpse of the skyline, a dizzying spectacle beneath me. Vertigo began to set in. He hit me again and I thought I would vomit. He struck me once more and I flipped over the rail.

With the wind whipping past me I tried one last, desperate stab of survival. I tried to force a pair of wings out of my back with Gunk's shapeshifting powers, hoping I could fly.

I'll never know if it would have worked or not, though, because just about then I fell out of range of the Gunk's powers.

The color drained out of my uniform and my hair lightened to brown. My gut softened, my shoulders narrowed and the ground got closer.

Worst of all, my flesh suddenly felt the impact of every blow I'd received. All at once it felt like I was being bludgeoned by a dozen hammers -- particularly in the groin. I'd rather let Dr. Noble use my ears as a wishbone than feel *that* again.

Through all of this, the ground came hurtling towards me. The speed and the wind and the pain finally overcame me, and I barely even felt the arms that caught me in the seconds before I finally blacked out.

CAPTIVE

When I could see again I knew I was dreaming. Annie was not only there, but she was smiling. "It's all right," she said. "We've broken out. We're free."

We were soaring high above Siegel City in the dream. The skyline was moving as though we were watching a time-lapse movie of the city growing and evolving -- beginning ten years ago and leading up to the present.

As the city flashed below me the sky remained the same. It was sunset, and the great yellow disc fell below the horizon while the sky around it erupted in a kaleidoscope of orange and red and purple. It reminded me of something I'd heard an artist say once: "never paint a sky blue." I don't know if it's precisely what he meant, but I took that as a warning to always look past the obvious.

"Exactly," Annie said as I thought that. "Watch."

The city still evolving beneath us, she pointed to Lee Park, where a figure was rising into the air with another in tow. It was Carnival, I saw, recognizing that frozen, blood-red armor that hadn't existed for ten years. He was flying too, with one arm extended in front of him and the other clutching a skeleton by its collarbone.

As he rocketed through the sky the armor began to glisten, then soften, then melt. It turned back into the slimy orange body the Gunk had always worn, even sprouting four extra arms. The slime flowed down his arm onto the skeleton. There seemed to be an endless supply of it. The skeleton was soon coated as well.

As he flew past me the Gunk fired a despicable grin in my direction. As he did it, his features solidified and a mask grew across his face. His body hardened and clothes appeared, a cape finally sprouting from his back. He was the phoney Lionheart again.

Laughing like a madman, he hurled the screaming goo-covered skeleton to the city below, rocketed off in the distance, and was gone.

I looked at Annie as if she would have the answer, but she wasn't there anymore. In her place were a pair of glowing purple eyes on a figure dressed in swirling magenta robes.

"What do you think?" Mental Maid asked.

Suddenly, my dream-self lost the ability to fly and I fell straight down towards Simon Tower, which was still under construction. I fell straight through the top floors, rocketing down through the building and into the complex beneath. I fell straight down, faster, finally falling into a room I'd never seen before and...

...then I was awake.

I was lying on a cot in a small, dark room with a single bare light bulb -- 40-watt, I'd guess. Morrie was such a damn cheapskate sometimes. The walls were a naked white and they ran about seven feet before cornering, then repeated the process. The single door, on the wall opposite the cot, was blue with a small glass panel set at eye-level. There was no doorknob.

As I shook my head and tried to squeeze the feeling back into my limbs, I realized my hands were bound together in front of me. This was one high-tech pair of handcuffs, with a center bar instead of a chain, covered with electronic energy read-outs and pneumatic clasps holding it on -- the thing was as close to escape-proof as anything ever designed.

These weren't handcuffs, I knew. I'd seen them once before, on a thawed-out Icebergg. They were power dampeners, and as long as I had them on, I was helpless.

I sat up, then hoisted myself to my feet. This was a mistake. I stumbled across the room and smashed into the far wall. Only the collision kept me from falling down entirely.

I slid myself along the wall until I reached the window in the door. Outside was the Justice Giant, his feet on a desk, watching a small portable television. It appeared to be showing the episode of *Happy Days* where the Fonz had to save Richie, Potsie and Ralph Mouth from some calamity or another.

"Hey!" I barked. "Hey, what's going on here?" I banged on the door with the power dampeners until I finally made a noise loud enough to get Justice Giant's attention. He looked back at me, frowned, and then motioned at somebody I couldn't see.

I craned my neck to catch a glimpse of who he was talking to. This was another mistake. The door opened and gave me a solid crash in the face, toppling me back to the floor. I felt a hell of a lot of pain, I noticed, but the biggest pain I felt was the realization that I wasn't getting a Rush from either of them.

"Dude! You can't *stand* there!" Ted bent down and helped me to my feet, Animan behind him. They pushed me back and sat me down on the cot.

"Those power dampeners can majorly screw with your sense of balance," Animan said. "Just sit down and *relax*, man."

"What's going on?" I moaned.

"You're waiting for your trial," Ted informed me.

"What?"

"Yeah, I know, Morrie wanted to start sooner, but you were unconscious and now he's all busy planning the press conference--"

"Press conference?"

"Yeah. Announcing Lionheart's return."

"He's *not Lionheart!*" I shouted. "Guys, he *can't* be Lionheart."

They glanced at each other nervously. "Josh... of *course* he's Lionheart," Ted said. "Who *else* could he be?"

"GUNK!"

"Gunk is *dead,* man," Animan said. "They found his skeleton in the morgue lying in a pool of... of that *slime* his body was made out of."

"Right. And *I* killed him. I forgot."

Ted shook his head. "No, no we don't think *you* killed him."

I jolted upright. "You *don't?*"

"No, Josh. Dude, we know you better than that."

"Oh, thank *God*, Ted. Then you believe your 'Lionheart' is lying?"

They glanced at each other again. "He's not *lying* man," Ted said.

"Yeah. He's... Lionheart."

"He must have just made a mistake. He doesn't know you like we do."

Mental Maid -- Gunk was using her powers to keep up his charade. Damn susceptibility field. "You're right, it was a mistake. But the *real* Lionheart *couldn't* make a mistake. Not about *me!*"

"Why not?"

"Because we--" I caught myself before the words came spilling out of my mouth. Even here, even now, I couldn't bring myself to tell them about the Heart of the Lion. It was too deep, too *sacred,* to share, I was almost mystically forbidden from speaking of it. And frankly, I don't think it would have mattered if I *did* tell them. Something that close to the soul couldn't be believed by those who aren't a part of it.

"I'm sure everything will be cleared up at the trial," Ted said.

The trial... God, I didn't even want to *think* about *that.* Mental Maid's eyes glowing... hitting me with that blindingly white Soul Ray-- I think that may have been what scared me the most about the whole thing. The prospect of learning what I really was. Would I be a dog? A lizard? Some ugly monster-thing? The real Lionheart wouldn't have had a problem, he was a prince, but I was pretty certain the rest of us would be unpleasantly surprised to discover once and for all who we really were in our hearts.

"Hey," I said, "where's Hotshot? Where's Annie?"

"Hotshot's been in Morrie's office all day trying to convince him to drop this whole thing."

"Thank God. Is he having any luck?"

"Not really," Animan said. "Morrie's been too busy getting ready for Lionheart's press conference."

"And Annie?"

They were awfully silent for a moment.

"She's in a bad way, Josh," Ted finally said. "She doesn't *really* think you could kill the Gunk but..."

"But what?"

"But she said she didn't really think Doc Noble would ever hurt her, either. Not at the beginning."

"Besides," Animan said, "all things considered, talking to Miss Sinistah right now may not strengthen your case much."

"Why not?"

"Well let's face it, brother, you haven't exactly been acting rationally where that girl is concerned. Everybody saw you chuck Noble through a wall over her."

"Your choice of targets hasn't been good," Ted added.

"What the hell does--" I saw the look in the Conductor's eyes and a light went off. "Ted," I said, "I know you used to have a thing for Annie--"

"Hey, I'm over that, buddy, I'm on *your* side--"

"That's not where I'm going," I said. "Who else around here did she know for a fact had an... interest in her?"

"Who did *she* know about? Oh God, nobody. She didn't even know about *me*. The girl is absolutely oblivious to how attractive she is."

"Well who did everyone *else* know about? Was Nightshadow one of them?"

"Well... yeah," Ted said.

"Hey, where *is* Nightshadow?" Animan asked. "You'd think he'd have shown up by now, what with all this commotion."

Damn susceptibility field. I decided it would be pointless to argue that point. "Who *else*?" I hissed, having a sneaking suspicion I would be able to guess every name.

"Well there was Flambeaux," Ted said.

"*And* Deep Six," Animan point out. "The brothers -- that almost got nasty."

"I heard a rumor once about Icebergg, too," Ted said. "It was so damn hard to *tell* with him, though..."

"Anyone else?" I gulped.

"Well... yeah, Photon Man. That was a pretty bad one, too, once Noble found out about it."

"Am I the only one sensing a pattern here?" I shouted.

"Pattern of *what?*" Ted asked.

Damn susceptibility field!

"Look, guys--"

I was about to launch into another futile attempt at reasoning with them, but just then Ted's eyes began to droop and his head started to nod. Animan fell back against the wall and slid to the ground. Ted toppled forward, bouncing his head on the cot before falling to the floor.

The blue door opened and, through it, I could see Justice Giant asleep at the desk, no longer paying attention to the *Happy Days* re-run he was watching.

In the door stood a purple woman with glowing eyes.

"We must hurry," Mental Maid said. "Both Morris and the Gunk are preoccupied with their press conference. There is very little time and much you must yet learn."

"*Aeeeeeeeeey*," said Fonzie in agreement.

THE SECOND BAR

Mental Maid had to step over Ted and Animan to get into the cell and close the door behind her. It was getting slightly cramped in my cell. "You put them to sleep?" I asked.

"Not exactly," she said. "I placed them in a dream-cycle during which they will relive their fondest memories until I restore them to consciousness."

"Mmm... Mindy," Ted moaned in his sleep. I heard an electronic synthesizer chorus resound from him. "*Bomp*-chicka-*waw-waaaaw*," it informed us. Mental Maid frowned at him, made a face, and the music stopped.

"A less... colorful memory," she said.

"*Thank* you," I said. "Now will you *please* tell me what in the living *hell* is going on?"

"I've been *trying* to tell you. *I* cleared Flambeaux's head so he could talk to you -- working on the topiary distracted him enough so that it was possible. I sent you your dream about the Gunk -- but now, for a few moments, I can act freely."

"If you can act freely, why don't you just drop the damn susceptibility field? It's going to get me *killed!*"

"*I* do not create the field," she said. "My brother does."

"*Morrie?*"

"Do you find it so difficult to believe a brother and sister could both be empowered?"

I thought of Annie and Tom and I decided it was not that difficult to believe. "So wait -- is Morrie a telepath too?"

"*Neither* of us are telepaths. I cannot read minds, Joshua. Mine is the power of *truth.* I can sense it, sow it, I can *reveal* it. I knew you were planning an exposé of this operation, just as I knew that, when the time came, you would be unable to go through with it."

"And Morrie?"

"My brother has always been a showman, a huckster. His is the power of lies. He can delete the truth from your memory. He can make you remember things that never happened. He can make you believe a lie and ignore reality."

"The susceptibility field."

"Precisely. And, true to form, he lies even about himself, attributing *his* powers to *me.*"

"I don't get it, though. If your powers come from the same source, then why is he... and why are you..."

"What?"

"Well... you're *purple*!"

"Oh. That. Make-up, prosthetic ears. Even electronic contact lenses -- Morris loves to put on a show, even if he is too dense to realize the show belongs to the Gunk. Ironic, isn't it? We get taken in by a monster and *I* am forced to live a lie, while Morris is as true to himself as he ever was."

"Yeah, something like that."

"It is the nature of my powers -- that is why I can resist his hold, if only for a short time. I also knew that you had the Heart of the Lion."

"You know--" I almost asked a stupid question, but caught myself.

"That was another reason I let you in. I knew that, when the Gunk made his move, only one with the Heart of the Lion would see the truth. And I knew Hotshot could not do this alone."

"What *is* his game?"

"He hasn't revealed himself to me, but I think it's clear. He's the same as any megalomaniac, he wants *control*. He will take over every Cape and Mask, one at a time if need be, until he has the power and the influence to rule this world -- even from the sidelines."

"It's been *ten years*," I said.

"The Gunk does not age. Ten years is *nothing* for an immortal. He has spent *hundreds* of years behind the scenes, waiting for this opportunity, pulling strings.

You don't want to know how many presidents have been in his thrall."

She was right, I probably didn't. "How many people *does* he have enthralled?"

"Many. But you must be careful, Josh, it is not *they* who are evil, it is their controller. Most of them, were they free to think, would fight by your side."

"Even the Goop?"

Her face clenched. "I... cannot speak... with freedom... about the Goop," she forced out. "Gunk's control over that area..."

"But he *is* just a pawn, right?"

She nodded. "But move wisely, Joshua. In *this* game, when you capture a black pawn, he may well become a white knight."

What about Icebergg? And Flambeaux and Deep Six? How do *they* factor in?"

"Icebergg's cold form was clearing his head too often. He was beginning to break free of the Gunk's hold." I remembered how freezing my own head had cleared my mind during Icebergg's capture and nodded.

"And the others?" I asked.

"He used Flambeaux and Deep Six to dispose of Icebergg for the same reason he once used Photon Man."

"*Why?*"

"As a favor. A show of good faith to his one partner -- the only one who knows his game and the very one he shall betray should he succeed."

The second BAR in my mental slot machine clicked into place.

"Noble."

"Gunk promises him power, Noble follows like a greedy pig."

"I've got to find Annie, I've got to get her out of here."

"She is already gone, Joshua."

"What?"

"After your capture she left the Tower, it was too much for her to absorb. She is with her family right now."

"Thank God," I said, thinking that at least she had Tom for protection. If that idea seemed ridiculous later, it didn't then. Tom wouldn't let anything happen to her. I believed that.

"Does she know?" I asked. "Does she know what really happened to Photon Man?"

"Joshua, *no one* knows what *really* happened to Photon Man. Except for Doctor Noble."

"And you?" I asked.

"Yes."

"Can you show *me* what happened?"

"Yes."

"Do it."

She nodded and her eyes began to glow. She placed her hand on my forehead and a sudden influx of images and sounds flooded my mind. I watched everything that happened in the last minutes of Photon Man's life.

I slumped to the cot, eyes wide open, mouth agape. I was still like that when Mental Maid whispered, "Do what you must," and left.

PRESS CONFERENCE

"Corwood? Hey, Copycat!"

I snapped out of my trance when I realized Justice Giant was standing at the door to my cell, smiling. Ted and Animan were gone -- I'd never even noticed when they left.

"What do you want?" I moaned -- not so much in an angry tone, but more like an exhausted person who just wants to be left alone with his thoughts.

"Morrie's press conference is coming on -- they're announcing the return of Lionheart. Thought you might want to watch."

I started to say that I'd rather use the Goop's skeleton as a chew toy than watch that bastard pretend to be Lionheart, but then I thought better of it. *Who knows?* I thought, *maybe I'll find some hole in his story or something.*

Justice Giant pushed the desk and television to a position where I could see it through the open door and he could watch from his chair.

The screen showed a dais in front of Simon Tower, where Morrie, DoubleGum Man (as a representative of the Spectacle Six) and Dr. Noble were standing in front of a large video screen with Morrie's corporate logo twirling on it. I took a small amount of pleasure in noticing that Noble's mask had been slightly modified to hide his broken nose.

Morrie went up to the forest of microphones at the podium and his name appeared at the bottom of the screen, along with the phrase "Superhuman Liaison." He was wearing a big, toothy grin, although his mouth looked kind of naked without a cigar dangling from it.

"As many of you have noticed," he said, "certain members of the Spectacle Six have been incommunicado for several weeks now. Some of you have suspected a fallout, a chiasm in the group. Some of you even went so far as to suggest that Deep Six has *fallen* in his neverending battle to protect the citizens of Siegel City.

I chuckled a little at how Morrie's speech suddenly became more refined when you put a TV camera on him. Master of lies indeed.

"Nothing could be further from the truth. The Spectacle Six have actually been working in conjunction with Dr. Noble," who was grinning like an idiot, "in a quest to recover something this city has sorely missed. A real Holy Grail. And I am proud to say that they have found the object of that quest, and all the people of Siegel City will be sleeping easier tonight."

Reporters' hands began popping up like targets in a shooting gallery, but Morrie just laughed and shook his head.

"I *could* just tell you what they found," he said, "but I'd rather *show* you. Come on down, big guy!"

As everybody looked up, the cameraman tilted his lens just in time to see a figure leap from the roof of Simon Tower. There was an instant murmur among the reporters, and as the figure got closer they began to murmur louder, realizing who it *was*. One man could even be heard to shout "Oh my *God!*" over the microphone.

Even *I* had to admit it, it *looked* impressive. The long-lost hero of Siegel was fluttering to the ground (buoyed up, no doubt, by Dr. Noble's telekinetic powers), landing by his fellow heroes, making a triumphant return. If I wasn't so disgusted by his presence I may have cheered.

"That's *not Lionheart*, you *idiots!*" I shouted.

"Awful cynical, aren't you Josh?" Justice Giant asked.

"Awfully *gullible*, aren't *you*?" I muttered, then I chided myself for it. He wasn't really gullible -- just *susceptible.*

The stunned murmurs among the reporters rapidly gave way to cheers and applause. It was Lionheart's face the Gunk was using, but it wasn't his smile. Lionheart's smile was warm, gentle and inspirational. The Gunk, even wearing Lionheart's face, couldn't manage a smile that was anything but harsh and merciless.

"Rotten bastard," I couldn't stop myself from grumbling.

On TV the Gunk-as-Lionheart quieted down the screaming press and fired off another of his soulless grins. "Thank you," he said, "Thank you. It's good to be back."

"Jesus, he's not even using the accent!" I shouted.

"Keep quiet!" the Giant barked. "I'm listening to this."

273

"Where have you *been*?" squealed one of the reporters in a very unprofessional tone of voice.

"I can't tell you that," he said. "Not *now*. Trust me, it's for your own protection. Suffice it to say I have eliminated a very *real* threat, and I have now returned to the city I love."

There was another chorus of applause and I snorted. "Knows how to play the crowd, doesn't he?" I said.

"Yeah," said Justice Giant in a dreamlike tone of sincere hero worship.

Hands began to reach into the air and the Gunk indicated one of them.

"What happened to Carnival?"

"That particular threat is long since dealt with," he said.

"Are you going to re-form the LightCorps?"

"I have every intention of reestablishing contact with my old comrades-in-arms," he said. "Whether anything comes of that will be entirely up to them."

I bristled at the thought of him getting a hold of Lightning, the Defender or the Tin Man again. The only reason he'd want to contact those retired heroes would be to eliminate the people who could pick his story apart.

"What about Copycat?" shouted one of the reporters. "Do you have any comment on *him*?"

"Yeah," I said. "*Do* you have any comment on him?"

"Ah yes," he said, "the ghost who's been wearing my emblem. I *am* up to date on current events. Copycat was recently captured by my old friend Hotshot. I trust he has been dealt with accordingly."

"Or shortly will be," Noble chuckled. Gunk shot him a look, but by and large I think the comment went fairly unnoticed.

"Okay, okay, ladies and gentlemen," Morrie said, taking back the podium. "We're all glad to have Lionheart back, but the man *does* need his rest. I'll be sending out a press release later with all the specifics. But suffice it to say, your hero has returned! And with him, I've got another announcement to make!"

With that, the video screen behind him flashed to reveal another version of Lionheart... a smaller, *plastic* version.

"As you know, out of deference to our fallen hero, we've never used Lionheart in our official 'Heroes of Siegel' line of merchandise before. Now that he's returned, though, he's signed an exclusive arrangement to license his likeness and trademark to Abadie Enterprises!"

"NO!" I lurched against my dampeners, smashing them pointlessly into the cell wall. Justice Giant raised an eyebrow at me

"Lighten up, man."

"Lionheart would never allow this," I hissed. On TV, the video screen moved on to show a line of Lionheart clothing, cereal, and other chintzy crap. The camera cut to a reporter who began blubbering about how the great, the *heroic* Lionheart had returned, seemingly from beyond the veil of death itself, to continue his neverending battle for truth, justice and--

"Turn it off," I said.

"What?"

"Turn off the TV. Or put it back where it was -- I don't feel like watching those morons gush about how great it is to have Lionheart back."

"Man, you have *got* to lighten up, you know that?" Still he did move the TV back and closed the door, leaving me alone with my thoughts.

And those thoughts were enraged.

For ten minutes, anyway. That's how long it was before the door opened again. This time, it was Dr. Noble and Hotshot. The latter looked exhausted, the former ecstatic.

"I wanted to be here, Josh," Hotshot said through weary, haggard eyes "You need a friend at your side."

"Come on *Copycat*," Noble said through a truly nauseating grin. "It's time for your trial."

"Lay on, MacDuff," I said. Then, smiling, I leaned in towards Noble and whispered,*"I know what you did to Photon Man."*

He looked a little taken aback by that, then chuckled. "You're bluffing," he whispered back so that Hotshot couldn't hear.

"Am I?"

He was visibly shaken by that, but then he shook his head. "Who gives a crap?" Then he raised his voice again. "You'll get soul-blasted in an hour anyway."

"Go ahead. Hold your kangaroo court. It won't matter. Your buddy screwed up *big* time."

"And how's that butt-munch?"

"He picked *Lionheart's* rep to destroy. I don't care if I have to come back as a *real* ghost. Didn't you know that's what a revenant was? A ghost who rises from the grave for vengeance."

"You going somewhere with this, Corwood? I'm a busy man."

I leaned in very, very close. And again, I smiled.

"*I'll stop you*," I said.

And as they led me away, for the first time, Noble looked scared.

And it felt *good*.

ISSUE THIRTEEN

ESCAPE FROM SIMON TOWER

My cocky attitude began to diminish as we approached the auditorium. Sure, Noble still had that uneasy look on his face, but there was a furrow just fighting to show up on *my* brow as the three of us walked in silence, Noble on my left, Hotshot on the right. Finally, we could see the auditorium door. The walk suddenly became slower.

"Don't worry, Josh," Hotshot said. "I'm gonna get you out of this."

"Yeah, right," Noble snorted. "Enjoy your last minutes on Earth, Joshie-boy."

"Hey Todd," Hotshot said, "who designed those power dampeners?"

"Particle, I think. Why?"

"And if they were suddenly -- I don't know -- turned into energy, Josh's powers would kick back in instantly, wouldn't they?"

"I guess..." Noble mumbled apprehensively. Where the hell was Hotshot going with this?

"So if I were to, say, charge those manacles up, Josh would be able to use *your* teke-field to protect his hands before they blew, wouldn't you say?"

"I suppose so--"

"Good. Got all that, Josh?"

I smiled. "I think so."

"Good." Hotshot's arm darted out and snatched the center bar of the dampeners, charging them up. I immediately felt power Rushing in from both sides, including Doc Noble's teke-field, which I used to sheath my hands, arms and the front of my head and torso.

"What the hell is *this?*" Noble shouted.

"What's it *look* like?" I asked, waving the glowing dampeners in Noble's face.

"Ah! Get *away* from me, you psychopath!"

"Gosh, Todd, what's wrong?" I asked in a voice like a three-year-old. He ran back down the hall and I chased him, twirling around the manacles. "What's *wrong*, Todd? Todd, can't we be *frien--*"

That's as far as I got before the dampeners exploded. I felt a clenching around my wrists and a considerable bolt of wind hit me in the face. There was no shrapnel to contend with, though -- when an explosion is caused by the violent disillusion of the ionic bonds of the source explosive, there really isn't any debris to worry about.

Noble babbled for a moment, then spun in midair and shot down the hall. "Ah, that felt *good*," I said, turning to Hotshot. "Now *you* -- what the hell do you think *you're* doing?"

He assumed a face like a character from a bad gangster film and said, "I'm breakin' youse outta heah."

"I appreciate it, Mugsy, really, but isn't this just going to make *you* a fugitive too?"

"Hey, you only live once."

"Not in this profession."

"Let's argue about that while we're on the run," he said. "That sort of blast is likely to bring company."

"Believe it!"

LifeSpeed whirled around the corner, pounded a solid hit to my jaw and turned to Hotshot.

"I can't *believe* you're helping this murderer escape!" he shouted.

"Come *on*, LifeSpeed," Hotshot said. "You should know better than that."

"We don't have time for this," I said. I reached out with LifeSpeed's own powers and made a mental twist. He screamed, clutched his chest, and fell over.

"What did you--"

"Sped up his heart," I said. "But just for a second. He'll be okay. I did *not* like doing that, Hotshot."

"Come on."

We ran to the stairwell and began flying up to the top of the building. We were on the second subterranean level and there were 40 floors above ground for us to race up through. That gave us a little time to talk.

"Why *are* you doing this?" I asked.

"Because that's *not Lionheart!*" he shouted.

"Not that I'm complaining, but why do *you* believe me if nobody *else* does?"

"We've got the Heart, remember? If that *were* Lionheart, neither of you would have been able to lift so much as a finger against the other."

"Well, at least *you're* not as susceptible as some people."

"What do you mean?"

"He's a mind-controller! He's already got a hold of Flambeaux, Deep Six, Mental Maid, Morrie -- hey, are we getting *heavier*?"

We were. Our ascent was rapidly slowing down as our bodies dragged through the air. I looked down to see Flux zipping up the stairwell.

"I didn't want to believe it, Josh," he called, "but an innocent man *never* rabbits."

"I'm not really *rabbiting*," I said, "this is more like *gerbiling.*"

Flux shot upwards and I only barely managed to dodge his rocketing fist. Hotshot, on the other hand, managed to *catch* that hand.

"You won't believe me," he said, "but I'm *really* sorry about this." He flipped the weightless Flux into a wall, hard. I don't know if it was enough to render him unconscious, but it was certainly enough to break his concentration -- Hotshot and I both lost our "extra" weight at the instant of the collision and shot towards the ceiling like a pair of bottle rockets. We screeched to a halt so fast I thought we'd leave skid marks in the air.

"In here!" he shouted, pointing at the second door from the top of the stairwell, the one that led to the top floor.

"We're not going to the roof?"

"They've probably already got somebody waiting for us there."

"But -- the top floor? Where the gift shop and restaurant are?"

"Yeah, why?"

"It's the middle of the afternoon, all that stuff is *still open!*"

"Witnesses. Let's go." He landed, opened the door and stepped through. I ducked in behind him. We darted through the hall into Simon's Sky-High Café and ran into a murmur among the patrons. Hotshot immediately took on his "calm down the folks" stance.

"It's all right, everyone. Just a routine superhero inspection... nothing to worry about."

"Hey, isn't that Copycat?" someone shouted, pointing at me.

"Isn't he a *Mask?*" screamed another incredibly helpful person.

"Um... he *used* to be," Hotshot said, throwing an arm over my shoulder. "He's reformed now. I'm training him to be my sidekick."

"Your *sidekick?*" I whispered.

"You wanna get out of here or *not?*"

My limbs started going all rubbery on me and I felt a now-familiar "pulled taffy" sensation. "DoubleGum Man is coming."

"Astute, isn't he?" The purple-clad rubber man began to flow out of a vent in the ceiling, wrapping me in one arm and Hotshot in another.

"Oh come *on,*" I said, easily turning my own body to rubber and slipping out of his grasp. By now the people in the restaurant were freaking out, wondering why all these Capes were fighting each other -- a situation that was only made worse a few seconds later when V3OL burst in through an empty elevator shaft and fired an energy-web at me from his robotic arm.

"Perpetrators located," his voice buzzed. He fired again and again I managed to duck. I couldn't copy powers from the robot, but I slithered in close and oozed all over his arm.

"Release me," he said in the calm, stupid monotone voice Morrie thought sounded "cool" coming out of the talking action figure. I wrapped my arms around his more powerful right one and jerked it through the air so it bore down on DoubleGum man, who was paying *no* attention to us but rather trying to stuff himself down Hotshot's throat and suffocate him.

"I will not fire at my teammate, perpetrator, if that is your intention," V3OL hummed.

"Fine," I said. "Hope you've got a spare arm."

With Hotshot's power I charged up the metal appendage and fired it at DoubleGum Man. He screamed and his body contracted, snapping back to its ordinary configuration like one of those stretchy dolls - - which is exactly what he looked like when he fell over. V3OL stumbled around, his torso sparking and hissing from the socket his arm was intended to occupy. "I'm really sorry about that," I said as he shut down. And I was, but I wasn't too worried -- Particle would be able to fix him up.

There was a rumbling sound and a huge chunk of floor fell away right in front of me. One of the few remaining patrons toppled backwards and would have fallen if I hadn't flown in and pulled him away. Once he was safe I saw a pair of red-clad arms trying to find purchase amongst the rubble. They finally gripped something and began to pull.

"Yo, 'Shot!" I shouted. "More company!"

"Funny," Hotshot said. "You'd think *Lionheart* would just *fly* up through that hole."

"The hole *he* created," I added.

"The hole that could have *killed* an innocent man," Hotshot pointed out.

"Stop trying to cloud the issue," the Gunk said, pulling himself to his Lionheart-clad feet. "I'm bringing you *both* in."

Hotshot and I glanced at each other, then back at the Gunk.

"Like *hell*," we both said. Hotshot whipped a pair of darts from his belt and fired them into Gunk's chest while I grabbed a steak knife from one of the tables and took aim at his head. He walked straight into them, taking the blasts like they were nothing, as civilians scrambled around like ants whose hill had just been kicked over. Apparently when he regained control over his malleable body (I *gave* him that control, I cursed at myself), he also gained the ability to make himself even denser than Noble's head.

"Firing around all these innocent people? For *shame*," he said. "You won't escape. Your kind never do."

"Go ahead, *Gunk*!" I shouted. "Play it up for the crowd!" I socked him in the gut, making my own body as dense as his. The result was that neither of us felt much of anything.

He swatted me aside like a roach and charged Hotshot. "And *you!* You were in my LightCorps! You're betraying everything we stood for."

"Lionheart *never* called it 'his'," Hotshot spat.

I leapt to help, but by now the few people left in the restaurant were charging for the door in a wave, pushing me back. I leapt over their heads and saw Gunk blocking a punch from Hotshot, delivering one of his own to the hero's jaw.

"Tsk, tsk," I said. "No manners at *all*!" I jackhammered his shoulders, knocking him away from Hotshot, and followed up with an aerial kick to the face.

"Come on, Lionheart!" I shouted. "Why don't you *fly* after me? Huh?"

"I don't *need* to fly to deal with the likes of *you*." He jumped at me, catching me around the waist. "Let's see how well *you* fly with a *passenger*!"

"I've got a better idea!" Hotshot flew up and grabbed the Gunk's ankles. "Josh! Make a wish!"

Catching his meaning, the two of us drifted in different directions, pulling the Gunk between us. Visible strain appeared on his face as he fought to keep himself solid and finally, let go of me, swinging through the air. Hotshot hurled him at the wall and he crashed, breaking through into the gift shop which, by now, was as empty as the restaurant.

I gave Hotshot a mid-air high-five and we both swept through the hole after him. We found him lying in a pulverized glass display case, picking shards out of his shredded (but non-bleeding) flesh.

I charged him and started pounding. My fists struck like sledgehammers and, the more blows I landed, the more it seemed to affect him. It was like touching a flat LCD computer screen -- the colors were all distorted wherever I would make contact, and the distortion flowed out in ripples.

"Josh! Fall back!"

Trusting my partner implicitly, I fell away. Hotshot leapt at the Gunk, holding a five-dollar, spire-topped model of Simon Tower. He drove it into the center of the proud Lion emblem on the shapeshifter's chest, then pounded it in further with both fists. When he dove out of the way I saw that the model was glowing.

"Hit the deck!" he screamed. Just as I managed to fall to the floor and cover my face, the model blew, spraying the entire gift shop with orange slime.

I looked up to see that the bottom half of the Gunk's Lionheart-body was still intact, black boots and all. From the waist up, though, drooped a skeleton dripping in goo, flailing about like a marionette having a seizure.

"Did that stop him?" Hotshot moaned, not really looking.

"Slowed him down," I said as the slime began to creep back in towards the skeleton. "I don't really think you *can* kill a shapeshifter like that. He's already starting to re-form."

"Okay, that's it, we're out of here." Hotshot charged up a ceiling tile and blew open a hole to the roof.

"Wait, why don't we just wait for someone to show up and *see* him?" I asked.

"He's probably using Mental Maid to keep anyone from coming until he's reformed!" Hotshot shouted. "Don't *you* feel the urge to run away?"

"Yeah, but I doubt that has anything to do with Mental Maid," I said. "Let's blow."

We flew up through the hole (Gunk had only reformed about an inch of his torso by then) and were about to blast into the sky when we got hit by the sound of a rising, sorrowful chorus.

"I can't let you go anywhere," the Conductor said. He was sitting on the rail with his arms crossed and his eyes blazing.

"Aw, *geez*, not you too, Ted," I said, landing by my friend. "You *know* me! Do you really think I'm capable of this?"

"I *thought* I knew you!"

"Just go look in that hole! You'll see I'm telling the truth."

For a second he looked like he was going to do it, but then he scowled and muttered, "I don't want to."

I cursed. "Do you really think you can *stop* us, Ted?" I asked. This was a foolish thing, because at that moment he cranked the volume on the choir up to ear-splitting and both Hotshot and I fell to our knees, clutching our heads.

"Okay, okay!" I believe you can stop us!"

The music fell back down to tolerable levels. Ted's voice was still loud.

"You're *rabbiting*, Josh! Didn't I tell you that's as good as an admission of guilt?"

"Not *this* time, Ted! Not *any* time! Come on, I've got to get out of here so we can find a way to prove I'm innocent. I trust you Ted. You know you can trust me. Please, *please* trust me now."

He exhaled and closed his eyes.

"Go."

"Really?"

"I couldn't stop you. You were too fast for me. Now get the hell out of here before I change my mind."

"Thank y--"

"*Go!*"

Hotshot and I only spared a glance for Ted, who looked more enraged and confused than anyone I'd ever seen before. With a silent prayer, we rose into the night and left him behind.

RABBIT

The phone rang about six times before a connection was made on the other end. Rather than the angelic female voice I'd hoped to hear, though, I got a horny teenage boy muttering, "--me *alone*, Tom, who'd be calling *you*?" Then in an artificially deepened voice he said, "Hello, Heather?"

"Sorry to disappoint you, Quentin," I said. "It's Josh Corwood. You know, Annie's friend. Is she there?"

"Oh," he muttered, not even attempting to mask the disappointment in his voice. "Nah, she's not here."

I cursed mentally and said, "Hey, let me talk to Tom."

Quentin snorted into the phone. "Whatever." Then, his mouth away from the receiver, "he wants to talk to *you* mushbrain."

There were sounds of a brief tousle on the end and finally I heard Tom asking, "Hello?"

"Tom? It's Josh."

"Josh! Hey, how're you doing?"

"I'm okay buddy. Look, can you tell me where your sister is? It's kind of important."

"Sorry, I don't know," he said. "When she got home this afternoon she was all upset and crying and stuff. Mom took her out somewhere." Then he fell to a hush and I could just picture him in the living room, eyes darting from side to side to make sure no one was watching. "I think she broke up with that creep Todd," he hissed, his voice equal parts informative and suggestive.

"Yeah," I said, "I think I heard that somewhere. Look, I don't suppose you have any idea where she went or what time she's coming back."

"Sorry."

"Do you at least know if she's okay?"

The other end grew silent for a moment and I heard a sharp breath. "Yeah," Tom finally said. "She's fine right now."

I shook off the strangeness of his reply -- I didn't have time to dissect it. "Okay. Look, do me a favor, if you see her *don't* tell her I called. I'll catch up with her later."

"I'll keep quiet, but what about Quentin?"

"Are you *still* on the phone?" a cranky voice bellowed.

"I think his mind is probably on other things," I said. "Thanks, buddy. Good-bye."

I hung up the pay phone – I didn't dare use my cell, Particle could track that effortlessly. Next to me Hotshot frowned and said, "No luck?"

"None. Dammit, if there were *anybody* I'm sure I could convince of my innocence--"

"We'll find somebody. But for now, let's get moving. We're not exactly the most inconspicuous fellas on the face of the Earth."

That was an understatement. We'd pulled our masks off, tucked our capes away and put on a couple of castoff jackets we dug out of a goodwill dumpster. In other words, we may as well have been wearing a neon sign reading, "Trying not to be noticed."

"Where do you think we should go? I've got an apartment--"

"Probably the first place they'd check," Hotshot said.

"Yeah, you're right. Hey, wait a minute, how *thoroughly* would they check it?"

"Pretty well. Why?"

"*Crap.* I need to make another phone call -- you more change?"

He dug into his pockets. "Here. What's going on?"

"Nothing, I hope." I dropped the change into the phone and pounded the keys. It rang once, then waited a supernaturally long time before ringing again. Then another excruciating pause before the third ring, when it was finally picked up.

"Hello?"

"Sheila, it's Josh."

"Josh? What's going on? You're all over the news! There's a manhunt for Copycat and Lionheart just rose from the freaking *dead* or something and--"

"Sheila! I can't talk long, just *listen*. First of all, that's *not Lionheart.* Second, remember when I told you never to break into my apartment again?"

"Yeah?"

"I need you to break into my apartment again."

I saw a flash in the sky that got me very nervous. "I need you to break in, find my notebook -- you *know* which notebook -- and *destroy* it. Shred it, burn it, *eat* it, but don't leave a scrap of paper big enough to read so much as a *vowel*, you understand?"

"Well no, but--"

"Gotta go." I hung up and looked at Hotshot. "Did you just see what I saw?"

"What did you see?"

I stepped out of the phone book and pointed to the sky. *"That."*

Spectrum was lancing through the sky over the streetcorner we occupied. At first I wasn't sure if he saw us or not. Then I decided he'd *absolutely* seen us and I was wondering if he realized who we were. This question was answered a few seconds later when a laser blast sizzled past my head and melted a hole the size of a silver dollar in the brick wall next to the phone.

"I think he may have noticed us," I said.

We shed our trenchcoats and blasted into the sky, yanking our masks into place. Another blast ripped at the air between us and we both tore off, giving Spectrum two targets to concentrate on.

"I don't suppose it would do any good to tell you I'm innocent, would it?" I asked.

"I've never met the man who admitted his own guilt," Spectrum said.

"I was afraid you'd say that." Then, taking a cue from First Light, I took his light-manipulation powers and turned them back on him, flashing his face with a high-intensity beam of pure white light. For a moment I shuddered to think how much it looked like the Soul Ray. The beam hit him square in the eyes, but he didn't even flinch.

"Copycat, I'm *king* of light manipulation!" he shouted. "Do you really think you could get me *that* way?"

I dodged another blast and looked around for Hotshot, who was buzzing the rooftops with his arms extended out from his sides, like a flying cross laid flat. "Hey!" I shouted, "a little help here?"

"You're fighting too literally, kid!" he shouted. I think he said something else, too, but I lost track of what it was when a laser clipped my shoulder. My largely-insulated suit protected me a bit, but I would still have to treat at least a second-degree burn there.

I spun in the air and aimed my good right first at Spectrum's jaw. Hotshot shouted something else, but again I missed it.

"Sorry, Scott!" I said, bumping up my speed so it would hopefully be enough to take him out. My fist made contact with his chin, right where I aimed it.

Then it passed *through* his chin.

Then, unable to stop in time, my entire body passed through *his* entire body.

"That's what I was trying to *tell* you, kid!" Hotshot shouted. "Spectrum controls light-rays! That doesn't mean he can *fly*! He turns himself invisible during a fight and *projects* himself into the sky! You're fighting a *hologram,* the real Spectrum is on one of these rooftops!"

I thought about how Spectrum's power must work - - he was bending light rays around himself so that Hotshot and I couldn't see him. But I had *his* light-bending powers. Dodging the occasional laser-burst projected from the hologram (I guess he was able to concentrate light from any point) I *felt* the light-rays in the area, trying to find a disturbance, a spot where the rays bent.

"There!" I shouted, pointing at the roof next to the one Hotshot was strafing. I tried to restore the bent rays to their natural position, but Spectrum fought me. He began flickering in and out, which only made him that much more noticeable.

Hotshot took my direction and charged Spectrum's *real* body, slamming him hard. The hologram vanished and Spectrum clicked solidly into view.

"Dammit, Copycat is *innocent!*" Hotshot was shouting as I landed. "Do you really thing I'd have broken him out if he *wasn't?*"

"'Lionheart' has you *all* snowed," I said.

"You're *insane!*" Spectrum wrenched himself from Hotshot and sent out a flash that temporarily blinded us both. When my eyes cleared there were dozens of Spectrums standing on the rooftop.

"That one," I said, pointing to the only one that didn't *feel* artificial. Hotshot slammed him again and this time he went down fast.

Blake M. Petit

"Hey, 'Shot! I think I see the Arachnid headed this way. Is he holding a *camera*?"

"Don't ask. I'm really getting tired of fighting my friends."

"We won't have to," I said. "Is Spectrum still woozy?"

"Yeah, I slammed him good."

"Then just stay quiet."

When the Arachnid crested the building a minute later, he didn't find a beaten Spectrum and two fugitives. He found me, a Spectrum hologram wrapped around my body, while the real Spectrum and Hotshot lay invisible.

"Did you see them?" he asked.

"They got my shoulder," I said clutching the wounded one. "I'm going in to get patched up. They're headed towards Barks Plaza."

"Got it," Arachnid said, and he skittered away.

"Neat trick," Hotshot said. I dropped the hologram and the invisibility shield. Spectrum, groggy, lifted his head.

"You won' get away," he moaned. "Why're you doin' this?"

"You'll thank us later," I said, and we both took off, leaving him there.

"He's right about one thing, Josh," Hotshot said. "We can't run forever. We can't even leave the *city* thanks to Mental Maid."

"Morrie," I said.

"What?"

"Nothing. We need some place we can stop and think. Do you know of anywhere we can go?"

"Maybe... no. That woman's been through enough. Only as a last resort. Is there anyone *you* trust to hide us for a while?"

I thought about it for a long moment. "Yeah," I said. "There just might be."

JUST THOUGHT WE'D DROP IN

I hovered outside the window of Annie's brownstone, my mask yanked down away from my face. "Are you *sure* this is going to work?" Hotshot asked, drifting above me and constantly glancing about for incoming Capes.

"Have you got a better idea?" I hissed. "Look, Tom's a good kid, okay. I'd trust him with my life."

"You sure this isn't just an excuse to be around when Miss Sinistah gets back?"

"Give me a *little* credit, will you?" I glanced in the window to see Tom sitting at his desk, shuffling through a deck of Cape and Mask cards. Quentin, I gratefully noted, was nowhere to be seen. Softly, hopefully light enough so that only Tom would hear it, I tapped on the glass.

"*Josh?*" he said, opening the window. "What are you doing out *there*?"

"I need some help, man! Can I come in?"

"But you're -- in the air, and... um... I guess so."

"Great," I said, drifting in the window. "Oh, by the way, I brought a friend."

My partner glided in and landed. "Hi, Tom."

"*Hotshot*! And Josh... you're *Copycat*? But... *you're* not *dead*!"

"Thanks for noticing. Long story, man."

"The guy on the news said you two were wanted. He gave us a number to call--"

"Not *this* again. Don't you trust me, Tom?"

"I... I *thought* I did, but--"

"Tom. I saved your life, for God's sake!"

"No you didn't!"

"I *did*. Tom, that was *me* in the Shift costume."

His face wrapped up in disbelief. "That's impossible."

"It's not. Look, get that 'Shift' card you got autographed, I'll prove it to you."

As Tom dug the card out of his binder I grabbed a scrap of paper and a pencil from his desk. "Watch," I said, my hand trembling. I'd never had the most consistent handwriting. I hoped it would be enough now.

"There," I said, shoving the paper next to the card. I'd written "Shift" on it, copying my earlier autograph as accurately as I could. Tom's eyes bulged.

"You *are* Shift!" he shouted. "Oh my *God* this is so cool I *knew* you weren't really a bad guy what's going on have you been *framed* yeah I'll bet that's it are you on the run do you need help what can *I* do?"

"Whoa, Tom! Slow down. And no more coffee for you. Is your sister home yet?"

"Naw, she and mom are still gone. And Quentin went to his *girl*-friend's house." His eyes suddenly lit up all over again. "Annie! She's a Cape too, isn't she? I *knew* it! I *knew* she was Glamour Girl!"

"Um... not quite. Look, I'll explain everything, I promise, but let me use the phone first, okay?"

"Oh... all right."

I picked up the phone (which was next to Quentin's bed) and dialed Sheila's number. Tom started offering Hotshot food -- everything from fruit to pot roast. Finally Hotshot agreed to a peanut butter sandwich just to get the kid out of the room for a few minutes.

"Excitable sort, isn't he?"

"Yeah," I said, putting the phone down, "but he's a good one. No answer from Sheila -- she must still be at my place."

"Unless they found her there," Hotshot added.

"So what's our next move?" I asked.

"I haven't the slightest idea," he said. "We should be safe enough for now, but it's really only a matter of time before they find us."

"So how do I prove I was telling the truth? Blow the Gunk up in front of everyone?"

"That'll be tough, getting close to him now," Hotshot said.

"Yeah, I know. God, it's just so *frustrating* to think about that son of a bitch traipsing around wearing Lionheart's face."

"But *how* do we expose the Gunk?"

"Freeze him?"

"Icebergg isn't around to copy powers from, remember?"

"Cut him up?"

"He's got an army to keep us from getting that close."

"Filling his shower with hydrochloric acid?"

"Tempting... no, how do we get back in there, get *close* to him, without looking like we're trying to assassinate Lionheart?"

There was a crash and we both turned our attention to the doorway, where Tom stood over a broken plate with a thick peanut butter sandwich and an empty glass surrounded by a pool of milk with so much chocolate powder in it there was sludge at the bottom.

"You're going to assassinate *Lionheart*?" Tom gasped.

"No! Tom, it's not like that," Hotshot said, but Tom pulled back, shouting directly in his face.

"You're going to try to kill Lionheart! Get him, Josh! Stop him!"

I let out an exhausted sigh. "You've got to trust me, Tom. That guy you saw on the news is *not Lionheart*. He's a Mask and he's hurt a *lot* of good people. We're running away so we can figure out a way to *stop* him."

As soon as I was done, Tom's face shifted from rage to shock. "Oh my God. What are you gonna do? Can I help? I've got these walkie-talkies--"

"Tom?" resounded Cynthia Harmon's voice from the living room. "I'm home!"

I swallowed. "You want to help, Tom, go make sure your mom doesn't find us here. Oh, and find out where your sister is."

Tom gave me a smart little salute. "Aye-aye, sir!" He spun on his heel like it was razor-edged and left the room.

"A *good* kid," I said, "but *way* too excitable."

Hotshot stared at me, looking considerably astounded.

"What? What is it?"

He did a double-take. "You don't *see* it?"

"See what?"

"He was ready to hand me my head when he thought I was going to hurt Lionheart, but *you* he trusts like you were Pope Josh Copycat the Fourth! It was the same when you proved you were Shift, his whole *face* changed."

"So?"

"That's because *Shift saved his life*, Josh. *You* saved his life."

I turned this over in my head for just a moment before it clicked. "No--"

"Yeah. He's one of *us*. Tom Harmon has the Heart of the Lion."

CAVALRY

It took Tom about ten minutes to get back, and when he did he was practically bounding off the walls. "Sorry I took so long, guys, but I had the toughest time convincing Mom I was tired and wanted to go to bed."

"I wonder why," Hotshot said.

"Annie's staying at our aunt's house. Mom said she just needed time away." My throat violently contracted as I wondered if she was, in fact, hiding from *me*.

Hotshot must have seen something in my face, because he put a hand on my shoulder.

"She'll be all right, Josh."

"I know. I'm just... I'm worried about her."

"Don't," Tom said. "I'll know if she's in trouble."

I raised an eyebrow at that. "Yeah... Will Quentin be home soon?"

Tom shook his head. "Nah, ever since he got to be a *teen*ager he stays out until he knows Mom is gonna get mad at him."

"Good," I said. "Why don't you take a seat, man? We've got a story to tell you."

"And it's not necessarily the nicest story," Hotshot said, "but you're a special kid, Tom, and you deserve the truth."

"But you've got to *promise* me you can keep this a secret, Tom. It's too important for you to talk about to anybody who doesn't already know."

He nodded. "Okay. I promise."

That was all we needed. All three of us knew that Tom Harmon couldn't possibly break a promise to *me,* even if he didn't know why.

Hotshot and I explained a lot to Tom -- about how Morrie's world was set up, about our place and his sister's place in it. Hotshot told what really happened to Lionheart and I punctuated it with what had happened to me, from the Gunk's appropriation of Lionheart's face through the truth about Morrie and Mental Maid (which Hotshot was hearing for the first time) and right through to our escape. And if you were to ask us later why we were sharing so much with a child, it would be because we simply couldn't keep the truth from someone like us.

"You see how serious this is, Tom?" Hotshot asked when we were done. "If we don't stop the Gunk, he's going to have everyone in the world thinking he's Lionheart."

"Until he moves to *crush* them," I said.

"I don't understand," Tom said. "Why would they do that in the *first* place? Aren't *real* heroes enough?"

I turned to Hotshot, giving him a "Do *you* want to field this one?" look.

"Just because fights are scripted doesn't mean the spirit isn't real, Tom," Hotshot said.

"And just because someone catches a Mask, that doesn't make him a hero," I added. "How many bad guys has the Gunk fought in the past ten years?"

"But... why *me*?" Tom asked. "Why are you telling *me* all of this? Is it just because you have a crush on my sister?"

Hotshot snickered and I felt my cheeks flush. "What, is *everybody* talking about that? No, Tom, it's a lot more complicated than that."

"Try me. I can handle it."

"I know you can," I said.

And for the first time in my life, I explained to someone what the Heart of the Lion meant. Tom nodded as he listened, keeping a smile on his face. It wasn't a look of realization -- it was more something he had always known was finally being confirmed.

He sat down at his desk and began flipping through his playing card binder. "So you guys need to find a way to get past a whole punch of brainwashed good guys to get to one bad guy, right?"

"In a nutshell," Hotshot said.

"Took us twenty minutes," I laughed. "Leave it to the kid to encapsulate the whole situation perfectly in one question."

"When I'm playing the card game," he said, "and my guys are outnumbered, the only way I can beat the *bad* guy is to hold him off until I pull more *good* guys out of the deck."

"A good thought," Hotshot said, "but who can we call in as the cavalry? Every superhuman in the city is under Gunk's spell, except for the two of us."

Tom turned another page and I saw two rows of older-looking, yellowed cards that leapt from the plastic at me. One of them I had seen before. The rest...

"No, 'Shot," I said. "Not *every* superhuman. Just the *active* ones."

There were six cards on this page, all artificially aged, labeled "Vintage Series." The first one was Lionheart, the card Tom had shown me the last time I'd visited him. The other cards completed the set.

Card two featured a man in gleaming silver-and-blue chainmail with a red tunic and a white star. He had no powers, according to the body text on the card, but was a master swordsman and skilled in almost every martial art. His shield had served as an inspiration to American servicemen in every war since the 1900's began, until he vanished after Lionheart was gone. He was the Defender.

The next card showed a flying man in black, red and brown. The one-foot warrior had a pair of wings, like an angel, but a razor-sharp pair of talons that could be brutal in combat. A brilliant scientist, the card said, his intellect was only rivaled by his rage at the injustices of the world. He was the Condor.

The card after that featured a woman in an identical costume, but her color scheme was orange, yellow and white. Her wings were not as harsh and her hands had no blades. Her calm demeanor and boundless compassion was a tempering influence -- not only to her husband, Condor, but to all who met her. She was called Oriole.

The fifth card was a modern knight in shining armor -- high-tech armor complete with Tasers, rocket-boots and bulletproof glass for the faceplate. The armor was gun-metal gray, but a slick paint job of red, black and blue racing stripes gave him a sleek, powerful look. It was the Tin Man.

The last card was an attractive, long-haired blonde woman in a black leotard with yellow leggings and a red-and-yellow electric motif. Her most obvious power was super-speed, the card said, but in fact that was only a manifestation of her ability to speed up or slow down time itself. She had been known as Lightning.

Those five cards, along with the Lionheart and a more recent Hotshot, would comprise the old LightCorps. None of the others, alone, carried quite the level of reverence that Lionheart did. But together... making a stand...

"Can you get them?" I asked Hotshot.

"Christ, Josh, those guys retired..."

"Because they didn't want to fight without Lionheart, I know. But this is different. We're asking them to fight *for* Lionheart. For his legacy. You can't tell me that none of them would be willing to fight for *that*."

He couldn't.

"Are any of them still in Siegel City?"

"Yeah, the Defender."

"Go to him," I pleaded. "Tell him what's happening and send him out to get the rest of them."

"Not *all* of them," Hotshot said, staring at the pages. I saw his finger trace gently across the Lightning card. "Some people have suffered enough. I won't call them *all* back. Not even for this."

"Okay, then," I said. "Get whoever you can."

"You're right," he said. "But I don't have to like it. Be good, Tom," he said. Then he climbed out on the window and then he was gone.

"Now what?" Tom asked.

"Now... I guess we wait."

We sat for about ten seconds before Tom couldn't stand it anymore. He picked up his game cards.

"Wanna learn how to play?" he asked.

TOM'S SECRET

After I finally had a marginal understanding of the game rules, Tom proceeded to soundly defeat me three times (twice, I grudgingly noted, with alternate versions of Animan.)

"Another round?" he asked with a mildly annoying grin.

"I dunno," I said. "There's only so many times a man can get whipped before he decides to move on to a new game. You don't have a cribbage set around, do you?"

"A who?"

"Never mind." I picked up the deck I'd been playing with and began shuffling through the cards, examining the pictures, reading the body text and getting a pretty good laugh over some of the things I saw -- Spectrum's flight speed, for instance.

I stopped shuffling when I came across a Miss Sinistah card. I gazed at it for a long moment before it spilled out of my fingers and on the floor. I sighed deeply.

"You're worried about her, aren't you?" Tom asked.

"A little, yeah," I lied. I was actually worried a *lot*. "I just have this nasty feeling that Todd's going to be after her."

"You can relax," Tom said. "She's all right."

"How do you know that?"

He smiled. "Can *you* keep a secret?"

"After today, you have to ask? Spill."

"Well... every so often I get this... *feeling*. This sensation -- I can't really explain it, but I always get this flash -- like I'm seeing through Annie's eyes, and I know she's in trouble. That's how I *really* knew she was a Cape... or... Mask, I guess. I never really saw enough to tell which side she was on. But she's always gotten out of it. She can take care of herself."

Was *that* it? I'd sensed the first time I ever met Tom that he had a power -- was it this "danger sense" that linked him to his sister? "How often does this happen, Tom?"

"Not often -- maybe every couple of months." That made sense. With Morrie's positively anal concerns about safety, the chance of Annie ever having been in *real* danger often were pretty slim.

"And you always have this -- 'feeling' -- before you get that flash?"

"Always. It kind of starts in the pit of my stomach, like I swallowed a feather duster."

"And then it moves up, right? Into your chest... into your throat?"

"How did--" then he choked, like there was something fluffy lodged in his windpipe. "Oh no... it's happening."

"I know," I gagged as the sensation traveled up my neck and into my head. "I feel it too."

As the sensation hit my nose I sneezed. When it reached my ears, I began to hear a sound like somebody breaking things.

When it reached my eyes, I saw.

It wasn't entirely clear -- it was like looking through a blue filter, but I could see a small apartment, meticulously decorated in a country motif. The color scheme, I'd be willing to bet, was either sunflower yellow or cream -- I couldn't tell.

Over the kitchen counter was one of those charming painted menus that read "Tillie's Diner. 1 -- Take it. 2 -- Leave it." In the corner was a water cooler with a knitted cover and fruit magnets peppered the refrigerator.

The images all clicked into place just in time for me to see Dr. Noble shatter the water cooler with a teke burst. Water gushed out of the fabric, which collapsed in on itself, shards of plastic ripping through. Then Noble spun around and glared directly at me and, for a moment, I felt a jolt of fear, certain he could see me. This was ridiculous, of course, I was just seeing what Annie saw.

Which meant, I realized with a churn of my stomach, that look of homicidal rage on his face was meant for *her*. Despite myself, I began to mutter, "I'll kill him, I'll kill him if he hurts her, I swear to *God*..."

"Where is he, you little bitch?" he snarled. His voice resonated through my ears, but it sounded empty, hollow, like someone talking through a balloon.

"I don't know, Todd!" she shouted, and my heart leapt. Not because she was angry or in danger, you understand, but because her voice did not crack or waver. She didn't sound afraid, she just sounded *mad*, and I was proud.

"Get out of my aunt's house!" she said. "How *dare* you barge in here and start *breaking* things?"

"Because I *know* you're hiding that little prick and *I want him.*"

"Go to Hell!"

"Yes!" I shrieked. "You tell him, Annie!"

My viewpoint suddenly darted around the room, as though I was frantically looking for something.

"Who said that?" Annie asked.

"She can *hear* me?" I squeaked.

"I didn't hear nothin'" Noble grumbled.

"Sometimes she can," Tom asked, "if I get really excited. I try not to do it, though. I don't want her knowing I can do this yet."

As we watched Noble continue to tear up Aunt Tillie's apartment looking for me, I reached out and grabbed Tom's shoulder. "There anything else about this you think you should be telling me, Tommy?"

"Well... sometimes, if I get *really* mad... I start to feel like I'm falling."

"*Falling?*" I asked. "What happens *then*?"

"I don't know... I've always pulled myself back."

"I swear, Todd," she was saying, "if you don't get out of here *right now*, I'll--"

"You'll *what*?" he asked, charging right up to her face. His breath was a mixture of tobacco and cheap beer and I suddenly found myself wondering how many stereotypes it was possible to cram into a single being.

"What are you gonna do, Miss Sinistah?" he spat. "Gonna call your new boyfriend? Sic that little psycho on me? He already killed the Gunk, who knows what he'll do to *you*?" Then the right side of his lip curled up into a nasty little sneer. "Then again, maybe you *like* whatever he's doing to you."

I saw a hand flash in front of me making solid contact with Todd's cheek.

"I can't believe I ever had feelings for someone who can't even use my real name," she spat.

"You *bitch*!" He raised his arm, clenched in a fist--

--and I was falling. Unlike Tom, though, I didn't even *try* to stop myself. I fell and fell and then--

--I was there, my left arm holding back Noble's right first, my right hand clamped around his incredibly thick neck.

"You're never hurting her again, do you hear me?" I raged. He choked and sputtered in my grip and I noticed all at once that the hollow quality of his voice was gone and the world was no longer blue.

"*Josh*?" Annie shrieked. "Where did *you* come from?"

"Your place," I said, driving a fist to Noble's gut and hitting his neck with a combination of Annie's strength and his own telekinesis. I smacked him across the face with my elbow and nailed him with a strategically-placed knee in the jaw as he fell to the floor.

"How did you *get* here?" Annie gasped. "It was like you just... *appeared*."

My immediate reaction was to tell her, "There's something you should know about Tom," but my jaw clamped shut before the words could even form. I'd promised him I'd keep his secret, after all.

"Long story," I said, but the point became moot a second later when I heard, echoing around in my skull, Tom's voice.

"Josh, look out!" he shouted. My head felt a little it was exploding for just an instant and he snapped into existence. There was no pop, no flash of light -- it was like someone spliced two frames of a movie together, one without Tom and the next with him.

He lashed out as soon as he was there, kicking at Noble's hand, which had been reaching for my leg while I was talking to Annie. I use Noble's telekinesis to mash him against the wall, and Tom and I both gave Annie a sheepish grin.

"Tom? Josh, *what* is going on here?"

I raised an eyebrow at Tom in a "we'd better tell her," look and he nodded. "The kid's been watching you for a while now, whenever you were in trouble," I said.

"Not just *her*," Tom said. "When Noble was about to attack, just before I jumped over here, I could see through *your* eyes, too, Josh."

I high-fived Tom as Noble growled. "I never *did* like that little freak," he said. "Come on, *Annie*. What do you do now? Harbor this wanted criminal?"

"He didn't do it," Tom shouted. "Copycat is *innocent*! *You're* the bad guy, he told me all about it!"

"What?" Annie cried.

"Thanks, pal." I looked to Annie. "You know it, Tom. I know it. Noble *absolutely* knows it. Question is... does your *sister* believe it?"

"You believe he's innocent, don't you Annie?" Tom asked.

She furrowed her brow and her eyes darted between the three of us. "Tom... I..."

"Annie?" I whispered. "Annie you *know* me. You remember what I said to you in the arboretum that night? Do you really think that guy could do the things they're accusing me of?"

Her lips turned in and quivered.

But only for a moment.

"Of course I believe you, Tom," she said. Then, turning to Noble, added, "Josh may not be perfect, but he'd *never* hurt an innocent man. If *you* weren't so thick-skulled, you'd know that too."

"He *does* know that," I said. "He's in on it."

There was a sudden smash against the back of my head and the "Tilly's Kitchen" sign showered my shoulders with splinters. It didn't hurt, really, but it was enough to break my concentration and free Noble.

"Word of advice, punk," Noble said, smacking my face. "Pinning a guy down isn't good enough when he's telekinetic."

"I'll remember that," I said, giving him a roundhouse blow to the gut, which I quickly followed with a good old-fashioned ear boxing. Noble shrieked and fell back, then telekinetically hurled me at the ceiling, which split apart on impact. I found myself outside, crashing to the roof of an apartment building not that far from the one where Hotshot and I had pulled our fire rescues.

Noble, as expected, popped up through the hole a few seconds later. What he *didn't* expect was for me to be waiting. I grabbed his cape and he executed an incredibly awkward arc, crashing face-first to the roof.

"Havin' fun yet, Joshie?" he said, picking himself up.

"Oh, *loads.*"

"I'm glad. You'll be short on it once you get a taste of the Soul Ray."

"I'll never feel it," I said, driving a kick to his jaw. I came in for a follow-up, but he caught my foot and spun me through the air, away from the building. I slammed into a smokestack one building over just in time to see Annie scrambling to the other roof, shouting at Tom (with absolutely no success) not to follow her.

Noble leapt across the chasm between buildings, aiming his fist at my head. I darted out of the way just in time to see him smash into the steel smokestack, which buckled with the impact. I hurled myself into the air, trying to get the battle as far away from Annie and Josh as possible. I lost track of how far I'd gone or even where the hell I was until Noble caught my cape and yanked down. I sputtered in the air and smashed face-first into a roof that was more ash and soot than any building material. It was the apartment Hotshot and I had helped evacuate. It seemed very long ago. At least no one would be hurt here.

"*Bas*tard," he growled. He piledrove his knee into my back and I'm pretty sure I heard something crack. I *know* I *felt* something crack.

He yanked my head back and began smashing my face into the roof, mixing my blood with ash, shouting all the while. "Think you can get away?" *Smash!* "You're *nothing!*" *Smash!* "Just a measly little worm." *Smash!*

He was then politely suggesting an anatomical atrocity he would like me to perform when two now-familiar Rushes came over me. Heroes were approaching -- thank God.

"That is quite enough, Doctor," said a high, proper voice. "*We* will see to it Copycat is taken into custody."

"He's whaling on the kid!--That's enough.--You're telling me.--No need to *brutalize* the guy.--What a jackass."

First Light and Five-Share had no doubt been combing the city for me, ready to take me in and send me to the stars. Showing up exactly when they did, though... they probably saved my life.

I only wish I could have returned the favor.

WHAT HAPPENED TO PHOTON MAN

Noble stood up from his position at my back and cracked his knuckles. "You folks better back off now. Copycat is *my* capture."

"If you were *just* capturing him, we *would* back off," said a Five-Share.

"You're *beating* the kid," said another.

"This is excessive.--Unnecessary.--Barbaric."

"Do you five share one *brain,* too?" Noble howled. "*I'm* taking him in. Now get out of here."

I pushed myself up and looked over at my would-be saviors. First Light was hovering just out of reach, looking more nervous than a Starfleet officer in a red uniform, while Five-Share had formed a semi-circle around Noble, trying their best to look imposing.

"Aw, let 'em stick around, Todd," I grunted. "Or don't you want them to see a replay of what you did to Photon Man?"

Noble's boot lashed out and made contact with my jaw. My lower lip split against my teeth and I felt the blood begin to trickle from my mouth. I didn't move to wipe it. "There you go," I gurgled. "Perfectly rational conflict resolution."

"What's he talking about, Todd?" a Five-Share asked. "Don't say he's lying.--Seems pretty sure of himself.--We can see right through you.--You suck."

"He's talking out his ass!" Noble yelped. "Come on, if *you* were rabbiting, wouldn't *you* say just about anything to turn folks to your side?"

"Well...--Got a point...--Who knows--"

I cut off the remaining Five-Shares. "Yeah, Todd?" I said. "Then why don't *you* tell them what happened?"

"Photon Man was rabbiting after he was caught burglarizing Morrie's quarters. I chased him down and I accidentally accelerated his energy production. That's a danger you gotta face when two guys with electromagnetic powers face off. That don't mean I did it on *purpose.*"

"Like hell," I said. "First Light... I've got to borrow something from you for a minute."

I pulled in energy from her and created an image in the air above the roof, the way she had done at Icebergg's trial. What I was displaying, though, were the images Mental Maid planted in my head right before Hotshot broke me out of Simon Tower.

"Here's what *really* happened to Photon Man," I said as the hologram flashed. It looked like a comet streaking across the Siegel skyline at first. As it approached, though, we could see it was a man in midnight black. His clothes were covered in swirls of yellow and milky white -- it was like he was *wearing* the night sky.

"You remember what Photon Man *looked* like before you nuked him, Todd?" I asked.

"You son of a--"

"Shut up!" I telekinetically lifted a stray support beam from the burnt-out shell of the building and slammed it into Noble's gut. He went down easy at that point -- we'd both been beaten to the point of collapse. He said it himself -- pinning him down telekinetically just wouldn't have been enough.

The hologram shifted as Photon Man got closer and a second streak appeared in the air behind him. "There's the Doctor," I hissed. "I know you guys can't hear this, but when Mental Maid dropped the scene into my head, I heard every word this mockery of a Cape said. Every syllable. Right now, Noble is telling Photon Man he'll never make it out of the city alive.

"And Photon there is screaming, 'I didn't do it. You *know* I didn't do it'."

In the hologram, Noble caught Photon Man by the boot and hurled him to a rooftop. "Oh, this is my favorite part. Noble's saying, 'I know you didn't. That's because *I* did it'."

Noble placed one large hand over Photon Man's entire face and smiled. "'Not that you'll ever get to *tell* anyone', he says."

There was a crackle of energy around Noble's hand and Photon Man began to glow. Noble dropped the man, now writhing in pain, and smiled. "Maybe *that* will teach you to lay off my woman."

I took a deep breath. "I'd tell you what Photon Man is saying," I said, "but most of it is just unintelligible screaming and the rest... well... you don't want to know."

We watched in mute impotence as Photon Man flapped around like a catfish on a pier. Energy sparked and danced, seeping from him like white blood.

Clawing about like a maniac, Photon Man finally tore the mask from his face and looked at the sky. He had a kind face, with light brown hair and a full beard. Crow's feet were just beginning to appear at the edge of his eyes, which were a crackling blue-white by now, and hemorrhaged energy into the air.

He screamed so hard I could almost hear it.

Then there was a flash and his body was ripped apart in a veil of sparks that looked like an electric snowglobe. The holo-Noble wiped his hands like he'd just finished working in his garden. He gave a quick glance to the "camera," then took off. Then the hologram ended.

"*God...*" muttered one of the Five-Shares. For once, only one of them could bring himself to speak.

"The man whose eyes we saw that through was hiding," I said. "He didn't think the good Doctor saw him. He was wrong."

"Who was it, Copycat?" asked a Five-Share.

"Who else? The next victim. Icebergg."

"Well..." there was a groan as Noble sat up, shaking his head. "Well ain't *you* slick?" He got to his feet. "You guys don't believe this crap do you?"

The Five Shares resumed their circular position around him. I joined them, and First Light drifted into a position above us, probably to keep him from escaping. She didn't have time to regret it.

"But..." Noble was sputtering, "the field--"

"The susceptibility field makes you more willing to accept the lie," said one of Five-Share.

"We've *always* known you were a jackass," said another.

"Fine," he said. "It don't matter. It's not like anybody's ever gonna hear it anyway." As often as he said that, I wondered what movie he'd seen it in.

Three of the Five-Shares were about to question this statement when Noble leapt from the roof in a cloud of ash. He was flying wobbly, like his head was still clouded from the pounding I gave him. That didn't stop him from flying high enough to grab First Light by the ankle, though. There was a blast of energy and he threw her to the roof. She was screaming and clawing at her leg like it had been dipped in acid.

"I'll get him," I said, ready to take off.

"Forget *him*!" Five-Share howled. "Look at *her*!"

First Light was twisting around like a feather in a hurricane. Light screamed away from her in waves and she gave off sparks like a downed power line.

"He did it to *her*, too!" somebody screamed.

I swear, I tried my best to save her. I used Noble's own power to try to reverse the flow of energy in her body and restore her to normal, but he'd boosted the output so high there was no way I could leech it away in time. I threw myself on the nearest Five-Share and put up the strongest teke-shield I could manage, what with Noble flying away like he did.

In the split-second before the blast, I could hear Tom's voice tearing through my head. *"JOSH! NO! JOSH!"* My head began to bloat again, like it did when Tom teleported before, but I forced the sensation back. I wouldn't let him through.

Then First Light convulsed, screamed and her entire body went off like a magnesium flare. The echo of the blast tore at my eardrums and I felt a white hot sensation consume my body.

It's actually surprising that the shield worked as well as it did. The Five-Share I'd protected was fine. And the upper half of my body didn't have a scratch on it.

The bottom half of my body, I cannot speak for. It no longer existed.

ISSUE FOURTEEN

DESPERATION

You would expect having your body vaporized from the waist down would be incredibly painful, but that really wasn't the case. The only way to describe the sensation is that it felt *white* -- my head looked down and I saw that I had no legs or feet, but my nerve endings were trying to argue the point. I supposed I was in shock. It's funny to think that I'd reached a point of panic so intense that I was completely rational, but that's really what it was like.

The blackened roof was now just a crater where First Light had been. A passerby would look into the gaping maw and not even guess the bomb that created the hole had been shaped like a human body.

There were charred bones and chunks of meat lying around the hole and rolling down into it. Of the four Five-Shares I hadn't been able to save, only one of them was even marginally intact. The entire front of his body had been scorched totally beyond recognition. His hands were burnt off and the blast sent him flying into the brick and mortar railing that enclosed the roof, snapping his back. I rather hoped he was already dead when he hit.

The remaining Five-Share crawled out from under me and screamed in a high pitched voice that betrayed her as the female. She ripped her mask off and grabbed her most intact brother, cradling him in her arms like a child with a shattered porcelain doll. She was sobbing too hard for me to make out most of what she was saying, but I could hear the occasional name -- "Stevie" was one, "Vince" another.

A few sentences did escape: "Oh you bastard I'll kill you, you *bastard*," over and over again. She rocked her brother back and forth. It was to be expected -- to say she'd only suffered a nasty shock would be a grave disservice, but I had a somewhat more pressing dilemma.

"Five-Share... Five-Share, help..."

She ignored me entirely. I clawed at the roof, dragging myself towards her, constantly trying to push with my legs and having no effect.

"Five-Share... *help*..."

I may as well have been talking to her brother. Five-Share was beyond panic, she was bordering on lunacy, and she was screaming for Noble's head.

My knuckles cut and bleeding from the crawl, I finally made it close enough to reach her. I placed my hand on her back, hoping it would jolt her back to reality.

Instead, it sent a jolt of energy into *me.* The Rush I got from her was stronger than before, perhaps because her power was no longer diluted between six people, and it made me think of a possible escape route. Screaming through gritted teeth, I grabbed at the air, collecting all the power I could from her, pulling it into myself.

Then I said a very brief, very fervent prayer that her remaining brother would be more rational than she, and I teleported.

I immediately regretted this decision.

As I remembered from the last time I did it, Five-Share's teleportation powers did not work the same way Tom's did -- a brief sensation of falling and you were just *there*. When I teleported with Five-Share's power it was a gut-wrenching ride, one that threatened quite persuasively to void my stomach of the cookies Tom had scrounged up for me (I suddenly realized I hadn't had a decent meal since before I visited Flambeaux in the infirmary, two days before.)

The transit somehow popped me out of my numbing shock and I began to feel the pain one would expect when his legs had been blown off and his groin shredded. It was like getting hit by fire and razors and clubs all at once, and the fact that I was even still *conscious* when I arrived is much more than a small miracle.

As the world re-formed around me, my stomach calmed and my legs continued to inform me they were no longer connected to my body. I struggled to get my bearings. I was obviously in Simon Tower, in somebody's living quarters -- the dorms didn't vary much -- but this living room/kitchenette was slightly larger than any I'd been in before. There was a full-size dining table near the kitchen and a large sectional sofa stretched through the living room.

It was on this couch that I materialized, right next to a familiar-looking man in blue sweatpants and a white t-shirt. His feet were up on a coffee table next to the remains of his dinner -- a half-eaten burger and a small logpile of fries -- and there was a scar on his cheek, but other than that the face was the same as four men I'd just seen die.

"Sweet *Christ!*" he shouted as I locked into existence. "Copycat? What's going on? What *happened* to you?"

"Noble," I moaned. Even *talking* hurt at this point. "Used your sister's powers... your brothers..."

"My brothers? What *about* my brothers?"

Damn my honest streak -- I probably shouldn't have brought up his brothers until *after* he got help. "Explosion," I grunted. "Please... help."

"An *explosion*? Are my brothers all right?"

"Five-Share, *please...*"

"Where are my brothers?" He shoved me off the couch and I crashed into the coffee table. The food he'd been munching spilled to the floor. I landed on a squeeze bottle of ketchup and a pool gushed out at my side.

He stood up and clenched his face in a look of concentration. Before I knew what he was doing, before I had a chance to stop him (not that there was much I *could* do), he vanished in a hiss and a spark.

"Help me!" I moaned as loudly as I could, which was actually pretty pathetic. I flailed out with my arm and wrapped my fingers around the ketchup bottle, hurling at the door as hard as I could. It made a good, loud "thump," but nothing more.

"Help me," I groaned again, as the world finally began to swim.

I'm not entirely sure what happened next, things began to mush together in my head, but I am certain the following events occurred:

There was shouting outside the door. I answered it with agonized moans.

There was a loud crash as someone broke the door down.

I looked up and saw a face that I hoped to God really was Animan and that I wasn't just hallucinating.

I managed to croak out, "Totem..."

"You want one of my totems?" he seemed to ask. "Josh, I can't--"

"*Please.* No time."

I think he shook his head. "Of course. Which one?"

I told him and he left me alone in Five-Share's apartment, shattered and bleeding.

The pain from my legs began lancing upwards and my temples started to throb. *Crap*, I thought, *all I need is a headache on top of everything else.*

I slumped to the ground and my head rolled to the side. I was looking at the door, but I was no longer seeing much of anything. I thought about the Gunk and I wondered who would stop him, although even at that point I had no doubt that *somebody* would. I thought about Dr. Noble and hoped that the girl from Five-Share would have a chance to tell people what really happened before he got her. I thought about Annie, and I prayed that Tom and Hotshot would make sure she was okay, and I knew that they would.

Somehow I became aware of a pair of feet racing towards me and I felt something press into my right hand. The five points on the object jabbed into my flesh as I clutched it as tightly as I could. I poured every ounce of concentration I had left into that hand, and I felt a tiny jolt, and the very act of thinking that hard was enough to make the world finally go away.

RECOVERY ROOM

The first thing that came to mind when I woke up was, "*Ow.*"

The second thought was, "Why am I still alive?" immediately followed by, "Why am I *complaining*?"

Why I was complaining was actually pretty obvious -- I felt like I had been hit repeatedly by a soft, fluffy pillow that was duct taped to the front of a Greyhound bus. I sincerely hoped that every portion of my body ached, because if there was anything left that *didn't*, the other body parts would likely gang up and beat it senseless out of jealousy.

My head pulsated like a snare drum. My lungs were on the verge of collapse and any attempt to lift my arms would have resulted in open revolt. My groin felt like the bottom of a mosh pit, my lip felt like I'd just attempted to play "Flight of the Bumblebee" on a sousaphone, and my earlobes hurt. My *earlobes* hurt. I didn't know earlobes *could* hurt.

Most amazingly of all, my *legs* hurt. I'd heard about amputees feeling "phantom limbs," but somehow I couldn't fathom why, if my brain was going to imagine legs that weren't there, it would imagine them feeling like they'd been run under a steamroller. With incredible effort, I opened my mouth and managed to vibrate my vocal cords just enough to convey the following sentiment: "Uuuuuuuugh."

"Hey, hey," said a deep, baritone voice. "Look who ain't dead yet."

Against my better judgement, I opened my eyes. Moving the lids proved to be an act akin to prying open a manhole cover with a popsicle stick. I was, however, grateful that I'd done it when I saw a warm, brown, grinning face over me. I felt the Rush coming down from him. "How you feelin', bro?" Animan asked.

"I am never... moving... again," I said.

"You just did."

"After... this," I forced out, and somehow we both managed to laugh. Whenever you turn up alive after coming that close to being dead, everything seems a lot funnier.

"Animan?"

"Yeah?"

"If I tried to look down, my head would probably roll off my body. Can you tell me if I've actually got *legs*?"

"Why don't I let you see for yourself?" He went to the door and removed his full-length mirror, which he held over me. The mirror was narrow, but wide enough for me to see that I was clad in sky-blue tights with darker blue trunks and a cape clasped around my neck by a golden seashell. My face was obscured by a star-shaped, purple mask, and my fist was still clenching a tiny, wooden totem.

My legs... *God*, my legs. Where nothing had been before, they had grown back to nearly three inches below the knees. At the bottom of the stumps I could *see* the new flesh creeping forward. Even the blue tights were slithering down after the legs, clothing me as they crept along. The process was slow, but it was happening.

"Interesting..." was all I could say.

"Slick as all *hell*," Animan chortled as he replaced the mirror. I realized, for the first time, I was in his quarters. Amidst the pain I managed to sort out an additional Rush coming from the Conductor, obviously in the next room. I wondered if anyone had seen him dragging me here from Five-Share's place. "The starfish totem, man, how did you know it would save your crazy ass?"

"Reporter's instincts," I grunted. "Gotta be able to recall insignificant details at a moment's notice. Like, for instance, if you cut off a starfish's limb, it'll grow back. Figured your starfish totem might amplify that ability."

"Big chance."

"Hey, if it didn't work, I was dead anyway."

He scratched his chin. "You know, I studied this crap while I was making that totem. If you cut up a starfish, *every piece* grows into an identical starfish."

"There weren't any pieces *left,* man," I said. "Everything was vaporized."

"I hope so," he laughed. "*Last* thing we need is *two* of your ugly face bobbing around here."

We both managed to laugh again and, while it did hurt like hell, it still felt pretty good.

"How long have I been out?" I asked.

"A few hours -- it's the middle of the night."

"What's been going on?"

"Doc Noble is back. *And* full of crap. He swept in not long after I got you here and started telling folks that *you* killed First Light and Five-Share, then you ran off."

I clenched my fist. "It wasn't me who killed 'em. I might as well have..."

"Wasn't your fault, bro."

"Sounds like you finally believe me."

"Hey, when I went in that room only *half* of you was there. You sure as hell didn't look like the dude that *won* the fight."

"You should have seen the *other* guy."

"I *did*. Looks like you got in your share of licks before the doctor took you apart. So spill, man, what really happened out there?"

"Probably just what he said, with the roles reversed. He juiced up First Light more than she could handle, and she blew. Just like he did to Photon Man. I managed to shield one of the Five-Shares and myself -- well, kind of -- and then we lost the rest of them."

Animan called Doctor Noble a string of names that he more than earned and then sat down at his work desk.

"I know," I said. "I agree. But I should have *done* more, man..."

"Don't start *that* talk, J-Man. We both know you did everything you could and we both know it wasn't your fault. This ain't no soap opera. So what's the plan, man?"

"Well, to start with, I'm planning to lie here until I have feet. After that, I'm getting a hold of some reinforcements."

"Reinforcements?"

As we waited for my lower extremities to grow back, I told Animan the plan. He nodded most of the time, accepting every word and I breathed a sigh of relief, figuring that the shock of seeing me blown apart had broken him from the susceptibility field. By the time I'd finished, as slow as I was talking and with Animan occasionally breaking in with questions, it was four a.m. and my legs had grown back to about the halfway point of my calves. Much of the pain was beginning to subside and, in the portions where body parts were actually regenerating, I felt an odd, almost pleasant tingling. If it weren't for the fact that it required the sudden, violent removal of my body parts, I wouldn't mind feeling it more often.

"So let's say Hotshot *does* manage to round up his boys. What good will that do? Won't they just swap over to the Gunk's side as soon as they enter the susceptibility field?"

"Not if they *enter* the field knowing Lionheart is a fraud," I said. "I'm hoping that seeing the original LightCorps will dazzle everyone else enough to break them out of the trance. When everything hits the fan, there are two things we have to do. We've got to expose Lionheart as the Gunk, and we've got to take down the field."

"And that means we've got to take down Mental Maid."

"No," I said. "Morrie."

For a second Animan looked stunned, then his bamboozled expression gave way to a chuckle. "Damn," he said, "Ain't *anything* around here what it seems to be?"

We laughed again. We laughed pretty damn hard. We laughed right up until the door opened and Ted Ossian stepped in, yawning.

"Who're you talking to, man? I'd think you'd want to get some sleep before we head out hunting again tomor--"

His eyes fell on me and he sucked in his breath. "Oh my God. That's him, isn't it? You took in that murderer and you gave him a *totem*!" He spun on his heel and leapt out of the room, hollering at the top of his lungs.

"Ted, wait!"

"I'll get him."

Animan snatched the wolf totem from its peg and charged after him. There was a snarl and a scream, and then the screaming stopped. A few seconds later Animan, as Wolph, stepped back into the room with an unconscious Conductor slung over his shoulder.

"This is beginning to turn into a habit, old boy," he said.

SQUARE ONE

Animan, as himself again, slung Ted into his desk chair and tied him up with an extension cord.

"Is that really necessary?" I asked.

"Hey, *you* ain't the one chasing him down," Animan said. "I'll let him go if he comes to his senses. Which I'm not counting on."

"What do you mean?"

"You haven't seen the way Ted's been acting since you left. He wanted to believe you were innocent, but he's also got a pretty weak will. And after Morrie found out you escaped from him, Ted spent an hour in the office -- probably got an extra dose of susceptibility."

"Weak-willed? He's a Cape, isn't he?"

"That's just it. Ted always wanted to be a superhero growing up -- same as most people here -- and when he found out he had his quasi-telepathic powers he thought it was a dream come true. But he's never been able to do any more with it than make a little music."

"It's not that bad a power."

"Try telling *him* that. He's so self-conscious that his will's been whittled down to just about nothing." He glanced around the room and realized there was nowhere left for him to sit. "Dammit... I'm going get a chair."

He walked out of the room and I was left alone with Ted, out cold. My limbs were starting to feel a bit more fluid by now, so I stretched out my arms and the three-quarters I had of my legs. I put my head back and began flexing the muscles, trying to make sure the blood was flowing properly.

As I laid back, my head began to swim and I was afraid I was going to pass out again -- but it cleared almost instantly and I was back to normal.

And then I started hearing the voice in my head.

"Josh? Josh, are you okay?" screamed the voice. I recognized it immediately.

"Tom?"

"Josh, thank God! I've been trying to find you again ever since... since..."

'Since the big boom?" I offered.

"Yeah..."

"It's cool, Tom. I suffered a -- minor setback, but I'll be fine in a couple of hours."

"Whew." Somehow, Tom managed to mentally sigh in relief. *"Where are you?"*

"Back at Simon Tower. A friend is hiding me, for now, while I recuperate. Have you heard from Hotshot?"

"Not yet."

"How about Annie? Is she okay?"

"She's fine."

"Good. Now why are you up so late? It's past your bedtime, man." He laughed in my head and I knew I'd calmed him down. "I don't suppose I'll be able to keep you from poking around in my head until this thing is over, will I? Just promise me you won't try to come here, okay? No matter what happens, I don't want you popping in."

"Aw, Josh..."

"No 'aws,' kid. *I* don't even want to be involved in this, I'm *sure* not dragging *you* in."

There was a stirring nearby and I looked up to see Ted lifting his head. "Who are you talking to?"

"Some guy who wants me to switch long-distance carriers. You okay?"

"Let's see, my two best friends have me tied to a chair, one's a suspected murderer and the other knocked me out -- I'm just ducky."

"Ted, you're not still on that kick, are you?"

"After you left, Lionheart and Morrie chewed me out for like an *hour*. Do you know what it's like to be chewed out by *Lionheart*?"

"Lionheart *doesn't* chew people out."

"No use, man." Animan came in with a folding chair tucked under his arm.

"Animan, how weak can his will possibly *be*?"

He shrugged. "When *he* had that thing for Annie for a while there, dude was nuts over her -- almost as bad as *you* -- but one dirty look from Doc S.O.B. and he acted like he'd never even *met* the girl."

"Bite me," Ted grumbled.

"You're just mad because it's true."

"Gentlemen?" I broke in, "can we focus here? Ted, you can't seriously think I'm the guilty one here. I mean... *look* at me."

"You look fine from here."

"I don't have any *feet*!"

"You have ankles."

"I don't ha-- hey, you're right. The regeneration process must speed up the farther along it goes. That's not the point, Ted. You think Noble would have been so brutal if he weren't trying to hide something?"

"He was brutal because *you* killed First Light and Five-Share!"

"I did *not*! Your skull *is* thick, isn't it?"

"The *thickest*," he snarled. Then, realizing that hadn't come out quite right, he proceeded to look down at his feet.

My own feet were regenerating nicely by now -- I had heels again and I watched for a moment as a pair of purple boots began to grow over them.

"Neat trick, bro," Animan said. Even Ted couldn't help but watch as the soles of my feet reappeared. The flesh, muscles and sinews continued to flow and finally I heard ten satisfying little "pops." I had toes. The boots flowed down over them and I was whole once more.

"Congratulations," Ted spat.

"You could be a *little* nicer," I said, swinging my brand-spanking-new legs off the bed and standing on them for the first time. They felt pretty good.

"Damn it, Ted," Animan grumbled, "will you just get over yourself? I should have known you'd have no willpower left, the way you always let goons like Noble walk all over you."

I fingered the starfish totem in my hand. "Well... here goes nothing."

"Josh, are you sure that those brand-spanking new legs are still gonna be there when you turn back? I mean... we really don't know how the hell any of this works."

"You know, Animan, the whole time I was lying there I was trying not to say that very thing so I wouldn't jinx it."

"Sorry."

I shrugged. My fist clutched as tight as it would go, I concentrated on the totem, on turning back into myself.

There was a flash and the starfish-man's body was gone. My costume reappeared and from the waist-up I was Copycat again. Even from the waist-down, everything felt new and strong.

And drafty.

Animan, in a futile attempt not to laugh, managed to say, "I guess... heh... the starfish-totem doesn't -- heh, heh -- doesn't grow back your *real* clothes. Heh... hold on, lemme get you some pants and shoes."

"Would you please?"

I wrapped myself in a blanket while Animan dug around. The new skin, while healthy, looked really pink and raw. It had sort of a strange, waxy sheen and I doubted I'd ever be able to grow hair on my lower extremities again. On the other hand, I had my legs and reproductive organs back. I decided to mark myself down as coming out ahead of the deal and dropped the subject.

Struggling a little against the extension cord, Ted was laughing. "Enjoying this, are you?" I asked.

"Oh, immensely."

"You know, Ted, you're lucky you aren't yourself right now. Otherwise I'd have to smack you around for being such a jackass."

"Or 'Noble-esque,' as the French say," Animan quipped as he tossed me a pair of jeans. I'd actually lost enough weight to fit in them very comfortably. I also pulled on a ragged pair of his tennis shoes.

"All dressed up and nowhere to go, huh?" Ted asked.

"Ted, I just had to re-grow half of my body, do you mind?"

"Oh, sure," he said, the look on his face turning maniacal. "Just thought I'd give you a little warning before."

"Before *what*?" Animan snapped.

We were both blown off our feet an instant later when Ted hiked up the volume on his telepathic jukebox to "earsplitting." A nasty brass chord threatened my eardrums and practically jellied my brain.

"What the hell are you *doing*?" I shrieked.

"He's sounding an alarm!" Animan shouted over the noise that only existed in our heads. "If he's broadcasting all over the complex--"

He didn't have to finish. Animan snatched a handful of totems and we both charged down the hall and out of the apartment.

"We're gonna make it," Animan said. "We're gonna make it, we're gonna make it, we're--"

"Screwed," I said.

We were flanked on one side by Spectrum, Justice Giant and Solemna and on the other by the Arachnid, Merlin Junior and -- still wearing Lionheart's face -- the Gunk.

"Ah *crap*," Animan said, fumbling for an ox totem.

"No!" I shouted, holding him back. The music had stopped and was replaced by a voice -- Tom's. And I liked what he was saying.

"We surrender," I said.

"We *what*?" Animan squeaked.

"Trust me."

Justice Giant took out couple of pairs of power dampeners and clamped them over our wrists. "Good move," Gunk said. "It'll go much faster this way."

"Have you lost your mind, man?" Animan said as we were led down the halls.

"Nope," I said. "Just got me a plan."

I didn't voice the addendum: "I hope."

ISSUE FIFTEEN

THE TRIAL OF JOSHUA CORWOOD

This time they didn't even bother throwing me in a cell, they took us straight to the auditorium and let Justice Giant and Merlin Junior guard us while the other roused the Tower and pulled us in for an assembly.

"I hope you're right about this, Tom," I grumbled.

"What did you say?" Gunk/Lionheart barked.

"I said, 'I hope an aardvark kissed your Mom'."

He raised his hand for a moment, like he was about to backhand me, then apparently decided what I'd said made no sense and let it go.

In the auditorium, Gunk sat us down at the table Icebergg had occupied for his own "trial." Every Cape and Mask in the city filtered in and glared at us, looks of hatred and disdain on their faces. This trial was just a formality. The verdict was already in.

"Wait here while we get your co-conspirator," Gunk said, marching off.

"What's he talking about?" Animan whispered. "You don't think he's caught Hotshot, do you?"

"No," I said, "Tom would have told me."

"Right, Tom. Remind me again why we're following a plan cooked up by someone who still wakes up at seven o'clock on a Saturday morning just to watch Bugs Bunny."

"I trust him," I said. Animan raised an eyebrow, as though he was still a bit wary, but eventually just nodded. That was enough.

That's about when "Lionheart" returned with someone else in tow -- someone wearing regular handcuffs instead of power dampeners, and someone who, I knew, had never seen this side of Simon Tower before.

"Hi, Sheila," I groaned as the Gunk sat her down.

"Hey, Josh," she said. "By the way, I'm never doing you a favor again."

"Okay," I moaned. "Are you all right?"

"Let's see, I'm halfway through burning the pages in your little notebook over the stove -- after having to disconnect your smoke detector, of course, when the goon squad breaks in, drags me here and throws me in a little room with no toilet all night. Right after I drank a pot of coffee. Do you *think* I'm all right?"

"Only *half?*" I moaned louder.

"Think that will be enough?"

"Oh, sure. Maybe they'll only send *half* of me to the penal colony."

"You know, a while ago that would actually have been an option," Animan pointed out.

Morrie came up to my table, wearing a "sorry about this" sort of grin. "You got any questions before we get goin', kid?"

"Yeah," Animan said, "how you planning on living with yourself once this is over?"

I scowled. That wasn't helping. "You're not gonna send Sheila off to the final frontier with us, are you?"

"When you're found guilty I'll get Mental Maid to wipe her brain an' send her back where she came from."

"*When* you find him guilty?" Sheila barked. "You've already got this decided."

Morrie frowned, but instead of responding he just turned away and joined the *faux* Lionheart between the United States and Siegel City flags on the dais.

"Who's your friend, Josh?" Animan asked. "She's got spunk."

"Right. Sheila, Animan. Animan, Sheila."

"Charmed," Sheila grumbled.

"Mutual," he said.

Morrie went to the podium and cleared his throat. "Okay, ladies 'an gentlemen, Capes and Masks, thank ya fer comin'. It's not a pleasant thing, these hearings, especially when we've had so many in such a short time. But it's somethin' that's gotta be done. We're here today, of course, to determine the guilt or innocence of Joshua Corwood, alias Copycat, an' his accomplice Eugene Torin, alias Animan."

"*Eugene?*" I whispered. "I thought no one used your real name."

"They *don't*," Animan said. "That's *why.*"

"Speaking fer the prosecution," Morrie continued, "is our recently restored cham-peen, Lionheart."

When the crowd began cheering, I leaned over to Animan. "Who speaks for us?"

"We speak for ourselves."

"*Great,*" Sheila said. "That means we've got a fool for a client or something, right?"

"Don't worry," I said. "I watch a lot of Court TV."

The Gunk stood up and cracked his knuckles. I wondered if I was the only one who noticed they didn't make any noise.

"Ladies and gentlemen," he said, "we all know why we are here. Joshua Corwood, known to you as Copycat these last few weeks, has willfully and without remorse committed innumerable crimes against his fellows including assault, disclosure and murder."

On those courtroom shows, this was always the part where the crowd started whispering excitedly. In my trial, though, everyone sat there, stone-faced, not making a sound -- except for the Goop, who was seated near the front, rocking back and forth on his haunches and whispering to himself.

"To begin with," the Gunk bellowed, "I have with me a notebook, found in Corwood's apartment, written in Corwood's own handwriting and being destroyed by Corwood's best friend." He held up the Spectrum-cover notebook, considerably thinner than the last time I'd seen it.

"Gee, that's sweet, Josh," Sheila said. "Why does Lionheart hate me?"

"That's *not Lionheart*," Animan and I said in concert.

"In this notebook Corwood, a member of the press, wrote down virtually every secret of this entire organization -- training routines, choreography, research and development. *Secret identities.*"

There was a slight murmur for that particular load of dung. I'd never written any secret IDs down. I made a mental note to chastise myself for ever writing any damn thing if I happened to have time later.

"But keeping the notebook, startling as it is, is by no means Copycat's most damning action. I *personally* witnessed, upon my return, the murder of the peaceful giant known as the Gunk."

This time the murmurs became a hiss and the Goop's whispers became a diatribe -- "No, that's not possible, no, it *can't* be right..."

"Now normally, the process here is for one of our holographically-empowered comrades to project a witnesses' depiction of events."

"You've been missing for ten years, 'Lionheart'," Animan growled. "How the blue hell do you know what the 'process' is?"

"This, of course, is impossible. One of our holographically-endowed friends, Spectrum, was beaten within an inch of his life by Copycat and his still-at-large accomplice, Hotshot."

What? That was ridiculous. Sure, we'd put kind of a hurt on Spectrum, but nowhere near as severely as he was making it out to be. What was he up to now?

"But far more grave is the fate of First Light and her teammates, Five-Share. I will allow my comrade, Doctor Noble, to explain."

Noble moved through the hissing, growling crowd. He paused at the defense table and whispered, "I don't know how you got your legs back, Joshie, but trust me, it won't matter for long."

He went to the dais and, without being sworn in or anything, launched into a rant about how he, Five-Share and First Light bravely fought me on the rooftop. I knew the last two Five-Shares, the absent ones, could refute his story, but that was assuming he hadn't found and dealt with them already.

"What we didn't count on," he said, "is that our opponent had done his homework. He knew what happened months ago, during my tragic confrontation with Photon Man. He knew how I accidentally accelerated his powers and caused his death."

Noble's voice cracked and I think he even squeezed out a tear. "Could this possibly sound more rehearsed?" I asked.

"Give him time," Animan hissed.

"Copycat used this knowledge to duplicate my abilities and deliberately accelerated First Light's powers beyond any levels she could tolerate. The resultant explosion killed not only First Light, but also Five-Share. I was lucky to escape with my life."

"You lying son of a bitch!" I shouted, and a chorus of Sheila, Animan and Tom (in my head) all shouted, "Josh, calm down!" at the same time.

"Are you ready yet?" I whispered.

"Not yet," Tom echoed. *"Stall."*

"Who is he talking to?" Sheila asked Animan.

"A telepathic Little Leaguer. Josh thinks he's gonna save our lives."

"Oh, good. For a moment there I was getting worried."

Noble and "Lionheart" became a tag team at this point, painting me as a spy, a killer and an enemy of mankind. I kept waiting for one of them to pull out a pointer and connect me to the grassy knoll theory. They rambled on for a good half an hour, and it was nearly five a.m. before they finished. The glares and looks of hatred cascaded down on me and, by proxy, Sheila and Animan.

"Tom," I moaned, "how long?"

"Soon," he said. This time I got the impression *he* was the one omitting "I hope."

"Joshua Corwood," boomed Morrie over the nasty, contemptuous mob, "do you have anything to say in your defense?"

I looked around at the blazing, hate-filled eyes. Only four people in the room wore anything but rage on their faces: Sheila and Animan, Mental Maid (who looked like she was desperately, and unsuccessfully, fighting the Gunk's control) and the Goop (who was looking more and more like somebody had just rolled over his kitten with a lawnmower).

"Yeah," I said, standing up. "I've got something to say."

"Josh," Animan pleaded, "these people are out for your blood! *Anything* you say, they're gonna twist to use against us. What are you gonna do?"

"What else?" I said, with what I hoped was a confident grin. "Filibuster."

I gulped and began.

"Ladies and gentlemen, my esteemed colleagues would have you believe that I was a killer, a murderer, a philanderer and a bunch of other big words that end in 'er'. And I would say to them, 'I know you are, but what am I'?"

Sheila groaned.

"If they have their way, my co-defendants and I will be spending twelve years in Leavenworth. Or eleven years in Twelveworth. Or five to ten at Woolworth's."

"What the hell is he *doing?*" Animan hissed.

"The Marx Brothers, I think," Sheila said.

"What's this all about, Corwood?" Morrie asked.

"If his honor would allow me a little leeway," I said, "I think I can make that quite evident."

Gunk and Noble both had fire in their eyes and for a moment I thought Morrie was going to break. Then I saw Mental Maid, her face clenched in concentration, and instead Morrie shrugged and said, "okay. But this better be good."

"You may be asking yourself why you should believe me when I claim this man before you is not Lionheart? Particularly when any fool can tell at a *glance* he's Lionheart. Well I ask you, who are you gonna believe, me or your own eyes?"

Animan moaned something that I believe included the phrase, "Gut us like a speckled trout."

"Oh Christ, he's gonna do Abbot and Costello next," Sheila whimpered.

And I did. I did "Who's on First?" I did "Niagara Falls." I proved mathematically that seven times thirteen was twenty-eight.

Once I ran out of old comedy routines, I did some Shakespeare. Hamlet's soliloquy. Romeo's balcony scene. Then the Gettysburg address. The preamble to the Constitution. The "Mr. Adams, Dear Mr. Adams" number from *1776*. A particularly moving speech I remembered Kermit the Frog making once. The assembled Capes and Masks kept scratching their heads, whispering each other, nobody knowing what was going on or what to do about it.

Finally, just when I thought I was going to have to go into my William Shatner impression, two things happened:

Morrie shouted, "*Mister* Corwood, is there a point to *any* of this?"

Tom's voice screamed, *"Josh! We're ready! We're coming through!"*

"Yes, there *is* a point!" I howled, staring right at "Lionheart" and Doctor Noble. "Bring 'em through, Tommy!"

My head suddenly felt like it was being pounded with a thousand jackhammers, from the inside. There was an eruption of pain and light and noise, but when my head cleared I could see between me and the dais half a dozen figures. The Defender, the Tin Man, Condor and Oriole, Miss Sinistah and my old pal Hotshot. The room screamed as a single unit and there was a mass of shrieking and confusion, and I was grinning like a maniac.

"The cavalry has arrived," I said.

JACKPOT

On my mental slot machine, I already had two BARs and the third roller was still spinning like a Ferris wheel. It seemed like it had been spinning forever.

But it was slowing down.

On the dais, Morrie looked like a guy who couldn't make out the last number on a winning lottery ticket.

Noble was muttering something I would have bet was along the lines of *"Now* what?" and the Gunk's Lionheart-eyes were suddenly flaring orange with rage.

"Stop them!" he screamed.

"Stop *what?"* asked the Defender, stepping forward. His voice was an echoing bass, the type of voice that makes speeches that send men off to war. "Have we done something wrong? Aren't we welcome here, 'old friend'? Or are you just afraid we'll uncover something you don't want getting out?"

As he debated with "Lionheart," the Tin Man fell back to the defendants' table and began picking the electronic lock on Animan's power dampeners.

"You can shut these things off?" Animan asked.

"You kidding me?" Tin Man said. "Who do you think taught Particle to *make* 'em?" Even though the only part of his face we could see through his faceplate was his eyes, I could tell they were both smiling like an old firehorse that's been called back to duty.

"If these young men are as guilty as you claim," the Defender continued, "what was their motivation? What have they *gained* from their supposed crimes? Or perhaps there were no gains at all, perhaps all the gains can be laid at *your* feet!"

"Is he making a *speech?"* Sheila asked.

"Ah, he used to do this stuff all the time," Tin Man said.

"Yeah," cooed Animan as his dampeners popped off. "Isn't it *great?"* Then, to Tin Man, he asked, "We're about to do something really stupid, aren't we?"

"You bet."

"Woo-hoo!"

Tin Man turned to me and began picking the lock on my dampeners. Unfortunately, Noble's eyes were a lot sharper than his sense of morality.

"He's breaking Corwood out!"

"Stop him!" Gunk spat even louder. This time I could actually *see* orange waves of energy coruscate from his head to those closest to him -- the Arachnid, Whipstar and Arrow Ace, among others. They all turned and charged us.

"Hold them back!" Hotshot shouted, and the LightCorps sprung to action. If being in retirement for ten years had lessened their skills any, they didn't show it. The Defender took Whipstar out in three swift chops. Oriole grew to her full size while delivering a flying kick to the Arachnid's solar plexus. Condor took the fight to the air, sweeping down at Doc Noble and dodging a series of teke bursts.

"Hurry!" I shouted.

"I *am* hurrying!" Tin Man yelled as the crowd erupted. Most of the Capes and Masks were frozen to their spots, confused, unsure of what to do. The Goop was actually ripping chunks out of his head, which were quickly reabsorbed into his slimy flesh, screaming like a child being forced to choose between his parents.

Some of them, though, the ones who weren't particularly bright or forceful (including, I'm sorry to say, the Conductor) began to zero in on us like the living dead.

"Hurry *faster!*" I bellowed, but the point became moot a second later when there was a twang, a clang and a spark. Arrow Ace actually banked a shaft off the Tin Man's chestplate and lodged it in the power dampeners before Miss Sinistah took him out.

"He destroyed the locking mechanism!" Tin Man cried.

"Well isn't *that* swell?" I yelled.

"Wait, let me!" The Defender leapt over the melee and aimed his sword at the center bar. Just before he brought it down in its arc, though, the sword leapt from his grasp and speared upwards, implanting itself in the ceiling.

"Telekinesis," Noble said, hovering above us. "It's a beautiful thing."

"Son of a--" the Tin Man fired his boot-rockets and launched into the air, shouldering Noble aside and racing for the sword. I didn't see what happened next, though, because just then the doors opened and Flambeaux and Spectrum bolted into the auditorium, both wearing hospital gowns.

"There he is!" Spectrum shouted, pointing straight at me.

"Damn!" I ran for the dais. "Mental Maid! Mary, help!"

She looked down, her eyes glowing purple. Then, her arm trembling like a weeble in an earthquake, she aimed at me.

"Hit him!" the Gunk shouted. "Hit him with the Soul Ray!"

"Yaaaagh!" I replied, leaping from the dais just before the Ray hit. Spectrum charged me, trying to trick me into retreating into the beam, but I held my ground and he passed right on through. Once the hologram cleared my vision, I saw Solemna leaping at me, her hands smoking.

I ducked and lashed out with a foot, flipping her onto her back. Then I smashed her on the back of the head with my power dampeners, knocking her cold but not turning the damn things off.

"I'll *kill* you!" Justice Giant announced, eyes flashing a bright orange. He shot up to twelve feet tall and tried to smash me with his huge fists. I darted to a clear spot and heard a snarl. Animan, now Wolph, had jumped on the Giant's back and was slashing with his claws.

"Murderer!" There was a blast of accordion music and I fell to my knees. The Conductor backhanded me and I fell to one side as the music subsided.

"I'll stop you!" he shouted. "I'll stop you if it kills me!"

"Ted, for God's sake, *listen to yourself*! Do you think the *LightCorps* would be here fighting if that was really Lionheart? You're smarter than that!"

"*No!*"

I rolled to my feet and lashed out with a kick, knocking him down. He looked up just in time to see the power dampeners falling down to his face.

And I stopped them there.

"I could have bashed your head in just then, Ted. If I was what you thought I am, I *would* have, I've got nothing to lose. For *God's sake, BELIEVE ME!*"

Ted's eyes flashed -- orange, just for the briefest second -- and his lip quivered. "Josh?" Then a look of rage appeared on his face and he launched his fist into the air, straight at my head.

Or so I thought. Actually, it went just a little to the side, drawing blood from the nose of Herr Nemesis, who had snuck up behind me.

"Josh?" Ted moaned, "what the hell is going on here? I was gonna kill you, man. Sweet God, what's *happening?*"

"You came around," I said.

"His loss!"

Noble swept down, batted Ted aside and nailed me in the gut with a teke burst. I went crashing into the first row of seats, now empty except for the Goop, who screamed when he saw me and buried his head in his arms. "No!" he cried. "No, you *can't* be bad, little guy, you *can't* be, but... but Gunk said... and Gunk... *YOU CAN'T BE BAD!*"

"Naw, of course not." Noble grabbed my cape and hurled me back to the dais, where Flambeaux and Spectrum each caught an arm. They slammed me against the wall and, between them, the dampeners and Noble's telekinesis, I couldn't move.

And the roller slowed even more.

"No!" Goop shrieked.

"Wake up!" I screamed. "Mental Maid, you showed me the truth! Spectrum, I *work* with you! Scott, you *know* me! *YOU KNOW ME!*"

Mental Maid raised her hand. It quaked and shook and I wondered how she could ever hit anything trembling that bad, and I knew she couldn't miss. The mental slot machine had almost stopped.

"Goop!" I howled, "this isn't you! What are you, some sort of pawn? You're a *doctor*! Your name is Edward Plante! Eddie Plante! Plante! *Plante!*"

I was screaming so hard I was out of breath after each syllable and gulped down air like water. When I started hysterically screaming Goop's last name, over and over again, it didn't come out "Plante! Plante!" Instead, I heard, "Plant-ah! Plant-ah!"

Plant-ah... Plant-ah... Plan-tag...

Third BAR.

Jackpot.

"PLANTAGENET!" I roared, the fear in my voice replaced with clarity. "That's *it*! The Crusades! Plantagenet! Richard the L--"

Noble's telekinesis clamped down on my jaw and tongue now, and the words I had been screaming were muffled into impotent howls.

"Have fun out there," Noble grinned.

"Fire!" the Gunk screamed.

Mental Maid's hand lit up. I wanted to close my eyes, but I didn't. I would face this with the Heart of the Lion.

Mental Maid fired.

And the Goop hurled himself into the beam.

"NO!" Gunk cawed. The beam didn't touch me. Goop stood before Mental Maid; I was safe in his shadow. The blinding white filtered through his orange slime-flesh, which began to grow translucent and then opaque.

The entire auditorium ground to a halt as everyone turned to watch, to see what the Goop was turning into -- to see what he really was.

Crouched down on the floor, he grew a pair of black trousers and boots. He grew a red tunic. A blue cape burst from his back and shimmied down his front, with a blue mask crawling up his face. A shock of raven hair sprouted from his head. His flesh was pink and healthy again, and a beautiful yellow emblem appeared on his chest. When he stood up, he smiled at me. It was the smile of a man who would fly into a burning building to pull out a ten-year-old boy.

In my head, in *everyone's* head, an English horn began to play, courtesy of the Conductor. First it blared out in a single, proud fanfare, and then it was joined by a chorus of brass, strings and finally percussion. It was like having John Williams in Simon Tower.

Throughout all this, nobody moved, nobody breathed, nobody said a word. Finally, it was Doctor Noble who found the words to express exactly what he was feeling.

"Oh *shit*," he said.

The man who was no longer the Goop winked at me, then turned to face the abomination who had usurped his identity.

And he smiled.

"Excuse me, sir," Lionheart said, "I believe that's my face you're wearing. I'd like it back."

GIANT-SIZED FINAL ISSUE

THE BATTLE OF SIMON TOWER

When the real Lionheart reappeared, nobody could even think of reacting. Once it sunk in it was like a cherry bomb exploding in an anthill. People jumped and screamed -- some in shock, some in joy -- and everything collapsed into total chaos. Half the people who'd been fighting us up to that point clutched their heads like a goddess was trying to burst out, fell to their knees and fought no more.

Gunk/Lionheart's face contorted into a maw of rage and venom. His eyes were glowing like a Jack O'Lantern, and he was sputtering so badly he couldn't even give his peons the command to attack.

"Get -- stop -- don't --" he hissed.

Of course, they got the message anyway. About half a dozen guys, including the ones holding me down, swarmed on Lionheart like maggots on roadkill. I dove out of the way of the rumble and began bashing the center bar of my power dampeners on the corner of the dais, trying to break them off.

"Josh! I'm coming!"

I looked up just in time to see Annie's fist charge in towards my head. I flinched a bit, but the arc of her hand brought it down directly between my hands, smashing the center bar and the energy source for the dampeners. Suddenly I felt Rushes coming in at me from every direction -- the manacles still dangled from each wrist, but they no longer bound me and they no

353

longer worked. Annie gave me her most incredible grin and said, "So, was it good for you, too?"

I spent a moment contemplating various responses, trying to find one that wouldn't make me sound like a total geek. Finally I gave up and settled on, "*Gosh, you're swell.*" She giggled and we both looked back to the dais. "Come on," I said, "we've got to help Lionheart."

"Wait, Josh, things just got a *lot* more complicated in the last two minutes. How do you know *that's* the real Lionheart?"

"Same way I knew the other one *wasn't,*" I said. I reached out with Noble's telekinesis and wrenched the Arachnid off Lionheart, who took advantage of the hole in the mob to spin DeVinity into Spectrum.

The Gunk started screaming orders, but most of them were drowned out when Noble, squealing like a kid trying to hog all the good toys, yelped, "Stop using *my* powers!"

He threw himself at me and I almost dove away, but I caught a glimpse of Fourtifier out the corner of my eye (he had just entered the fight between Condor and Whipstar and seemed to be trying to determine which he should be hitting). Pulling the rock-man's powers, I turned myself to stone and allowed Noble to smash into me at top speed. He slumped off and I was about to follow up with a burst of flame, but I couldn't seem to summon any up. Flambeaux wasn't at the battle site. Instead I stretched my arms out like DoubleGum Man (dropping the inert dampeners in the process) and slingshot him into the ceiling.

There was a thud behind me and I turned to see Ted, backing towards me, clubbing Silverfish over the head with a flag he'd retrieved from the dais.

"Josh," he said, "am I going totally insane here?"

"Not at all," I replied, delivering a blow to the Arrow Ace, who was still looking a little dazed from the pummeling Annie had given him earlier. "You really *are* fighting alongside a bevy of retired heroes while two different versions of a man who died ten years ago duke it out."

On the dais, the two Lionhearts were facing off, one with a warm, friendly smile, the other with cold, Halloween fury in his eyes. "I've been taking your marching orders for quite some time, Gunk. Or Carnival. Or whatever it is you're calling yourself these days. I rather think it's time to stop marching."

As he talked and approached his imposter, I tried to contain a belly laugh. Hearing the real Lionheart speaking in his crisp, British accent while the Gunk could have spilled out of Anytown, U.S.A. just made the whole thing seem ridiculous somehow.

I felt a new Rush approaching and the doors to the auditorium exploded in a curtain of fire. Three forms barged in, one in the air -- Flambeaux. On the ground were two new goop-men, one clad in the shredded remains of a diving suit.

"Deep Six and Nightshadow!" I shouted. "He sent Flambeaux to the morgue to thaw them out!"

"*Nightshadow?*" Ted yelled.

"Who did you *think* was playing the role of Gunk's corpse?"

"Josh!" A heavy mass slammed into me and I, in turn, slammed into the ground just as a screaming white blast seared the air.

"Look out, old chum, Gunk's still got Mental Maid firing at you with the Soul Ray."

When I rolled over I didn't recognized my rescuer at first -- he was a big, furry creature with fangs, a squat nose and heavy, leathery flaps on his arms. Then it hit me -- Animan was using a bat totem.

"Thanks for the save."

"No problem, friend of friends! Just remember, I can't watch your back *all* the time!" He then took to the air after Flambeaux and I frowned at Ted.

"What kind of personality is *that* for a bat to have?" I said. "I mean... *chum*?"

My diatribe was interrupted in the next second by a horrified scream coming from the direction of the defense table. Sheila had been backed up against the table by the Jackal, who was crouched over her and fumbling with the front of his pants.

"He's going to *rape* that girl!" Ted shouted. He ran a few feet with the flagpole, then jammed the tip against the floor, pole-vaulting over the unconscious form of Herr Nemesis, and pounded both feet into the Jackal's back. He crumbled like a good pie crust and Ted was left standing, amazed.

"I did it! I stopped him! I saved somebody!" He laughed like a hyena, then jumped back into the fray. "Hey! Yo, *Squid*! Remember that day you cut in front of me in the cafeteria..."

I rushed over to Sheila, kicking the Jackal out of the way. "Are you all right?" I asked.

"Well, yeah," she said, her handcuffs dangling. "But... I didn't really need any help."

"*What*? Then what was that scream all about?"

"Oh *that*. It was the Jackal after I kneed him in the crotch."

I looked down at the fallen Mask's face and, to be certain, the look of pain was far more intense than he would have felt being slammed in the back by a 150-pound band director.

"Do me a favor," I said, "don't tell the Conductor that. Now come on, I've got to get you out of here."

"*Out* of here? Are you *nuts?* This is the best story *ever!*"

I shot her a glare that would go down in the Dirty Looks Hall of Fame and she weakly grinned. "Kidding, kidding..."

"Come on..."

We were almost to the door when a shout stopped us. "Look out, Josh!" I spun around to look for the voice, only to see Lionheart running towards us. "Don't head out that door! The Gunk went that way!"

"Oooh, good save. Hey, there's something I've always wanted to tell you."

"What?"

I drew my hand back and, combining the strength of virtually every super-being in the city, cold-cocked him. He slammed into the wall, orange gunk exploding from his form, and the Lionheart facade cracked a little.

"Your accent *still* sucks," I said.

"Maybe... why don't I try it with *your* tongue?" Gunk re-formed the Lionheart disguise except for his right arm, which was now a three-foot sword -- he was aiming at my head. I grabbed at him with Noble's telekinesis and pounded at him, sending him breaking through the ground. Without stopping to think, I leapt after him.

THE PLOT

I landed in the hallway on the bottom level, near the morgue, next to the warehouse. Although I could feel the Rush, there were so many of them flying around at this point I didn't notice the Gunk's, specifically, until he grabbed me and began smashing me into the wall. The drywall outside of the Tower's storage facility couldn't hold up to the relentless onslaught of my face being pounded into it. Soon the wall cracked, then splintered, then burst apart. The Gunk's momentum helped carry me through, and I broke into the room, crashing into a cardboard box. The box broke apart too, and I found myself suddenly cushioned. When I stood up, there was something red covering my face. I whipped it off and was about to throw it aside when a flash of gold caught my eye.

It was a t-shirt, a red one, with Lionheart's emblem on it.

And in the box I'd drawn it from: at least a hundred more.

And as I looked around, bewildered, I realized the room was full of cardboard boxes, each one bearing Lionheart's stamp.

The Gunk smiled at me, again disgracing Lionheart's face. "Something wrong?"

"The garbage Morrie showed off at the press conference. What *is* all this?" I said.

He laughed. "What do you think?"

I grabbed another box and ripped it open, and a dozen Lionheart lunchboxes spilled out. Another had fruit snacks in the shape of his symbol. Next was the back-to-school pen-and-pencil set. Breakfast cereal. Silicone "What Would Lionheart Do?" wristbands. I picked up a talking Lionheart action figure with light-up chest emblem, and turned to stare at the villain. "What the hell *is* all this?" I screamed.

He started laughing. "What does it look like? It's the cornerstone of everything I've been working for. Well... the *economic* cornerstone at least. The lying and killing people parts are pretty important too."

"Lionheart *never* allowed himself to be licensed like this. Even after he was gone, Hotshot--"

"Yes, yes, he managed to keep that short-sighted policy in place for ten years. I was there, remember?"

I picked up a Lionheart coffee mug. The handle came off in my hand and the cup shattered to the floor. "Even merchandise this crappy couldn't have been made overnight."

He smiled again. "When you've been alive as long as I have, you don't need to do anything on the spur of the moment."

"Why?" I felt outside of the room, looking for just the right Rush, and when I found it, I turned it on. "For God's sake, *why*?"

"I've been alive for a long time, Josh. And there have always been people like us... people who are *different*. But we used to be *decent* about it. We hid. We stayed in the shadows. We became the stuff of myth and legend, and eventually, people forgot how to believe in us. And I *liked* it like that. The world was *peaceful* then."

"So?"

"So, then came Hitler. And Roosevelt. And your 'Good War' and your 'Greatest Generation' and the costumed goons in the thrice-damned United Statesmen. A few of us got it into their heads to put on stupid clown suits and risk their lives to help the stupid, short-lived, short-sighted *normals*, and the next thing I knew, the world was full of them!"

"Full of *what*?"

His voice exploded: "SUPERHEROES!"

"Superheroes?"

"Superheroes! Self-righteous fools in their garish costumes parading around what used to be *different*! What used to be *special*! Things were fine before that. No fighting, no warring amongst each other, none of these humans assailing us, wanting our favors, wanting us to take up their fights—I had *peace*, boy! But now, there is no peace. There will *never* be peace again, and it's all because of the stupid, stupid *superheroes*."

"You think there was *peace* when there were no heroes?" I said. "I only *read* history books and I know that's not true. I thought you *lived* through it."

"War for *humans*, fighting for *humans*," he said. "I got to *rest*."

"So who said you had to get back into the game?" I asked. "You could have stayed in your cave or whatever you were doing. No one made you jump into the fray."

"No. He *did*." He picked up a water bottle in the shape of Lionheart's head and crushed it in his fist. "A few dozen villagers as servants, that's all I wanted. Maybe a world leader or two to pull strings for me. I have to blow out the energy after a few months to keep my cohesion anyway. Lionheart brought me into the fray, boy, and now I'll finally get peace again."

I didn't comprehend how he could pull this off, but I would keep him talking as long as possible. He didn't realize yet that I was drawing on Mental Maid's powers from elsewhere in the complex to make him ramble about his plans like a Bond villain, but as long as I could keep him going, I would keep listening.

"Even after Lionheart was gone, even after I got *rid* of him, he was *still* the fuel for this city. He's *still* the one everyone wants to look up to, wants to be like, wants to see racing in to save the day. Getting rid of him didn't *end* him, any more than it did John Lennon or Martin Luther King. So if I can't end his influence by eliminating him..." he squeezed his hand tighter and ground the plastic water bottle into dust. "I have to *destroy* him."

"By putting his picture on a lot of crappy toys?" I said. I started to chuckle, and he started to frown.

"What are you laughing at?"

"How somebody so *old* could be so *stupid*," I said. "You think superheroes are about fighting and wars and t-shirts? You don't know *anything*. You were already inhuman when superheroes – *real* superheroes – were invented. You don't have the slightest idea what they really mean." I picked up one of the Lionheart action figures and pointed it at him. "People like Lionheart aren't here to beat each other up or sell a bunch of dolls. They aren't even here to get cats out of trees or kids out of burning buildings."

"They--"

"That's what they *do*. That's not what they're *for*. Superheroes are a *goal*. They're an *ideal*. They do amazing things to remind us that things can be better, that *we* can be better. Just like every hero in history, from Joan of Arc to Jesus Christ. They're all here for the same reason. They're all here to remind us that we can be *better than you*." The little lion emblem in my hand flashed, and my grip tightened. "You almost made me forget that. But not all the t-shirts in the world can make people forget what Lionheart did."

"Oh, lovely. Truly a lovely sentiment. But I won't make people forget Lionheart's legacy by selling them cheap toys."

The toy in my hand began to vibrate, began to hum. With the number of heroes in the Tower who were lending me varying degrees of invulnerability, I was pretty tough, but the doll exploding in my grasp still stung so badly I thought it would take my head off. The blast hurled me through the mountains of cardboard, and I wound up crashing through a huge carton of the action figures. As they rained down on me, the Gunk stepped forward, smiling.

"I'm going to make them forget Lionheart's legacy by *killing* them with cheap toys. Officially endorsed death machines, each one with the Lionheart seal of approval. Once Lionheart is the most hated man in America, I spread out. I'll destroy every hero and villain in the city, then the country, and then..." he exhaled, a deep sigh of anticipation. "Then I'll finally have peace again."

The emblems on the dolls around me all began to flash in perfect synchronization. And with each flash, my blood boiled hotter. I charged in, punching upwards this time, and he burst back up into the higher levels of the complex.

I rocketed upwards through the new hole he'd created, back into the chaos of the upper battle. It only took me a second to find him, arm again turned into a glittering silver blade, but he was faster than me. This time, he was aiming for Sheila, aiming at her throat.

"Leave her alone!" I roared. I was about to grab some telekinesis from Noble to deflect it, but as it turns out, I didn't need to. In mid-swing the Gunk was picked up off his feet and hurled through the ceiling. Where he stood seconds before was the *real* Lionheart, dusting off his hands.

"That's three you owe me, little guy," he said.

"You *remember* the first one?" I said, amazed, thinking of the flames licking at the tub, the water heating up around me and the sense of relief when I saw that beautiful, golden emblem.

He smiled and tapped that same emblem on his chest. "You never forget," he said. "Nice outfit, by the way. Denim was a bit of a fashion risk, though, don't you think?"

"These are my emergency back-up super-pants."

He laughed at that. "Say, my memories of, oh, the last ten years or so are a bit muddled, including the layout of this place. Can you tell me exactly where I threw that git?"

"Well, if you threw him hard enough, he could have made it into the Tower proper... which means -- oh no."

"What?"

"We've got to stop him before he gets outside. Sheila--"

"I can take care of myself, flyboy," she said. "Go save the world."

FIREWALL

When we made it outside, following the path of destruction Gunk had left, the sky was the clean blue of a summer morning just before the sun came up. There weren't many people on the street at all -- a couple of garbagemen, a kid dropping a letter into a mailbox, a newsstand vendor, a stray dog.

I pointed to the mailbox. The girl had to hop up to reach the handle. Her worn, pink sneakers left contact with the ground several times, and her already-torn jeans snagged the metal edge.

"I'm thinking a kid that young shouldn't be out this early in the morning," I said.

"Unusual," Lionheart said, "but not unheard of, particularly not in a city this safe. Besides, she's too short. Gunk's skeleton has to remain solid, only his flesh morphs."

"That also rules out the dog," I said, "and the guy driving the garbage truck, he's too short."

"Do you sense anything?" Lionheart asked.

"Oh yeah." I reached out -- definitely feeling a Rush from *some* direction... the girl at the mailbox. I pointed. "It's definitely that way, but you said the girl was too short."

"No, not the girl," Lionheart said. "But when she dropped that letter in the mailbox, it coughed."

We glanced at each other just for a moment and, without a word, formulated and executed our plan. I jumped first.

"Look out, sweetheart!" I shouted, grabbing the girl and, using Lionheart's power (and how *good* that felt!) flew her to a safe distance. Lionheart aimed just a tad to my left, hitting the mailbox as though it had a target on it. The sides collapsed in and Lionheart pounded a blue and white humanoid shape that belched out the card the little girl had mailed.

The girl in my hands first shrieked, then cheered as she started to enjoy the ride. "Hey," she said, "why is that man fighting the mailbox?"

"Because the mailbox was bad," I said, putting her down at a safe distance from the rumble. "Now go home as fast as you can. I've got to help my friend... er... beat up the mailbox."

I executed a backflip in the air and bore down on the fight. By now Gunk had reverted to his orange slime-form and Lionheart had driven his fist through the orange flesh, clutching the Gunk's skeleton's bony neck.

"How many people have you subjugated, Gunk? *Why*? What the bloody hell is the *point*?"

The orange flesh around his mouth pulled back into a grin. "Because of *you*."

"He's a lunatic," he said. "He wants to destroy everything you are because he blames superheroes for making the world messy."

"And you let me *live*?" Lionheart said. "How stupid *are* you? You can't possibly have believed it would work."

"Oh *do* calm down, it's not as though I killed anyone... not *this* time, anyway--"

"What about First Light and Five-Share?"

"I'm afraid the good Doctor did that entirely of his own accord. I thought it would be an interesting lark to have an accomplice in this particular scheme, so I brought him in. At first he really only wanted the fame that accompanied being the city's premiere Cape but after a while he really turned out to be quite mad."

"Well thanks for clearing that up," I said. "What tipped you off, when he tried to beat his girlfriend or when he nuked Photon Man?"

"Temperance, Copycat," Lionheart said. "Believe me, I want to see this monster pay as much as you do, but anger will serve only as a distraction. We need our faculties."

"Yeah, I know... Well, we've got him now, let's bring him in."

And the Gunk laughed harder.

"You really think I'll let you incarcerate me?" he said. "I'm going to leave this city, I'm going to establish a new identity somewhere else and I'm going to start all over again with the *next* plan. And even if it takes me fifty years to establish myself and a century to make my move, so what? I've got the time."

"And precisely how do you think you're going to get away?" Lionheart asked, almost finishing the whole last word before the bottom floor of Simon Tower exploded.

A wall of flame actually seemed to push at the glass doors and windows lining the ground floor before they rushed out, splashing broken glass across the sidewalk. Virtually every potential opening erupted with fire and shards.

"This isn't good," I said to Lionheart.

A body came hurtling out of the smoke. Since Lionheart was still holding onto the Gunk, I took off and caught it.

"Joshua..." it moaned through a beak. I hadn't even recognized him until he spoke -- probably because all his feathers had burnt off. He was Aquila. Underneath he was Animan. "Joshua, look out. He's coming for you."

That's when the swarm hit. Everyone -- Cape and Mask, free man and pawn, came scrambling out of Simon at the same time. Some were being dragged, some pushed. Oriole, at one-quarter size, was carrying an unconscious, fully-shrunk Condor. Ted kept trying to help Sheila, who was insisting quite loudly that she didn't *need* any help. I landed by Lionheart, gently laying Aquila down.

"What the hell happened?" I asked anyone who was listening. Annie came running up to me.

"Todd -- Doctor Noble," she said. "He threw him straight into the fire, then held him there. I think he's still in the complex."

"Son of a *bitch*," I hissed. "You happy, Gunk? You've turned him into a full-blown serial killer!"

"Animan's not dead," Annie said.

"He's close."

"Will he be all right?" Lionheart asked.

"Maybe," I said, "I'm no doctor. But I'm going to help him."

Drawing on Flambeaux, Annie -- *anyone* with powers that could shield me long enough to get down there, I charged into the fire.

I couldn't see much between the smoke and the dancing flame, but I knew right where I was going, even inside the inferno. The floor in the lobby of Simon Tower had been almost totally ripped apart, a gaping hole extending all the way to the auditorium below. I jumped into the hole, drifting down into the auditorium, which was completely ablaze. This must have been where the blast originated -- in my mind's eye I could see Flambeaux going five-alarm and Noble chucking Aquila into the blast like a rag doll.

Every Rush I could feel faded out as I began running through the halls. I was too far away from the surface to be picking up energy. This one was going to be up to old Josh, all by his lonesome.

I raced to the dormitory level and smashed open the door to Ted and Animan's quarters. I vaulted the furniture in the living room to make it to Animan's pad and burst in to find it had been totally ransacked.

The books and models were scattered, charts were ripped apart, the workbench had been overturned and paints, tools and sawdust covered the carpet. All of Animan's totems were in a heap on the floor, some smashed, some broken. Few intact.

I didn't have a chance to even silently curse the Gunk before I felt a now-familiar Rush approaching from above.

"God no, not him, not *now*."

I fell to my knees and begin sifting through the totems, tossing them aside -- seal, dolphin, owl, llama... it was like a zoological encyclopedia in 3-D.

The Rush got closer as I dug -- orangutan, tiger, sloth, penguin, beetle -- was the thing still here? Was it still in one piece?

Hyena, come on, antelope, caribou, please *God*, marlin, kangaroo--

Starfish.

"*Thank* you!" I snatched it up, counted five complete legs and no significant scratches, and spun around to get the hell out of there.

But Dr. Noble was in the doorway. Any trace of sanity his eyes may once have held was gone. His gloves were scorched and his cape had bloodstains on it.

"You don't get out of here in one piece, little boy," he said.

THE RACE

We stood in the door to Animan's room, Noble circling me like a cat toying with its prey. "I don't suppose if I just forfeited we'd be able to walk out of here hand in hand and consider the whole thing over with, huh?" I asked.

"Probably not." Noble lashed out with a teke burst which I managed to deflect with one of my own. I returned the blow, dropping the totem into my jeans pocket, freeing up both hands to club him over the head. He staggered for a bit, but came back by ramming me in the gut. Soon we were on the floor, scrabbling to our feet and slapping and pounding each other like kids on a playground.

"You took *everything*!" he screamed, slapping at me. "The plan, Sinistah, my *respect* -- I'm a laughing stock because of you! You know what they're saying about how you beat me? They said I don't have what it takes anymore. They've been calling me 'Doctor Numbnuts' behind my back! They've been--"

I cracked Animan's work bench over his head telekinetically, beating him off. "They've *always* called you Doctor Numbnuts behind your back," I said. I sent a kick across his face. "This is Siegel City, Todd, home of heroes; your 'blame the victim' crap isn't going to fly here."

With him sprawled on the ground it was tough to resist the urge to simply beat him into submission. Animan needed the totem in my pocket, though. I flew over Noble's bruised, bloody form and raced for the ruins of the auditorium. Before I made it to the doors, though, I heard a scream of blind, stupid rage and was teke-shoved into the wall.

Noble charged up behind me and began pounding my back, trying to create a fulcrum point with his telekinesis to crack my spine. I think he was so crazy with anger he didn't even realize I was using his own shield to cushion the blows -- I still felt them, but not enough to do any real damage.

I thrust outward with the shield, hurling Noble into the opposite wall. He broke through the fire-damaged plaster into the burning auditorium. The flames regurgitated through the hole into the hallway and the sprinklers kicked in.

I was trying to decide if it would be smarter to follow Noble through the hole or just cut through the doors when he leapt out of the flames, arms extended, racing towards me. He was still instinctively shielding himself and not doing a very good job of it. His cape was on fire.

My plan was this: fall to the ground and telekinetically shove him upwards, therefore avoiding a collision. Unfortunately, he was moving faster than I'd anticipated. The first part of my plan, the falling, started out rather well, but when I was at eye-level with his fists he added a burst of speed and smashed me in the face.

I saw a flash that was compounded a second later when he pounded my head with his elbow. As he hit me, repeatedly, he began shouting obscenities and blaming me for pretty much everything from his mommy not hugging him enough to his upcoming male pattern baldness. If he weren't trying so hard to give me a concussion, I may have pitied him.

Fighting off the urge to black out, I sheathed my head telekinetically and let him pound the shield while I regained my senses, a superpowered rope-a-dope.

"I'll kill you," he whinnied. "I'll *kill* you!"

I lay there, sprawled out, hoping he'd leave or wear himself out if I didn't react -- or that I'd at least have time to come up with a better plan as he screamed, "*Say* something! I'll *kill* you if you don't *say something!*"

I'd decided to aim one all-out teke burst at his head, hard enough to take him down if he was unshielded, when my *own* head began to ache and split. By the time I realized it wasn't just the beating I'd taken making my head rumble, it was too late to fight it back. Tom came spilling out of my brain, directly between me and Noble.

Holding a baseball bat.

Which, in turn, was aimed at Noble's crotch.

He smashed it into Noble's groin like a kid beating up robbers in a bad movie. Then, when the lunatic Cape bent over in agony, Tom swung upwards, probably breaking the guy's jaw in the process. He flopped backwards into the water pooling on the carpet. The sprinklers rinsed the blood from his face and the pool turned pink.

"Nice one, Mantle," I said. "I thought I told you not to come here."

"And you thought that would *work*?" he said. I couldn't possibly argue with that.

"I was fine on my own," I finally settled on.

"Oh, *right*. That's why you were just lying there?"

"I *had* a *plan*!" I said. "Look, we don't have--"

"--time, I know. You say that a *lot*. Let's just get the totem to Animan."

I tapped into Tom's powers and looked outwards, at the battle going on outside the tower. I finally settled myself behind Annie's eyes. She was holding on to the badly hurt Aquila while watching the chaos around her. Fire trucks, cops and camera crews were swarming outside the tower as the Gunk's last few holdouts fought the LightCorps. I saw Oriole take down Whipstar, Tin Man dousing Flambeaux with flame-retardant foam from his armor, the Defender slashing at the men who used to be Deep Six and Nightshadow, trying hopelessly to reason with them the way I'd reasoned with the Goop.

"Annie? Can you hear me?"

"Josh?" She started looking around.

"No, no, I've got Tom with me down here. I've got something for Animan. Hold on, I'm coming through."

I fell forwards, spinning around through the ether, finally materializing in front of Annie. She jumped back as I appeared, Tom by my side.

"Josh? *Tom*? What's going on? Why are you wet? Why does Tom have a baseball bat? What -- oh God, Josh, what happened to your face?"

I suppressed a gleeful smile as she tried to clean the blood from my face. "Not that your concern isn't appreciated," I said, pulling the starfish totem from my pocket, "but let's worry about *him* for a while."

I knelt by Animan and found the eagle totem dangling from his neck, wrapping his hand around it. "Come on, buddy, I need you to transform, just twice, okay? Can you do that?"

"Joshua..."

"Change! Change, dammit! Just *change*!"

He closed his eyes and there was a spark. Aquila was gone, the burnt, broken wings were gone, and he was replaced by a just-as-damaged, impossibly burnt Animan. He shrieked with renewed pain and began convulsing. I pulled the eagle totem from his hand and shoved the starfish in as he flopped and howled.

"One more!" I screamed. "Just *one* more, can you do it? *Please*, man!"

His hand began to quake and he screamed, thrashing about. Light spilled from his hand and washed over his body, and once it passed he'd stopped thrashing. He was wearing the starfish uniform I'd regenerated in and, although still badly burnt, I could see his skin beginning to heal.

"How did you know to use that?" Annie asked.

"After Noble made me half a man back there, the starfish grew back my legs. I just hoped it could regenerate him, too."

"Can starfish really regenerate from *burns* like that?" she asked.

"I have no idea. Let's pretend they can, though, it seems to be working."

"Josh!" Hotshot came in for a landing behind me. "Where's Lionheart? I thought you went after him! And -- why are you wearing jeans?"

"Everybody's so concerned about the blasted jeans," I said. Then, after a glance, I added, "where *is* Lionheart?"

"Gunk slipped away from him," Annie said. "They were going in the direction of Lee Park."

I nodded. "Tom, watch Animan. We're going after Lionheart."

"Not without me you're not." Annie said.

"Annie, how long has it been since you rested? Don't you need to rebuild your powers every so often?"

"I'll make do," she said. Arguing, I knew, would have been pointless. I scooped her up in my arms and took off after Hotshot. This had gone far enough.

CHILDREN OF THE LION

It wasn't quite six a.m. yet, but in a city like Siegel the park was, at that precise hour of the morning, the worst public place Gunk could have gone. While most of the city was slithering out of bed, having coffee or getting ready for the drive to work, Lee Park was rife with early-morning joggers, cyclists and roller-skaters getting their daily workout amongst the trees and statuary. At the just-post-dawn hour there was nowhere in the city with more places to hide and more people to blend in with.

I don't know what happened before we got there, but when I pointed out the area I could feel Lionheart and the Gunk's Rushes coming from, the park was in total chaos. People were off their bikes, skaters were trying to pull themselves to their feet and runners were trying to get the hell out of Dodge. What's worse, neither the Cape nor the Mask were anywhere in sight.

"Think they've been here?" Hotshot asked. We landed under a tree and I put Annie down.

"Safe bet," I said. "Let's see -- I *know* I 'felt' both their Rushes around here somewhere..."

"Hey! Hey, you're Hotshot, right?"

We turned to see a jogger in red high-tops rushing towards us. He was a big man, with a beard and sunglasses. "Yeah!" he said. "You were Lionheart's old partner, right?"

"So?"

"I just saw your friend fighting that slime-monster guy... whadda they call him... the Gunk? They're over there!" He pointed to a bank of trees nearby, too thick to see into.

Hotshot was about to say something to the guy, but I interrupted, stepping on a fallen branch and swiveling it up into my hand.

"Not *twice*," I said, twirling the branch. "I don't know what's worse, your stupidity or your low opinion of *me.*" I borrowed a jolt of power from Hotshot, charged up the branch and blasted the jogger dead center in the chest. He screamed and threw back his arms, flailing about. His shirt and chest did the computer-screen ripple effect and chunks of orange flesh began to drip away.

"How did you expect to fool *me?*" I asked, using Annie's strength to deliver a blow to the head. "Now where's Lionheart?"

The ground beneath Gunk broke apart and a red-clad hand grabbed his slimy orange foot. Lionheart burst through the soil, executed a graceful arc in the air and smashed the Gunk into the ground, finally knocking him out cold. He landed and began brushing dirt from his uniform.

"This is really beginning to inconvenience me," he said. "First ten years as a zombie and now my uniform is an absolute *mess.*"

"How did he drive you underground?" I asked.

"He's an immortal, he was bound to pick up gardening skills *somewhere.*" He smiled at Hotshot and I realized the two of them hadn't really had a proper reunion in all the insanity. "I see you got them together again," he said.

Hotshot's lip trembled and his voice cracked. "Not *all* of them," he said.

I felt a tug on my arm and Annie pulled me away. "Come on. I think we should leave them alone."

"I guess so." As we moved away I put my arm around her shoulders. She made no move to remove it. "How are *you* holding up?" I asked.

"Okay, I guess. It's a lot to take in just a day or two. First you're a killer, then you're a rabbit, then my baby brother has powers and -- Todd. God, what he did to First Light--"

Her lip quivered and she sniffed. A tear rolled down her flushed cheek and I simply didn't know whether it was for First Light or Dr. Noble. She'd honestly loved him and the realization of who he was would be difficult to bear. I was still trying to decide what, if anything, I should say when I felt a tingle of Rushes in the distance.

"Aw no, don't we *ever* get a break?" I grumbled.

"What?" Annie asked, but I was already heading back towards Lionheart and Hotshot.

"Guys! Heads up! Playtime isn't over yet!"

Over the trees came the last stragglers of Gunk's brainwashing -- Flambeaux, Mental Maid, Justice Giant and the gooified Deep Six and Nightshadow. Except for Flambeaux, none of them could fly, so I wasn't particularly surprised to see Dr. Noble, wide-eyed and soaked, bringing up the rear, using his telekinesis to keep them aloft.

On his coat tails was the LightCorps -- or most of them, anyway. Tin Man carried Defender and Oriole flew behind. I remembered seeing her carrying Condor out of Simon Tower, and I just hoped he'd be okay.

"I'm sick of being on defense," I said. Stealing a Rush from Justice Giant, I pushed my body outwards, growing to a height of fifty feet. (To my relief, my clothes grew with me.) With one massive hand I plucked Noble from the air and reared back, planning to hurl him into the ground.

"Hit him, Double-Em!" he shouted, and I looked up just in time to see a white Soul Ray roasting the air. I couldn't move fast enough to dodge it, so I dropped back down to normal size, falling past the beam and losing my grip on Noble in the process.

"I can't believe you morons are *still* trying to toast me!" I shouted, flying through a spray of fire and hitting Flambeaux in the gut.

"Careful, lad," Lionheart said, joining me in the sky. "These men aren't in their right minds."

"Not to sound cold-hearted," I said, "but at this point I'm finding it particularly hard to give a damn."

Deep Six and Nightshadow leapt at me, abandoning Noble's telekinetic lift, and each grabbed onto an arm. I was dragged down to the ground by the added weight, then thrust outwards with a burst of my own, hurling them away. Annie caught Nightshadow, clocking him over the head hard enough to shove through the slime and concussing his brain. He collapsed.

"The girl's got heart," Defender said, landing on Deep Six's back. In his years of combat, the Defender had learned nearly every form of combat known to man and developed a few of his own, but none of them had ever taught him to hit at superhuman strength. Cutting through the slime, trying to make contact with Deep Six's skull through the broken, battered helmet, was as useful as trying to anesthetize a rock. Kick, twirl, slash with the sword, thrust with the shield -- for every one blow Deep Six landed the Defender landed six more, but they were beginning to wear him down.

"I've got him!" I shouted, leaping at the fight, but before I moved a foot Annie tackled me from behind. A split-second later a Soul Ray churned the Earth just about where I would have been at that point if she'd let me go.

"Thanks," I said. "I don't know if a telekinetic shield would be any good against one of those or not."

"Hey, if I'd let you get hit Tom would never have forgiven me," she said. I smiled and looked up, trying to figure out where Mental Maid was, but I couldn't see her anywhere. I still felt that strange, vague Rush I'd always gotten from her, but it was bold and fuzzy, and I couldn't tell where she really was.

The exercisers in the park were running around like survivors of a train wreck, half of them trying to get away, the other half trying to get a better look. One of them shouted out, "Dude, it's the LightCorps!"

"No way."

"That's the Defender, man, my dad told me all about him!"

"If that's the Defender, how come he got whupped up by the Goop?"

"Man, that ain't the Goop..."

But I ignored the rest of the conversation, looking instead for the Defender. In the grass in front of me, the Defender and Deep Six's wrestling match had ended. And not favorably. Deep Six simply wore him down until he worked in a gut blow that wasn't deflected. From there it was a short matter to take him out.

"Son of a bitch," I said, jumping Deep Six and ripping his helmet off like it was aluminum foil. I landed a blow right to his temple, dropping him for the duration of the fight.

"Two down," I said.

"Two of yours, too!" boomed Justice Giant, and there was a "whump" sound as a black-draped figure fell to the ground next to me. I rushed over and pulled the cape back to find Hotshot barely conscious, his arm clearly twisted in a configuration God hadn't intended. I spun around to charge the Giant, but Annie was already climbing up his body, delivering strategic blows to the knees, back and finally making it to his head. She kicked him hard in the back as she climbed and he wasted time swatting at that little spot you can never quite reach, never even realizing she was making for his neck. She wrapped her arms around his neck and began to squeeze, cutting off an artery to the brain. Justice Giant's eyes rolled back in his head and he toppled forwards.

"The bystanders!" Tin Man swept in and grabbed Justice Giant by the back of the collar, trying to slow the descent enough for the idiot onlookers to get out of the way, but by the time the massive brute was at a ninety-degree angle to the ground, the fall began to speed up again.

"Christ, *no!*" Tin Man shouted. I flew up next to him and grabbed hold, helping him slow the fall. Annie, who was never trained to watch out for civilians the way someone in Cape did, was near panic.

"Oh God, no, I'm sorry, I didn't mean--"

"S'not *your* fault, girl..." Tin Man groaned. His eyes were clenched shut behind his visor and his arms were trembling.

"What's wrong?" I asked.

"Damn suit's been out of commission for ten years," he said. "I didn't have time to recharge the power cells fully... I'm gonna--"

Justice Giant slipped totally out of his grasp and the weight tugged at me, but I managed to set him down without hitting anybody, and just barely avoided being hit by a lancing Soul Ray. Annie cursed herself. "I thought I could help, Josh, I'm sorry. I'm running out of gas too -- if I don't rest soon my powers are going to short out on me."

"It's okay," I said. "How's Tin Man?"

The armored Corpsman had rolled off Justice Giant when he hit the ground and was discarding his gauntlets and boot-jets. "It's worthless, there's no power in this thing at all. I'm a sitting duck."

Just as he said it, branches that looked like they'd been ripped off trees by a charging rhino hailed down about us, driving themselves into the ground.

"My favorite kind of duck!" came Noble's voice. I threw up a telekinetic shield around myself and was about to guard the exposed Tin Man, but Annie jumped in front of him. The first few tree limbs shattered against her skin, but they were starting to leave welts wherever they made contact.

"Annie, look out!" I was about to throw another teke shield up, covering the both of them, but I was forced to dodge another Soul Ray blast. I was about to jump out anyway, and Soul Ray be damned, but the matter was quickly settled. Two more snapped, broken branches ricocheted from Annie's body.

The third hit her, and hit her *hard*, lodging itself in her shoulder. She screamed, clutched her shoulder and fell to the ground. She'd gone far too long without resting and her invulnerability was nil. With her down, the shower of branches stopped. I never noticed.

"Annie!" I was at her side in an instant, even before the Tin Man had time to kneel down.

"She was protecting *me*!" he shouted. "That bastard. You know, your friend Morrie had her in the wrong uniform -- girl had the heart of a Cape from the start."

"Annie..." I moaned, unaware that there was another voice in my head saying the same thing. Tom was there in the blink of an eye.

"Weren't you watching Animan, son?" Tin Man asked.

"She's my *sister*!" Tom screamed. "Animan's gonna be fine, he's got that Conductor guy with him."

I looked up at the sky through tear-stained eyes and saw Noble streaking away. "You got a medical kit in your armor?" I asked.

"Of course."

"Help her." I took off so fast the grass probably burnt beneath me. No less than three Soul Rays ripped through the air around me, but I didn't even try to dodge them -- I was aiming straight for Noble, adding up every jolt of speed and energy available to compound my acceleration. I hit Noble hard enough to powder bones in anyone who didn't have a telekinetic shield. I'm pretty sure I at least cracked a few ribs, but the maniacal Noble just grunted and spun in the air to face me.

I hit him with a fire-blast that could have slagged iron. It barely singed his eyebrows, but the distraction was enough for me to grab his cape and charge it up with Hotshot's power. It detonated a second later and he pitched through the air, narrowly missing a Soul Ray himself. He began to fall. I followed closely behind, avoiding the final, aerial battle between Lionheart and Flambeaux, but didn't even try to catch him.

He hit hard on the concrete walking path in the middle of a pack of roller skaters who had stopped to watch the festivities. I landed nearby and moved to pick him up.

"Hey, back off, man!" One of the roller skaters moved herself between me and the fallen Noble. "I've seen you on the news, you're that Copycat guy! After everything Noble's done for this city, if you think we're gonna let you lay a finger on him--"

"He's a killer," I said, very calmly. "He's a murderer and he may have just killed again. I'm putting a stop to it. Now *get out of my way.*"

"No." Noble pushed his way through the crowd, not looking nearly as beaten up as he should have. "Let him through."

Even though I didn't think before hitting him in the gut with everything I had, I was kind of surprised when my fist went through his stomach, gouging a hole into his chest cavity. I screamed even louder than any of the bystanders.

I screamed again when I tried to pull my hand out, only to find it held tight. That's probably when I noticed that the fluid covering my hand wasn't red, but orange.

The Gunk dropped his Noble face and smiled a big, gooey, orange smile. Then he nodded and I felt my free arm grabbed from the other side. It was Noble, looking a lot more battered than Gunk's facade had. They were holding me, stunned, with my chest fully exposed.

That's when Mental Maid dropped out of the trees, her arm aimed at me. It was still quivering tremendously, and fat tears gushed down her cheeks, but she didn't say a word before she fired.

The Soul Ray didn't hurt at all.

Gunk and Noble both let go of me as I fell forward, my body twisting and mutating. My stomach lurched a bit and my legs gave out underneath me. I trembled and shook everywhere until it was over and I was finally able to look at what I had become.

I was the same height as before, and my jeans and sneakers had been replaced by black trousers and boots. I was still wearing the Copycat costume, complete again. But I felt slower... heavier somehow. I realized that the weight I'd shed during my time amongst the Capes at Simon with the high-octane metabolisms had returned with a vengeance. My old gut was back -- baby fat I'd never worked off, my mother called it -- and I wasn't quite as spry as I had been seconds ago.

But I could still feel the Rushes. My powers were the same. In short, the Soul Ray had changed me to exactly what I had been at the start of the whole mess. Not a monster. Just... *me*.

Mental Maid fell to her knees, weeping, and Gunk and Noble both stumbled backwards as the bystanders screamed, not knowing what the hell had just happened.

"That's *impossible*," Gunk cried. "You should be a monster by now."

"Did *Lionheart* turn into a monster when you zapped *him?*" I asked, starting to find the reality of the situation even a little funny.

There was *one* other thing that changed as a result of the Soul Ray, though. Suddenly that big, diffused power Rush I felt from Mental Maid was comprehensible. I knew every nuance of her powers. I knew how to use them.

I looked at Noble and *saw* him, really *saw* him for the first time, and I laughed. "You're just a bully." I said. "A stupid, scared, piggish bully who thought nobody liked him and decided to make *sure* of it. The only difference between you and the kid who stole your lunch money is that the kid *grew up*."

I shot one arm forward and impacted his face hard enough to beat him into another dimension. He slumped to the ground and didn't get back up until the battle was long since over. Then I looked at the Gunk and smiled. He started to run.

Back at what had become the *de facto* battlefield, Lionheart tossed Flambeaux onto Justice Giant's inert form. Tom was helping patch up Annie, who seemed to have come around, and Oriole was with Hotshot, trying to reset his broken arm. Condor had arrived in my absence, and he was helping tend to the fallen Defender.

"One to go, big guy!" I shouted. A smile broke Lionheart's face when I picked up Gunk by the clavicle, swooping in with Lionheart's power. His feet waggled in the air, helpless to move, and he fell backwards. I pinned all his bones in place and he stopped moving.

"Well done, little guy," he said. "Where's the Doctor?"

"It's naptime," I said. "Anybody got a pair of power dampeners?"

Condor whipped out a pair and held them out. I grabbed Gunk's arms and forced them back into the dampeners. When they shut his orange flesh contracted and turned pink, and he rolled onto the ground, a bald, naked, pathetic heap.

"So *now* is it over?" I asked.

"Oh I hope so," Lionheart laughed, and I knelt by Annie.

"Hey," I whispered. "Nice job."

"You didn't do too bad yourself," she said. "Maybe once things calm down--"

Whatever she was about to say, she never got the chance. She was interrupted by a ridiculous laugh from the Gunk.

"Oh what the *hell* do you have to be laughing about?" Tin Man asked.

"It's just that Lionheart was right all along!" he guffawed.

"About *what?*" Lionheart asked, and the flash in the Gunk's eyes scared the hell out of me.

"I *should* have killed you when I had the chance."

Condor shimmered suddenly, and his body fell away, revealing Spectrum standing in his place. And his eyes were glowing a bright, nasty orange. The power dampeners on the Gunk's wrists vanished too, and the flesh on his arms quivered and transformed into long, metal spikes. He leapt forward, swiveling his arms to the front, and charged Lionheart.

The spikes ripped straight through the gold lion emblem on his chest, jutting out his back covered with torn cloth and blood. Lionheart's head quaked and flopped forwards, his eyes big and blank. Gunk's lip curled up. "Guess I've rectified *that* mistake."

"*YOU SON OF A--*"

I reached out for Gunk, ready to rend him limb from limb, but Lionheart raised his hand and stopped me. A thin trail of blood dripped down from his lip and he raised his head, looking the Gunk straight in the eye. He grabbed the spike in his chest and air began to swirl around them.

"*I do not die easily,*" he said.

Energy sparked around Lionheart's wound and sputtered around them both. The Gunk tried to pull himself away, but Lionheart would not let go. Together, they lifted up and shook in the air. Blood trickled from them, but as it rained I saw that the blood was not red at all, but instead an incredible silver that seemed to roll off dry matter and sink away as if to some other place.

It was as though the wind itself was pushing them up, there was so much of it, and the silver energy carried them like a net. They shredded the atmosphere, racing to the sky, until they were nothing more than a couple of dots higher than we would have been able to see if not for the energy dancing about them.

Then there was the explosion.

The silver energy, whatever it was, raced outwards, encompassing everything I could see, touching everyone it could. As soon as the energy made contact with me, I felt a sudden jolt, a *connection,* the likes of which I'd never felt before or sense. It was a feeling of unity, of *oneness* that words couldn't even describe.

It was the Heart of the Lion. And in that instant, every man, woman and child on Earth that possessed the Lion's Heart, those I knew, those I didn't, those I knew about and those I never suspected... was One.

*I **was** Lionheart, (and my heart soared) and he had a message for me: Thanks, little guy. I'm proud of you.*

*I **was** Hotshot, (and I was sorry) and there was a quick exchange. I/Hotshot said I was sorry, and Lionheart said it was never my fault.*

*I **was** Tom, (brave Tom, someday he'd be more of a hero than me, of that I was certain) clutching my/Tom's sister's bleeding arm, and Lionheart told me I would do great things someday.*

*I **was** Animan, (Animan was one of us? I should have known) slowly regenerating back the Tower and, for the first time, realizing I/Eugene was a part of something greater than myself.*

And more... so many more --

-- in Manhattan, a man prepared to run twenty-six miles, wanting nothing more than to bring America an Olympic marathon gold --

-- in Las Vegas a jazz trombonist played a song of love found and lost and the journey to regain it again --

-- in Louisiana a girl, not quite a woman, sat at the edge of a glistening pond, debating whether to dive into the unknown --

-- at a college a drama student was questioned for a murder he didn't commit--

-- in Idaho a young man learned he had cancer --

-- in a forest somewhere a little old woman stirred a pot of stew, waiting for her sons to return --

-- a child screamed as he saw his bullet-ridden parents hit the ground --

-- a Kansas farmer tilled his soil as a bolt appeared in the sky--

-- a police officer was struck by lightning --

-- a man grit his teeth against a sandstorm--

-- more... hundreds more...thousands... --

-- until finally, in Boston, a woman sat in a darkened apartment, clutching a scrap of colored paper to her breast, crying with a pain I'd never known, and for all her gifts she could not freeze that moment in time, making it last forever.

The energy faded and the light in the sky darkened. Tom, Hotshot and I trembled. Nearby, Spectrum's eyes were returning to normal. Deep Six and Nightshadow's flesh turned their natural colors again, and Nightshadow was lying on the ground, naked and cold. Hotshot, clutching his arm, wrapped Nightshadow in his cape, looking like he'd had the weight of the world lifted from his shoulders.

"What was *that*?" Tin Man asked.

Those of us who knew, and understood, didn't say a word. Instead, I went to Annie, who leaned on me. I didn't argue.

"Does *that* mean it's over?" she asked.

"Yeah," I said. "I think it does."

And we began to laugh. We laughed long and hard, until the tears came, and I don't think either of us ever noticed when they changed from tears of hysteria to tears of pain and sorrow and relief.

THE SUMMIT

The smoke was still settling literally and figuratively, when several of us collapsed in the lounge that afternoon. The whole press corps came out in force, and this time the susceptibility field wasn't going to be enough to keep them at bay. Finally, Morrie gave them a harsh, forceful, "NO COMMENT," along with a stern mental push to tell them to get the hell away from us. When Morrie's brain pushed, people listened.

Back in the tower, though, Morrie was all smiles. "Oh, this is just too cool for school, kid. The old Lightcorps, back in action? People are going to eat this up!"

Morrie was talking to Hotshot, who was leading his old teammates around the facility. Animan was there as well, and Annie, cradling her injured arm. It would be a while before Miss Sinistah swung that club of hers around again. We all exchanged looks at each other when Morrie started talking about the Lightcorps – part exhaustion, part frustration.

"Abadie, right?" Oriole said, walking up to him. "Morrie Abadie? The mentalist? I remember you. What are you talking about?"

"I'm talkin' about you and your crew! I'm talking about you guys signing on with my crew! Come on, you can't tell me you didn't enjoy the rush you got out there today. You want back in the Cape game, right? Well, little lady, I'm the guy that's gonna make it happen!"

The Defender sheathed his sword, somewhat more forcefully than was strictly necessary. "He's joking, right?"

"Morrie," I said, "all this... this whole setup... how much of the charade was you and how much was the Gunk?"

Morrie shrugged. "Look kid, he wasn't runnin' my show from the beginning'. He just knew how to use a good thing when he saw it."

"This can't stand," Defender said. He picked up a Lionheart shot glass someone had left on the counter. "We've always had power, but... *this*. This *economic* power... it's no good."

"I'd rather get a mountain dropped on my head," Tin Man agreed.

"It's worse than that. It's not right, it's not *honest*. It's... is this what Lionheart would have done?"

"Oh, I don't know," I said facetiously. "Let's ask." I took one of the WWLHD rubber bracelets that lay about in abundance and stretched it back, firing it over to the

Defender. He caught it, read it, and dangled it from his fingers like a dead fish.

"This can't stand," he repeated. "This obscene organization has to end *now*."

"What, so we can go back to throwing masks into a revolving door prison like you guys did back in the old days?" Animan said. "Look, I respect you guys. You're my heroes. And Morrie may be the bottom-crawling, scum-eating crud of the Earth, no offense."

"None taken," Morrie said, using a Lionheart cutter to nip the end off his cigar.

"But whether you approve of his motivation or not, Morrie's system *worked*. Siegel City is one of the safest places in the world. If we get on television and tell everyone it's fake *now...*"

"Riots," Annie whispered. "People would go crazy."

"Every villain in the country – every *real* villain – would come here looking for a piece of us," Hotshot said. "The city would be a warzone."

I picked up one of the Lionheart action figures, turning it over in my hand, looking my lost hero in the eyes. "People would lose faith."

"Well right now the entire city is *brainwashed*!" Condor shouted. "I'd heard things... rumors about what was happening here... but until Jay called us yesterday I had *no* idea how bad it really was here."

"And all it takes is one Gunk at the top to bring down the whole system." The Defender dropped the bracelet in the trash. "Think about the raw power in this building. If we hadn't stopped him, he would have turned the entire planet against Lionheart, then against the rest of us. Then it would have been his."

"All right, all right," Annie said. "We can't get rid of it and we can't leave it the way it is. What's left?"

"We change it," I said.

Everyone turned to look at me. Tin Man, Defender, Condor, Oriole... waiting for what *I* had to say. It was just a wee bit intimidating.

"*Change* it?" Morrie said. "Kid, you been here about five minutes. What makes you think--"

"He's *earned* it, Morrie," Hotshot snapped. "Or maybe you forgot that you'd still be the Gunk's sock puppet if it wasn't for Josh."

"Go ahead, lad," Tin Man said, a faint Irish brogue echoing in his helmet. "Make your case."

"We can't shut things down overnight. People would realize something happened. Even with the susceptibility field, sooner or later *someone* would notice all the Masks going away at once. But it's too dangerous to leave things the way they are. Plus, I think we've pretty well established this set-up wouldn't exactly sit well with Lionheart."

"So what option do we have left?" Annie asked.

"We take our time," I said. "Next week – after I've had time to take the mother of all naps – we announce that the heroes of Siegel City are cracking down. Then, over the next two years, we publically capture every prominent Mask in the city and put them away for good. The revolving door is out of business."

"Are you nuts, kid?" Morrie asked. "I'm runnin' a business here. I've got merchandise to sell. I've got employees to take care of. How many hard-workin' Masks are gonna be out of a job?"

"They're not all bad guys, Morrie. In fact, most of them aren't. So we'll 'rehabilitate' some, we'll give others a new identity, and in a couple of years, this will be a legit city again."

"What about my company?" Morrie growled. "We go 'legit,' and how do you plan to bankroll all this?"

"Morrie's not the only concern. Decent people would suffer too," Hotshot said. "Half of Siegel City's economy is based on tourists coming to see our heroes and the stuff people buy with our faces on it, Josh."

"There's nothin' wrong with a little capitalism," Tin Man said. "I see no reason ye can't keep using the merchandise to fund the operation and pay people's salaries."

"Are you serious?" Oriole asked.

Tin Man shrugged through his armor. "Even a Cape has to eat, after all."

"Actually, I think there are a few around here who don't," I said, "but point well made."

Oriole nodded. "Okay, but there needs to be a public face to the money as well. Something that can be held accountable."

"A foundation," I said. "In Lionheart's name. The fake heroes cleaned this city up. With a little financial muscle, maybe the real heroes can make even more changes... improve the schools, fix the roads... make the city even better. Look, ever since you guys went away, ever since *Lionheart* went away... things just didn't seem right. I didn't know what it was until I found out about Morrie, but it was always that little nagging voice in the back of my head telling me that something in this city was *wrong*. And everybody else in town feels it too. Let's get rid of that feeling, guys. Let's give Siegel City *real* heroes to believe in again."

There was a quiet for a few minutes. Everyone was rolling it over in their heads. Finally, it was Hotshot who spoke. "I think... I think Lionheart would be okay with that."

"You know, once the Capes are real again, the real Masks are gonna come back too," Morrie rumbled.

"We'll be ready. Hell, Morrie, don't you see what you've done? You built the biggest superhero team on Earth. We can take all comers. We don't even have to stop with Siegel City. Once we're finished this model can change *every* city. Detroit, Miami, New Orleans... they can all go legit again."

"You're taking a big chance, kid," Morrie said.

"So what? Come on, Morrie, can't you feel it? This is our chance to finally do what heroes are *supposed* to do."

"And what's that?"

Hotshot laughed and threw an arm over my shoulder. "Isn't it obvious, Morrie? We're gonna save the world."

JOURNEYMEN

Hotshot, Annie and I stood on the roof of Simon Tower, drinking in the sun, both of them with their arms in slings and Annie with a bandage around her shoulder as well. Work was still going on to repair the bottom floor of the tower (not to mention all the levels beneath), but the support structure was fairly secure and the building was in no danger of falling down. There was a slight mist hanging about in the air as if it just finished raining, although the sky had been clear for days, and the light of the sun refracted through the clouds, painting the whole sky as red as a newborn babe.

"Sure you don't want to stick around?" I asked. "See what happens?"

"I'll be back," Hotshot said. "There's a debt I need to repay first."

The rebuilding was going to be hell. After we finally rid ourselves of the Gunk I would have been perfectly willing to sleep for a month. Things didn't quite work out that way.

The first and most visible problem was that half the city had seen the battle -- Capes fighting Capes and Masks fighting Masks and the sides so jumbled nobody knew what was going on. As expected, it was Morrie who came up with the solution. Apparently (the press releases said) the Battle of Simon Tower had actually been a concentrated effort by all Siegel City's superhumans -- Cape and Mask alike -- to turn back a subversive alien invasion. These were the same aliens from whom Lionheart had escaped only days before, the ones who held him captive for a decade. The beams of blinding white light people saw were actually used to *reverse* a person's nature, turning bad people good and good people bad. It was the aliens' main weapon against us until the LightCorps came out of retirement to drive them off. It was real crappy, B-movie stuff. The public ate it up like candy.

This was undoubtedly due, in no small part, to the susceptibility field, which Morrie reestablished as soon as his head was clear, the pretense of Mental Maid keeping it up abandoned. This made me sort of nervous, but Morrie assured me that with the Gunk gone everyone who had been transformed changed back and everyone whose mind was controlled had their free will restored. Things were back to normal, such as it was. But they wouldn't be for much longer.

The "war against the aliens" was not without its casualties, of course. A memorial was being erected to First Light, Five-Share and Dr. Noble in Lee Park. It churned my stomach to see the murderer paid tribute alongside his victims, but I understood the necessity of it. Nothing could be gained by telling the citizens what kind of unbelievable bastard they were already beginning to canonize. Let them think he was a martyr.

The real Doc was gone. That was the only part of the whole mess that still ate at me. Sometime between me laying him prone and Lionheart being gutted, Noble woke up and managed to stagger away from the park. We couldn't find a trace of him, anywhere on Earth, and the fact that there was somewhere he could hide from people with our resources bothered me for a very long time.

The two surviving Five-Shares had left Siegel City, probably for good, and gone home to their mother. The woman lost four children in a blink of an eye; the two she had left were refusing to put their lives on the line again, for her sake. Nobody blamed them.

The remaining members of the Spectacle Six, now four strong with Deep Six's return, did not take on any new members right away, even though Morrie urged them to. In memory of the fallen, they would go on and accomplish the fantastic on their own.

Things weren't all gloom and mourning, though, as those of us touched by the silver power knew something no one else could possibly believe.

Lionheart was alive.

We didn't know *how* we knew, but we knew. That blast when Gunk tore through him had expelled almost all of his power, but more than that, it had ripped a hole open to somewhere else. For a second, I even caught a glimpse of it -- a vast field of trees and pools filled with the same sort of silver water I thought fell from him as blood. He was out of there somewhere, weak, helpless and perhaps in grave danger.

But he was *alive*.

To say Morrie made a big deal out of the LightCorps' decision to look for him would be a criminal understatement. There were bands and celebrities and the mayor gave each of the "intrepid explorers" keys to the city. Hotshot, the Defender, Condor and Oriole were all making plans to head out and find Lionheart, wherever he was.

The Tin Man, however, was staying behind. He'd elected to head up an all-new LightCorps back in Siegel, consisting of Nightshadow, Mental Maid (who was a lot less mysterious and a lot happier with the Gunk gone),

Aquila and the Conductor. There were also two "probationary" members, former Masks who'd been zapped by the aliens and whose reversion to the Cape side seemed to be permanent -- Copycat and Turnabout (formerly known as Miss Sinistah). Together, we announced our plan to clean up the city once and for all. The Battle of Simon Tower had convinced us to tighten security and hit the bad guys like never before. A couple of groups, as would be expected, started calling us Nazis and fascists and insurance agents and the like, but public opinion was on our side – over 85 percent, and that was *without* Morrie fudging the numbers. We could do this. We could make this work.

Annie said she was going to try to keep up her "bad girl" image, even as a Cape, but personally I didn't believe it would last. Capes all wind up as media darlings at one point and as scapegoats at another -- once the press got a hold of Turnabout and realized how sweet she really was, everyone in the city would love her as much as those of us in Simon Tower already did.

Tom's mother was absolutely manic about her little boy running about all night, but Annie eventually managed to quell the inevitable storm, feeding her a story about a car accident (explaining her bandaged arm) and needing Tom as a blood-type match. A little nudge from Morrie got her to believe it.

Tom kept calling me up, asking me if I wanted a sidekick, and finally I made a deal with him -- if he'd stop bugging me I'd put in a good word for him when he turned thirteen. It at least calmed him down for a little while.

Animan recovered nicely, and was a lot more enthused about seeing *his* place torn apart than I was by mine (whoever had been looking for my notebook had really ripped the place to shreds and had even, for no apparent reason, stolen my spare Copycat uniform). When Animan heard that half his totems had been destroyed, he bubbled up like Santa Claus getting a huge order for tin soldiers. "Hell, bro," he said as he helped me move my stuff into Simon Tower a few days after he'd healed up, "half the fun of having this power was researching the animals and crafting a character to go with 'em. Now I get to do it all over again. Fix some glitches, you know?"

"Like the glitch your bat-guy has?" Ted chuckled.

"What glitch?" Animan asked. "There's nothing wrong with Flapper."

"Whatever." Ted snickered, slitting open a cardboard box. Rather than trying to restore my apartment to livable conditions, I'd just decided to move into the apartments in the Tower, which had suffered some water damage, but nothing that couldn't be fixed in a couple of weeks. If anyone would still have been prejudiced against me or bothered by the notebook thing, seeing me fighting with Lionheart seemed to have cured them of that.

"Hey Josh," Ted asked, "are you still going to see your friend Sheila now that you quit working at the magazine?"

The job had just been far too time-consuming to keep up with, especially if I was going to be in the new LightCorps. "Are you kidding?" I laughed. "If I stopped hanging around with her she'd track me down and neuter me like a cat. Why?"

"Well... I mean... I was just thinking, you know, maybe I could hang out with you guys sometime."

I rolled my eyes as I saw where this was going. Animan could barely control his amusement. "Here we go again."

"What?" Ted said. "She's not seeing anybody, is she?"

I thought about Sheila's longstanding on-again/off-again infatuation with Spectrum and wondered if her sudden, violent introduction into the underside of Siegel City might have cured her of that. "Not *exactly*..." I said, then I just shrugged. "Good luck, man."

Sheila wasn't the only one whose love life was as confusing as hell these days. Annie and I had become closer than ever after Lionheart's powers connected us all, and there were definite sparks whenever we saw one another, but after everything she had been through I wasn't about to make a move until I knew she was ready. Unfortunately, if there's one thing even super-powers can't help a man with, it's understanding women. Unless she started wearing a sign sometime soon, I didn't have the first clue how to tell if she'd be open to anything.

I expressed how I felt about that in a long, positively Olympic-level sigh as we stood on the roof, watching the sun burn the sky. Annie gently touched my arm with her good one.

"What's wrong?"

"Just thinking," I said.

"Well don't think *too* hard, Josh," Hotshot said. "I won't be around to put a stop to that for a while."

"I'll do okay, old timer."

He put his free arm around me and we embraced like two brothers as the elder went off to boot camp. Once we let go, he turned his attention to Annie.

He planted a kiss on her cheek. "You'll keep him out of trouble, right?"

She nodded. "Count on it."

The communicator clipped to his belt crackled and he tapped a button on it. "Hotshot here."

"Where *are* you rookie?" asked a female voice with a distinctly Bostonian accent: "Wheah *ah* yew?"

"Saying good-bye to some folks."

"Well shake a leg, huh? We're waiting over here!"

Hotshot smiled. "Lightning," he said to Annie and me. "That woman is going to still call me 'rookie' when I'm ninety years old in a rocking chair."

"Lightning?" I said. "Where did *she* come from?"

"She wanted in on the rescue mission," he said. "She's got some unfinished business of her own." He stepped to the edge of the building, then turned back for one last look at us. Even through his mask, I'm pretty sure I saw his throat quiver as though he was forcing himself to swallow a baseball.

"I'll see you later," he said, and I'm certain the reason he turned away so fast was so we wouldn't see his eyes watering up. Then he stepped off into the sky and drifted away.

Annie and I took a seat on a bench and watched as he floated off. I felt myself sighing again.

"What?" she asked, her voice a mixture of teasing singsong and genuine concern.

"Tired," I said. "I'm moving a little slower these days. Feeling a little heavier."

"Oh relax. As long as you're around these hopped-up metabolisms you'll be slim and svelte again in no time."

"Are you sure about that? The Soul Ray may have made me like this for good."

"So what if it *did*?" She patted my stomach. "I think it's kind of cute. And it suits you... makes you look jolly."

I laughed. "Right. It's just a little sobering, I guess. Lionheart comes out of the Soul Ray perfect and I come out as... well... little ol' me."

"Oh come on. Perfect gets real boring *real* quick." She threaded her arm through mine and rested her chin on my shoulder, staring up into my eyes. "So you didn't come out perfect," she said. "*I* still think you came out pretty damn good."

She gave me a dry, tender kiss on the cheek, placed her head on my shoulder and we sat there, watching Hotshot become nothing more than a mote on the horizon. I felt the weight of her, smelled her hair, I was warmed and electrified by her. If I could have made that moment last forever, I would have.

It wasn't everything I wanted from her, but it was a start.

BONUS CONTENT

Lonely Miracle

*Shortly after I finished the first draft of this novel, I happened on the idea of crafting a new short story every year as a sort of "Christmas Card" to my friends and family. I was still very much in the mindset of Siegel City when I wrote it, and it should be no surprise that my first attempt at a Yuletide tale took me back there. From a historical standpoint, this story takes place the Christmas immediately **before** the events of the novel you just finished reading.*

Thanksgiving dinner again consisted of a cold turkey sandwich and a glass of milk at the diner down the street, the same as it had for three years now. She used to be quite a cook -- probably still was, she supposed -- but Nancy Drake never had an excuse to cook for anyone anymore. She didn't let herself think about that. She just sat there, idly playing with her sole piece of jewelry -- a sparsely-decorated charm bracelet -- and finished off her milk.

A waitress was coming between the red-upholstered booths carrying a tray laden with coffee and a club sandwich for the only other customer, an old man who looked like Nancy, at least in that he was spending Thanksgiving in a diner because he had no one to be with. The fluorescent light had a cold flicker, making the waitress appear as though she was walking through a lightning storm.

Right as the waitress walked past Nancy's stool, her feet slipped away and she pitched forward. Her tray fumbled from her hands and the coffee fell out into the air. The sandwich, in four segments, tumbled off the plate and a spray of potato chips followed, spinning in space.

Where everything hung.

The coffee appeared frozen in place, the sandwich hovering as though gravity had suddenly changed its mind about claiming it. It wasn't just the food, either. The waitress was motionless and frigid, the fluorescent light stopped flickering and the other customer was idly looking out the window at cars in the street that were not going anywhere. Even over the grill, jumping grease bubbles stayed in the air instead of falling back down to the steel surface. Nancy got off her stool and physically shoved the waitress aright, plucking her tray from the air and re-balancing it in the woman's hands. She took the sandwich segments and the potato chips and replaced them on the tray as well. The coffee was a little trickier, it had already begun to spill, but by dragging the cup at angles through the air she managed to scoop up most of the liquid. A few drops may still find their way to the linoleum, but no more. Nancy sat down and repositioned herself the way she had been sitting when everything stopped. Then, with a blink, everything began again. The waitress staggered for an instant, but kept her balance.

"What... I thought I tripped..." She looked back and forth between Nancy and the old man. "Didn't you see that?"

"Nice car," the old man said, paying no attention. Nancy just shook her head and lay a five-spot and three singles on the countertop. She got up to leave.

"Um... Happy Thanksgiving, ma'am," the waitress said, still trying to figure out why the floor wasn't covered in coffee and sandwich.

"Same to you," Nancy said, stepping outside. A shadow passed over her and she looked up to see a man in red, white and blue with a flowing cape flying across the sun. The Liberator, Boston's resident superhero. The Capes couldn't take holidays off, after all. Nancy knew she never had.

She only made one stop on her way back to her apartment, at the greeting-card store where Christmas ornaments and decorations had been on display since September. She made this stop once a year, and if it ever occurred to her to cease the tradition, she dismissed the thought. The line of figurines was expanding, each a happy pair of children with round, cherub faces, arms locked or hands held, each holding a little sign that read "Our 1st Christmas Together," or whatever year was appropriate. Nancy had always been impressed at how thorough this particular shop was, the figurines went all the way up to year 25. She didn't think it cynical of them to not go any farther. If you were lucky enough to make it to 25, you didn't need figurines. She shuffled through the figures and picked out the little ice-skating pair that designated year number 13.

"Hey, don't I know you?" asked the girl at the counter as Nancy went to pay. For a moment, Nancy's blood chilled. Oh sure, she'd worn a mask up until ten years ago, but it was just a small one, and her long mane of blond had stayed essentially the same since her early twenties. At 35, she occasionally thought about cutting it, but Edward always liked it this way. Ten years... this girl must have been about nine the last time Nancy was in uniform, but she was always half-afraid of some anonymous person coming up to her on the street and saying, "You're *her*, aren't you? You're *Lightning*."

"Know me? Oh, I don't think so..."

"No, it *is* you. I'm sure of it." The girl bent down under the counter and produced a small, pink paperback volume with a blue bookmark hanging about at page 250 or so. The title was *Matilda's Waltz*, and the picture on the back undeniably familiar.

"You're Nancy Drake, right? I *love* your books, I've read them all."

Nancy let out the breath she hadn't realized she was holding. "Yeah, that's me."

"Oh *wow*. You're so great... how do you come up with all those *ideas*? I mean... I've read Jackie Collins and like that, but the people in *your* books are so *real*. I mean you can *feel* their hearts breaking, you know? How do you do that?"

"Practice," Nancy said. She managed to escape what threatened to be a long and tedious conversation by means of a quick autograph and a hastily-imagined social arrangement, which the clerk was more than willing to accept. Then she headed out of the store and went in the direction of her apartment building.

She should have known the girl was just a reader -- nobody remembered Lightning anymore. She preferred it that way. And while Nancy Drake was something of a well-known figure, she kept up her hermit's life. It suited her. She found it comically ironic that the best-selling romance novelist in New England hadn't so much as brushed hands with a man in over a decade... not since Edward.

As she walked past an old, abandoned bookshop, letting this thought through her mind, she started to feel the corners of her cheeks curl up. Then she started to giggle a little. Then she stopped walking and looked at the shop. It wasn't natural for her to start laughing like that. Something was wrong. She brushed some of the dust away from the shop window and peered in at a dirty, dusty, empty room. Nancy took a quick glance at her hand to make sure it was clean then ran it across the doorjamb. Her fingers came away with a slight rusty orange residue.

"Soul Wraiths," she said. It had been twelve years since she and the rest of her team had thought these emotion-consuming spirits exterminated from the Earth. If they were back... well... this was bigger than her problems. Something needed to be done.

She rushed back to her apartment and ran to the telephone, not even bothering to unwrap her figurine. She picked up the receiver and dialed one of the few personal numbers she still knew, although she rarely bothered to call it. There were a series of rings and finally a connection was made. A young male voice resonated in her ear. "Haaaaappy Thanksgiving, this is Jay."

"Jay. It's Nancy."

"Nance? Oh, wow, it's good to hear from you. What's--"

"This isn't a social call, Rookie. Soul Wraiths in Boston. Your people should check up on it."

"Oh, are you kidding? We'll be right out there. Say, do you--"

"I'm not getting involved anymore, Rookie, you know that. This is just a heads-up, for old times sake."

"Well... if you're sure."

"I'm sure. Happy Thanksgiving." She hung up the phone and, satisfied that her civic duty was fulfilled, went to the closet and began taking out her Christmas decorations.

Her decorations were pretty meager. The tree was an artificial one-foot sprig that she put away in its box each New Year's Day, still fully decorated, waiting for the moment in eleven months when she would allow it to see the light again. She put it in the center of her dining room table and plugged it in. All the lights were good this year. Good, she wasn't up for replacing them.

Then she took out the box with her collection of figurines. The first-year figure, a boy and girl on a holly-decked swing together, she put on her bookshelf facing the room -- after getting a small lion on her charm bracelet caught in the figure and untangling it. The only other charm on the bracelet, a tiny bolt of lightning, escaped. Year two, where the couple was building a snowman, also faced out, as did the dancing couple of year three.

Beginning with year four, the couples faced backwards. She lined up nine of the figures this way, then carefully unwrapped year thirteen and put it at the end of the line, also facing away.

That last figurine was lined up exactly with one of the few magazines she kept on her bookshelf, an old edition of *Powerlines*, the first news magazine devoted exclusively to Capes and Masks. Edward was on the cover. Oh, she was one of the few people on Earth who would call him that, but beneath the red and black uniform, the proud golden emblem, it was her Edward. He, like Nancy and Jay, had been a Cape too, perhaps the finest of them all. But for all that none of the other heroes on Earth had ever been able to do something so simple as avenge him.

"Another year, Edward," she said, "ten of them now, and we still haven't found him. I'm sorry. I hope you can forgive me."

It wasn't her fault, everyone always said. They all knew the risks. Capes were like cops or firemen, sometimes they fell in the line of duty. And while death, for a superhero, sometimes turned out to be a temporary condition, in ten years there was no sign that Edward could possibly have survived.

She put away the magazine and turned back to her Christmas decorations, although she was already nearly finished.

She picked up a the next few weekly editions of *Powerlines* to see if there was any news about the battle with the Soul Wraiths. She didn't bother with a television and she didn't trust newspapers, but *Powerlines* was pretty reliable. It *should* be, their top reporter was really the superhero called Spectrum in disguise. Sooner or later, Nancy was certain, someone would figure out he just created a hologram beard when not in costume and his entire cover would be blown, it was such a lousy disguise. Until then, at least she knew his magazine could be counted on to get the story right.

When the story with the Wraiths broke the week before Christmas, it was Jay who nabbed the spotlight, and the cover. "Hotshot to Soul Wraiths: Get Out of Siegel!," the cover blurb read. There was also a photo that showed him in midair, delivering a roundhouse blow to one of the glowing red creatures. That would go straight to the Rookie's head, no doubt. Not that he didn't deserve it. He'd tried his damndest to fill Edward's shoes in the past ten years. He couldn't, of course, but at least he tried.

The battle, it seemed, hadn't taken place in Boston after all, but in Siegel City, where 99 percent of all superhero activity seemed to center these days. The Wraiths, according to a the story, had tried to leech away the citizen's "Christmas Spirit" to power their latest attempt at world domination. And as always seemed to be the case, at least once a year since she'd lost Edward, some second-stringer had died in the fighting. A villain this time, a guy named Photon Man. Nancy hoped he didn't have any family, for their sake, but at this point the news of a death just didn't faze her that much.

She tossed the magazine aside and turned to her computer, where chapter six of her latest novel was waiting for her. Writing what her mother had always called "trashy romances," even as she read them by the truckload, turned out to be the perfect occupation for the post-Edward Nancy Drake. Human contact was limited to shopping excursions and the occasional conference call with her editor, plus she had an outlet to focus all the scenarios she kept imagining where Edward miraculously returned. Her first few books had followed pretty much the same pattern -- the long-lost boyfriend or husband or fiancé returned from certain death, each scenario getting more elaborate and unlikely. Sometimes they were reunited. Sometimes not. Nancy didn't restrict herself to the happy ending. Eventually she got out of the trap of the long-lost hero and began conjuring up more creative plots, but her earliest works were, for the most part, blatantly autobiographical. She suspected the same held true for most writers.

Her powers made the job even easier. Most media outlets -- even *Powerlines* -- had screwed that up pretty consistently over the years. Everyone seemed to be under the misconception that she had super-speed powers. In fact, she had the ability to speed up or slow down time itself, like she'd done to the waitress on Thanksgiving. After only a few hours worth of trials, Nancy had learned how to synchronize her personal typing speed exactly to the rate that her computer could process what she was inputting. She could literally write as fast as she could dream up the stories. In the nine years since her first sale, she'd turned out twenty-six lonely heart novels and, to her utmost shock, people actually seemed to be reading them.

Time slowed down around her as she shifted into the writing groove. A shadow crawled across the window as, in regular time, a bird flew by. The second hand on her clock moved infrequently at best. She and the computer were a perfect match for the time she was going to spend writing.

She'd made it five pages into chapter seven, where the tortured Monica Gacey was finding evidence that her husband had died at the hands of her own father, when the room began resonating with a low, thrumming sound. It was like a drawn-out "whump." Nancy recognized it at once -- it wasn't the first time she'd heard this particularly sound while in her writing zone. She restored time to its usual flow and the "whump" shortened and the pitch rose until it was a rapid tapping on her window, which she reluctantly opened. "Come on in, Jay."

The red-and-black clad Cape drifted into her office from her sixth-floor window, pulling back his mask to reveal the grinning face Edward had recruited only a year before they lost him. "Hey, Nance," he said. "How are you."

"Same as usual. What brings you to Boston?"

"Air currents. Heh." His grin vanished in about as much time as it took him to accept that his joke had fallen flat. "I wanted to let you know we took care of those Wraiths for you."

"So I read," she said, pointing to the magazine on her desk. "Good work. How much damage did they do before you got them?"

"It was pretty bad, actually," Jay said, "they managed to set up shop in nearly every major city in America before we caught them, but we should recover. Particle ran some calculations, said that the worst that will happen is a few less crappy Christmas specials this year. I say as long as they keep rerunning Charlie Brown, I'll be happy."

Nancy allowed herself one of her few genuine smiles. The kid (she didn't care if he *was* 29 now, he'd always be "the kid" to her) always *did* know how to make her laugh. "You could have told me that on the phone, you know. And don't try to convince me that you just happened to be in the area. You guys never leave Siegel anymore if you can help it."

Jay sat down. "Truth? Some of the guys wanted to check up on you. I volunteered for the job. We just wanted to make sure you were okay."

"Hey, *Frontier Trace* just hit number four on the New York Times list. I'm fine."

"That's not what I mean."

"I know."

"We just... hell, *I* just know how tough this time of year is on you. It was always... his favorite."

"Yeah. It was."

Jay's smile dimmed a little with guilt -- guilt that he'd survived when Edward didn't? Yeah, Jay was that type. He glanced over at the mini-tree that served as her primary decoration. "Hey, at least you're keeping things festive."

"I try my best. If you don't mind, Jay, I was in the middle of a chapter. Cut to the chase?"

"Right. Well, Harrison and Erica are having a sort of reunion thing on Christmas Day. Most of us don't have a family, not in any traditional sense, anyway, and they asked me to extend the invitation."

Nancy turned it over in her head for a moment... the prospect of seeing Harrison and Erica, known to the world at large as Condor and Oriole, of getting together with her old teammates, of the whole team, the whole LightCorps being reunited.

With one exception.

"I... I don't think so, Jay. Give 'em a big 'thanks anyway,' but I just don't think I'll be up for it."

"Are you ever going to be 'up for it,' Nance?" he asked. She didn't answer.

On Christmas Eve, Nancy went to church more out of habit than out of any remaining faith. She saw a police chase on the streets and, just for an instant, felt the urge to leap in and interfere, but Liberator arrived on the scene and put a stop to it himself. Call it a Christmas present, she thought -- her overactive sense of responsibility didn't have a chance to flare up and her exhausted guilt complex didn't suffer an added burden.

There was a Santa Claus on the streetcorner, and a poor excuse for one, too. He was rail-thin, and his beard looked tired and scruffy. His eyes were a deep blue, but sunken into his head, and his cheeks could only have been described as "rosy" if the roses in question were pale as the snow. Nancy tried to walk past him without incident, but as soon as she was within five feet of him, those cold eyes locked onto her. She felt her neck tilting against her will and she stared at him, looking straight down those eyes like a tunnel.

"Help," he whispered.

"Um... I don't have any change," she said. She tried to sidestep him, but he moved in front of her.

415

"*Help*," he repeated.

"I really don't think I have anything," she said, even as she dropped her hand into her pocket, searching for even a single to give him.

"No," he said, "help *me*."

Nancy felt a chill race through her that had nothing to do with the nip in the air. She shuffled past the old man without a word and headed for her apartment, a good five blocks away. She didn't use her powers, but she got there as fast as any normal human could.

She fished the key to the building out of her purse as she ran, hoping to get in before the strange man -- if he was so inclined -- could catch up to her. She tried to slide the key into the lock, but her hands were quivering a bit more than they should have been. He was probably just some homeless guy trying to get a meal or something, after all. Had it really been so long since she'd dealt with the unexpected that a simple plea scared her?

"Nancy?"

The key fell from her hand and clattered to the concrete steps. She turned remarkably slowly for someone once called the fastest woman on Earth. Five words, that was all she had heard of this tired, gruff voice before. It was unmistakable.

The old man was standing next to her, right up next to her. On the right. She'd been running from the *left*.

"Please, Nancy. I need your help."

Secret identity be damned.

Nancy dropped time down to a crawl. At this speed a snail at a greyhound track would only have two to one odds against it. She scooped up her key, opened the door and charged up six flights of stairs to her apartment. She slammed the door, flicked the lock and deadbolt closed, secured every window and only then restarted time so she could set the security system. She slumped behind the chair in her office and looked at the telephone, briefly contemplating calling Jay. Then she realized how absurd that was -- she had six years of experience on him, even if she *had* been out of practice for ten years. If she called him for a creepy old man, she'd never hear the end of it. Even a creepy old man that could teleport or something. A creepy old man who knew her name.

"I need your help, Nancy."

She didn't turn around this time. She didn't need to. She was looking into the monitor of her computer, which was off, and quite clearly showed the reflection of an anemic Santa Claus with a glowing nimbus of light around him.

"I need *Lightning*, Nancy."

She turned around, feeling her throat constrict. "Who are you?" she managed to hiss. A small smile upturned his lips.

"Who am *I* Nancy? Surely it hasn't been *that* long."

She flicked her leg outwards, tripping him. When he hit the floor she catapulted out of her chair and landed on his back, twisting his arm behind him. "No. I hasn't been that long, only ten years, and I haven't forgotten everything. Now you tell me who you are and how you know who I am or you carry your right arm away with your left."

"I'm *Santa Claus*. Kris Kringle. Saint Nick. I'd show you my driver's license, but they don't make you carry one for the sleigh."

"I'm supposed to believe a skinny Santa Claus that breaks into my apartment uninvited?"

"I apologize. I'm used to having an open invitation in pretty much every home on Earth. You used to extend the same."

"I'm sure I did," she said, twisting the arm a little harder. The Santa Claus grunted.

"*Must* you do that?"

"Must you feed me your line of crap?"

"Easy Bake Oven!" he shouted. Her eyes opened wide and her grip involuntarily loosened a little.

"What did you say?"

"Easy Bake Oven," he said. "That's what you wanted for Christmas when you were seven years old."

"Yeah, and I didn't get one," she said.

"That's because on December 23 you tricked your little brother into climbing the storm gutter outside your house. He could have been hurt. I even had the oven packed and ready to be loaded into the sleigh when I got the notice that I had to switch you off the 'Nice' list. I didn't *like* doing it, Nancy. If you had waited 36 hours the loot would have been in your hands."

She let go of his arms entirely at that, standing up, her jaw open. He flexed his arm and pulled himself to his feet. "Does this mean you believe me?" he said.

"Not necessarily," she said. "I've seen enough shapeshifters and mind-readers not to believe any weirdo who shows up knowing things about my childhood. But I've seen too much strange stuff to refuse to believe you, either. Convince me. Start with why Santa Claus is skinny this year."

"The Soul Wraiths," he said.

"What?"

"You didn't think I only lived off cookies and milk, did you?" he said. "My power -- my very existence is dependent on the faith people have in me, and in this season. Those Wraiths ate up so much of the hope and love that exist this time of year. It's causing me to waste away, Nancy. I don't have the strength to do it this year... not on my own, anyway."

"So you're telling me your power wouldn't build up eventually? Why come crawling to me?"

"A thousand years ago, it may not have mattered, Nancy," he said, "but we live in such cynical times... times where people believe only in what they can see and touch. The faith of the children in a Santa Claus is one of the few intangibles left. If I miss even one year's worth of my rounds, the loss of faith would be so devastating I may never recover."

"And that would be the end of Christmas, I take it?" she said. "I've seen this Rankin-Bass special, I think."

"Not at all, child," Santa said. "I am not vain enough to believe this season exists because of me, or even that I am the primary participant. The season would survive, even if Santa Claus were to die."

"Then why should I help you?"

He smiled again, and in that smile she caught a hint of a twinkle, one that almost made her think there was something to this after all. "Oh, Nancy, I saw the way you almost tried to stop that car chase this evening. I was listening in on the phone call when you warned Jay about the Soul Wraiths. I see a thousand other things you do every year, even out of costume, that prove to me you haven't stopped caring entirely. Wouldn't be enough for you to know you helped save a life?"

She folded her arms and gave him a skeptical smile. "You know what buttons to push, mister, I'll give you that. What are you asking?"

"The toys are made," he said, "and the route prepared. And I've found the help for the deliveries -- never you mind how. But I need your power, the power of Lightning, to slow down time for me this evening, or the toys will never be delivered in time."

"You want me to slow down the *entire world*? I've never tried anything that big, I don't even know if I *could*."

"You *could*," Santa said. "If you *believe* you could."

"Oh man, this *is* a television special, isn't it?"

"Nancy, *will you* help me?"

"I still don't know that I believe you."

His red-gloved hand reached into his natty beard with a scratching motion. Then he smiled and waved his hand in the air, a sack appearing from nowhere. She couldn't help noticing that it wasn't quite as full as she would have assumed.

"How about this," he said, reaching into the sack. "I have two presents for you this year, if you help me. One, you may open now, as evidence. The other will have to wait for Christmas morning."

He pulled his hand from the sack holding two brightly wrapped parcels. They were both about six inches long, thin enough to be candles, and wrapped at the top with a bow. He placed them side-by-side on her desk. The wrapping of the one on the left looked like it consisted of a many multicolored cords wrapped together all the way up the package. The one on the right, on the other hand, looked like the cords hadn't been woven at all, and were branching out in all directions with no discernable pattern or logic to them.

"What are they?" she asked.

"Something you want."

She considered this for a long moment, then reached out and picked up the package on the left. She took the ribbon between her fingers and was about to pull, but looked up at Santa first.

"Go on," he said.

She slid the ribbon off and opened up the paper. She never saw quite what was inside the package, because the light that consumed her at that moment was far too bright.

"I love it," Edward said, holding up the sweater she gave him to his chest. It was orange and brown striped, and looked like something someone's nearsighted grandmother would have crocheted just to get rid of the extra feet of yarn that was cluttering up her sewing closet. "It's absolutely grand."

"You're lying," she said.

"I most certainly am not." His British accent still gave her gooseflesh, and the smile he wore was quite possibly the most beautiful thing she had ever seen.

"Yes you are. You're a wonderful man, Edward, and you're the most beloved superhero on Earth because you're so good and honest. And part of the reason you're so honest is because you're the worst liar I've ever seen. You *hate* the sweater."

"I do *not* hate the sweater," he insisted. "I'm not particularly fond of the way it *looks*, I admit, but I don't hate the sweater itself. What is it, wool?"

"Cotton."

"Oh, good. I'd hate to think innocent sheep are wandering around naked for this monstrosity." She laughed and hit him at the same time. That was the sort of relationship they had, where either of them could slap the other on the arm or shoulder and it meant the same thing as a kiss, which is what he gave her in response to the blow. "All right," he said, "my turn now."

He stood up and walked around the apartment, which looked the same as it did when, in another time, Nancy wrote solitary novels about broken-hearted damsels. The only significant difference was the much wider array of Christmas decorations, including a four and a half-foot tree, and the bare bookshelf. He picked up the bag he'd brought in with him, which began beeping as he started rummaging through it.

"Edward, you're smart enough to know not to give a woman something electronic."

"It's my mobile, darling." He said "darling" in that wonderful, sarcastic tone that he only used when he knew she'd hit him with a particularly clever wisecrack.

"Uh-oh. Which one?"

"LightCorps."

"I'll go suit up."

"No, don't." He turned off the device and dropped it back into his bag. "I made arrangements with Condor and Oriole tonight."

"What kind of arrangement?"

"The kind of arrangement where they remember what their first Christmas together was like and graciously agreed to supply us with something of the same. Don't worry, they promised to call if something tremendously difficult should come up, such as a giant alien threatening to eat New York or something. But no less, if the alien's only going to munch on New Jersey I say let him have the bloody thing."

She laughed and he smiled -- they had a particularly good arrangement in that respect. He took out two packages, both about the same length but one considerably thicker. "This first one is actually a present for the both of us. Here."

She took the package and opened it up to reveal a small white box. When she unfolded the top she pulled out a figurine of a little boy and a little girl out ice-skating together. They held a sign between them that read "Our 1st Christmas Together."

"Oh, Edward, this is so sweet."

"I thought it might be nice to establish a tradition or two. They had an entire line of these things at the store.

I thought perhaps we can go out next year and purchase the next one together."

"Next year?" Nancy said. "So... there'll be a second Christmas?"

"I certainly hope so," he said, and she kissed him for that, and he accepted. Then he handed her the second package, which was opened to reveal a gold charm bracelet.

"A lion and a lightning bolt," she said. "Is this us?"

"Oh, you're *so* smart," he said.

"I love it. This is wonderful."

"I thought it would be nice for you... just in case."

She slid her hand into the bracelet and latched it. "In case what?"

"Well... let's be honest, Nancy, you and I aren't exactly in the safest line of work. I'm sure police officers and firemen often give their girls sort of... 'in case' gifts."

"Most firemen don't have their girls putting their lives on the line *with* them," she said. "I'm not saying nothing *could* ever happen, but hasn't it occurred to you that I have just as good a chance of... not making it as you do?"

"It has," he said. "But frankly, I think I'd rather fall myself than let anything happen to you."

"Don't talk like that."

"Sorry."

It was, in fact, the first conversation either of them had about the chances of one of them dying in the three years they had been members of the LightCorps together. Of course, it was the first Christmas they had being a "them" instead of being two teammates, two comrades, but nothing more. Nancy didn't quite remember what happened to change it, but she knew that the initial moves had been hers, and she had

423

always been mildly nervous that he was only reacting to her affections rather than expressing his own. A silly paranoia, she knew, but one she couldn't avoid.

"I know it's possible, Edward," she said, "but... the thought of losing you now, just when we've become something... really special."

"I think we're special too," he said. "But the lunatics that are out there trying to kill us won't care."

"I know," she said, taking the figurine and putting it on the bookshelf. "Do we have to have this conversation, Edward? It's Christmas Eve."

"I'm sorry, I didn't want to upset you. I'd jump off bridges to keep from upsetting you."

"Well yeah, but *you* can fly."

He laughed. "You know what I mean."

"Yeah." That's when something inside her bubbled to the surface and forced its way out of her mouth, something neither of them had said before, at least not since their attraction had been confessed. "Edward?"

"Yes?"

" I love you."

His face grew longer in a look of unmistakable surprise and she spun around, pretending that she was adjusting the figure. Stupid, stupid, how could she have said something so stupid? "God, I'm sorry--"

"Sorry? Dear God, don't be sorry." His voice was cracking, and when Nancy turned around she saw the most powerful man on Earth coming up behind her with a single tear rolling down his cheek.

"Are you crying?"

"I... I just didn't expect that."

"Edward, you've had girlfriends. Do you mean no one has ever said that to you before?"

"Well..." he placed a hand on her should and turned her until their eyes met. There were still a few tears in his. "No one else has ever said it *first* before."

As he kissed her, the light roared up again and he was gone, but she could still feel him on her lips, twelve years later.

Nancy's mind crunched as she absorbed the revelation that it was *now*, not *then*, that the man holding her by the hand was not Edward, that although the memory she had just tasted was wonderful it was only that, a memory. "What was..." she started to ask before she realized that was the wrong question. "Why did you give me *that*?"

"Because you needed to remember," he said, and she noticed that his cheeks were a little rounder, that they had some of their pink back. And the twinkle in his eye, before only hinted at, was now quite evident.

"Will you help me, Nancy?"

She smiled -- one of her first genuine smiles in a long time.

"Hey," she said, "who could say 'no' to Santa Claus? So... what do I do?"

"You're already doing it."

She glanced around and saw he was right. The clocks were not moving, the refrigerator was not humming. She had become so lost in the memory of Edward that she'd tried to preserve it the only way she knew how -- by freezing time.

"It's not quite enough," he said, "not yet. Time has only slowed for us, in this room. Now reach out. That's all you have to do. Just... reach... out."

Nancy sent her power out and she felt the world's spin change to match her own slowed-down time. First, here in Boston, cars stopped, drinks were frozen in mid-pour, parents hastily attempting to assemble toys were trapped trying to untangle a bicycle chain.

Elsewhere, birds stopped flying but did not fall. Hearts stopped beating but no one died. Everywhere there was a great freeze, a great Slowing, and the whole world, in very literal terms, grew still.

The strain was enormous. Nancy had never expended so much power before and she had no idea how long she would have to hold it.

"Now what?" she asked.

"Now," he said, "my friends go to work."

Nancy could feel, in the middle of the stillness, motion. It began somewhere in the north and it spread, branching out like roots, creeping down the whole of the world.

And he knew everything. Each time one of the roots stopped and touched a child, it asked the same question. The answers were almost never the same -- building blocks, a teddy bear, a football, a video game. She was feeling the entirety, the *now*, and with each stop, each time her companion gave of himself, his smile grew larger.

But for all her power, Nancy had to remember that she did not really *stop* time, just slow it down so much that its passage became imperceptible. And as time *did* creep, and as the first children woke up and found Christmas morning, the visitor's smile grew brighter, his figure fuller and more robust and finally, after what felt to Nancy like centuries, the job was done and the twinkle in his eye was so bright that she had only seen its like once before, in Edward's last moments, and she cried out in grief and joy as she finally released her power and allowed the world to begin again.

When she awoke to a larger, warmer world, she was surprised to find her friend still there, looking plump and jolly and quite convincing, even to a faithless cynic like herself.

"You're still here," she said.

"I owed you a thank you."

"No you didn't. But you're welcome."

The sun shone in her window and she realized she'd slept the whole night right there on the floor of her office. And although she was tired, she'd never felt more alive.

"What are you?" she asked. "What are you really?"

"I'm old Saint Nick."

"Oh I know that," she said, "But *what* are you? You're not normal, not a man... not even a jolly old elf."

"Oh, and I suppose you've met elves?"

"I have, actually," she said. "I used to be in a pretty eclectic line of work, you may recall. But you're something else. What? An alien? Ghost? Some sort of funky interdimensional spirit?"

"I'm a spirit all right," he said. "Let's leave it at that."

"Okay."

"I suppose I'll be going home, now. I'll be more than well enough to do this myself next year."

"Good-bye, then."

He stood up and shook himself. He lifted a hand to his face, but before he made contact, he nodded to her desk. "It's Christmas morning, Nancy. Open your present."

And then he lay a finger aside of his nose, and he was gone.

Nancy lifted the small package from her desk, the one with the wild, multicolored cords in the wrapping. The other one was a memory, was the *past*. What then, was this?

She opened the top and peered in and, like before, she was consumed by light.

The vision was different this time, not a memory, not even something that definitely belonged to *her*, but she knew it was real. She saw Jay, first, not as he was years ago, but as he was now, stronger and prouder, but with sadder eyes. He was in uniform, in battle, the way she always thought of him.

And he was not alone.

At his side was a young man -- no older than she herself had been when she last became Lightning -- wearing a modified version of the uniform Edward used to wear, only darker, with muted colors. He wore it well.

And standing with them both, clad in his own uniform, looking not a day older than he had the last time she saw him, looking even stronger and prouder than ever, was Edward himself. Alive, and breathing, and fighting on.

And the vision ended. The package and the wrapping glittered away into thin air, and she felt a rush of warmth envelop her.

If the first package was the *past*...

She got up, showered, and dressed in her most warmest, most festive clothes, then turned her powers on herself, speeding up enough so that the journey to Siegel City would take no time at all. Walking through her living room, she stopped and looked at the row of figurines on her bookshelf. Before she left she took the newest figure, "Our 13th Christmas Together," and turned it around to face the room and the decorations, turned it away from the magazine on the shelf with Edward's picture on the cover, turned it so that the little boy and the little girl were finally looking ahead.

Inciting Incident

Last summer I received word from Scott Roche, a fellow podcast author whose work I quite admire, that he was working on a new eBook science fiction anthology called Flagship. When I heard the theme of the first issue would be "Origins," the following story came to me I was honored to be included in the first edition of Flagship, from Flying Island Press. You can check out Scott's stuff at www.spiritualtramp.com or buy back issues of Flagship as an audiobook or an eBook from www.flyingislandpress.com. This story takes place a few years prior to Other People's Heroes.

According to his figures, if he jumped from the roof of Simon Tower, it would take Ethan Hellig approximately 47 seconds to hit the ground. He had no intention of hitting the ground, of course, but standing as he was on the precipice, it was rather impossible not to ponder the numbers.

The experiment was untested, after all. He had every reason to believe it would work, that the apparatus he was wearing would perform perfectly, that the variables would all align as predicted... but even the most assured prediction was just that until he put it to the test. And this wasn't exactly the sort of test he could attempt on a gerbil first. It would have to be all him.

He checked his helmet, checked the straps on his mechanical wings and rocket booster, triple-checked the status of the energy reservoir. "Here goes nothing," he mumbled, mostly because he felt such a moment called for words of some kind and nothing better occurred to him. Holding his breath, he stepped into the air.

He'd been skydiving before, but this wasn't really the same thing. Jumping from a plane, you were completely out in the open, falling through nothing. Now he was falling down through a chute of steel and concrete, acutely aware of the buildings on every side of him. In the open air, you could fool yourself into thinking you were flying. Here, most definitely, Ethan was falling.

He pushed the button and the apparatus around his body began to hum. He closed his eyes and waited for something to happen.

Six seconds later, he was still falling.

Eight seconds later, he wasn't.

His wings did nothing, the rocket he was wearing did less, but he'd stopped falling. He looked around to see the buildings drifting down, the ground becoming distant, and he looked up to see Dr. Noble. The top hero of Siegel City, at least for the last year or two, had caught him under the arms and was carrying him upwards, away from what would probably have been assured destruction.

Noble was your all-American superhero – he flew, he was strong, he even draped himself in the colors of the flag. As he caught Ethan, though, Ethan felt a tickle of static and the hair on his arms stood up. Noble had some considerable energy powers in his repertoire as well, and although he wasn't throwing around energy bolts right now, there was a constant buzz in the air around him. Ethan could hear a buzz coming from the energy reservoir on his chest, which started to glow green and it didn't stop until Noble dropped him off on the roof. The Simon Tower observation deck was closed for the evening, but Ethan was small in stature and had gotten very good at hiding in places he shouldn't be until people were gone. Simon Tower was the hub of superhuman activity in Siegel City, but despite that the villains rarely attacked the building itself. It was strange, but for what he was trying to do, Ethan was more interested in the heroes anyway.

"Let me guess," Noble said, looking him over, tapping the metal wings. "You built a jetpack that's supposed to let you fly so that you can become a superhero too."

Ethan stammered. "Uh... well..."

"Oh, take off that stupid helmet." He grabbed the shell around Ethan's head and pulled it off, leaving a red mark on Ethan's chin where the strap rubbed against it. He handed the helmet back. "I've seen it a thousand times. Let me tell you something, buddy, ninety-nine percent of the people who build something to make themselves into a Cape fail. About seventy-five percent wind up in the hospital. You want to know what happens to fifty-five percent?"

Ethan did not.

Noble examined the device he was wearing more closely. "You got some smarts, I can tell. If you can build something like this, you can build something that will make you rich. Why don't you focus on something like that instead?"

He gave a salute and floated off into the air, leaving Ethan alone. As he vanished from sight, Ethan smiled.

"Maybe I will."

The encounter with Dr. Noble left Ethan a bit perplexed, but undaunted. Noble wasn't exactly what he'd expected. On television, whenever he made a public appearance, Dr. Noble came across as the all-American corn-fed paragon that everybody wanted him to be. In person, his voice was gruff and he felt a bit dismissive. Why not, though? If movie stars and professional athletes could have a clean public image and a dirty smear underneath, why wouldn't the same apply to superheroes?

Back in his shop, Ethan's attention returned to his work. The energy reservoir was reusable, of course, but the rest of his next device was completely new construction. Under his black bodysuit he wore a thin copper alloy mesh – uncomfortable against his skin, but necessary for what he was planning. A black ski mask would help protect him from the cameras, or at least slow down any investigators enough that it wouldn't matter who he was by the time they found him.

At 11 o'clock, he slipped out of a hiding place in the Ditko Medical Pavilion, where he'd been hiding in various supply closets and unoccupied rooms for several hours now. A fiber optic camera attached to a PDA allowed him to peek around corners and under doors, helping him avoid detection. Word was there was a failed cancer treatment that had been attempted here… failed in that it did not cure any cancerous cells, but a success in that it altered the bioelectric field of a medical researcher, giving him incredible healing abilities. The device may not still be there, but even if it wasn't, Ethan was hopeful that he would at least find *some* useful files he could adapt for his own experiments.

In the end, he didn't find the cancer treatment or any device or files related to it. He found something even better. In a glassed-off observation room was a large, blue-skinned man glowing with a cold fire. He had no idea what was wrong with the man, but if there was even the slightest chance Ethan could put it to use, he had to investigate.

The readouts on the computer bank were a bit out of his wheelhouse, but he'd studied enough biochemistry (out of necessity) to get together a basic understanding of what he was looking at. This guy – he recognized him now as Catalyst, one of the heroes of nearby Centerville – was going through a series of bodily transformations due to an unstable metabolism. Ethan's eyes grew wide – there had to be *some* way he could put that to use. If only he—

There was an electric blue sizzle and Ethan felt a shock across his entire body. The copper mesh suddenly began to sear, and he knew he'd look like he'd fallen asleep on a grill when he took it off. After what seemed like hours, the surge of electrical power stopped and Ethan fell down to his knees. A hand grabbed the back of his shirt and lifted him up.

"Well what have we here? Paparazzi looking for a story? Industrial thief? Or just a good old fashioned supervillain?"

The man looked at him through a white mask that flowed down into his red-and-white costume. On his chest was a large red cross – medical, not religious – and Ethan couldn't suppress a smile. He'd been found by STAT, the self-styled "medical marvel." On Ethan's chest, the energy reservoir hummed again and the display on the front shifted colors to a soft, lightning blue.

STAT shook him again. "Come on, buddy, you've got nothing to say for yourself?"

"Just goodbye," Ethan said. He kicked out and hit STAT in the kneecap. The sudden pain made the Cape drop him and Ethan rolled away. It was a gamble, but STAT didn't see a lot of combat, mostly spending his time in the field healing up other heroes who got shot, stabbed, Karate'd, whatever. He could use his bioelectric shocks offensively too, obviously, but his attacks weren't nearly as strong as his defensive powers. Back on his feet, and with STAT bending over to clutch his knee, Ethan punched him in the face, sending him onto his back and holding his chin. He felt bad about brutalizing the good doctor, but just a little. STAT had interrupted *him*, after all. He wasn't there to steal anything... at least nothing they would need.

He rushed down the hall, easily evading the few nurses and orderlies roaming the halls at this hour. There was a security guard at the entrance who waved a Billy club in his direction, but Ethan whipped out a telescoping staff he'd kept strapped to his thigh. With the flick of a wrist, he swatted the club out of the guard's hand. With a second swing, he'd connected to the guard's forehead and put him down. He felt worse about him than STAT, to be frank, but he wasn't going to let either of them put him in jail for trespassing in the hospital after hours.

He pulled out a Hawaiian shirt from his backpack and put it on as he ran, peeling off his black ski mask and gloves and throwing them in a dumpster. It may not be the greatest camouflage in the world, but at least anyone who saw him leave the hospital wouldn't automatically connect him to the man in black. The Hawaiian shirt also neatly covered his energy reservoir, although if you looked closely at his chest, you could still see a small, blue glow.

The next pieces of his device snapped onto the energy reservoir easily. And why not, hadn't he designed them that way? The hard part was disguising all of the pieces under his clothing – a few plastic cases the size of a pack of cigarettes weren't that hard to disguise, but other pieces were a little bigger. No big deal when he was on his own, hiding in the Clinic or sneaking up to the roof of Simon Tower after hours. This was different. It was taking a risk, going out in public for this next attempt, but there would be no better time to try to test it on Lifespeed than at this charity race. The super-speedster from Siegel City was racing Centerville's resident racing guru, Speedburn. Actually, studying her powers might work too, but Ethan had spent more time studying Lifespeed and felt

435

he had a better understanding of just how his powers worked. Speedburn would be a wild card, and if her running speed didn't come from the same place as Lifespeed's, he could be putting himself at terrible risk if the two were incompatible.

The race track was laid out in a circle between Siegel City and Centerville. Either of the heroes could traverse the distance between cities almost faster than it takes to tell, so they were going to do a 500-lap race, tracked and verified by the Swiss timer company that was sponsoring the event. The start and finish lines were both in Lee Park, and Ethan had to get there two days ahead of time to ensure a spot close to the track. V3OL of the Spectacle Six was there to serve as the starting pistol for the race, literally, as he had a cap gun attachment in his huge arsenal of weaponry. The advantages of being a combat android, Ethan supposed. He knew the robot could also detect weapons, and as he came out to the starting line he was clearly looking over the crowd. Ethan wasn't wearing anything that could be used offensively, though, and he'd have to hope V3OL's sensors wouldn't register the rest of the advanced tech on his body.

The two speedsters stood at the starting line, leaning over and waiting for the signal to begin. As they did so, Ethan slipped a hand into his pocket and touched a switch that activated his device. V3OL fired his starter pistol and the two racers vanished in the blink of an eye. A few seconds later there was a tremendous wooshing sound, signaling that the first lap had been completed already, followed by another woosh seconds later still. According to the timer, the split from which was displayed on a huge plasma screen set up in the park, Speedburn was ahead of Lifespeed by 0.0000007 microseconds. To someone who moved as fast as they did, Ethan supposed, that was a huge margin.

By lap 50, the energy reservoir was already beginning to tick away underneath Ethan's shirt. He dared a peek down and saw a red light glowing close to his chest. That was no good – for the sort of energy he was trying to pick up from Lifespeed, it should be glowing *orange*. He would need to get closer. Shaking his head, preparing himself for something that would severely suck if it went wrong, Ethan shoved his way through the crowd and flipped over the safety rail onto the track.

"Hey, somebody get that guy out of there!"

Ethan timed it so that he made it into the track between the gusts of wind and streaks of color that signaled the passing speedsters. He made it into the air tunnel that had developed in the gutter in the middle of the racers. There were a few gasps of surprise, a few people yelling at him, but nobody moved to pull him out and the streaks that marked the paths of the speedsters continued their race. Against his chest, the energy reservoir began to glow and spark yellow. He didn't feel anything, of course, he'd shielded himself too well for that, but he *could* almost sense the batteries charging, filling up, and—

He broke free from his trance when a hand grabbed the back of his shirt. There was a whirlwind around him, and the world didn't stop spinning when the wind ended. He almost couldn't tell that Speedburn was holding him up, and although she was wearing a full face-mask, there was something about the shape of the jaw and brow beneath that suggested extreme agitation.

"Look, buddy, I don't know if you've heard, but this is a *race*. Even if we're really just playing for bragging rights, I get kind of irritated when somebody stumbles onto my track."

"I – I fell down," he said, sounding dazed. "What happened? Where am I?" He hoped that the vertigo from Speedburn's "rescue" would make him sound convincingly perplexed about how he got there.

Lifespeed stood next to Speedburn, arms folded. "What's that fancy box he's holding? It looks like something Particle would put together with Legos."

"It's nothing! It's—"

Ethan tried to tighten his grip on the device, but even if his head wasn't still spinning, he couldn't have matched the woman's liquid motions. He didn't even know how it happened, but soon she was holding him in one hand and his invention in the other, dangling it from the handle like a dead fish. If he couldn't get it back from her and get away, everything he'd done so far would be wasted. It was time for a desperate ploy – he would tell the truth. Or at least as much of it as he could.

"It's an energy sampler," he said. "I'm trying to study superhuman abilities. Trying to figure out how they work."

Lifespeed drew Ethan's face close into his own. "And why would you want to know something like *that*?"

"You're a whole new field of science! I just want to know where the power comes from, how you generate it, how you *control* it! The guy who figures out how super powers work is going to go down in the history books next to Isaac Newton and Benjamin Franklin. Who *wouldn't* try to figure it out?"

The two Capes looked at each other, then Speedburn gestured towards the assembled viewers. From out of the mob, another Cape appeared – this one in a dark coat and black mask. His eyes were shielded, but the expression on his face was intense. "Have you met my partner?" Speedburn asked. "His name is Sleuth. And he can tell a few things about you. Sleuth, is this guy holding any weapons?"

Sleuth looked Ethan over, and then turned his gaze towards the device. As he did so, Ethan saw a small bubble of light blue appear in the energy reservoir. Sleuth looked back at Speedburn. "Nothing here."

"Anything that could be used *as* a weapon?"

Another few moments of scrutiny, another blue spark. "I don't think so."

Speedburn looked at Ethan, then put him down. "I still don't trust you. I'm going to take this little toy down to Particle. If he says it's okay, you'll get it back. Until then, just sit tight. We'll be in touch with you soon."

"In touch?" Ethan tried not to show the panic on his face. He didn't know if his explanation would satisfy

Particle or not, but the thought of letting his work in the hands of one of the city's most well-known scientific minds was horrifying. "How are you going to be in touch?"

Speedburn smiled and held up Ethan's wallet, handing it over to him. She really *did* have fast hands. "I've got your contact info," she said. "Don't worry, you won't be needing mine."

He was not terribly surprised later that day when he got a phone call that told him, without any trace of ambiguity, he was to report to Simon Tower at exactly 5 p.m. He wasn't wild about going back there, to the heart of the city's Cape population, but if he didn't get the device back he would have to start all over again, and he'd put entirely too much work into this to do *that*.

He *was* surprised, though, when he saw who was waiting for him when he stepped into the mostly-empty lobby: the flag-draped Dr. Noble, looking just as pleased as he did the last time Ethan encountered him. "Lookie lookie who's back at the Tower. I thought I told you to drop this superhero stuff, pal."

"Did you?" Ethan asked. "Sorry, I guess I was preoccupied with my little toys."

Noble rolled his eyes and ushered Ethan into an elevator. Instead of turning to push a button, he spoke a command that started the vehicle: "Laboratory." Then, instead of feeling a slight tug down as the elevator moved up, Ethan was startled to feel his stomach leap into his throat as the car plunged into the earth.

The doors opened and Noble practically shoved Ethan out into an enormous room full of computers, monitors, scanners, half-constructed devices of a thousand potential uses, and a small, smiling black man in a blue-and-red suit. His costume, unlike the tights most heroes wore, was plated with body armor, and equipped with more gadgets and doodads than Ethan had ever seen before. On the table in front of him was Ethan's device.

"Ethan Hellig!" he said gregariously. "So nice to meet you. They call me Particle."

"I know," Ethan replied. With the Tin Man retired, Particle was the undisputed tech king of Siegel City's Cape population. And *he w*as studying *Ethan*'s device. Ethan's hands started twitching.

"Calm down, Ethan, you're not in any trouble."

"Don't tell him *that*," Noble snapped.

"Relax, Doctor. So, this is an interesting little apparatus Speedburn brought in. You told her it was an energy sampler. That's not quite right, is it?"

As sincere as Particle sounded, Ethan didn't feel much better being told he wasn't in trouble. Still, he decided it was best to stick to the truth. "No, it's not. It's actually an energy *collector*."

"That's what I thought. And that's why you've been walking all over the city, having encounters with as many different Capes as possible. This thing is designed to gather different energy types and synthesize them into something else. You want to use this to figure out how to give yourself our super powers."

Ethan didn't answer. That was close enough to the truth that he knew Particle would never surrender the device.

"Moron," Noble said, and Ethan didn't think he was directing his ire towards Particle. Again, the pristine public image was gone, and Ethan felt like he was in the presence of a schoolyard bully. "What did I tell you about trying something stupid like this?"

"Now, Doctor Noble, let's try to be understanding here. Don't you remember what it was like before you got your powers? You can hardly blame the man for trying to aspire to great things. But Ethan, here's the thing I don't understand. This device of yours is designed to collect several different forms of energy, but there's only *one* kind in here."

"Huh?"

"I'm not sure who you've tried using this on, but I'm not detecting different signatures in the energy reservoir. So either this thing has a leak, or the most recent type it's encountered has overtaken and neutralized the rest."

"What's the most recent type it's showing?"

"Well, Speedburn didn't know how to shut it off, so it kept collecting different energy samples until it got to my lab. And since I don't have any powers myself – I'm strictly a techie, you understand – that means the last person whose energy readout it detected was the man in the room with me at the time. That would be Doctor Noble here."

Ethan had to fight back a smile.

"I like your elevator," Ethan said. "Voice activated tech is a lot of fun, isn't it?"

"What are you talking about?"

Ethan barked out one word: "DEFENSE!"

From its perch on the table, Ethan's energy collector suddenly sparked. A jolt of energy struck Particle in the chest and shocked him unconscious. Ethan broke into a run, dodging a few jolts from Dr. Noble as he ran. He made it to the device, but Noble sent a searing blast into the table, right where Ethan's hand would have been if he hadn't pulled it away. Noble let fly with a few more shocks. "Sneaky little bastard. Keep your hands off that thing!"

"SHIELD!" Ethan shouted, and the device threw up a cube of energy around both itself and Ethan. Noble's next attack sparked against the cube, but it had no effect on either Ethan or his prize. The cube lasted only for a second, but it was long enough for Ethan to get a hand on the device and dive down behind Particle's table. Another jolt of energy burned the air above him, and he smelled an electric tinge in the air.

Noble started to hurl blasts above the table and to both sides, blocking any possible escape route Ethan could have used, but that was okay. He turned around so that he was facing Noble, keeping the table in-between them of course, and put both hands on his device. The hidden grips on either side fit his fingers just as he'd designed them, and both thumbs rested on the triggers that, to Particle, had probably looked like valves. He faced the front display away from his chest and, holding his breath, stood up so that he was facing Noble directly.

"Guess what this little toy is going to do next, Doc."

Noble didn't answer, but instead trained his energy directly against the device, aiming at the blinking readout like a dartboard. When Noble's next bolt struck, the device did exactly what Ethan wanted it to do. The device tugged on Noble, leeching more energy out of his body and mingling it with the power already contained in the reservoir. It kept tugging the energy like a vacuum until Ethan let go of the left trigger. Noble, literally drained, fell to the floor in a heap.

The glow on the energy collector was white now. It was time to hit the trigger on the right side.

All of the energy contained in the device turned backwards, pouring into Ethan's body. The copper mesh wasn't nearly as uncomfortable since he found a way to weave it into a body stocking, but it was just as effective. The energy spread out through the mesh and into his skin. It felt like he was being stung by a thousand bees, everywhere at once. The bees didn't stop at a sting, though, they were almost *burrowing* into his skin. He held on to the device as long as he could, even falling to his knees to keep the strength in his hands, but after torturous minutes, he released the trigger and the pain stopped. The device clattered to the floor and he slumped over, his body crackling.

It worked. Oh, he would run the tests, he would go through the trials he had set up back in his own lab, but he could tell. It *worked.*

He was ready to test it when he felt the kick in his gut. Noble was standing over him, face twisted into an expression of rage, a slight glow in his eyes to indicate where his power used to be. It would come back, Ethan knew, Noble generated it from within, but it had served its purpose.

Noble kicked him again, spitting on Ethan's cheek when the blow made him roll onto his back. "Nice try, Tinker Toy. Looks like your little Trojan Horse backfired, though."

Ethan laughed, wiping the saliva from his cheek with a sleeve. "Oh, Noble, don't you wish?"

The energy – not exactly the same as Noble's, but close enough – brimmed inside of him and erupted from his hands, lancing out and consuming the Cape in tendrils of pure white light. Noble shrieked and fell down. Ethan was on his feet before Noble could look up, and he hit him with another blast, then one more just to keep him down.

"Don't worry, Doc, I'm not here to kill you. Not worth it to have an entire city full of Capes hunting for my blood. No, I'm actually gonna do you a favor."

"Favor?"

"Well sure. You want everyone in Siegel to recognize you as the top hero, right? Well how do you ever expect to get that status without a good, old-fashioned arch enemy?" Ethan laughed, picking up his device, then another wire-covered cube from Particle's work table. "No idea what this is, but I'll bet it's worth something. Remember how you told me to use my brain to make money? Pal, I was *way* ahead of you."

Ethan walked over to the elevator, forcing the doors open with a burst of energy, then using another burst to force the car down below him. Stepping into the empty shaft, he hovered in the air and began to glow.

"Money's not everything, of course. Sometimes it's just about proving you're the smartest guy in the room."

"We know your name... We know your address..."

Ethan shrugged. "Neither of them matter to me anymore. I'm going to do things Ethan Hellig never could. Call me... call me... Oh, damn, I was supposed to have a good exit line, wasn't I? Oh... call me Photon Man, I guess. Not exactly accurate, but it has the right theatrical ring to it. Have a good one!"

With a push, Ethan shot up the elevator shaft, leaving the stunned Dr. Noble and Particle to pull themselves up. Noble looked over at Particle, who by now was using the table to pull himself up.

"You heard that?"

"I heard." Particle laughed. "Mr. Ethan Hellig has a lot to learn about what it means to be a villain in Siegel City, doesn't he?"

"Yeah," Noble said, but the grin on his face was unmistakable. "But he was right about one thing. I could use a villain. Come on. This could be fun."

About the Author

Blake M. Petit is a freelance writer, columnist, reviewer, podcaster, actor, director, teacher, and unlicensed tree surgeon from Ama, Louisiana. He is the author of the novels *Other People's Heroes* and *The Beginner* (coming soon to eBooks), as well as the podcast novel *A Long November*. His weekly comic book column, *Everything But Imaginary*, has appeared Wednesdays at CXPulp.com since 2003. He co-hosts, with whoever the hell is available that week, the *2 in 1 Showcase* comic book podcast, appearing every weekend at CXPulp. Blake is a member of the board of directors of the Thibodaux Playhouse theatre company in Thibodaux Louisiana, where his original stage play *The 3-D Radio Show* was produced in 2004. In a former life as a newspaper editor, his weekly *Think About It* column won the Louisiana Press Association Award for best column in 2001. In his free time, he teaches high school English, which at the moment pays better than the rest of his more impressive-sounding endeavors put together.

Contact Blake at BlakeMPetit@gmail.com. Visit him online at www.EvertimeRealms.com.

CPSIA information can be obtained at www.ICGtesting.com
Printed in the USA
LVOW100320160612

286430LV00007B/60/P

OCT - - 2013